THE CAPITOL GAME

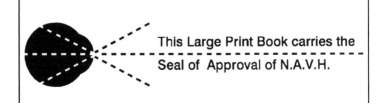

This Large Print Book carries the
Seal of Approval of N.A.V.H.

THE CAPITOL GAME

BRIAN HAIG

THORNDIKE PRESS

A part of Gale, Cengage Learning

GALE
CENGAGE Learning·

Detroit • New York • San Francisco • New Haven, Conn • Waterville, Maine • London

Copyright © 2010 by Brian Haig.
Thorndike Press, a part of Gale, Cengage Learning.

ALL RIGHTS RESERVED
The events and characters in this book are fictitious. Certain real locations and public figures are mentioned, but all other characters and events described in the book are totally imaginary.
Thorndike Press® Large Print Basic.
The text of this Large Print edition is unabridged.
Other aspects of the book may vary from the original edition.
Set in 16 pt. Plantin.

LIBRARY OF CONGRESS CATALOGING-IN-PUBLICATION DATA

Haig, Brian.
   The capitol game / by Brian Haig.
     p. cm. — (Thorndike Press large print basic)
   ISBN-13: 978-1-4104-3255-1
   ISBN-10: 1-4104-3255-6
   1. Corporations—Fiction. 2. Scandals—Fiction. 3. Washington (D.C.)—Fiction. 4. Large type books. I. Title.
   PS3608.A54C37 2010b
   813'.6—dc22
                            2010033689

Published in 2010 by arrangement with Grand Central Publishing, a division of Hachette Book Group, Inc.

Printed in the United States of America
1 2 3 4 5 6 7 14 13 12 11 10

To Lisa
Brian, Pat, Donnie, Annie

Special thanks to:

My family for their love and support . . . and especially the kids for mostly behaving while I wrote this book.

My good friend and agent, Luke Janklow.

Everybody at Grand Central Publishing for everything they do.

1

Abdallah shuffled and squirmed a little deeper into the dark, dirty culvert. The day was hot, almost blisteringly so, though slightly more bearable in here. He drew a deep breath of air, cupped his ears, and listened hard for the noise of loud engines.

Hadi, his best friend of twelve years, and currently his partner in crime, was holed up in a room on the third floor of a large building abandoned during the bombings, then gutted and neglected ever since. For generations, the building had belonged to the Fadithi clan, a private enclave surrounded by lush gardens nurtured and tended by half a dozen workers.

The Fadithis were richer than anybody; they rarely slipped a chance to let you know it, either. Big, fancy imported cars, scholarly tutors for their tribe of rottenly spoiled kids, and they escaped every summer to long, luxurious vacations in the cool hills of Lebanon.

The farthest Hadi had ever traveled was to the tiny village two miles to the south, a tiny lump of dirt-infested squalor that bore a disappointing resemblance to his own sad pile of dust and concrete.

Local lore had it the Fadithis had fled out of their house during one of the American air raids and blindly dodged straight into an American bomb. Like that — boom — pulverized into mist, the richest family in town, nothing more than a revolting smear on the street.

Inside two days, the big building hosted a raucous neighborhood bash — the furniture, the clothing, the wiring, the heaters from the backyard, even the windows torn out and hauled off by the laughing neighbors.

Allah did indeed have a cruel but just side.

Abdallah and Hadi had rehearsed this stunt the day before, a brief run-through before their attention shifted to a pickup soccer game three blocks down and they spent the remainder of the afternoon booting around a ball given to the neighborhood boys by one of the American invaders, a large man in dark glasses with a fierce sunburn and a bright smile loaded with phoniness. The ball had a queer shape. It quickly proved worthless, like somebody had grabbed it at both ends and tugged so hard that it never snapped back. With each kick, it flew off in weird directions, bouncing and bobbling and skittering in the dust. What a hoot.

Americans! Whatever made them believe they could conquer and rule this country when they couldn't even design a workable soccer ball?

Abdallah gently fingered the device in his right hand — a trigger, the man who provided it had called it. Didn't look like a gun trigger, though: Abdallah had seen plenty of those, he bragged to the man, and this, well, no, this definitely wasn't a trigger. The man got mad, poked him with a mean finger in the stomach, and reminded him who was paying the money; it was whatever he decided to call it. Well, whatever it was, the funny device fit cleanly into the palm of Abdallah's small fist. It was not in any way he could see connected to the big bomb stuffed inside the large garbage barrel beside the road. No wires, no fuse, nothing. But the man swore the slightest squeeze would produce a terrible explosion.

And afterward, he warned with a deep scowl, Abdallah had better drop the trigger and scatter as fast as his chubby legs would carry him.

The man doing all the talking, Mustafa, was a two-bit loser who had rolled in and out of Saddam's prisons with disturbing frequency. He had tried his hand at forgery, bribery, holdups, a little drug dealing, and failed pathetically at all of them.

Mustafa's last incompetent attempt at crime was a harebrained holdup at a local shop that ended badly and was still the topic of great laughter among the old men at the local tea shop. The shopkeeper leaped over the counter, easily took the knife out of Mustafa's hand, and stuffed it in Mustafa's leg. Mustafa howled and bled, and tried his damnedest to crawl away. The shopkeeper sat on his back and slapped him on the head till the cops showed.

In consideration of all his past illicit deeds, Mustafa got twenty long ones in Abu Ghraib, far and away the most appalling sewer in Saddam's sprawling prison system. Few survived even ten years there, and Mustafa, being small and definitely unlikable, was deemed less likely than most to make it to the other end. The village breathed a sigh of relief and thought it had seen the last of him.

Allah, though, in his infinite wisdom, had

other paths for the small-time hood. Only six months later, in the hard, tense weeks leading up to the American invasion, Mustafa found himself dumped back onto the streets along with all the other crooks, pimps, and kidnappers — a gift from Saddam for the Americans.

They might win, but they would regret it.

Mustafa emerged a new man. A reformed man. Amazing what a few brief months could accomplish. He now sported a thick black beard and called himself an Islamic warrior, a patriot, a freedom fighter dedicated to ridding Iraq of its loathsome invaders. He took to carrying around the Koran though it was well-known that he couldn't read a whit. Turned out Mustafa had met new friends in prison, generous sorts, men who weren't picky and happily paid three thousand American bucks for every American he killed. Five thousand if the corpse happened to be an officer.

Mustafa wasn't into the killing game himself. Subcontracting was his preferred method — in truth, his only method — primarily using small kids to handle the dirty work. He was particularly partial to street orphans, like Abdallah and Hadi, who brought along a few big advantages. They were poor and indescribably desperate, for one thing. They came without baggage, for another — no pissed-off parents, no angry brothers, no vengeful uncles or clans to worry about when things went wrong.

And in Mustafa's case, things often went wrong.

Abdallah glanced up. Hadi was furiously waving with one hand, pointing wildly to his left with the other. This wasn't the signal they had agreed to, not even close. Hadi, though, was only twelve, small for his age, slightly daft, and tended to get carried away at moments like this. At thirteen, Abdallah was far the more seasoned, cooler, and ambitious of the pair. It was he who had talked Hadi into this little job. Hadi put on a good front, though it was obvious he was scared out of his wits and well over his head. Abdallah had to keep reminding him that Mustafa had promised five hundred dollars if they pulled this off, a fortune they would split fifty-fifty.

The bounty for dead Americans was six hundred, Mustafa swore, and out of fairness — he was a religious man after all — he would limit his own share to a paltry one hundred. But five hundred, theirs to keep, all for squeezing the tiny device in his hand. Easy money.

A few local boys warned them that Mustafa was a notorious cheat and was getting much more than that. Who cared? Five hundred was a fortune. They would eat well for a year.

Captain Bill Forrest munched loudly from a bag of Lay's barbecue potato chips. He washed them down with deep sips from a bottled water that, over the past twenty minutes, had gone from lukewarm to nearly a boil. The day was a scorcher, never dipping below 115 degrees. He was aching to get out of the body armor, aching to catch up on his sleep, aching for the tour to be over. He dreamed of air-conditioning, of cold ice cream, of long walks in cool woods without anybody shooting or trying their damnedest to blow him up.

The idea of a week without sweat — or explosions — was almost more than he could imagine. He was trying his best, however.

"Two more weeks of this crap," his driver, Private Teddy Davis, loudly complained, banging a hand hard off the steering wheel. "Know what I'm gonna do the second I get back to the world?"

"Pretty sure I do." Forrest crunched loudly on another chip. Why ask? Same thing every single guy in the unit was swearing to do. Look for naked ladies. Fat, ugly, skinny, didn't matter — female and disrobed in any shape or form would do the trick. "Keep your eyes on the roadsides, Davis."

The driver stared straight ahead, and so did his brain. "There's this girly house, sir. Just three short blocks from the front gate. Gorgeous ladies. They strip down to nothin', I hear."

"Sounds promising. Then what?"

"Then, well, I dunno." Good question, he realized. "What're you gonna do?"

"I'm married, right?"

"Yeah, so?"

"So first I'm gonna spend a few minutes playing with my two pretty little girls."

"Sounds fun," Davis commented, not meaning a word of it.

"Then, well, then I'm gonna take their pretty momma upstairs, lock the bedroom door, and play with her, too." The captain smiled and Davis couldn't resist joining him.

Bill Forrest was twenty-nine, a big man with broad dark features and thick dark hair, who had played linebacker in college, at Notre Dame, a fact that thoroughly impressed his men. On a lark, between football and classes, he had dabbled a little in ROTC in college. And though his degree

16

was in finance, with an ambition to get seriously rich, and despite no tradition of military service in his family, he had enjoyed the military camaraderie and decided to try his hand at infantry life for a few fast years. Brief years, he had promised himself.

The last day of the third year, it was sayonara, boys, on to Wall Street.

The money would come, later.

Senior year he had married Janet, the hottest property in South Bend that year, or, for that matter, any other year anybody could remember. Janet was blonde, lovely, and quite pregnant by graduation, then almost immediately pregnant again, spitting out two pretty blonde-haired girls ten months apart, Irish twins, which seemed quite fitting for a pair of hard-knuckle Notre Dame grads.

Year three, 9/11 and war intervened, and Bill found himself unable to run out on his friends and his country. Just two more years, only twenty-four months, then it was adios, baby, he promised Janet. Year five it became one brief tour in a war zone and Bill would never have to look back with regret.

Janet weathered his military stint with good grace and well-managed patience. She liked the other Army wives and enjoyed the hardy sisterhood of military life. A hot dusty post in Texas, on the other hand, left much to be desired. Janet was a city girl, born and bred in downtown Chicago; she could put up with the cramped Army quarters, the dust storms, even the severe summer heat. The whole pickup-truck, country music scene, however, grated powerfully on her northern sensibilities. She preferred constant noise, traffic, inescapable human contact, and all the other questionable intrusions of urban life.

Bill had a wonderfully attractive long-term offer from a big financial firm in New York City, a raucous, lively city she yearned to be part of. The partners in the firm, two of whom happened to be rabid Notre Dame fans, vowed to keep it open so long as Bill didn't exhaust their patience. Bill was good at the Army, though. She didn't press.

Truthfully, she didn't dare. The wives of the soldiers in his company would've hanged her from the front gate had she tried. His men adored him. The same quick wits that made him a terror on the gridiron translated nicely to the battlefield. Over eleven months in battle, so far. Eleven long, bloody months in some of the worst battle zones and festering sores in Iraq, and not one of his 150 soldiers had made the sad trip home in a body bag. The other companies in his battalion were wracked by casualties and funerals. Not Bill's, though. A few were wounded, some quite horribly. But better a hospital ward than a lonely grave on a quiet hillside.

And now, only two weeks to go and the perfect record appeared within reach. An entire year of exploding bombs, drive-by snipers, roadside ambushes, more close brushes than anybody cared to remember, and amazingly, everybody would make it home.

The wives were knocking thrice on every piece of wood in sight, squeezing their rabbits' feet, and planning a big bash for the day their men returned.

The radio squawked, Captain Forrest picked up the handset, and a long, soothing discussion ensued. Had to be another futile attempt to calm the jangled nerves of that aggravating lieutenant four vehicles back in the convoy, Davis decided, fighting back a big smirk. The lieutenant was young, brand-new, so nervous his eyes trembled. A wet-nosed babyface sent down from headquarters to replace a battle-hardened platoon leader who had lost his legs to a grenade. Sad. With only three weeks to go, too.

Now the poor guy would spend the rest of his life hobbling about on phony legs.

Less than a mile ahead loomed a small

village, another decrepit, cramped, run-down, sandblasted pisshole. What a sad, sorry excuse for a country, Davis, not for the first time, thought, swabbing the sweat rolling down his cheeks. A product of one of the poorest back hollows in Mississippi, he hoped he'd seen the last of poverty. The money in his house got snorted up his papa's nose, or paying down his mama's considerable bar bills. He had worked at a shoe factory after school, labored hard at the coloring booth, but the messy, cramped trailer he called home was so small his parents easily found his money and used it to their own ends. He enlisted at the first chance, fled to the Army and a new life. So long, Mama; bye-bye, Papa — go ahead, sniff and drink yourselves into the grave. Then he came to this place.

Their Humvee struck a deep rut that caused a hard, jarring bounce. Their heads knocked solidly against the roof and the captain let loose a loud curse. "Sorry," Davis mumbled, melting into his seat, trying to avoid the scowl he knew he was getting. "Worn-out springs," he said, rather lamely.

Of course the springs were worn out; hell, it was overloaded with so many sandbags and pasted-on iron plates, it was a wonder that the jerry-rigged heap could move at all.

The Humvee was eight terrifying months overdue for a replacement by one of the newer, uparmored models. Every month opened with fresh promises that the company doing the upgrades would meet its contract. And every month closed with stale excuses about why the contractor was still behind.

The replacement they had been praying for had a heavier suspension and reinforced armor that offered some hope of surviving a bomb blast. Now, after almost a year of rolling around Iraqi streets in this thin-skinned death trap they had finally given up hope.

Now they were just trying to survive time.

Hadi now was jumping up and down, flailing and gesticulating like an army of biting bugs was crawling around inside his drawers.

Abdallah pushed forward and squirmed out a few feet. He looked up at Hadi and held out his arms. How many, he was asking.

Hadi stuffed his tiny head out the window and peeked right. With his left hand he appeared to be counting. Eventually he flashed ten fingers, then waved his arms like windmills.

Settle down, Abdallah wanted to scream

21

at Hadi. Ease back from that window, take a long breath, relax. He now could hear their noisy engines without any help from his friend. Could almost picture the convoy of targets less than half a mile away. Any moment, the Americans would come rolling down the main street in their huge vehicles lined up like arrogant ducks straight into Abdallah's sights.

He reminded himself to bide his time and take his pick. No need to rush. Would it be one of those boxy, odd-looking things called Humvees? Maybe a Bradley Fighting Vehicle?

But if Abdallah was really lucky, there'd be a fat fuel tanker he could really light up. The blast would be monstrously huge, a massive fireball that would be seen for miles. It would burn for hours and be the talk of the village for weeks. He swatted at a fly on his nose and dreamed about it.

He had chosen his culvert with the pickiness of a master chef. The road to the village fed directly into the main street, a skinny thoroughfare without turns, bordered on both sides by buildings that channeled the convoy straight to Abdallah. After long and careful consideration, he had positioned himself twenty yards short of the first intersection, a four-way and the first opportunity for the Americans to change direction.

They had no choice but to pass directly by Abdallah, no option but to drive by the lethal trash barrel ten feet back from the road.

Abdallah couldn't resist a smile. What a nasty surprise they were in for.

The four men in robes peeked over the edge of the building. The street was clear and quiet, no traffic, no pedestrians wandering aimlessly. A perfect target zone, a perfect day to kill.

They had, three hours before, patiently observed the big barrel being rolled into place, then later watched one tiny urchin enter the neglected building and reappear a few minutes later in an upstairs window. They laughed as the bigger, fatter one fought and squeezed his way into the narrow culvert.

They watched and they waited.

They had slipped up onto this rooftop in pitch-darkness the night before. For the past seven hours, between cigarettes and quiet sips of hot tea, between sweating and boredom and baking under the broiling Iraqi sun, they had watched and waited.

They whispered among themselves, arguing quietly and sometimes heatedly about the quality of the bomb below. Would it work? How well would it work? This was a test, a vitally important one, though this news had been slyly withheld from Mustafa and the two street punks he had hired to do this job. That fired-up, true-believer patriot act he put on fooled nobody. Mustafa was a selfish, self-indulgent crook, plain and simple.

A mercenary who killed for the cash, nothing more.

He would've pressured for more money had he known. Probably a lot more.

The bomb was the newest thing, smuggled in a week before from Iran with lots of loud promises about what it could destroy. Supposedly, the device was manufactured to be triggered through the open air, though the four men on the rooftop had no idea how that actually worked. Nor did they care. An Iranian bomb mechanic had babbled on about the particulars — something to do with penetrating rods, and secondary explosives, and sound waves, and signal receptors. All four men were yawning and nodding off long before he finished.

Who cared? The long-winded blowhard was squandering his breath and their patience. They merely needed to know if it worked. Did it trigger a blast or no? Would it allow them to kill more Americans or not?

One of the four men edged forward a little. He positioned his video camera against the ledge. He pushed zoom, narrowed the picture frame to the road space directly abutting the barrel, punched start, lit up a smoke, and waited for the fun to begin.

Bill Forrest had his nose stuffed inside a map. Fifty yards out from the village, he pointed straight ahead at the narrow street. "Follow that until the first intersection, then turn left," he told Davis, who pumped the brakes and slowed up a bit as was their usual custom anytime they drove through built-up areas.

Roadside bombs could be hidden anywhere, in animal carcasses, in broken-down cars, or even dug into shallow holes in a road out in the middle of nowhere. Towns and villages, though, offered plenty of camouflage and were particularly dangerous.

"What a dump," Davis remarked. The streets weren't even paved, just flattened-down dust.

"Slow down a little more," Forrest warned him, looking worried and tense.

"Why?"

"Do you see anybody on the streets? Locals always know when it's too dangerous to come out and play."

Davis scanned the village and saw a few faces poking out of windows. "Well, it is the hottest part of the day. I'd hide inside, too."

Just then the radio barked, the same young lieutenant again, the same whiny, needy tone. The captain shook his head, rolled his eyes, and lifted the handset. "Listen," he told the young officer, "take a deep breath and settle down. I'm trying to watch the road, and you keep interrupting me."

Davis stifled a laugh.

Abdallah held his breath, kept his hand loose, and watched as the convoy approached the barrel. Mustafa had told him not to squeeze the trigger too soon. It had happened twice before, Mustafa warned, young idiots overcome with excitement or nerves who clumsily wasted a bomb and killed nobody. No corpses, no money, Mustafa had threatened with a mean grin that showed where his front teeth had been kicked out in one of his many failed attempts at crime.

Abdallah glanced up at Hadi, who was leaning out the window, craning his neck and straining to watch the big boom.

A moment later, the lead vehicle was directly beside the barrel. Abdallah could actually observe the men inside, one talking into a handset, the other, a bit younger-looking, chuckling to himself and steering the vehicle. He vowed that he would wait for a vehicle with more passengers, a much riper target, but in that instant his hand developed a mind of its own and squeezed hard on the device.

The response was immediate and over-whelming. Abdallah felt the blast literally drive him back another two feet into the culvert, until he felt like a cork stuffed into a bottle. He squealed with pain and clenched his eyes shut to block the barrage of dust from the road. His ears hurt, and though he did not know it, the drums had burst.

When he opened his eyes, he saw that the Humvee had been blown over, sideways, and now was teetering on its side, like some giant Tonka toy tossed by the wind. It was on fire and he could feel the surge of intense heat even from fifty feet away. He watched a man crawl out, a big man, pulling himself up through the side opening, trying desper-ately to escape the flames. After a moment the big man in an invader's uniform ended up on the ground, flopping and pulling himself forward with his arms, which really was the only way he could since his legs were gone.

The big American seemed to be staring straight into Abdallah's eyes with a mixture of shock and recognition. Then he lay still for a moment, bleeding and suffering. Abdallah couldn't hear, but could clearly picture his groans and his pitiful attempts to draw breath. He saw his hand move, go inside his shirt, and he pulled something out and stared at it hard.

Abdallah used all his might to get out of the culvert and edge forward. The big American just stared at the thing in his hand, and Abdallah strained to see what it was. Clearly the man was dying, and Abdallah wondered, what was the last thing a man on the cusp of death wanted so desperately to see?

He was out of the culvert now; to his surprise he discovered he could barely walk. Blood was trickling out his ears. He stumbled forward until he stood swaying above the American.

In the man's hand was a picture of an attractive blonde woman, hugging two little blonde girls who were laughing and giggling.

2

The folder had been passed around the conference table four times, read, dissected, debated, scrutinized, and rescrutinized by the three men for nearly an hour.

The biography of Jack Wiley held their attention for the first thirty minutes. An impressive man, no question about that. A 1988 graduate of Princeton, peculiarly he had entered the Army, fought in the first Gulf War, then traded his boots for loafers a few months after the last shot was fired. A Silver Star and a Bronze Star: a combat vet and genuine hero to boot. A few intense years drinking the Kool-Aid at Harvard Business School, then he shot straight into the labyrinth of a big Wall Street firm, bouncing through three big firms in ten years.

A few calls by one of their executives posing as a corporate headhunter to those firms revealed that Wiley was restless, but a steady rainmaker wherever he went. His former employers described him as pleasant, smart, energetic, but also cautious and diligent, all values the men around the table intensely admired. He produced profit by the bushel wherever he went; this quality they admired even more. That success brought a flood of offers from competing firms, and he jumped without compunction for better pay and more exalted titles.

For the past three years he had been a partner and senior VP at Cauldron Securities, a small, elite private equity outfit with a solid though stodgy reputation.

Elite because it invested only in midsize, already profitable companies.

And small by choice, because Cauldron was picky. It hired only the best of the best, only from the top five business schools, drowned the associates in work and unbearable pressure for five or six years, spit out nine out of ten, and spoiled the keepers with fat bonuses and perks.

And stodgy because it avoided risk like poison.

The partner, Edward Blank, put a finger in the air and guessed, slightly dismissively, "Probably made two mil last year."

"More like five," countered Brian Golightly from the seat directly to his right.

"Cauldron had a great year and Wiley got a partner's split. Five even might be a little light."

Golightly had taken the initial call from Wiley and, only after a little checking, referred the proposal upstairs. The résumé had been slickly culled from the executive recruiting firm that handled Wiley's switch to Cauldron. Confidential material, of course, but the headhunters wanted to do a little business with the Capitol Group, favors beget favors, and broaching the trust was, after all, a trifling technicality.

"Wiley's single," Golightly continued, filling in a few details not included in the file. "Army brat, born at Fort Benning, straight A's through high school, two points from perfect on the college boards." Then, after a brief pause, "Played lacrosse in college. All-America, attackman, nerves of steel."

The other two men lifted their eyebrows. His academic performance, combat heroism, and business success were impressive, but his prowess on the sports field definitely hit the mark.

Golightly had acquired this valuable tidbit from a Princeton classmate of Wiley's who happened to belong to his country club. The man was a pompous know-it-all, an unremitting bore, and to boot, an awful golfer.

Enduring nine holes of his incessant hacking and slicing and almost endless babbling had been worth it, though. Wiley had started all four years, fearless, lightning reflexes, very quick around the net. Second team All-America his senior year. He also dated the same girl all four years, an English lit major with killer legs and poetic eyes, who now was making her living pushing weepy romance drivel onto the best-seller lists. She said adieu at graduation, when he chose the Army.

"So what's he want?" Blank asked, squirming in his seat, a study in festering impatience.

"He described it only as an opportunity. An incredible opportunity — those were his exact words," Golightly replied, repeating the same answer he had offered the previous three times Blank had asked. This mystery had occupied most of the past thirty minutes. A quick glance at his watch. "In another minute, you can ask him yourself."

Golightly had tried his best to pry this information from Wiley and been politely and insistently brushed off. For whatever reason, Wiley preferred to play it close to his vest until he met directly with the LBO boys.

The leveraged buyout section of the Capitol Group was the tip of a large, very prosperous, enormously powerful spear. In a firm that viewed business as warfare, they were the assault troops. All were hand-picked, chosen for their hunger and their relentless ambition; most important, they had to be cold-blooded and ruthless. They made the deals. They found the targets and kicked down the doors. They located the vulnerabilities and ratcheted up the pressure until the other side caved in to whatever the Capitol Group was willing to pay.

They borrowed money by the boatload and bought companies, nearly always heavily distressed ones in financial decline, then turned them over to management to be squeezed, downsized, bled dry of impurities and imperfections, refurbished, and sold off for usually three times the cost. Sometimes five. Only those companies that proved wildly profitable — and appeared destined to stay that way — were kept, added to the Capitol Group's swelling stable of permanent properties.

The Capitol Group was a factory. An enormously profitable factory. It was privately held; the owners preferred it that way and stubbornly resisted the urge to rake in billions by going public. It spawned a

bewildering array of products, from rubber tires, to electronic devices of all sorts, to airplane engines, to defense equipment — almost more products than anybody could count.

But nobody cared to count. Why bother? The mix of companies turned over so fast, it would be senseless.

CG owned factories spread around the globe, from Pennsylvania to Hong Kong to the tip of Africa, and raised capital wherever wealth congregated, from New York to Dubai, and most recently Moscow, where ex-Marxist billionaires were now growing like poppies. There were twenty directors at the top, forty so-called partners, and four hundred lesser executives who bought and oversaw a diverse collection of companies employing nearly three hundred thousand workers.

But had anybody cared to count, CG's arsenal at that moment included sixty-two companies, a figure that churned and changed weekly and, had it been listed on the stock exchange, would've been valued at $110 billion. It was a staggering figure by any measure, and all the more remarkable for an outfit founded only twenty years before by a few penniless, insanely optimistic ex-government types.

"I think he's bringing us a takeover deal," guessed Barry Caldwell, an accounting assassin brought into the meeting at the last minute to act cold and hard. Spreadsheets were his specialty. His froglike eyes could chew through the debits and credits, gauge the assets and liabilities, dart through the income and expenses, and in lightning speed spit out an amazingly precise portrait of corporate health or disease.

"If not, he's wasting our time," Blank answered, slapping a hand on the table. Of course he was bringing a deal. Why else the insistence on meeting the LBO group?

"It's time," Golightly announced, standing and buttoning his jacket. He tucked the folder in a briefcase. The other two men stood and buttoned their jackets as well.

The door opened, and after a moment, in walked Jack Wiley hauling a buttery tan briefcase in one hand, a stack of slides and spreadsheets in the other. He was taller than they expected, probably six-one or six-two. They took note of the soaked-in tan that spoke of long days on the golf course, along with a build that suggested plenty of gym time. Full head of sandy brown hair, a sprinkling of gray showing at the temples, cold blue eyes. The briefcase and slides landed heavily on the conference table. The usual handshakes and nice-to-meet-yous were quickly and insincerely exchanged.

The three men were impressed. Without being asked, Wiley fell into a seat, coolly crossed his long legs, and, as if he owned the place, suggested, "Why don't you all get seated and we'll start."

"Good idea," Blank answered for all of them. At forty-five, he was the senior man and the only CG partner in the room. He wanted Wiley to know it, too.

As if on cue, a comely assistant poked her head in. "Good morning, gentlemen. Coffee, tea, soda?"

Wiley produced a polite smile and, before anybody could produce an answer, announced, "Not yet, thank you." His eyes roved across the faces on the other side of the table. "First let us find out if we have anything to discuss."

Yes, yes, another good idea, the three men across the table agreed. If the meeting was a bust, why prolong the pain with forced small talk and refreshments? Then it's thanks for stopping by, Jack, don't let the door bang you in the ass.

Blank edged forward on his elbows and took charge of the conversation. "So you're a partner at Cauldron."

"That's right. Three years now."

"I'm not familiar with Cauldron. Small, isn't it?" In other words, You're lucky to be sitting here with the big boys, Jack — and don't you forget it.

"Yes, tiny, actually." Jack took the put-down in stride and nodded. "We like to think of ourselves as a boutique firm. We're very selective. We pride ourselves on being nimble, and in our view, size would only hamper us." After a beat, he smiled lightly and added, "It would also water down the profit share for the partners."

Big smiles from all three CG boys. This outright profession of greed warmed their hearts. "What's your firm's specialty?" Golightly asked, as if they hadn't just spent thirty minutes hashing over this very issue.

"Good question," Wiley answered. "Our investors tend to be old money, mostly inherited. Mostly from New York, upper New Jersey, and New England. They have their fortunes, they appreciate it, and they want to appreciate it next year as well. We buy one or two properties each year, no more. Our focus is on lean, well-managed, steadily profitable companies in need of a little capital to expand. Nothing exciting. It's a good formula, though, and it works."

The men across the table smirked and made little effort to hide their disdain. They lived and died on the mantra of no big risks, no big payoffs. Cauldron sounded like a bunch of wimps. Little Leaguers hustling for chump change.

"You don't find it stifling?" Blank couldn't resist asking. Obviously, it would kill him.

Wiley smiled and ignored the insult. "I spent ten years on the treadmill at the bigger firms. A full decade running the halls, fifteen-hour days, no weekends, plenty of canceled vacations. Ten years of midnight deals hanging by a thread, then trying to turn around turkeys we never should've gone near. You boys know the life."

The three men nodded. Damn right they knew.

"I wasn't burned out," Jack continued. "But I can't say I was enjoying myself, either. When Cauldron offered a fast-track partnership, I jumped at it. Understand, Cauldron is very laid-back, a low-pressure outfit. Lots of long lunches where drinking isn't off-limits. Weekends are sacrosanct. The partners can often be found napping in their offices. And why not? Our investors are content with ten percent growth a year. They throw a wild bash for us if we hit fifteen." He produced a weak smile for the hungry sharks across the table.

As he and they knew, at CG, ten would

be a disaster. The directors would turn up the heat, pink slips would fly — life would become intolerable for the survivors. This had happened, once, only once, twelve years back. A painful recession had set in. Growth sank to a mere eight percent that year. Blank was the only one in the room with enough tenure to have lived through it. A bloodbath, 365 days of unmitigated terror, twelve torturous months without a day off, a full year of unbearable stress. His blood pressure shot up forty points. He still had nightmares about it.

"Sounds ideal," Golightly commented, obviously not meaning it.

"Yes, doesn't it?" Jack replied, matching his insincerity ounce for ounce.

"So why don't you explain this irresistible offer you were bragging about?" Blank asked. Having cut Wiley down to size, it was time to cut to the chase.

"In a minute, Mr. Blank. Let me start by telling you, you're not the only people I'm talking to. I developed a model. Four firms fell out. You're one of those four and any or all of you could fit the bill. It doesn't mean only four firms will do, but four of you are ideal."

Casual nods from across the table. Standard fare, and also empty bluster. Nobody with a noodle of sense ever confessed up-front that CG was the only firm they were talking with. Offers always came juiced up with a little competition. The boys from CG heard it all the time. Nice try, Jack.

They nudged one another under the table and played along. "But we do fit the bill?" Blank suggested, straight-faced, as if there was any chance in hell they might not.

"You might even be the best fit," Jack agreeably allowed.

"What a relief."

"Should I go on?"

"Yes, do."

Jack uncrossed his legs and leaned forward. "It's a company that came to my attention a few months ago. At first glance it looked like a perfect fit for Cauldron — midsize, profitable, well led, courting an infusion of capital. Their CEO and head financial guy were making the rounds through a few firms like ours. Call it a road show."

"And you met with them?" Golightly asked.

A fast nod. "It wasn't my meeting, but I was present, yes. Forty-five years ago, the CEO founded this company. Built it from scratch, the usual story, sweat, smarts, and his bare hands. His life's work. He's now in

40

his late seventies, has two sons and a daughter. He's in fairly good health, but a realist. He had two heart attacks in his late fifties. He quit smoking and watches the cholesterol, but long lives don't run in his genes. Either of his children could succeed him. He wants to leave them set up for success."

"So this company's his property?"

"No," Jack said. "Not exactly."

"Meaning what?"

"It's listed. A penny stock, though. Through his stock and a few friendly stockholders he controls slightly over half of the voting shares."

Caldwell suddenly developed a deep frown. "If you'd done your homework, Wiley, you'd know we prefer private companies."

"Who doesn't? Less complications, less mess."

"Plus," Golightly — also frowning — stiffly noted, "it doesn't sound like management wants to relinquish ownership. You mentioned that this geezer intends to hand it over to his kids. CG never shares. We buy it, and it's ours to do with as we please."

Jack leaned back in his seat. The legs crossed again. He smiled at the three men and let a little more cockiness show. "Do you want to hear the setup or should I find my own way out?"

"We're asking fair questions," Golightly replied. His tone made it clear he wasn't the least bit apologetic.

"No, you're nit-picking before you've heard the pitch."

"No, we're —"

"If I'm wasting my time, Brian, let's call it quits now."

Blank had cleared his calendar for this meeting. He had an hour to kill with nothing better to do. He cleared his throat and decided to hear him out. "All right, continue."

"Good decision. As I said, this is a midsize company. About four hundred million in revenue, and fifty mil in profit two years ago. It's lean and efficient, but competes in a low-margin business. They were asking for a hundred mil. See where I'm going with this?"

The three boys from CG exchanged looks that quickly turned into shrugs. No idea.

Jack smiled again, and exposed a little more of the chip on his shoulder. "I asked the CEO what he intended to do with the money. About half for plant expansion, a quarter to hire more salespeople, the rest for updating a few systems."

"And what bothered you about that?"

Golightly asked.

"According to him, his company was already clearing fifty million in profit annually. Do the math, Brian. That means a hundred and fifty million for investment, minimum."

"So?"

"So, for fifty million they accomplish the same goals, without selling any ownership. For a hundred and fifty mil they could build an entire new company."

This point seemed to arouse some interest. "You think he was hiding something?" Golightly asked.

Jack nodded. "I was sure of it."

They focused on his lips and waited to hear what was being hidden. Come on, Jack, spill it, their eyes were saying.

Instead, Jack said, "I think I'd love a cup of coffee."

3

The woman returned and filled three cups with coffee. The cups were fine china, boldly embossed with the large gold letters CG. Jack chose black and took his first deep sip; the coffee was watery and weak.

The accountant drank tea, no cream, no sweetener. He made loud slurping noises as he sipped.

Once they were settled, Blank decided it was time to shift control. He opened by asking, "If this is such an incredible opportunity, why aren't your partners at Cauldron taking advantage of it?"

"May I be frank?"

"You better be."

"Not a good fit, Mr. Blank. Cauldron never involves itself in unfriendly takeovers, for one thing."

"Why not?"

"My partners regard it as unseemly. They're pretty old-fashioned that way, and so are our clients. They don't like getting their fingers dirty."

By inference, the boys on the other side of the table had no compunction about wallowing in mud.

"If that rubs wrong, I meant no offense," Jack added quickly, nodding contritely at the men across the table.

The apology was wasted — absolutely no offense had been taken.

"Are we the first firm you've approached?" Blank asked.

"Yes. But don't think that means you'll be the last."

"Why us?"

Jack appeared to contemplate this question a moment. He took a long sip of coffee. "It happens that you share one or two common markets with this company, an essential quality in whoever I team with."

"Why is that important?"

"I don't intend to get into that yet."

"That's it?"

"No, there's more, plenty more. The Capitol Group obviously brings a lot to the table — influence, marketing muscle, deep pockets, a track record for doing what it takes to win." He quickly added, "And so do several other firms."

Blank shared a wink with Golightly that

Jack was obviously meant to catch. "Why don't we go back to this big secret the CEO was supposed to be hiding?"

"All right. I did a little digging after our meeting. The more I dug, the more convinced I became the CEO was concealing something. I was right."

"What kind of digging?"

"Later. Once we have a deal, I'll lay it all out for you."

Not *if,* but *once* — as if the option belonged to Wiley. Who did this guy think he was dealing with? The boys from CG exchanged a few more looks.

Blank planted his elbows on the table and bent far forward. "Look, we're very busy people, Wiley. I think you better tell us what it is."

"Sure." Jack smiled, as if to say, Lousy timing, but if you insist. "The CEO is a chemical engineer. He and a few of his people spent years working on a new product. They called it Project Holy Grail. For reasons that will become evident, the past two years they threw everything they had into it. They worked around the clock. Weekends, no holidays, late nights, they nearly killed themselves."

"But they found it?"

Jack nodded. "Unfortunately, it's a new

market for them. One I think will be very difficult for this company to break into. It happens to be one where CG is a dominant player."

"Look, we're all getting tired of the vagueness, Wiley. It's about time you tell us what this product is," Golightly prodded, tapping the table, clearly speaking for his friends.

"If you like." Jack paused. He let the suspense build for a moment. "It's a polymer coating. Paint it onto a combat vehicle, any vehicle really, and it pretends it's thirty inches of armor."

The three faces across the table displayed complete indifference. Blank shifted his rather broad rear forward in his chair. Big deal, his posture said. "Right now, the market's full of crap like this, Wiley. If I had a dollar for every nutcase who claims to have invented a new lightweight armor, I'd own CG."

"I didn't say it was armor," Jack patiently corrected him. "Here's the important point. This polymer is also reactive. Do you understand what that means?"

Three collective shrugs.

"Embedded in this polymer are millions of, well, for simplicity's sake, call them beads. Tiny little beads. The concept is unique and performs beautifully. They act like explosives. When a penetrating rod hits the polymer, these little beads explode outward. Do you understand the physics of this?"

"Why don't we listen to you explain it," Blank replied, giving the impression that he could write a textbook on the subject.

Jack leaned forward on his elbows and explained, "Every time we invent a new type of armor, or improve on an old form, the bad guys initiate a mad scramble for a way to defeat it. It's a game, a long game without end. The most common way to attack modern armor is through designed stages. Sometimes the explosive strikes first, maybe softens or ruptures the armor, then a penetrating rod hits and punches through. Sometimes the rod isn't designed to penetrate, but to turn the tables, to use the armor against itself. The idea is to inflict spalling, to cause the armor to lose its integrity, to break apart, then these big chunks of metal bounce around inside the vehicle. It's a tanker's worst nightmare."

"And these beads prevent that?" Golightly asked. He specialized in defense industries; to his discomfort, though, his expertise was aviation systems, and this was way over his head.

"Exactly, Brian. Remember, these beads

explode out, tens of thousands of them, simultaneously. The force merges, becomes collective, dynamic. It counters, in fact, it defeats any of these so-called penetrators. Best of all, there's no inward force; thus, no spalling."

"And you just paint it on?"

"It's slightly more complicated than that. But yes, essentially. Two coats, applied in a sterile, high-pressure environment, ten hours to congeal, and voilà — the equivalent of thirty inches of steel coating."

"And you could put this stuff on, say, a Humvee?"

"Sure. A Humvee, a tank, a Bradley Fighting Vehicle, your grandmother's car. It's surprisingly lightweight. Coat an entire Humvee, you add only fifteen pounds to the overall weight. Its adhesive quality is almost miraculous."

"Has it been patented?" Golightly asked, the predictable question regarding all new developments.

Jack obviously anticipated it. "As research progressed, the company filed every time it made a breakthrough. It's a complicated formula and a long chemical process. Years of work and progress, a lot of small breakthroughs that add up to a seismic invention. All told, we're talking twenty-one U.S. and sixteen approved international patents."

"But is the overall product patented?" Blank asked rudely, as if Jack had evaded the question.

"No, not yet."

"Why not?"

Jack, hesitated then released a heavy breath as if to say, I shouldn't have to explain this, but . . . Instead he said, "Patents are public domain, Mr. Blank. The instant they're approved, they're posted online. Lots of firms hire researchers who study every new patent. File the finished product and you announce to the world what you've got. The CEO played it smart. He found a watertight way to protect the confidentiality. The entire process is wrapped in ten tons of legal protection, but nobody knows it exists."

"Has it been tested?" Blank asked in a tone that was growing increasingly antagonistic.

"Yes, under very realistic conditions. Only by the company, though."

"Then you have only their word that it works?"

"For the time being, I'd prefer not to disclose what I know, or how I know it."

"So we have only *your* word."

"That's right." Jack pushed his coffee cup

away. With a few loud snaps, he opened his briefcase — they were sure he was going to withdraw filched lab results or a spreadsheet, some form of incontrovertible proof to back up his remarkable claims. He instead picked up the stack of slides and began stuffing them in the case.

Blank watched him. "What are you doing?"

"What does it look like I'm doing?"

"Leaving."

Very coolly, Jack said, "You finally got something right today, Mr. Blank. Congratulations."

"You're not finished, are you?"

Jack smiled and continued packing his briefcase. "Uh-oh, back to the dumb questions again."

The accountant looked at Blank and explained the obvious. "I think leaving usually means finished."

"I don't get it, Wiley. You asked for this meeting."

"You're right, Mr. Blank. My mistake."

"What are you talking about?" Golightly asked, unnerved by how quickly this was unraveling.

Jack snapped shut his case and looked up. "I hope you enjoyed the insults, because they were very expensive. Now allow me to

51

leave you with something to ponder. This company can be had for as little as a hundred million. One-fifty at the outside. The first year, sales will almost definitely hit the four billion range. The second year, at least six. After that, it depends on a few variables."

"Variables?"

Jack looked at them as if he was tired of having to explain such simple concepts. "The U.S. Army and Marine Corps are the obvious first customers. They'll be pleading for all the polymer you can produce, as fast as you can manufacture it. And did I mention this polymer can hold dye? Take gray, for instance; a prosperous color. Imagine now if the Navy was persuaded to paint its ships with this polymer. Twelve aircraft carriers coated, head to stern, then a hundred destroyers, and three hundred assorted other warships."

The jaws on the other side of the table were dropping. The numbers struck like bullets.

Jack continued in the same assured businesslike tone. "And that's only the beginning. There's a large private market as well — corporate limousines, police cars, bulletproof vests. And of course, the United States isn't the only country with military vehicles that need protection. Marketed properly, I envision sales to reach the fifteen billion a year range." Jack smiled. "Of course, I come from a small, backward firm. Meekness is bred into me. Regrettably, I tend to underestimate these things."

The three men across the table suddenly found it hard to breathe. Their knees went weak. Had they heard right? The magic numbers hung in the air. The accountant was noisily scribbling figures on his beloved legal pad.

Four billion the first year alone — a two thousand percent return in only twelve months. Four billion! Why hadn't Jack announced that at the start?

"Jack, sit down and stay a little longer. Please," Blank pleaded, suddenly overwhelmed with affection for Jack Wiley. "There's a lot more for us to discuss." He tried a smile that came across like a tree tortured by the wind. "Please, Jack."

Jack glanced at his watch. "My flight leaves in thirty minutes. I meet with a firm in New York in three hours. At five, I have to be in Pennsylvania for another meeting. Sorry, boys, busy day."

"These meetings wouldn't be about this polymer, would they?" Golightly asked, overcome with a sudden feeling of nausea.

53

If this deal walked out the door, if it turned out to be half what Wiley promised, and if some other firm bagged Jack Wiley, he might as well throw himself out of the window.

If, if, if — three big ifs. A sickening feeling was telling him the ifs were about to become whens.

At least it wouldn't be a solo flight: Blank would splat in the parking lot right beside him.

"I tried to warn you, Brian," Jack said. "Three times. You blew it. It wasn't an empty bluff, you should've listened."

"Don't be that way. It's not personal, Jack, it's business."

"Exactly, it's business." Jack now had his case packed and was standing by the door. He turned his back on them and said, "I'll listen to what the other firms offer. Then, maybe, I'll get back to you."

With that parting shot he was out the door, gone.

Like that, the fifteen-billion-dollar man disappeared.

The three men huddled together for a terrifying moment. Agreement came quickly and unanimously; a few frantic, sweaty handshakes and a firm bargain was violently sealed. What a disaster.

"You blew it," he'd said — and he was right.

Their only prayer was to keep this calamity from the big boys upstairs.

They swore a solemn oath to carry this secret to their graves.

4

The existence of the taping system was known to barely a handful of CG's most senior executives. Beyond that, there was just the small crew of closemouthed listeners hidden in the basement who monitored the action, sifted the nuggets from the useless chatter, and red-lighted anything alarming or worthy of interest to the big bosses upstairs.

Only the LBO boys were targeted. Only their conference rooms were wired. Consideration had once been given to a wholesale expansion, to tapping their phones, bugging their desks, even planting a few listening devices in nearby bathrooms. Put in enough bugs and wire to match Nixon's White House. No way. As quickly as it was raised, that dangerous idea was discarded. The overhead of listeners would multiply sixfold. The chance of exposure would become immense. Why risk it?

The real action took place in the conference rooms anyway.

The system was a necessary precaution, the senior leaders of CG felt. At first, anyway. Over the years some of the LBO boys had been caught wheeling-dealing, cutting side deals, or committing CG to things that weren't technically or even mildly legal.

More than perhaps any other firm in the world, the Capitol Group had a reputation that needed to be protected, whatever the costs.

Over time, the taping system acquired wonderful new purposes. The CEO and a few select directors frequently listened in to decide which of their aspiring LBO cutthroats had the right stuff and which needed to be booted out the door. Truth was, they enjoyed listening to the kids bicker and quarrel, raise the pressure, and go for blood. They loved having ringside seats at the most profitable game in town.

The full-time tenders worked out of a cluttered room in the basement, a small nook fitted with security cameras and a highly sophisticated taping console. They came and went through the service entrance at the rear of the building. They wore grease-stained coveralls, carried pails and brooms, and were coldly ignored by the snooty executives on the upper floors.

Mitch Walters, the CEO, had his big feet planted on his desk. His two big hands gripped the armrests as he craned forward and strained to hear every word, every nuance. The instant they heard Wiley's farewell threat and the door close behind him, Walters punched a button.

The noise stopped. "Idiots. They underestimated him. He's smarter than they are. Much smarter," he announced for the benefit of the older man in the room.

Daniel Bellweather produced a weary nod. "You have to admire it."

"You're right, a perfect ambush. Didn't let on till the very end."

"Just let them act stupid, play like loudmouthed braggarts, then handed them their balls on a plate."

Daniel Bellweather, or Mr. Secretary, as everybody in the firm still called him — without the slightest trace of affection — was a former three-term congressman and, for four years, secretary of defense under a mildly unpopular former Republican president. His tenure in the Pentagon had been somewhat rocky. There had been runaway spending on a few multibillion-dollar hardware programs that produced useless belly flops the military hated. Two martial misadventures that went horribly wrong and resulted in lots of corpses and hasty retreats. Then came the quiet revolt by a bunch of Army generals that had to be brutally quelled.

The former president he had served was now in the grave; dead, he became far more popular than when he was breathing. An average president on his best day, compared with the sorry losers who followed in his stead, he had been lionized as one of the greats, an afterglow that trickled down to his retainers and aides.

They were the sage architects, the wise elder statesmen of an administration notable for one unforgettable achievement: it produced no great disasters. Two full terms. Eight years without a single market meltdown, no big wars, and, in a modern record, slightly less than half his cabinet ended up under indictment or in prison.

No successive administration had even come close.

Mid-seventies, craggy-faced, tall, thick white hair, portly, but not too much, Daniel Bellweather had weathered nicely into the picture of an eminent Washington mandarin. For eight years before Walters, he had been the CEO. He steered the ship and attended to the details. He roared into the office screaming at six every morning and didn't mellow out until six in the evening. He stoked the ranks with as much greed, fear, and insecurity as he could manage, and kept the immense profits flowing.

His tantrums were legendary. Firm lore had it that after one of Bellweather's calmer tongue-lashings, a senior VP fled down to the parking lot, withdrew a pistol from the glove compartment, and reupholstered the interior of his Mercedes with his brains.

That myth was a wild fabrication. The man had flung himself from an upper-floor window and painted the car's exterior.

But after eight years at the helm, eight years of steadily increasing profits, and after getting richer than he ever believed possible, Bellweather suffered his first stroke. A mild one. Little more than a bad headache, really; his first scary glimpse, however, that all good things come to an end. In shock, he stepped back from the unrelenting pressure and retreated into the fringe role of director.

Time to kick back and relax, he told himself; enjoy the fruits of thirty years of juking and jiving around Washington, of draining the swamp of as much cash as he could stuff into his pockets. It had been a terrific run; flee now, enjoy the good life, go on an epic spending spree, escape before it killed him.

A year rolling through the coastal enclaves of enormous wealth followed. Then six months bouncing around the Caribbean on his mammoth yacht — a full year and a half of lovely tranquillity, eighteen months removed from the mad hustle-bustle of D.C. — before he decided he had made a horrible mistake. He became bored and miserable. Always a pathetic golfer, if anything, he became more terrible.

And hanging around with a bunch of rich has-beens only reminded him of his own sorry diminished status. The perks, the sense of self-importance, and the action were calling him back. Plus, with all that time together, his rather young third wife suddenly discovered what her predecessors had learned: she loathed him. She took to sleeping in another bedroom, which was fine by him because the sex had turned dull and he was tired of her snoring anyway.

Also he learned about the yardman, Juan, a handsome young Latin hunk who trimmed a little more than the hedges.

Bellweather promptly sold the yacht, fired the gardener, dumped the wife, and had himself installed as managing director, a vague title that required very little work, yet

61

gave him carte blanche to nose into any nook or cranny that interested him. The position of institutional magpie suited his tastes immensely, the exquisite privilege of looking over his successor's shoulder and second-guessing him at every turn.

"Think it's real?" Walters asked, sounding deeply depressed.

"Maybe. Who knows?"

"Good question. Who knows?"

"Well, Wiley — I guess he knows."

"Yeah, and he didn't sound like a guy who's shooting blanks."

"The Holy Grail project," Bellweather repeated, letting the sound roll off his tongue. "If Wiley's even half on the mark, that's exactly what this polymer is. Do you know how much the military would pay for this miracle coating?"

Walters rolled forward in his chair and pinched his eyebrows together. He had a pretty good idea, and that depressed him all the more. "Who's this company he's talking about?"

"Could be anybody, really. He was very cagey."

They had both listened to the tape, three times, replaying certain key sections until they thought they'd be sick; Wiley had never once slipped. Not once, not a clue, not a breadcrumb. Walters quickly summed up the little they knew: "The CEO of this mysterious company is a chemical engineer. Two years ago, his firm pushed sales of about four hundred million. It's a penny stock." He rubbed his shiny forehead in frustration and said, "Any of ten thousand companies fit that bill, Dan. Could be Hostess Twinkies, for all we know."

"Who do you think he's meeting with now?" Bellweather asked after a long moment of staring at the walls.

"No idea. But they probably look a lot like us. He mentioned New York and Pennsylvania. Could be corporate, say, GE or United Technologies. I hope it's not another big takeover outfit."

The names of a dozen fierce competitors rattled through their brains and for a long ugly moment they shared the same depressing thought. In the small, intensely competitive world of big-league equity firms, word would spread like a flash fire that CG had let the biggest catch of the year slip out of its grasp. Worse, CG, for a variety of reasons, specialized in defense work. It dabbled in countless other areas, diversifying to protect itself against the eventuality of an outbreak of world peace, unwelcome and unlikely as that might be. War, however, was its mainstay. Gouging a large chunk of defense pork remained its bread and butter.

Oh yes, the story of how CG clumsily let Wiley and the most remarkable defense product of the decade walk out the door would roar around town.

It would be more than Walters could bear. He could almost hear the snickers from his buddies at the Congressional Club. Could almost picture the insufferable smirks. "Yo, Mitch, what does fifteen billion slamming the door sound like?" — he could make up the sorry insults himself. Maybe he'd give up golf for a month or two.

Actually, a decade or two might be more like it, he sadly admitted to himself.

"We need to find our boy Jack," Bellweather announced very firmly, an idea that got a quick nod from Walters. "Tonight. Before he has time to settle on somebody else."

"He's going to make us eat dirt," Walters prophesied with a mournful scowl.

"We deserve it. Let him rub it in till he gets tired of it. Who do you want to handle it?"

"Keep it low-key, for now. He's got us on the ropes and he knows it. But we can't afford to cede leverage." Walters folded his arms, recovered his composure, and calmly said, "Bill Feist. He has a real gift for this sort of thing."

"Yep, a born ass-kisser. Send him up on the jet. Not the small one, the big one. Tell him to forget the normal wine-and-dine, and forget the half-measured approach. Think fifteen billion dollars."

"Bill's good at that, as you know."

"This time, it's worth every penny." Bellweather pushed off from the wall and over his shoulder said, "And find out whatever we can about this Jack Wiley."

Locating Jack turned out to be loaded with more complications than anybody expected. This task was handled by a private security firm located in Crystal City, a midsize, discreet outfit loaded with washed-up former Feds and spooks who often did work for CG.

TFAC, it was called, a cluster of initials that stood for absolutely nothing but seemed to have a nice ring to it. TFAC was among a growing number of private outfits in D.C., fueled by the explosion of clandestine services and operations after 9/11 that slid easily in the shadows between government and private-sector work. The Capitol Group was their second largest client, right behind Uncle Sam. The U.S. government could wait; the snoops dropped everything and promised instant results.

Locating Jack was kid's play, or so they thought initially. They focused first on New York City, especially Manhattan, the normal habitat of single young millionaires. Just to be on the safe side, they also weeded through the other boroughs as well. Eleven Jack Wileys turned up. After two hours of running down the prospects, ten of the eleven fell out: six married; two tucked away in retirement homes; one ensconced in jail; one in the hospital coughing out his lungs and dying of AIDS, of all things.

Jack Wiley number eleven lived in Queens.

Queens! — no way could this be the right Jack. No self-respecting young bachelor millionaire would be caught dead living there, and he was quickly dropped before anybody wasted further time on tracking him down.

More troops were thrown into the breach and the search widened to northern Jersey, Long Island, and Westchester County, the usual burbs for well-to-do New Yorkers.

Dead ends piled on top of more dead ends. Then, voilà: a likely prospect popped up with his phone number listed, along with his address.

It looked right and it smelled right. The area code hinted at big money. They needed to be sure, though.

A female researcher claiming to be the dispatcher for a national delivery service called Jack's assistant at the main Cauldron office, two blocks off Wall Street. "It's a package marked urgent we've tried twice, unsuccessfully, to deliver," she explained, sounding very distressed — the white foam container probably had some of those mail-order steaks that cost a fortune and turn rotten and stinky in the blink of an eye. "The address must be off," she complained, loudly playing up her frustration. "Just thank the Lord Mr. Wiley had thought to include his work number with his order."

The TFAC researcher rattled off the address, deliberately mixing up two numbers; the assistant promptly and sharply corrected the mistake.

It was him!

The address was punched into a computer, then, via the wonders of Google and its satellite service, they found themselves ogling a top-down satellite shot of the neighborhood. A technician adroitly expanded, shifted, and manipulated the picture until they were staring at a grainy, blown-up image of the roof of one Jack Wiley.

Jack, it turned out, lived in a large, roomy

brick two-story in the town of Rumson, a leafy, very well-to-do northern Jersey suburb, one block from the Navesink River, and a ferry shot from the Big Apple.

One of the former Fibbies knew the police chief of a nearby borough. A friendly phone call and a nosy local cop was immediately dispatched for a quick look-see. He snapped pictures of the front, then left his cruiser and snuck around to get wide-angle shots of the sides and rear.

Georgian in style, red brick all around, about seventy years old, three chimneys, perhaps eight thousand square feet, with a large walk-out basement. One entrance in the front. One in the rear. Twelve ground-level windows.

A sticker on the lower corner of a front window declared that Jack had devices and security provided by Vector, a national outfit that happened, by happy coincidence, to belong to the Capitol Group.

A different group of snoops in a large room two floors below was laboring to unearth everything that could be learned about Jack Wiley.

The order was vague and nonspecific. Information of any nature or form on Wiley would be appreciated. They knew their client, though: dirt, as much as could be found, would be even more richly appreciated.

This team was led by Martie O'Neal, a former FBI agent who once ran the background investigations unit for the Bureau. Martie was a legendary snoop with a legion of helpful contacts in government and the private sector. Digging up dirt was his specialty and his passion. Given two weeks, he could tell you the name of Jack's first childhood crush, whether he was a Jockey or boxer man, his preferences in extracurricular drugs, who he diddled in his spare time, any medical issues, his net worth, and how he voted.

He was given only five hours. Five fast and furious hours to unearth as much detail and dirt as could be found. He cherished a challenge and dug in with both fists. His squad of assistants gathered around and Martie began barking orders. The phones and faxes were kicked into gear and information began flowing in.

By one o'clock, Martie had Jack's report cards from college down to elementary level; as advertised, he was a very smart boy. Twenty minutes later, Jack's home mortgage was splayed across Martie's desk: a fifteen-year jumbo at five and a half percent. The home had cost four million; Jack plunked down three mil, and now owed $700K. Never missed or even been late with a payment.

Jack was not only smart and rich, O'Neal decided, he was also tidy and diligent, and a savvy investor with a good eye for the deal. The most recent assessment listed the home as worth nine million.

By two, after calling in a big favor, Martie had his rather large and crooked nose stuffed inside Jack's Army record, as well as his father's. Jack's ratings from his Army bosses were uniformly exceptional. The common emphasis was his coolness under fire, his exceptional leadership qualities, and his care and concern for his men.

His father served thirty-three years, a mustang who battled his way up from private to colonel and retired after twice being passed over for brigadier general. Nothing to be ashamed of there; the old man's record was quite impressive. The old man was dead, after a long, spirited battle with cancer, buried in Arlington National right beside Jack's mother, who had passed away five years before of a stroke that left her debilitated and nearly comatose for three horrible years as her husband and son cared for her. Army medical insurance had paid her bills until Jack and his father decided to go outside the system; Jack covered the rather hefty expenses after that. O'Neal even had the grave numbers in the event anybody cared to check, unlikely as that seemed.

By three, Jack's love life was being peeled back. This was accomplished the usual way. From the report cards, O'Neal's snoops began speed-dialing Jack's old teachers, a path that led directly to childhood chums, and from there to his present acquaintances. They identified themselves as FBI agents. A routine background check for a security clearance Jack had applied for, they explained ever so casually with a heavy splash of boredom as though they cared less about Jack, and didn't really care to nose through the old closets of his life. From prior experience, four out of five people typically accepted this at face value. The usual odds held and they hung up on anybody questioning their legitimacy.

Gullibility and the call of patriotic duty nearly always got the tongues wagging. How nice it felt to smear and spread rumors, to tarnish and trash reputations — anonymously, of course, and all in the name of Old Glory.

The names of Jack's classmates began pouring in, more phone calls that yielded more names. Old friends begat newer friends, and the stampede was on.

A large board on a wall was created: the "Put-Jack-in-the-Box" profile, some wag named it, and that drew a big chuckle from the overworked searchers. The room quickly became wallpapered in yellow Post-it notes and a large spiderweb that linked together the widening network of Jack's friends and business associates. By five, the researchers had more information than they could handle, with hundreds of leads that needed to be followed up.

A cursory profile had taken shape, though. Handsome, Catholic, no glitches in his career. No drugs, no medical problems, no arrests. Jack had never been sued, nor had he ever sued. He drank — fine imported scotch seemed to be his beverage of choice — but rarely to excess. There were a few college tales about Jack tying one on and whooping it up, all harmless fun, but nothing since then. He enjoyed the ladies, they enjoyed him.

He voted Republican, with one exception, a college roommate who made a hard run for a New Jersey Senate seat. Jack contributed the legal limit, and even did a little volunteer work in the campaign office. The roommate proved too radical even for New

Jersey's champagne liberals and got shellacked anyway.

The previous year's tax return had been easily acquired and quickly evaluated by a financial forensics stud. That effort produced the following estimates: minus his real estate holdings, Jack's net worth nested between fifteen and twenty-five million, probably around twenty; the previous year, his pretax income was six million and change; he invested carefully and conservatively, tucking the bulk of his money in tax-free municipal bonds; aside from his home mortgage, no debts, no child support, no alimony.

In short, after a superficial five-hour peek, Jack was discovered to be moderately wealthy, a wholesome, apparently well-adjusted, red-blooded, healthy American male who drove a three-year-old Lincoln (this was the only surprise; his profile nearly screamed Beemer or Mercedes). He had dated serially his whole life, tapering off a lot the past few years. Why was an open question. A good-looking, wealthy bachelor who had never been married raised obvious questions about his sexual disposition. The evidence, though, simply did not support a man who didn't enjoy the company of women. Perhaps boredom, or an emotional setback, or plain disinterest accounted for it. Maybe he just enjoyed being single. His four-year fling at Princeton had been his only long-term romance.

If he had a current love interest, nobody knew about her.

Also, he owned a small, quaint cottage on the shore of Lake George; occasionally he spent weekends there, and all his vacations as best they could tell. No Vail, no Aspen, no Hamptons. No hobby ranch out of the middle of Nowhere, Montana, where he raised hobby horses and prattled around in cowboy duds, playing at Roy Rogers on the big range. None of the usual enclaves where the rich and hyperambitious mingled and vied to show off the swankest house, the biggest yacht, the gaudiest toys.

O'Neal was satisfied with the amount of information gathered and deeply concerned about the utter vagueness of it all. A lot of traits and colors that added up to barely a sketch: it remained anything but a painting. The absence of dirt or bad habits was particularly annoying.

O'Neal held out hope, though. After only a few hours of digging, what did they expect? Martie was confident he could find it, given enough time. He had vetted Supreme Court nominees, cabinet members, even a number of senior generals and admirals in need of background clearances. There was always something. Always. Some dark secret. Some hidden fantasy life or regretful sexual escapade, some concealed addiction or crime or loony aunt tucked away in an attic.

If it was there — and Martie O'Neal was sure it was — he would find it.

A terse written summary was sent by messenger and hand-delivered to Mitch Walters.

A scrawled directive from the big man himself shot back an hour later: Spend whatever it takes, do whatever it takes, keep looking.

In other words, find the dirt or concoct it.

At six, the taxi dropped him off, and Jack stepped off at the curb to discover a long, shiny black stretch limo idling, dead center, in his driveway. A rear door flew open and out popped a silver-maned man dressed in an elegant black tuxedo, who eagerly and noisily closed the distance. "Bill Feist," he barked before he was all over Jack. A crushing handshake accompanied a huge smile: Jack quickly lost count of the backslaps. "Listen," Feist told him, frowning tightly, "about that thing this morning, we couldn't be sorrier. An awful embarrassment. Edward

Blank, what a horse's ass. We let him go this afternoon."

Before Jack could react to that news, the frown flipped into a smile that seemed to stretch from wisdom tooth to wisdom tooth. "So, Jack, what are your plans for the evening?"

"Oh, you know. Slap a little dinner in the microwave. Catch up on the news. Then I thought I'd slip into my office and digest the offers I got today."

"Time for that later. Hey, you got a tux?"

"Yes, why?"

"Don't ask, just believe me, you'll have a ball. I mean, literally, a ball." A pause and the smile seemed to widen. "Incidentally, the tux has to be black."

"Forget it, Mr. Feist. I have another meeting in the morning."

"It's Bill, and of course you do. Where?"

"In the city, but it's early," Jack replied, digging in his heels.

"I'll have you home by midnight, promise."

"Look, I appreciate the —"

"Don't make me beg, Jack. Think of the kids I'm trying to shove through college. Spoiled brats, both of them — if I get sacked, they'll come home, and my life will turn miserable." He paused before he whispered, almost an afterthought, "Ever met the president?"

"What president?"

"Good one, Jack. We're going to the White House. Come on, grab your tux."

Whatever reservations Jack had felt instantly disappeared. "Give me a minute." Inside five minutes, he was sinking comfortably into his seat in the rear of the long stretch limo, his tux packed neatly in the trunk, his new friend Bill shoving a scotch with two cubes in his fist. "Glenfiddich on the rocks," Bill announced with a knowing wink. "Your favorite, right, Jack?"

"You've done your homework since this morning," Jack noted, accepting the drink.

"We got off to a slow start, but we'll catch up. I'm aware you don't smoke, but would you care for a cigar?"

"Don't overdo it, Bill."

Feist chuckled. Unable to stop himself, he held up a paperback novel; the cover displayed an inhumanly handsome man with engorged muscles wrapped tightly around a lusty-eyed woman. The girl was dressed, or barely dressed, in an impossibly tiny string bikini; the guy wore an even skimpier loincloth. They stood knee-deep in the frothing waves of a white beach, a large orange sun setting gently behind some generic jungle paradise. *Ecstasy in the Wild,* screamed the luridly suggestive title in large silver letters.

"Read the first ten chapters on the way up," Bill reported, slapping the cover. "Tammy Albert — lovely girl from the jacket picture. You actually dated her at Princeton?"

Jack took the question in stride. "How was the book?"

"Truthfully?" Bill didn't wait for a response. "Awful, I mean really pathetic. Women actually read this weepy crap?"

"She can buy and sell both of us. Tammy's sold over forty million copies."

"For real?"

Jack smiled. "In college, she dreamed of writing the great American novel. Apparently she changed her mind." Jack paused. "What's this about, Mr. Feist?"

"It's Bill, and forget business tonight. I'm only here to make amends for the morning."

"Won't be easy."

"Didn't think it would."

"Well, give it your best shot."

The large limo swept through the dying remnants of rush hour and nearly sprinted to the airport. Feist handled Jack like a pro;

the banter and jokes and scotch never abated for an instant. After ten minutes, Jack was Jack, my boy. After twenty, Jack's arm was limp from being squeezed and massaged.

Call-me-Bill's best shot turned out to include a Boeing 747 parked at Teterboro Airport, fueled up, ready to launch. An armada of corporate and private jets was littered about, a convention of shiny Lears and Gulfstreams and Embraers. Beside the 747, the entire lot looked cheap, like a puny third world air force. Large gold letters — THE CAPITOL GROUP — were splashed on the side to be sure everybody knew exactly who to envy.

Bill bounded up the stairs and nearly danced into the expansive cabin, as if he owned the plane. Inside were only eight chairs, a large conference table, an entertainment console with a gigantic flat-screen television, two workstations, and a gleaming oak bar, all surrounded by enough burled wood to make a rain forest blush from envy. Designed to seat hundreds, the plane had been gutted and gentrified with enough luxury appointments to satisfy the wildest fantasies of only eight. "It's often used for overseas flights," Bill mentioned, as if any explanation was called for. "CG believes in taking care of its people."

Speaking of people, two striking young women in cocktail dresses — one brunette, one blonde — occupied two of the seats. "Jack, this is Eva and Eleanor," Bill announced with a wave of his hand.

It was impossible to tell which was more fetching. Tall, bare-shouldered, high-cheekboned, matched blue eyes — both were nothing short of stunning, with incredibly long pairs of legs that seemed to stretch to their earlobes. If they weighed two hundred pounds together, it would be a miracle. There was barely any back to Eleanor's dress, barely any front to Eva's.

The brunette, Eva, carefully eased out of her seat and approached Jack with her hand out and a dazzling smile, one that disclosed a spectacularly talented dentist. "I think you and I are together tonight. I hope you don't mind."

Before Jack could jump to hasty conclusions, Bill explained, "This shindig is a couples affair. Eva works at CG, the accounting department, if you can believe it."

Jack didn't believe it — the idea of anybody wasting legs like that on numbers defied reality. But he nodded and said, "I don't mind at all." Really, how could he?

Eva pretended to act relieved, as if there

was any chance Jack would be disappointed.

The instant they fell into their seats the jet sprinted smoothly down the runway, lifted off, and gained altitude. A smiling young lady in a handsome blue uniform materialized out of nowhere. She was hauling a tray with four flutes of bubbly and a large silver bowl overflowing with black beluga caviar. Bill threw a wink in Jack's direction. "We're quite serious about making up for this morning."

Jack took the first slow sip from his flute. There was no label, but from the profusion of spirited bubbles, Jack calculated at least a hundred dollars per flute. He dug a cracker into the caviar, pulled out a large dollop, and inhaled the first small nibble. The caviar was so fresh it made loud pops when he chewed.

Eva reached across Jack toward the caviar. "You played lacrosse in college, I hear," she said by way of opening a conversation.

Jack nodded.

"So did I. Harvard, class of 1999." Not only Harvard undergrad, it turned out, also the B-school, and Eva threw out a few of the professors' names she was sure Jack would recognize. It further turned out that she happened also to be an Army brat and an All-America, three years, first team, goalie.

She flirted shamelessly, and laughed and smiled at the slightest tinkle of humor. Their life stories were nearly identical: military brats, MBAs from Harvard, college lacrosse stars, with a million common interests left to be discovered and explored.

Just another all-American couple brought together by the wonderful, caring folks at the Capitol Group. By Delaware, they were swapping names of Army posts where they had lived, and Eva was treating Jack to hilarious stories about a legendary B-school professor who had chased her around the classroom a few times.

He had been one of Jack's favorite teachers. You never knew.

Thirty minutes after the limo departed, three men dressed in black and wearing gloves and sneakers quietly eased up to the rear door of Jack's house. The door led to Jack's walk-out basement; as they were warned it would be, it was locked. One man briefly studied the lock, withdrew a small kit from his pocket, and selected the perfect pick. The door swung wide open inside a minute.

The alarm was silent and connected

directly to a Vector Security branch office in Red Bank, about twenty minutes away.

One of the three, a crackerjack at electronics and alarms, barely gave the alarm system a glance. Who cared? Howl for all you're worth, he wanted to scream. The night crew at the Vector branch office was under orders directly from the regional headquarters to ignore it. A test, they were told, one requested by the owner. A technician shut it down a minute after it went off.

The three men climbed the stairs to the ground level. They paused and began a cursory survey. Enormous house for a bachelor, they agreed. Nicely furnished, too, and in a decidedly masculine fashion they all liked a lot — dark leather, wood paneling, and heavy furniture were the predominant theme, the kind of decor a girlfriend would loudly admire as she quietly schemed about replacing everything with whites and flowery pinks the instant she moved in.

They paused briefly to envy Jack's cavernous family room — a massive walk-in fireplace; heavy, ornately carved pool table; and a mammoth flat-panel hanging off a wall. This is why you get rich, one remarked, and they all laughed. One man climbed the stairs to begin nosing through Jack's bedroom and bath. The other two raced to the large home office, where the real work would be accomplished.

Jack's tan buttery briefcase was located on the floor, wedged awkwardly between the trash can and desk. They attacked this first. The paper slides concerning this company with the miracle product were withdrawn then, one by one, photocopied on the portable copier one man had hauled in. Odd, one remarked, that the papers never yielded the name of the company. But so what? The slides were no doubt loaded with hints and clues that might be unraveled later, to reveal the name.

Next, Jack's black book was located and also photocopied; the snoops down in D.C. could mine it for more information and leads. One man began digging through desk drawers, the other rifled through the big wooden file cabinet against the wall. Fortunately, Jack was the neat and organized type. They appreciated this. The files were alphabetically organized by topic — dental, financial, medical, social, and so forth. Three years of credit card purchases and four years of old tax returns were also withdrawn and efficiently photocopied.

O'Neal had given them a detailed inventory of topics to search for; they marveled at how easy Jack Wiley made it.

By then the upstairs man had finished with the bedroom — nothing the least bit interesting, certainly nothing incriminating, a place to sleep, nothing more — and was preparing to switch the search into the bathroom. On Jack's dresser sat a silver-framed black-and-white photo of a handsome military officer with his lovely, adoring wife, Jack's parents, no doubt.

But there were no photos of any other women, which certainly seemed to support the existing theory that Jack was currently unencumbered in the romance department.

He eased into the bathroom, stuffed his pug nose inside Jack's medicine cabinet, and began poking around. Nothing worth noting here, either — the normal array of shaving supplies, mouthwash, toothpaste, and a spare bottle of shampoo. The strongest medicine in the cabinet was a bottle of aspirin — unopened and two years past the expiration date.

They would continue the search for two more hours. Everything — every paper, every paper clip — would be put away just as they found it. They were pros. They would leave only two traces of their presence.

Before they snuck back out the rear door, the electronics man would stuff bugs into all of Jack's phones.

The other two would plant a five-pound sack of marijuana on a storage shelf at the back of Jack's expansive three-car garage, slightly behind a mulch bag Jack might never touch, but certainly not before spring. An insurance policy; they had done this before and it worked like magic.

If it was needed, fine.

If not, they would sneak back at some later date and retrieve it.

The instant the jet cruised up to the private terminal at Ronald Reagan Airport, another black stretch limo raced up and cruised to a stop at the bottom of the steps. Jack, Bill, and the girls piled in, laughing at another Feist joke and having a ball. Feist began doling out the booze before they were rolling. He was a heavy drinker, matching Jack at least three for one, but he obviously had had plenty of practice, and he handled the booze well. A brisk ride ensued before they were idling at the side entrance gate to the White House parking lot. Bill rolled down his window and shoved some type of magic pass in the faces of the uniformed security guards. "Thanks, Earl, Tommy," he made a point of saying quite loudly as they were whisked through without a second glance.

"Nice to see you again, Mr. Feist," one barely had time to mumble back as the limo shot by.

"You've been here before," Jack observed.

"I worked here, under two different presidents," Bill noted with an obviously insincere attempt at modesty.

A young naval officer packing enough ribbons and gold braid to capsize a battleship escorted the foursome upstairs, then across a broad hallway, straight into the spacious state dining room, where more than a hundred guests in resplendent finery were already congregated, sharing drinks, stuffing hors d'oeuvres down their throats, and gabbing about important subjects.

Eva and Eleanor were instantly adored by every male in the room. By far the two youngest guests, the most scantily dressed, and the loveliest, half the room admired them with every cell in their body.

The other half plainly detested them.

On just one side of the room alone, Jack picked out the secretary of state, secretary of defense, and chairman of the Joint Chiefs huddled together with their wives. Slightly to their right, the clutch of bespectacled gents whispering seriously among themselves were either Supreme Court justices or excellent imitations.

Bill and Eleanor split off, leaving Jack and Eva to drink, chat, and ponder the incredible fact that they were in the White House. The White House!

Bill immediately launched into a fast-paced whirl, virtually dancing around the room, gripping illustrious hands, complimenting the ladies, flitting from group to group, pollinating laughter in his wake.

If he was trying to impress Jack with who he — and by extension, the boys of CG — rubbed shoulders with, the performance was nothing short of impressive.

On several occasions Eva pointed out some luminary. "Who's the big man Bill's talking to? Isn't he a movie star or something?"

"Was. I think now he's governor of California," Jack answered.

"What about the lady beside him? I'm sure I recognize her face."

"On his left, the attorney general. The other one, the good-looking blonde, she's the intern the president's sleeping with."

"You're kidding, aren't you?" Eva asked, looking more closely at the woman.

"I am, and you can stop now, Eva. The room is loaded with ridiculously famous people. I get it. Any moment they'll notice I don't belong here, and I'll be forced to start waiting tables."

"I don't know what you're talking about."

Jack smiled. "Are you supposed to hustle me all night or can we have fun?"

Rather than pretend embarrassment, Eva laughed. "Am I that obvious?"

"I had you at hello."

"I'm wounded," she said, smiling coyly, apparently relieved to surrender her duties.

Suddenly the president and First Lady, accompanied by another couple, entered; the military band in the corner launched into a gusty version of "Hail to the Chief" and the roomful of powerful people began filtering dutifully in the direction of a reception line. Jack overheard somebody mention that accompanying the president and First Lady were the king and queen of a country he had failed to catch the name of, but where apparently everybody was tall, cadaverously thin, and had terrible complexions.

The royals stood shuffling their feet, making no effort to disguise that they were already bored out of their minds.

Eva grabbed Jack's arm and nearly dragged him to the line. They found themselves crushed between a famous movie producer and a handsome, scowling senator who had run against the president and got creamed. The campaign had been long and nasty, an ugly mudfest. Together, they had polled the lowest voter turnout in history. It was the most expensive, and by general agreement, least inspiring campaign in history.

There was only one conceivable reason the senator was invited here tonight: "Hey, you sorry, loudmouthed loser, how do you like my digs?" they could picture the president asking him with a spiteful grin.

And the rampant rumors about the senator's love life appeared to be accurate. He quietly ignored everything and everybody — that is, everything but Eva's long legs and admirable fanny. The movie producer, on the other hand, launched into a long, simmering diatribe about the appalling situation in Swaziland. An obscure tribe of pygmies was apparently at risk of extinction from an equally indistinct disease the director pronounced differently each time he mentioned it. If only Americans didn't care so little about the world, he moaned with a light flip of his hand, a miracle cure could be found. But for American indifference and stinginess, the tribe could be saved. Indeed, the only reason he had deigned to come here tonight, he confided loudly enough to be heard by everybody in the line, was to bring this abominable issue to the attention of Washington.

"A whole tribe? How awful," Eva remarked, pinching Jack's arm.

"Isn't it?" the by now red-faced director snorted. "A whole line of DNA lost forever. What a terrible, terrible waste."

"Maybe you should make a movie to bring it to the world's attention," Jack suggested, trying not to laugh.

The famous director's face instantly shrank into a wrinkled scowl. "Yes . . . well, unfortunately, there's no money in it."

"How sad," Jack said and he meant it.

The movie director was politely but firmly pushed and shoved through the handshakes before he could get out a half-strangled sentence about this poor ignored tribe and the poisonous microbe — like that, an entire tribe doomed to the dustbin of history.

Eva went next: nobody shoved or hurried her through. In fact, the president awarded her an extra ten or twenty hardfisted pumps with a smile that nearly broke his jaw.

Then it was Jack shaking the most powerful hand in the world. "Nice to meet you," the president said, gripping and grinning with vigor.

"My pleasure, sir," Jack replied, trying gracefully to ease out of his clasp and move on.

The president wouldn't let go. He bent forward. "Hey, ain't you the fella with that miracle goop I been hearing about?"

"Actually, it's —"

"Jack, our boys are dyin' like cattle over there."

"Yes sir, I know."

"Oughta get that stuff over there soon as possible."

"I believe it might —"

"You know, you couldn't do better than the Capitol Group." The president's free hand landed on Jack's shoulder and squeezed. The smile widened and the grip tightened.

"I'll definitely think about it, sir."

"Do that, Jack," he said, suddenly quite serious, before he flashed his trademark silly, lopsided, dismissive grin. "Anything I can do, be sure to let me know."

The ambassadorship to the Court of St. James's would fit the bill rather nicely, Jack was tempted to say, but a well-practiced shove from the president's shoulder hand interceded and Jack found himself walking beside Eva to their dinner table.

"That was amazing," Eva announced, shaking her head, leaving it unclear whether she meant meeting the president or the arm-twisting over CG.

Actually, it wasn't at all unclear. "Absolutely amazing," Jack agreed. The president of the United States had just hawked the Capitol Group. How much did that cost? he wondered.

"He's right, you know."

"That might be a first," Jack replied. "Hasn't been right about much so far."

"I promise I won't say another word after this," Eva told him, placing her hand on his arm as they walked. "CG has the strength and resources to make your dreams come true, Jack."

"I'll take you up on that."

"You'll sign with CG?"

"Don't say another word. More champagne?"

The dinner was lovely and delicious, the speeches predictably horrible, with the president mangling the names of the pimply king and queen, and they danced till eleven before Jack reminded Feist of his promise to have him home by midnight.

Eva offered to fly back up with him, Jack politely and regretfully declined, said his thanks to Feist, and by twelve-thirty was sleeping peacefully in his bed.

5

For seven long days and even longer nights, they did not hear a word from Jack Wiley. He ignored them completely.

But he was anything but ignored by them.

On day four, the gang at TFAC, CG's contract security outfit, eavesdropped on an incoming call to Jack's house phone. The call came at eight in the evening. The caller vaguely identified himself as Tom. No last name, just Tom.

There was a moment of empty pleasantries before Tom came to the point. "I just want to clarify our offer," he told Jack, never quite identifying what firm he represented. "We'd really like to get a deal nailed down."

"Make it better than what I heard this morning and we might," Jack answered a little coolly. "Three of your competitors are offering more. Considerably more," he emphasized, sounding like a man who was holding more offers than he could count.

"You're the bottom of the barrel, Tom. Step it up a notch, or this is a farewell call."

A long, awkward pause. "How did you enjoy Bermuda?"

"It was nice, thanks."

"*Nice,* Jack? Jesus, that was our five-star treatment. The private jet, that glorious estate on the beach, the boat, the big party."

"I told you, it was nice."

"We spared no expense, Jack. The CEO and half the board flew in to meet you. You looked like you were having a ball."

"Okay, Tom, it was *very* nice."

A brief pause, then trying to sound more upbeat, "I spoke with the CEO and board this morning. They want this deal."

"That's good to hear."

"They want it very badly, Jack," Tom said. "They like you, and they love the product. I've never seen them this excited."

"Good. Now remind them how to spell 'excited' — twenty percent ownership for me. Not a percent less."

"Jack, Jack, don't be greedy or near-sighted. Focus on how quickly we can bring the product to market. How much we can sell. How many doors we can kick open. We're big and powerful, and we're prepared to make you a very rich man."

"I'd rather be greedy, Tom. In fact, it's fun."

"Then focus on our resources and reach. We didn't get this big by thinking small."

"Give it a break. A firm of idiots will have the polymer on the market inside a month. You know that, and so do I. The product sells itself. I'll say it again: twenty percent. Are you listening, Tom?"

"Look, Jack, you're putting me between the rock and hard place. Left up to me . . . hell, you'd have it, the full twenty percent."

"But . . . ?"

"Well, sadly, the board just doesn't believe your part's worth that much."

"So now we're down to good cop, bad cop. Don't patronize me, Tom."

"Look, it's —"

"No, you look. My role's worth whatever I say it is. I'll make some other company a boatload of money, and you'll stand on the sideline and watch."

"All right, all right."

"What's that mean?"

"Give me time to canvass them again."

"Fine. Call me at ten tomorrow morning, at the office. Unless your board doesn't meet my demands, then don't bother."

"Jesus, Jack, that's impossible. It's after eight. There are twelve board members, mostly old men. They need their sleep."

"What makes you think I care? This is what you pay them for. After ten, I won't be taking calls from you."

Bellweather and Walters listened to the tape with growing horror. By the sound of it, Wiley was rolling in offers, pitting at least four companies against one another and having a ball. A bidding war, and a rather brutal one, plain and simple. And Jack, holding all the cards, was clearly going for the kneecaps.

"Why hasn't he called us back?" Walters groaned. The past week he had been miserable to live with. His mood alternated between despair and rage, favoring the latter. He banged around the office bullying everyone in range. He'd fired an assistant, screamed at the head of the LBO section, and broken two phones after flinging them against a wall.

None of it made him feel the least bit better.

"Settle down, Mitch. He'll call," Bellweather, the older sage, assured him. It wasn't his tail on the line, after all; he could afford to stay cool and unruffled.

"What's he waiting for?"

"What would you do in his shoes?"

"I don't know. I'd want to have the best

offer in my pocket, I guess."

"So there's your answer."

Walters loosened his tie and fell back in his chair. "He's a real smart boy."

"We already knew that."

"Yeah, but it's not nice to see it in action."

Bellweather moved across the office and leaned casually against his old desk, the same desk shaped like an aircraft carrier, now manned by Walters's rather ample rear end. "Give him two more days," the old man said, looking and sounding quite sure of himself.

"And then?"

"Then we'll make him call. Then we'll order our friends over at TFAC pull out the stops and turn up the heat. What is it this time?"

"Five pounds of marijuana, planted in his garage."

"Nice."

"We debated whether to use the dope scheme or the child porno scam. I opted for the dope. Fits his profile better, I think."

Bellweather grinned his approval. "So in another two days he gets a nasty little visit by our friends at TFAC. The usual routine."

Walters bit back a smile and nodded: the "routine" nearly always worked like a charm. Four of five times, the targets had collapsed like bowling pins. The more they had to lose, the faster they dropped — and Jack had a great deal to lose. Oh yes, it was a perfect little trap.

They avoided each other's eyes a moment, and both dreamed of how it would go down.

As easily with Jack as it had with the others, both men were sure. A few of the TFAC boys would arrive at Jack's doorstep, late at night, unannounced and unexpected. Out would come the authentic-looking search warrant and genuine DEA identifications. They would show up dressed as undercover cowboys: unmarked cars, shabby clothes, cute ponytails, earrings, tattoos, the whole nine yards. Before Jack could stop them or call his lawyer, they would push their way inside, he would be shoved up against the wall, patted down, and slapped in cuffs. Next a hurried search that would finish up, inevitably, in Jack's garage. "Hey, looky-looky what I found," one of the phony agents would declare, gleefully holding up five pounds of high-octane Mary Jane. "My goodness, Jack here's been a naughty boy."

Jack would be understandably shocked; he would rail and scream, protest his innocence, the whole act — that he was legitimately innocent would only add to the fun. But he would eventually grow tired of being ignored, shut up, and insist on a lawyer.

Once Jack brought the "lawyer" word into the discussion the TFAC boys would retreat into a quick whispering huddle. Eventually, one would approach him and, with a knowing grin, initiate a hard-edged, intimate conversation. From a "tip" they knew Jack was a big-time peddler, a two-bit pusher in a fancy suit. All that money, and yet, for whatever perverse reason — perhaps thrills, perhaps to act young and hip — he had chosen an unhealthy little sideline.

And five pounds of marijuana shoved him clearly beyond the legally mild user gallery, into the far more dangerous territory of big-time distributor.

Ten years was the max. Five was the usual, especially for first-timers, but who knew how the judge or jury felt that day. Rich boys don't elicit much sympathy or mercy.

The case was ironclad — two reliable informers had fingered him. Both swore they had bought from him on multiple occasions. They testified to the quality of his "supremo shit" — the Juan Valdez of the dope business, they called him. They identified him by name, knew his address, and described him and his house to a tee.

Plus, DEA now had the goods. Incontrovertible evidence. Five pounds of it, high-grade stuff packed in a nice big sack located in his garage. Oh, you're going down hard, Jack.

We can and will gladly nail you on a golden cross, he would be warned with a solemn shrug. Big Wall Street guy in a lavish house in a fancy neighborhood in a plush little town filled with celebrities and the hyper-rich. Wow, don't Springsteen and Bon Jovi live around here? You see, Jack, you have a lot to lose. Go ahead, call the lawyer; then we call the local cops. Won't the neighbors be happy when your driveway floods with flashing blue lights? How many will peek out their windows and gawk at the spectacle as you are dragged out your front door in cuffs and stuffed in the back of one of those cars?

And how will your Wall Street chums and bosses react the next morning when the DEA crashes into your office, flashing another warrant and poking around for more evidence? Imagine the horrified looks on their rich, stuffy faces. What's the matter, guys, didn't you know your partner was a pusher? Wouldn't that do wonders for business? The clients would love it.

DEA just adores guys like you. A Wall Street hotshot, a big-deal millionaire taking a careless stroll through the gutter. Maybe not page one news. But an honorable mention in the *Wall Street Journal* is the least you can expect, and the last thing you can afford. They will do their best to smear you across every rag on the East Coast and make you the toast of New York.

DEA has you by the balls, Jack would be assured once again with a confident sneer. If you wish to call your lawyer — okay, fine, it's your constitutional right, go ahead. Be sure, though, to tell him to meet you at the local police station after you're already booked and charged with possession with intent to distribute, and the reporters are already jockeying in an unruly mob outside the station waiting to get a nice photo of the celebrity pusher.

So what will it be, Jack? Your lawyer or us? A noisy mouthpiece who can't lift a finger as you're publicly flayed and disgraced, you're fired from your job, and have to sneak in and out of your own home — or will you be an upright citizen and work with us, Jack? We want the pusher you bought this from: the big-time guy at the top of the dope chain. And the names of every one of your customers sure would be nice. A big fish or two would really hit the sweet spot.

No rush, Jack, relax, take a day or two,

think about it. Then we'll be back.

They would let Jack suffer and stew for a day or so — let him lock himself into his house, blow off work, imagine the terrifying possibilities, and scream at the walls about the injustice of it all.

Then would come the surprise visit from smiling Bill Feist, world-class fixer, all jokey and amiable as ever. Just dropped in to see how you're doing, he would inform Jack. Hey, he would add with thinly feigned innocence, an old buddy in the DEA mentioned that you got your tit in a wringer. Sounds serious, Jack. Five pounds, huh? Those fellas don't mess around, but maybe I can help. Pull a few strings, call one of my many old White House chums, you know, make this whole mess disappear.

At CG we value our friends: of course, it's a two-way street.

It was crude and brusque, but it would work; Jack had far too much to lose for it not to. The house, the job, the all-American reputation — best of all, as Jack would eventually figure out, this sweet deal he was flashing around would go out the window. As a felon, he would lose his broker's license and certainly be barred from directorship of a public company.

He would know he was being framed and

blackmailed, and be understandably outraged. But so what? What choice did he have?

It had worked like magic four out of five times. It hadn't exactly failed the fifth time, it had simply worked in a way nobody anticipated. In that case, the CEO of a large rubber company CG was interested in, a proud, stubborn, and resistant man who had just been informed by the ersatz agents of TFAC of the stiff punishment for being caught red-handed with kiddie porn on his computer hard drive, had sneaked into the dark shed behind his house, tossed a rope over a rafter, and hanged himself.

Maybe he had a guilty conscience.

Too bad.

Fortunately the amenable man who succeeded him the next day promptly accepted CG's offer.

"Two days?" Walters asked, pushing back his chair and clasping his hands behind his head. "Why not tonight?"

"Don't rush things."

"Maybe he'll accept another offer in between."

"He won't."

"How can you be so —"

"Because I know how he thinks," Bellweather insisted with a confident grin. "Jack

104

intends to gather the offers, then he'll be back at our door. We have time."

Early in the morning of day eight, Jack gave his watchers the slip. It did not appear intentional, certainly not planned, but a car whipped into his driveway at 5:05, Jack dashed out the front door and jumped in the passenger seat, and the car squealed away.

The watchers strained to get the license number, but between the darkness, their drowsiness after another long dreary night, and the fact that the plate was splattered with mud, it was hopeless. The car was a late-model Mercury Sable, dull gray in color, assuredly not a hired limo, and thus presumably was driven by a friend or acquaintance of Jack's.

By the time the watch car idling around the corner received the order to give chase, any hope of catching up was futile.

Floyd Thompson, the driver, turned to Jack and said, "Long time no see, Captain."

Jack smiled at him. "Four years, Floyd. What've you been up to?"

"Same old, same old."

"How was Afghanistan?"

"Is that a question?"

Jack laughed. Fifteen years earlier he had

served beside Floyd, back when Floyd was a newly promoted buck sergeant, E-5, and Jack was his commander. Now Floyd was an E-8, on the list for promotion to sergeant major, the highest enlisted rank in the Army. The first wisp of gray salted his temples, though he still looked as fit as he had at 23.

"Ike and Danny can't make it this time," Floyd informed him. "Ike's in Afghanistan, Danny's doing Iraq."

"Some guys will do anything to get out of this."

Floyd smiled. "Miss it?" he asked with a quick glance at Jack. "I mean, the life."

"Which part? The early morning five-mile runs, sleeping on the ground, lousy pay? Frequent tours to countries I wouldn't send my worst enemies to? Being shot at?" Jack paused, then smiled. "Sure, who wouldn't?"

Floyd laughed and they caught up on their lives and drove generally westward for two hours, eventually ending up in Allentown, Pennsylvania, at a small, obscure country cemetery on the outskirts of town. The morning was cool and blustery. A light drizzle was coming down. A small knot of people had already arrived and were milling around in the rain by the parking lot.

Like Floyd, four of the men wore Army uniforms bedecked with ribbons and military merit badges and a long procession of time stripes on their sleeves. And two, like Jack, wore suits appropriate to their current status as former soldiers, now civilians.

The men filed over and they all shook hands but said few words. Next they all marched solemnly to a gravesite where a woman, Selma Gaither, was standing, using the moment of solitude to share private thoughts with the man in the grave, her husband, Thomas Gaither, former staff sergeant and a former comrade of the men in the group.

It was a ritual they adhered to every four years, coming together at Tom Gaither's final resting place, a way to honor a fallen friend. Floyd shuffled behind the gravestone and managed to produce a few simple words, then started crying; he just managed to choke out a barely coherent amen. He and Tom had joined the Army together, a pair of stout defensive linemen at Salisbury High School looking for a new life. They had grown up on the same block, raised hell as teenagers, barely escaped high school, then gone off to war under a stint the Army called the Buddy Program.

They all stood in an awkward silence another five minutes, each man remembering what scraps and remnants he could of serving beside Tom. The memories became dimmer with the passing years, though nobody cared to admit it. Two of the men owed their lives to Tom and both cried quietly but unashamedly.

Finally, Jack led the procession back to their cars. They drove five miles in a caravan over twisty back roads to The Gut, a remote roadside eatery that had somehow become part of this little ritual. The Gut was little more than a shack, a shabby collection of cramped booths and chipped, linoleum-topped tables. Someone had called ahead and four tables had been jammed together and reserved for the party. Except Jack, the offspring of a military professional, the rest of the men came from hardscrabble back-grounds and were quite at home there.

Jack sat at one end of the tables, Selma at the other. She also had grown up with Tom, had had her pigtails pulled by him in kindergarten, had flirted shamelessly and relentlessly with him throughout elementary school, had dated him continuously through high school, then broke it off when Tom left for his Army Basic training.

Selma had deep roots in Allentown, her family having settled there a hundred years before. They were immensely prolific types and there was barely a block in the city without her kin. She had no intention of leaving her family and friends, of living the gypsy life of a military wife. The night before he left for boot camp, she and Tom had a loud, raucous fight. The first battle in their relationship, it was also the last, both swore resolutely to themselves when the brawl ended. That firm divorce lasted all of three days, before Selma hopped a train for Georgia and they were married, till death do they part, the day after Tom completed basic training.

Selma was a large black woman, big-hearted and fiercely independent. It was clear that Tom would be the only man in her life. They had produced two lovely children, Jeremy and Lisa, and raising them had occupied whatever loneliness Selma felt.

A gargantuan breakfast was served — ten plates piled high with flatcakes, five dishes overloaded with greasy bacon and greasier grits, ten pots of stiff black coffee, and an assortment of local side orders. The Gut was no place for the health-conscious.

Conversation flowed easily as the men caught up on their lives — who had gotten married, divorced, had children, and so forth. The men had all gone their separate ways, those who got out jumping into various professions, and those who stayed in, buffeted by the Army's chronic wartime needs, bouncing through an assortment of assignments. But they had survived a war together. They had fought and bled and nearly died together. That bond was more special than a common college or fraternity brotherhood: it lasted a lifetime.

"Remember the day it happened?" Floyd eventually asked, sipping his coffee and staring at Jack. It was time to get down to business. The table was loaded with empty dishes. A sullen waitress in the corner eyed the mounds of empty plates but made no move to retrieve them.

"Like I could forget," Jack answered, giving a look down the table at Selma, who quietly produced a resigned nod. She eased back in her chair, cupped her coffee in her hands, and settled in for the talk.

Pete Robbins, two seats down, muttered, "Tell you what I remember most. There was a sandstorm like I never seen before or since. Stuff filled your ears, crawled up your nose, couldn't see two feet."

"Yeah," Willy Morton joined in, "the third day of the war. We had that big fight the day before, the one at that sand dune, remember? Still can't believe we all made it through that fight."

Three or four men began nodding. Yep,

they remembered.

Floyd put down his coffee and leaned back in his chair. "And then Captain Wiley got ordered to move to the next village. They said by the radio emissions there had to be a big headquarters there. We was supposed to knock it out."

Selma, at the other end of the table, sipped from her coffee and patiently let the men ramble on. It was the same thing every time, the men recounting the day Tom died, going through the painful details as if it happened yesterday. She knew what it was, survivor's guilt. They needed to return to that day and explain what happened because it was too late to change it. Well, nothing would change it, so she guessed talking it out had to suffice.

Willy Morton, then the team medic now a doctor with a razor-sharp brain, performed most of the narration about that day, about Jack planning their assault, making the exhausted men rehearse and rehearse again, treating them all like packhorses, forcing everybody to haul a triple load of ammunition and six canteens of water. By the time the captain had finished adding more of this and a lot more of that — extra claymore mines, extra AT-4 rocket launchers, and so forth and so on — each man was hauling

111

well over a hundred pounds through the hot desert. Jack had seemed to have a premonition, Willy explained, but nobody objected or complained.

Yeah, that's right, Walter Guidon chirped in. A crusty, foulmouthed Cajun, he'd been with Jack in the Panama invasion, too, and quickly recounted a similar incident there when Jack had a hunch — a seer's eye, he called it — and changed the plan at the last minute. Good thing, he said. The old plan would've gotten them all butchered.

Then Willy took over the story again. A furious sandstorm hit and left them all blinded as they moved in for the attack. Selma heard again how Jack made them all lash one another together with a piece of rope, how Jack led the team like a staggering mule train through the driving sand straight to the objective, and how the sand obscured what an intelligence catastrophe they were walking into.

It was a headquarters for sure, but left out of their briefing was that it was guarded and protected by nearly three hundred Iraqi soldiers, outnumbering Jack's ten-man team by thirty to one.

Evan Johnson, the heavy weapons man, picked it up at that point. A simple southern country boy with a flair for homespun phrases, after describing what a big, nasty surprise it was, he said it was like sticking your fist in an "uptight hornet's nest." Four years before, Evan had used the metaphor of sticking your fist in a "big pool of bone-starved piranhas"; the reunion before that, like landing in a pit of "seriously annoyed snapping turtles."

Selma vaguely wondered what it would be in another four years.

But before they knew it, the attackers were the defenders, surrounded and, as a result of the blinding sandstorm, unable to receive air support, or helicopters, or artillery, or even reinforcements. The battle raged for six hairy hours. Both sides pounded away with enthusiasm. Had Jack not ordered every man to carry triple the normal ammunition load, they would've been slaughtered after only an hour or two.

Like Selma, Jack sat quietly and allowed the men to recount the horrors of a day when by all reason they all should've been killed.

There was a reason for the prolonged story, though, and at the appropriate point the others fell silent and allowed Floyd to pick up the thread. He and Tom had been boyhood friends, after all; it was by now part of the tradition that he got to narrate the sad ending.

The battle had raged over five hours by the time Floyd weighed in with considerable drama. The team now was desperately huddled inside two small buildings on the far edge of the village. They were little more than huts, but the walls were thick mud that swallowed whatever the Iraqis shot. The noise of bullets and explosions had long since grown monotonous. Evan and Willy were wounded, barely conscious; the tourniquets Jack had tied were all that kept them alive. A few others had been nicked and bruised, but nothing too severe. Ammunition was now precariously low, a few rounds, then they'd be throwing rocks and spitting at the Iraqis; Jack had long since given the order to fire only at the sure targets. Iraqi bodies littered the ground around the two buildings, including two large piles of corpses where the enemy had twice tried to outflank Jack's position and rushed straight into lethal blasts from the claymore mines he had added to their packing list.

The only hope was to collect some of the Iraqi weapons from the dead in the large stacks. After telling the others to give him cover, Jack made a mad dash out the door, dodging a hailstorm of bullets and rushing to the piles of bodies, using the corpses for cover as he stripped their weapons and whatever ammunition he could grab.

Tom made a decision to join him. He dove out a side window, rolled a few times, then stood and sprinted for the second pile, where Jack was hunkered down, gripping a stack of weapons and ammunition. About ten yards from Jack, he went tumbling through the air and landed just short of the pile of bodies.

From Jack's face, Floyd said, they knew Tom was hurt, and that it was real bad. Jack threw Tom over one shoulder, hauled the weapons and ammunition with his free arm, and sprinted for the building.

He laid Tom on the ground, distributed the Iraqi guns and bullets, then returned to kneel beside the fallen man. Tom hollered at him to ignore his wounds and get back to fighting. Jack instead yelled for Floyd to come over and didn't need to explain why. There was nothing to be done; Tom only had minutes left.

He began talking about Selma and the kids. He said Selma had given his life meaning and happiness, and he swore he wouldn't change a minute of it. He was sad he was dying, but happy he and Selma had created two lives, Jeremy and Lisa.

By the time Floyd finished, all the men

were sniffling and acknowledging how Tom's sacrifice had saved them all. He was a certified hero, they all agreed.

And it was all a big lie. The truth was that after five hours of unrelenting fire, Tom had snapped. Whatever it was — the direness of the situation, the ammunition dilemma, the hopelessness of Jack's desperate effort to collect guns and ammunition — he just seemed to outrun his mental tether. When Jack made the dash out the front and drew all the Iraqi fire, Tom made a foolhardy sprint out the back, hoping to use the distraction and the cover of the sandstorm to make his escape.

He was cut in half by an angry hail of bullets before he got twenty feet. There had been no final words. No dramatic farewell, no last thoughts about Selma and the kids. They collected Tom's bullet-riddled corpse after the fight ended.

At the time, the mood of the team was fury at Tom for trying to run out on them that way. But Jack gathered them all together and made them swear a solemn vow; Tom had a wife and kids, after all. Sure, in a moment of weakness he might've tried to escape, but they wouldn't run out on him. They'd been through lots of tough fights and scrapes together. They wouldn't let one moment of cowardice be his shameful legacy.

Now, after all these years, a number of the men had actually convinced themselves that Tom's final act of heroism was a stone-cold fact, absolutely the way it happened. Selma thanked them for coming and for honoring the memory of her husband, then slowly the group began to break up and go their separate ways.

Finally, it was Selma's turn and she asked Jack to walk her to the parking lot and see her off.

Outside, she took his arm and said, "Strange how that tale changes every four years."

"Memory is a funny thing."

"Yep. Last time, they all swore Tom went out the door for the weapons first. They said you followed him." She was looking at Jack's face with her eyes narrowed.

"They're getting older, Selma. Another four years and Tom will be wearing a blue cape, rushing the main Iraqi position, and pulling the weapons out of their living hands. How are the kids?" Jack asked, quickly changing the subject.

"Fine. Jeremy made the basketball team at Lafayette College."

"I heard. He called me after the cut. And Lisa?"

"Got all her applications in. Straight A's, that girl."

"Gets it from her mother."

"Who you kiddin'?" They both chuckled and continued walking in silence to the car. Selma had barely made it out of high school; her children would be the first of her family to graduate from college, much less such fine colleges. Lisa was hoping desperately for Princeton, Jack's alma mater. She was smart, athletically gifted, popular, and best of all, a minority. The admissions people were making promising noises. Jack opened Selma's door, but before she got in, she gave him a strong hug. "The kids and I thank you. Without that fund, I don't know if they'd of got this chance at college. It means more than anything, Jack."

"They all threw in some money to get the fund started."

"Uh-huh." Maybe it was true, maybe everybody threw a little cash into the Gaither kids' college kettle, but Selma was not the gullible sort. At best the team might've been able to pinch together a few thousand dollars. They were all soldiers back then, living paycheck to paycheck,

118

barely able to afford their car payments. And maybe, as Jack always swore up and down, his investment of that hoard might've fallen into a gold mine and multiplied a few times — but no way did he grow a few thousand dollars into half a million, enough for both kids to go to any college in the country, without a second thought to the cost.

"You're a fine man, Jack Wiley. When are you gonna find a fine woman? The kids are always askin' when Uncle Jack's gonna settle down."

Jack laughed. "You have a sister?"

"Yeah. A real uptight bitch. She's too old for you. Already been married and divorced three times, anyways. Can't hold a man."

Jack smiled. "Can I have her number?"

6

Bellweather was right. It was nearly five in the evening the next day when Jack called. Walters's assistant, Alice, unfamiliar with his name, swore up and down her boss was out of the office and in any event was too busy to speak with him. But Jack loudly insisted that she interrupt whatever her boss was doing and mention his name.

Walters at that moment had a putter clenched in his sweaty palms, having just lined up a shot, when his cell phone rattled. He was on the back nine of the Army Navy Country Club, hosting two admirals and a high-level assistant secretary of acquisition from the Pentagon. A shipbuilding company down in Pascagoula, owned by CG, was a year late and now two hundred million and counting in cost overruns on a pair of Navy destroyers. Walters was using the occasion to talk them out of a full-blown audit, doing it the usual way, hinting at the job openings that were expected to come open right about the time the three men were in the window for retirement.

He blew the putt, an easy five-footer, threw down the putter, cursed, and jerked the phone off his belt. "What?" he yelled, wishing he could strangle the caller.

His knees almost went rubbery when Alice, after apologizing profusely for breaking his concentration, mentioned who was calling. Alice's predecessor had been fired only the week before. Divorced, three kids, a big mortgage, she was walking on eggshells, trying desperately to avoid that fate. The betting pool around the office gave her two weeks. Three at the outside.

Walters barked, "Put him through."

A moment later, he heard magic. "Mr. Walters, I suspect you've heard about me," Jack said in a very friendly tone.

Walters tried to smile into the phone. "Sure have, Jack. Couldn't be sorrier about that stupid meeting with Ed Blank. What an ass."

"I was hoping you and I could meet," Jack said abruptly.

"Love to. Say when."

"Okay, 'when' is tonight."

"Tonight?"

"Yes. I'm afraid my schedule's gotten very

cluttered."

"Yeah, well, my schedule's pretty loaded, too," Walters snapped back. The idea that this uppity punk was busier than him was ridiculous. But he quickly regained his composure, and in a tone that was only mildly friendlier suggested, "Why not to-morrow? I'll tell my secretary to find me an hour."

"Tell her not to bother."

"What's that mean?"

"You know what it means. Good-bye, Mr. __"

"No . . . wait!" Walters nearly screamed. The clutch of admirals and the assistant secretary politely edged away.

Wiley made no reply. Not a sound, not a peep. At least he hadn't hung up, though.

"Listen," Walters said, trying not to sound desperate and failing miserably. "Maybe I can make time tonight."

"Maybe?"

"Okay, I can. What time?"

"I won't be free until about nine."

"Then nine it is."

"And bring along some of your directors, Mr. Walters. This is a fast train. I want to be sure you can commit to a deal."

Walters was fiercely tempted to tell him to cram it. Who did this guy think he was, ordering him around like some snot-nosed junior executive? He worked up every bit of his nerve and said, "Sure, no problem. Where?"

"I'm in town, so how about your headquarters?"

Walters was about to reply when the phone line suddenly went dead. One of the admirals sank a thirty-footer. "Good shot, sailor," Walters yelled over his shoulder. "Sorry, gotta go, boys, finish without me," and he jogged back to the clubhouse, howling into his phone for Alice, the temporary assistant, to arrange champagne and snacks, and to contact three directors and tell them to be there at all costs.

Tell them the fifteen-billion-dollar man is back.

Dan Bellweather was personally awaiting Jack in the downstairs lobby when he arrived, alone, hauling a small black suitcase. Bellweather shook his hand with great enthusiasm, escorted him past the security people and up in the elevator to the tenth floor, where the spacious senior executive suites were located. "We're glad you came back," he happily informed Jack on the way up.

"I'm not exactly back, Mr. Secretary," Jack

replied, polite but poker-faced.

Bellweather smiled nicely. Oh yes, boy, you're definitely back. After a moment, he said, "I understand you were a military brat."

"I grew up bouncing around Army posts. Fun life."

Bellweather could almost recite from memory the many places Jack had lived. "And you were in the Army yourself," he noted, "and your father was a lifer. Why did you leave it?"

"The war was over. I did my part, time to enjoy the peace."

"You mean make money, huh?"

"Sure, why not."

"I admire that motive," Bellweather said, and his smile widened and sparkled. Nice to see Jack had honorable ambitions.

They had reached the tenth floor and Jack encouraged Bellweather to step out first. After a fast trip down a long hallway, he ushered Jack into a large wood-paneled conference room where three other gentlemen in a mixture of thousand-dollar suits and blazers were picking at snacks on a side table and waiting.

"Jack," Bellweather said, almost gushing with pride, "I'd like you to meet Alan Haggar and Phil Jackson, two of our directors.

And of course Mitch Walters, our CEO."

Like nearly every other CG director, Alan Haggar was a former high government official, a deputy secretary of defense, number two in the mammoth Pentagon hierarchy, who had left the current administration only six months before. He was short and flabby with a pinched face and narrow, indistinct eyes blurred behind thick bifocals: he appeared to have been hatched in a bureaucracy. His smile was tight, obviously forced and slightly nervous. He was the newest and, at forty-five, the youngest CG director.

To his right, Phil Jackson, a lawyer, had been a close confidant to many presidents — Republicans or Democrats, he went both ways — particularly when they got into legal trouble and needed a slick operator to stonewall, obscure, twist elbows, and finagle a way out. In a town loaded with powerful fixers, Phil Jackson had written the textbooks they all studied. He was tall, skeletally thin, entirely bald, stone-faced, with severely narrowed eyes that looked slightly snakish.

The four men quickly gathered around Jack in a tight huddle, hands were shaken, then Bellweather led Jack to a wall upon which hung twelve photographs in elegant gold frames. "Our directors, Jack" — he waved a hand reverently across the gallery

— "I think it would be fair to say we're led by a rather distinguished, illustrious group."

What an understatement: at one time or another the heavyweights on the wall had ruled and/or misruled a healthy chunk of the planet. The engraved plaques attached to the bottom of the frames were a waste of space and money; few of CG's directors required any form of introduction.

Included in the august group were a former French president, an Australian prime minister, a former British defence minister, a former secretary of state, even a former American president. Jack spent a politely dutiful minute moving down the line, gazing at the photos, before he glanced at his watch and suggested, "It's getting late. Why don't we get started?"

"Okay, fine," Walters said. "Would you care for a glass of champagne?"

"Maybe afterward," Jack answered, pausing briefly before he pointedly added, "if there's something to celebrate."

Only thirty minutes before, they had all listened to — or in several cases, relistened to — the tape of Jack running circles around their LBO boys. The four men couldn't help smiling at one another. We know your games now, Jack, they felt like saying; nice try, but don't think we'll fall for your tricks again.

They quietly sat around the conference table, the four CG heavyweights on one side, Jack, alone and seriously outgunned, on the other.

Jack carefully placed his suitcase on the floor, unbuttoned his jacket, offered a nervous smile, opened by briskly thanking them for meeting with him on such short notice, at this late hour, then came right to the point. "I have met with four other firms about this offer. All four are intensely interested, all four are making seriously generous bids."

A quiet moment of mild confusion ensued while Mitch Walters glanced at his directors and they quietly decided who would take the lead. Nobody seemed to feel this was a bluff. This mistake would not be repeated. Bellweather cleared his throat, edged forward in his chair, and said, "I don't wish to be rude, Jack, but it's not clear exactly what you're offering."

"A takeover. I'm sure you've all heard the particulars about the company, so I won't waste your time with a regurgitation."

"Yes, I think we're all aware of the polymer and its remarkable qualities." Nods from the others on his side of the table — Yes, yes, we want this deal. Come on, Jack, let's get rich together. "Please continue," Bellweather plunged in very politely.

"All right, here's what I'm offering. I know the company, and I've mapped out a way to take it over. It's vulnerable and ripe. Make the right moves and it'll fall into our lap in no time. I've done a lot of research. It will work."

No mights, no maybes, no probablys. It *will* work, simple as that.

"We have plenty of in-house expertise at takeovers," Bellweather noted, careful not to sound pushy or dismissive.

"I know you do. And I'm open to better ideas, though I doubt your people will improve on my plan," Jack replied, looking and sounding quite sure of himself.

Mitch Walters came to the point they were all wondering. "What do you get in return, Jack?"

"For starters, I intend to resign my partnership at Cauldron. It would be a conflict of interest for me to remain there."

"A job, is that what you want?"

"A job, no. Call it a limited partnership, and I'd like an office in this building. A small out-of-the-way cubbyhole will suit me. No assistant, no staff; I don't intend to be a burden. I don't plan to be here often, but I'd like the accessibility."

"Easy enough."

"And I want to personally orchestrate the takeover. I'll need help from a few of your people, of course. But it's my baby and I want to bring it home."

Sure, why not? If he screwed it up, they'd simply take it away from him. Maybe they'd take it away on general principle. "We're agreeable to that," Walters answered, a vague assurance at best.

"And a twenty million finder's fee for bringing you this deal." Jack paused and searched their faces, then specified, "Payable the moment we complete the takeover."

The heads from CG looked at each other a moment. Twenty million? That's it, only twenty? Peanuts for a deal that would quickly grow in magnitude to billions. He could've demanded fifty and they wouldn't have blinked an eye. A hundred million was worthy of negotiation. Was he really leaving that much on the table?

Probably not, they collectively thought. Obviously the boy with a diamond in his pocket had something else up his sleeve, something much bigger. Jack waited until all the eyes were fixed on his face, then said very firmly, "And I want twenty-five percent ownership."

A long moment before the mouths fell open. Bellweather actually squeezed his arms against his sides and popped his lips. Jackson and Haggar rolled their eyes and exchanged incredulous looks.

"Out of the question," Walters snorted, speaking loudly and insistently for all of them. "We're perfectly prepared to give you a larger finder's fee. And certainly, a piece of ownership isn't out of the question. A few percent, fine. But a quarter? Forget it," he repeated, shaking his head emphatically. "I mean it. Not even negotiable."

"Think again, Mitch," Jack answered, not giving an inch. "I have two offers of twenty percent burning holes in my pocket. That and considerably larger finder's fees."

"But you wouldn't be back here if you didn't know we're your best bet, Jack," Mitch persisted with a sneer. He crossed his arms, worked his lips into a tight pucker, and made clear he meant it.

Instead of debating that point, Jack bent over and started rummaging through the small black suitcase he had hauled in and placed on the floor. He popped back up after a moment and tossed a green canvas bag on the conference table. The bag slid, then stopped almost dead center. Walters and Bellweather took one look, just one short look — with sinking stomachs, they knew exactly what was inside the sack. They didn't need to be told — they knew!

Jackson and Haggar, the other two directors, stared at it. "What's that?" Haggar demanded, clueless.

"Oh, this?" Jack asked, as if the question surprised him. "A nasty present I found in my garage," he mentioned with maddening casualness. "Five pounds of marijuana. High-grade stuff, planted in my home to frame me. Enough to get me five to ten, my lawyer tells me. Can you imagine anybody doing something so slimy and stupid?"

Apparently not; at least, nobody ventured a response. Blank expressions all around; two sincere, two faking it for all they were worth.

Jack pushed back his chair and gazed thoughtfully at their faces. "The boys you sent were good, but lazy. Here's one of the things they overlooked: electronically activated cameras in the ceiling that switch on in the event of a break-in."

Walters took a stab at playing innocent and with a loud show of indignation declared, "I don't know what you're talking about."

"And I don't like being treated like I'm stupid."

"I'm not —"

"Mitch, listen before you open your

mouth. I have some expensive artwork, and in addition to the cameras, my alarm is dual-wired and my home is flooded with infrared beams. It gets me a nice discount from my insurance company. A signal is sent to Vector, with a simultaneous signal to a private security firm I'd prefer not to disclose."

"So what?" Walters said as if he could care less.

"So my security firm dispatched a few people to my house. For over two hours the burglars rummaged around inside. Naturally, my people became curious. Where was Vector's response? And why did the burglars remain inside so long?"

Jack let the questions linger in the air for a moment. Bellweather and Walters weren't about to surrender or retreat, and both shrugged as though it was a complete mystery and they were dying to hear the answer.

Jack looked directly at Walters. "It was as if they knew I was in Washington and wouldn't be back till midnight. So my boys staked it out until the burglars were finished, then trailed them."

"Jack, Jack, I have no idea what you're getting at," Walters protested, his tone up about three octaves, nearly vibrating with innocence. He was battling an irresistible temptation to get up and flee. "You're not inferring we had anything to do with this?"

Jack ignored him and pushed on. "Here's where it gets more interesting. Afterward, these burglars — three of them, if you don't already know — checked into a Best Western on 95, a few miles outside Princeton. Spent the night, had a nice leisurely breakfast at a local diner, and left plenty of fingerprints and DNA traces in their wake. The DNA and prints were collected, then run through a national database. One was a black hole, a cipher. The other two are former military. Their prints and DNA are on file and easily accessed. After the Army, they fell off the map, though I would bet they continued in government service of some sort. Probably CIA. What do you think?"

Bellweather, in his most deeply paternal tone, and with a frown so sorrowful it verged on tears, took his best stab. "Look, we're sorry to hear about the break-in, Jack, all of us."

"Are you?"

"Sure. It's a lousy world filled with crooked people. I'm sure you live in a big, prosperous house, the kind that attracts burglars. But don't go paranoid on us. CG doesn't do this sort of thing."

"The burglars work for a security firm here, in D.C.," Jack continued — the denials were expected, his expression said. "TFAC, it's called. Can anybody help me out? I'll be damned if I can figure out what the letters stand for."

By now Bellweather's face was red and his jaw was clenched. "That's enough, Jack. You're barking up the wrong tree. It's a disgrace coming in here accusing us of this."

Jack stared at him a long moment, then bent down and dug around in his suitcase again. He flipped a large black-and-white photo onto the table. "The TFAC headquarters," Jack said. Then, in an effort to be helpful, he pointed at the building in the background. "Who does that look like leaving the building two days ago?"

Four heads jerked forward. Four sets of eyes collectively gawked at the picture. The photo was slightly grainy and out of focus, but without question it was Mitch Walters, actually grinning stupidly at the cameraman as they passed on the sidewalk outside the entrance.

Grinning!

The last attempts at denial or phony innocence shot out the window. Why act any stupider than they already looked? Why issue more denials that were obvious lies?

Walters was now staring down at the photo, dumbfounded, gaping in shock. How had they caught him? He wanted to sink into the woodwork and disappear.

Bellweather, now exuding anger, stared hard at Walters — how idiotic could he be, getting caught like that? He wanted to reach over and strangle the CEO.

Phil Jackson, the lawyer, reacted with the instinctive violence honed by decades of D.C. political brawls and scandals. "This proves nothing," he yelled, on his feet and shaking his finger like a half-cocked pistol. "There are a million possible explanations. Nothing you've showed us will stand up in court. It's all circumstantial conjecture," he roared.

Jack relaxed back into his chair. He smiled pleasantly at Jackson. "You might be right, or you might be wrong, Phil. It doesn't matter. It's irrelevant."

"Why's that?" Haggar asked.

"What good would it do me to see you prosecuted? And if it were my intention to sue you, I wouldn't be here tonight. My lawyer would, spewing threats and dropping subpoenas like confetti."

"Okay." Jackson dropped the finger and the bluster. He straightened his tie, struggling to conceal a considerable sense of irritation and relief. "Why are you here?"

"This is your last chance at this deal. As I said, others are offering twenty percent. I'll be a billionaire inside three years, and I can live with that." Jack paused before he added, "It won't hurt to speed it up, though. Considering the circumstances, I thought you might see your way to up the ante another five percent." Jack pointed at the picture and offered them a cool smile. "Call it the cost of getting caught. I think it's a fair price, don't you?"

"Are you threatening us?" Jackson asked, pinching his eyes together.

"Threatening is such an ugly world. Just say I'm adding a little more to the pot than I offered the others."

"If you don't mind, we have to talk," Walters quickly intervened, avoiding the eyes of his three directors.

"Good idea." Jack stood and adjusted his coat. "Five minutes, then I'm gone." He picked up his horrible little suitcase filled with terrible things and looked perfectly ready to bolt. "I won't be back after this, gentlemen. Remember, five minutes."

The moment the door closed, Jackson snapped at Bellweather and Walters, "I can't believe you were stupid enough to walk into such a simple trap."

"It worked before," Walters insisted weakly, knowing full well how dumb that sounded.

"Yeah, and it worked great this time, too — for him, you fool."

"Think he was expecting this?" Haggar asked, pointing at the picture. Good question, and everyone stopped to consider it. Was it possible? Was Jack Wiley really that clever? Or were they just that clumsy and dumb?

"No, no way," Bellweather eventually responded with his typical sense of certainty. "He's zealous about security. A lot of people are. He has some nice things in his house and added a few extra layers of protection. He got lucky, and our boys made some sloppy mistakes. Why, what do you think?"

"Maybe you're right. Either way, you underestimated him."

Walters preferred not to dwell on that inarguable sentence and switched instead to the prominent question that was occupying all their minds. Facing Jackson, he asked, "Could he make a convincing legal case out of this?"

"No, not a chance. Not on the evidence he just described. He could embarrass us, not convict us."

"Are you sure?"

As only a lawyer can do, Jackson began speaking out the other side of his mouth. "One, we have no idea how much more evidence he might've kept from us. I think we all agree he's very smart." A quick glance around the table — yes, Jack was definitely smart. Maybe too smart.

"Two, he could subpoena our records and TFAC's. Look for pay transactions, any hint of a relationship. If it's there and he finds it, we've got big problems." He examined Walters's face and got the answer to that question — it was definitely there.

"Three," he continued, "for sure, he has the burglars on film. In court, in front of a jury, that would be very damaging. Imagine nearly three hours of videotapes, probably showing the burglars searching every nook and cranny in his home. Not stealing. Just searching, then planting the drugs. It would be very difficult to explain."

Jackson fell quiet and allowed them all to consider how ugly this could become. It was a real mess. They were all creatures of Washington; dodging scandals was the major industry and, to a greater or lesser degree, they all had experience with it. A federal investigation was a possibility — actually, for a firm loaded with so many power hitters, more in the realm of a likelihood. The press would pile on and have a ball, delighted to throw fuel on the barbecue.

Oh yes, the Fibbies would have a field day, crawling around the headquarters, grilling possible witnesses, pitting CG against TFAC, sweating the three burglars and promising a sweet deal to the first one who ratted out everybody in sight.

What were the odds the burglars would take the fall for a bunch of rich old men?

Plus there were three burglars: one was all it took to bring down the house; one blabbermouth and they were all cooked. This could get very, very ugly.

Mitch Walters, particularly, could feel a trickle of sweat running down his back. Wiley had left that horrible photo lying in the middle of the table, a terrifying reminder. Walters tried his best to ignore it, but couldn't wrench his eyes off it. It was him in that damned photo, him grinning and looking smug and self-important as he left the TFAC premises.

Any jury would stare at that photo and make the inevitable jump to the same conclusion: guilty as hell.

From the corner of his eye he caught Jackson's mean, skinny little eyes staring at him. It was so obvious what the coldhearted legal thug was thinking. If worst came to worst, in order to protect CG and themselves, they would throw Walters to the sharks. The CEO was wild, on his own and out of control, a rogue agent who had done something spectacularly stupid and embarrassing.

"I think we go twenty-five percent," Walters blurted out, before anybody else could say anything, suddenly eager for a deal, any deal. Hell, give Wiley fifty percent if that's what it took to shut his yap. When nobody made a reply, he pushed on. "That still leaves us the lion's share of what promises to be an incredibly lucrative deal. If he walks out now, we get nothing. Nada." When nobody bit at that reasoning, he added, now sounding desperate, "He already has two offers for twenty percent."

"No, he says he does," Jackson noted, his voice dripping with skepticism, enjoying the sight of Walters's misery.

Bellweather stood and said, "Mitch is right." Thinking of the call TFAC had intercepted of Jack talking with Tom from the mysterious company, he added, "Wiley has at least two twenty percent offers. We know this for a fact."

"How do you know this?" Jackson

snapped.

"Damn it, Phil, don't ask. We just do."

"You need to get this under control," Jackson warned, now eyeing both Bellweather and Walters with fresh malice. "You're getting sloppy."

Walters quickly insisted, "It wasn't us, okay? The TFAC guys did this on their own initiative. I asked them to dig a little into Wiley's background. That's all. A little research, a little background, all perfectly legal. The dirty stuff was their idea."

He was lying and it couldn't have been more obvious. "Try saying that in court and see where it gets you," Jackson warned, stabbing a finger at the photo.

"Relax. It's not going to court," Bellweather announced quite firmly as he bent across the table and seized the moment. "One minute left. Is it a deal or no?"

Having most recently left public service, Haggar, the newest, least secure, and poorest of the partners, said, "I say yes."

Without hesitation, Walters loudly seconded him.

Jackson straightened his tie again, cleared his throat, then said, "Bring him back in."

7

To his credit, Jack was not smirking when he reentered the room, fell into his seat, and crossed his legs. "Well?" he asked, watching their faces.

Jackson, trying to match Jack's poised air, said, "Let me start by assuring you, Jack, that nobody in this room had a thing to do with the break-in. Apparently somebody in the LBO section got a little carried away. You know how that can happen."

"Do I?"

"Hear me out, Jack. One of our junior executives, a man known for being a little overeager, well . . . just say he encouraged TFAC to pressure you. He'll be taken care of first thing in the morning. We don't abide with that kind of behavior. As for that picture of Mitch . . . uh, Mitch went there to tell them to back off and leave you alone."

They watched his face and waited for the reaction. There was no reaction. Not a snicker, not a frown. "Let's talk about the deal," Jack said.

"The deal, yes, good idea. We're willing to meet your conditions, all of them. Including the twenty-five percent." Jackson paused, then scrunched his lips together. "Subject, of course, to reviewing your plan, assuring ourselves it will work, and is worth our efforts."

Jack sat quietly and took that in. Finally he asked, "Are you willing to sign a contract to that effect?"

Arguing that Jack should simply trust their word or seal their agreement with a gentlemanly handshake seemed like a waste of time at this point. "Sure," Walters answered quickly for all of them. "Of course, it will take us a little time to prepare one."

Jack reached into his dreaded suitcase again, withdrew three copies of a draft contract, and casually tossed them on the table. For a moment, the four heads from CG ogled them in disbelief. They were incredulous — he already had contracts drawn up — what nerve! Then three sets of hands immediately snatched them. Nobody spoke. The CG boys dove into the conditions; predictably, all of the stipulations Jack had just laid down were there, in black and white. The office, the twenty million finder's bonus, twenty-five percent ownership in what the contract termed a limited liability partnership.

The partnership would be incorporated in Delaware, a business-friendly state with wonderfully hospitable corporate laws, one where any problems could be speedily and fairly adjudicated. But CG's usual preference regarding partnerships was to park them offshore, where taxes were nil and oversight wonderfully lax.

On the other hand, Jack's stipulation made good sense: for such a high-profile defense contract, it was undoubtedly best to have a U.S. imprimatur on the partnership. Red-white-and-blue all the way.

Jack crossed his arms, sat quietly, and watched them read. His face was expressionless, his body motionless. He looked neither angry nor jubilant. If anything, he looked slightly bored, even a little disconnected.

He looked, in fact, very much like a man with at least two perfectly good offers already in his pocket. Go ahead and object, his posture seemed to say; it'll cost you billions and I'll laugh all the way to the bank.

Jackson, the lawyer, was first to speak. "Legally speaking, the contract appears acceptable."

Jack nodded. The signature at the bottom was for Mitch Walters. Jack slid him a pen. "You first," he said. Walters had to fight back a smile as he slipped on his reading glasses and scrawled his name three times. He pushed down so hard he nearly slashed through the paper. What a relief.

Jack's turn, and he methodically attached his own signature to the bottom of all three copies. He slid one copy across the table to Walters, then neatly tucked the other two back inside his lethal suitcase.

"Before we get started with the details," Bellweather said, "why, after this break-in, did you choose us?"

"Aside from your willingness to give me twenty-five percent?"

"Yes, that's what I mean."

Jack uncrossed his arms and leaned forward. "To tell the truth, your attempt was the tipping point. It was stupid and clumsy. That part didn't impress me in the least."

"I don't understand."

"You cared enough to go the extra mile, Dan."

"You're serious?"

Jack nodded. "This takeover is going to take a little of the right kind of elbow grease. It won't be totally clean. I need a partner that doesn't sweat the small stuff."

"I see."

"You'll see better in a moment," Jack promised.

Walters reached across the table and handed Jack a flute of champagne. "Congratulations, partner," he offered rather pathetically.

Jack raised his glass and took a short sip. Bellweather planted his elbows on the table and said, "Now convince us it's a deal worth pursuing."

Jack took another sip, and they all watched him and held their breaths. At last, after nine days of chasing and wooing him, after raking through his past, trying to frame him and get their hands on this gold mine, they were about to hear the particulars.

Jack put down his flute. "The name of the company is Arvan Chemicals. Named after its founder and CEO, Perry Arvan. It's located in Trenton, New Jersey."

Blank expressions all around. This name did not register with any of the men.

Jack nodded and continued. "Here's the story. Arvan makes products that feed into the munitions and automobile industries. Principally chemicals for bombs and supplying adhesives that bind paint to car components. This intimate familiarity with two of the basic workings of this polymer

led to the breakthroughs. Perry Arvan is a thermochemist with expertise in chemical explosives. Nitroglycerin, C4, RDX, and HMX are a few of the key products his chemicals go into. Other chemists on his staff specialize in adhesives for metals. They pooled their expertise to create this polymer."

Walters edged forward in his seat. "You said it took years."

"It's a difficult design challenge, Mitch. The biggest roadblock is stability. The beads have to be high-explosive, meaning that heat or force causes them to release all their energy at once, rather than just burn or expunge gas. By necessity, the explosive is nitrogen-based. But nitrogen is inherently unstable, and subsequently the military has very stringent requirements. The explosive has to be able to withstand smaller shocks, high and low temperatures, friction, even sparks. Perry toyed with a thousand variations before he found the perfect product."

"But it works?"

"Yes, quite well."

"You know this for a fact?"

"It definitely works," Jack assured them again, more firmly this time. "Perry worked out a confidential arrangement with a contractor in Iraq. It's a company that does security work, bodyguarding high-level Iraqi officials for the most part. Ten months ago, Perry coated their vehicles before they were shipped over. Over ninety explosions later, not one contractor or protectee was killed, or even seriously injured. A few nasty concussions from the shock, which is unavoidable, but it certainly beats the alternative. The coating was never penetrated or even fractured. They've been hit with everything. IEDs. Rockets. Grenades. Plenty of direct hits, and yet not one vehicle was punctured, much less destroyed."

"Has this been verified?"

"Glad you asked." Jack bent down, pulled a thick black notebook from his suitcase, and dropped it on the table. "Perry did the smart thing. He hired an independent outfit to examine the results. Here they are. They're quite impressive."

"How impressive?" Haggar asked, eyeing the report.

"After each explosion a technical team examined the vehicle and assessed the impact. A few lessons were learned. For example, two coats work better than one. As you'll see, the results exceeded the most optimistic expectations."

Haggar picked up the book and began flipping pages. The laundry lists of highly technical details only confused him, so he flipped to the photographs of vehicles taken post-explosion. After a moment, he whistled.

A few scorch marks; otherwise the vehicles were completely undamaged. Not even dented.

Jackson looked down his long nose at Jack. "How did you get this material?"

"You mean, did I do something illegal?"

"Exactly."

"Why would you care?"

"As your partner, we have the right to know our level of legal exposure."

"Relax. At the moment you have no exposure."

"Let me be the judge of that," Jackson snapped, tightening his eyes and glaring at Jack.

"I thought a lawyer would know better. Whatever I did occurred before the fact. Only if I tell you now do you become legally culpable or vulnerable."

Touché. Jackson actually flinched and looked away.

"Does Arvan know you're interested?" Walters asked, a good question.

"No. I met Perry Arvan once, in New York. I doubt he remembers me."

Bellweather walked around the table and

refilled Jack's flute with champagne. "What makes you think Arvan's ripe for a take-over?"

Jack raised his eyebrows and smiled. "There were things Perry Arvan failed to disclose when he visited Cauldron."

"Like what?"

"Well, for one, Arvan had a revenue of four hundred million, not last year, but the first year of the war. Demand shot through the ceiling. Between Afghanistan and Iraq, the intensity of operations went sky-high. The Army and Marines were blowing up two armies the usual American way, throwing millions of bombs and rockets and artillery shells at everything in sight. High explosives became desperately short, so Perry expanded his factory and almost doubled his workforce. He stocked up on chemicals to get ahead of what he was sure would be demand-driven inflation in the prices."

"Those sound like good judgments," Walters noted.

"Except all good things come to an end. And that's exactly what happened. A year later, both wars sank into low-intensity stalemates. The insurgents still use plenty of high explosives, American military demand, though, has cratered. Last year, Arvan's net sank to slightly over two hundred million."

"How bad off is he?" Bellweather asked, almost rubbing his hands together. Arvan's net was down fifty percent; this sounded so good, so filled with possibilities.

"I haven't talked to him about it, right? But he's done his best to avoid bankruptcy, taken the usual steps. Laid off a few dozen workers. Tried to restructure his debt, squeezed his suppliers, all reasonable measures, but in the end, it's finger-in-the-dike stuff. His only prayer is this polymer."

"Then it is, in a very real sense, his holy grail," Walters observed.

"Yes, it's well named."

"What are his chances?" asked Bellweather.

"If he can hang on long enough to get a contract and swing into production, he won't just survive, he and his company will be drowning in profits. He'll have to hire ten accountants to keep track of the billions. The past two years will be a bad memory."

"How close is he?"

"We have to move fast," Jack replied, then paused before he admitted, "frankly, this is why I put this process into overdrive and turned up the heat."

"Describe fast, Jack," Walters said, nearly drooling with anticipation.

"Perry is initiating negotiations with a few low-level officials at the Army munitions command at Rock Island."

Jackson, still licking his wounds from his earlier drubbing, said, "You seem to have unusual inside knowledge, Wiley. Do you have an inside source?"

"None of your business, Phil."

"You signed the contract, Wiley. It is now."

"Is it true you cheat on your wife?" Jack asked with a tight smile.

"What?"

"Any extramarital affairs? Share the dirty details, Phil. We're your partners, tell us about the bimbo. Do you use a hotel? Is she hot, Phil?"

"Watch your mouth, Wiley."

"And you learn to keep yours shut," Jack snapped back and the temperature in the room instantly cooled a hundred degrees. "You're my partner, not my owner."

Jackson had taken his best shot at intimidation and come up empty. Not many people beat him at his own game, much less mugged him to a bloody pulp. Jack had accomplished this not just once but twice, and in such a resounding fashion. They were even more impressed with Jack, their fifteen-billion-dollar man.

"Why did he go to the guns and bombs

people?" Haggar asked, trying to get the discussion back on track. Jack and Jackson were still staring each other down. "The force protection and threat reduction guys, that's who he should be talking to."

Jack looked away from Jackson, toward Haggar, and smiled. "Remember, Alan, Perry Arvan is a scientist, not a businessman. Because of the polymer's qualities he figures the military will categorize it as an explosive. He's a novice at the military procurement game. Always been a subcontractor, never a direct supplier."

The CG boys took a moment to absorb all this inside information Jack had just unloaded on them. It sounded so promising. Inside only two years, Arvan had sunk from $400 million in revenue to just over $200 million. What a disaster. They could picture Perry Arvan slapping on Band-Aids, reeling from the shrinkage, trying to stem the bleeding long enough for the big bonanza that would save his hide.

The idea of stealing it all out from under his feet — and at the last minute — was immensely satisfying.

"So what's your plan?" Bellweather asked, openly admiring Jack for finding such a plump target. Better yet, it was clear that Jack had an incredibly knowledgeable inside source. He was dying to hear the plan; it was bound to be great.

Jack got up and worked his way to the side table laden with food and snacks. He picked up a plate and loaded it with cucumber sandwiches, a few sweet pickles, some chips. "Perry is surviving a day at a time. He borrowed heavily for the expansion and to build his stockpile. He emptied his equity, leveraged himself to the hilt. I understand he owes 150 mil on five-year notes at seven percent. Do the math."

Walters, only too happy to express the obvious, said, "Any setback at this point will be disastrous."

"So do you have a plan to squeeze him?" Bellweather quickly asked. He was sure he had a whopper.

Jack selected a pickle and bit down hard. "You're going to do it."

"Us?"

"That's right, and here's a happy coincidence I think you'll savor. Perry's largest account is a munitions company located in Huntsville, Alabama. Globalbang. Perhaps you've heard of it."

Big smiles instantly erupted on the other side of the table. Globalbang, they all knew, happened to be one of the many subsidiaries of the Capitol Group. It produced, among other things, Air Force bombs and Navy missiles and an assortment of other things that go boom in the night. No wonder Jack had set his sights on CG. They spent a brief moment admiring how cleverly Jack had walked them into this, then another moment, leaning forward to hear the details.

After nearly inhaling a sandwich, Jack continued. "Last year, Perry sold seventy million in chemical explosives to Globalbang. You can find out more easily than I, but assume his contracts this year are roughly equivalent." He paused and let the moment build. "Imagine now if those contracts are canceled."

"He would sue us," Jackson snarled, still smarting from his earlier humiliation. It was time to even the score, and he knew how to do it. He worked up a condescending scowl and said, "And you know what, Wiley? He'll have an excellent case. In fact, he'll cream us."

"So what?"

"That's a stupid question."

"Let him hire the meanest legal shark he can find. Sue to his heart's content. It would take at least a year or two for resolution. Perry hasn't got a prayer of surviving two months, much less two years."

The light finally came on and Jackson

blurted, "And if we take him over —"

"Then why would we sue ourselves?"

Bellweather began gliding around the table, topping off their champagne flutes. They had already toasted the partnership: now it was time to toast a victory that was all but in their laps. They could see it, smell it, taste it. After a moment, he lifted his flute and, smiling broadly, said, "Here's to Jack and his holy grail."

"Hear, hear," they all chanted.

8

Tuesday night meant chicken barbecue at the plant, a weekly event that nearly all of Perry Arvan's employees and wives made a point to attend. It was a tradition, a ritual. Something Perry had instituted decades before, back when Arvan Chemicals was a desperate start-up with five employees struggling to build a long-shot dream.

In the early years, Marge, Perry's lovely young wife, kept the books and performed the secretarial chores. Then the kids came and she stepped back and encouraged him to hire a professional bookkeeper. His sons and daughter worked at the plant almost from infancy. Now his grandchildren were dropping by after school, doing odd jobs and learning the trade in the bottom-up route Perry insisted they follow. It was a family place, cradle to grave, always had been, and he fought hard to keep it that way. Nearly three-quarters of his employees were relatives of each other, in one way or another. Sons and daughters hauled vats of chemicals right beside their fathers and mothers. "Uncle This" and "Auntie That" were frequently bellowed about the plant. These days, increasingly, grandchildren of employees he'd known for more than forty years were on the payroll.

As always, Perry stood by the door, warmly greeting everybody who entered. He knew them all by name. He knew their children, where they lived, had attended many of their weddings and stood somberly at the funerals of their kin. They came to him with their problems and tragedies, and he knew those, too.

The world around him had changed, not much for the better, Perry thought. After attending Princeton University for his undergraduate, his master's, and his doctorate in thermochemistry, he had made the easy decision to plant his dream a few miles down the road, in Trenton.

Trenton was a roaring factory town back then, home to countless small, bustling firms, like his, that fed the fabulous appetites of larger companies, from the great automobile manufacturers in Detroit to the vast array of large chemical firms sprinkled around New Jersey. "Trenton makes, the world takes," boasted the proud lights on the big bridge that spanned the sluggish, muddy Delaware River to Pennsylvania.

A sad joke these days. A glittering homage to irony. Trenton had long since been eclipsed as a manufacturing center, then entered a period of steep decline. A city that once bragged of almost as many diemakers as Detroit could now only boast of having almost as many murderers, drive-by killers, and muggers. It seemed to Perry that the town had become little more than a swamp of abandoned warehouses, blighted blocks, and unhappy, desolate, drug-addled people.

Perry had watched it all with sad awareness; the decay came fast and cruel. Once-bountiful parks became drugstores where the hopeless bought from the desperate, snorting white stuff up their nostrils or pushing dirty needles in their veins. The only businesses that expanded were bars, racing to keep up with the swift upsurge in drunks. The abrupt eruption of crime and gangs simply overwhelmed the police force. Kids were shot down in school. There was a flood of muggings and rapes and stickups. The local hospitals overflowed with addicts and overdoses and shooting victims who, too often, were children.

He mourned the passing of a once great

town. Perry had been sorely tempted to pack up and move a thousand times. But he stayed. Trenton was his home. Arvan Chemicals was one of the last of the breed and proud of it, a place of employment from birth to death, where hard work was rewarded, where families stayed and struggled together.

"Evening, Perry," Marcus Washington said, pumping hard with his left hand. Perry smiled back and offered his customary "Welcome to the big bake." One of the many old-timers, Marcus had joined Arvan back in 1968 after an ill-fated tour in Vietnam, where he lost his right eye and the lower part of his right arm. He was desperate for work, horribly scarred, and despite his mangled condition and the manual nature of factory work, Perry took him on. Marcus had never once given him cause to regret that decision.

"Marcus, Angela. Chicken's still on the grill, but you know where the drinks are."

"That's exactly what I need, a drink," Angela grunted as she stoutly shoved her way past. "Maybe two or three."

A drink? Oh no, that's the last thing you need, Perry was tempted to shout, but pursed his lips and smiled at her anyway. It wouldn't help, wouldn't make any difference at all. She and Marcus had met in the plant. He worked on the floor, Angela clerked in shipping. They actually held their wedding in the factory, a big to-do with the whole place bedecked with flowers and shiny gold crepe, the works. Back then Angela was a pretty girl, petite, flirty, a smile-a-minute type. After three dispiriting miscarriages, they finally produced a little boy, a tousle-headed, freckly little redhead named Danny, who was their pride and joy.

Poor Danny lived to the ripe age of eight before he fell ill with a painful blood disease nobody could identify or treat, much less cure. Perry and the workers scraped together what money they could afford to help defray the increasingly expensive treatments. In the end, though, young Danny passed away, screaming in agony. Marcus swallowed the pain and soldiered on. He'd lost pieces of himself in Vietnam; he'd learned to endure loss. But Angela turned moody, sour, and unhappy, ballooned in weight, and adopted booze to assuage her grief. She was so big now she waddled. She took to wearing spandex tights and was quite a sight.

She frequently got drunk at these events and made a damn fool of herself. And that was okay, too. Family. All one big family, they understood, and forgiveness came easy.

Marge sidled up beside him. "Seven o'clock, dear," she whispered, seizing his arm and tugging him inside. "Time for you to get a drink and eat."

Perry stole another glance at the parking lot. He saw no latecomers so he nodded and allowed Marge to drag him through the big doors. They held hands and strolled together through the reception area, then entered what the workers fondly called "Perry's Versailles."

Arvan had started out in a small red-brick building on a corner lot. Over the years, more buildings had been added to the cluster as the business grew from a drip of a dream into a prosperous midsize enterprise, and the plant expanded from one small building into a vast maze of vats and mixing tanks and labs. Perry had personally overseen every detail of the expansion, always adhering to his red-brick rule; every building had thirty-foot ceilings, red-brick walls inside and out, large swinging windows for safety purposes, with everything situated around a large green courtyard, which now was totally surrounded and enclosed. Given the array of dangerous chemicals, safety and security were always foremost and no expense was spared: the complex now resembled a fortress.

On Sundays, he and Marge and whatever workers cared to contribute tended the gardens inside the courtyard. Trees and bushes and exotic shrubs had been imported from around the world, meticulously chosen by Perry; no matter the season, something was always in bloom. But in springtime the little courtyard exploded with colors and leaves and tendrils of unimaginable assortment. A dozen fountains and ten koi ponds were sprinkled around, along with too many stone benches to count.

It seemed that as the streets around the plant grew rougher, uglier, and more dilapidated, Perry's gardens flowered into even more of a paradise. The barbecue was always held in the courtyard, and tonight was no different. Two hundred workers and their families were already milling about, drinking and spreading whatever hot rumors they had picked up this week.

Years past, the rumors were harmless and mostly ambled around common themes: office romances, promotions, and corporate politics, such as they were in a small, inbred company. But the past year, a new theme had taken hold. Terror was the only word to describe it: the layoffs struck like a fist. One year, business was booming like never

163

before: the warehouse was crammed with a massive chemical stockpile, new equipment was ordered to chase the sudden demand, and Perry could hardly hire enough folks to handle the load. Then everything dropped off a cliff. The first layoff in Arvan's history. Pay cuts across the board. The tremors were still being felt, leaving everybody edgy and faintly resentful.

Eddie Lungren, a big, interminably happy Swede who worked in mixing, manned the bar, a job he was quite proud of, though mostly it entailed little more than handing out Budweiser in bottles and cheap boxed wine in flimsy plastic cups. "The usual, boss?" he asked Perry, and after a nod, Eddie's big hand pushed an icy diet Pepsi across the bar. After a health scare twenty years before, Perry had quit smoking and drank very rarely.

Mat Belton, Arvan's financial officer, eased his way over. "Nice turnout," he mentioned, nodding in the direction of the grills where a gaggle of workers were hungrily eyeing the chicken. Tuesday cookouts were strictly informal affairs. Most workers were still wearing their grungy coveralls, and it was strictly jeans and T-shirts for the wives. Before the purge, the turnouts were twice as large.

Perry took a slug of Pepsi. "How were the numbers this week?"

"Don't ask."

"Will we make payroll?"

"By a hair. It was touch and go. Had to sell five trucks and six mixing vats on eBay to make it."

"Won't be much longer," Perry assured him, trying to sound confident. The past year Perry and Mat had employed every desperate trick they could think up in a jarring race against bankruptcy. Everything that wasn't nailed down had been sold or auctioned off — usually for a tenth its worth — in an endless, increasingly reckless effort to raise cash. They had fallen behind on bank payments a few times. For a while Perry's charm and solid reputation had bought a reluctant form of patience from the banks. Eventually, though, the calls turned threatening and vicious. Mat was forced to play hardball to get the bankers to back off. Go ahead, he had snarled at one particularly obnoxious lender — push harder, we'll declare Chapter 11, and you and the other buzzards can scratch each other's eyes out over the scraps, which won't be worth squat.

Poor Mat had also been the one to make the job cuts. Perry simply didn't have the heart, so wielding the scythe and delivering the harsh news fell to his financial man. Predictably, Mat's popularity took a terrible drubbing. The tires on his car got slashed so many times he now took a taxi to work, sneaking up the back stairway and through the rear hallways to his office. He brought bagged lunches to avoid the nasty stares and snide comments in the company cafeteria.

"How long is not much longer?" Mat asked, taking another long sip of wine. A year ago wouldn't be too soon.

"Hard to say, Mat. Monday, Harry and I went up to Rock Island Arsenal."

"I heard. How'd that go?"

"Okay, I guess. They were impressed. I think we might be talking with the wrong people, though."

"All right, who are the right people?"

Perry stuffed his hands in his pockets. "Who the hell knows? That Department of Defense is an octopus, a massive bureaucracy sprawled everywhere. Left hand doesn't seem to know anything about the right hand. I asked the fellas at Rock Island. No idea."

"I don't like the sound of that, Perry. Every day counts. We're tiptoeing on the edge of bankruptcy."

"Hell, I know that, Mat. We could afford

it, I'd hire one of those slick operators from down in Washington. You know, someone to cut through the red tape."

"That would be wonderful." Mat drained the wine from his plastic cup. "You're right, though," he concluded somberly. "We can't afford it."

Timothy Dyson, the besieged CEO of Globalbang, could feel the damp sweat mark spreading on the back of his red leather chair. He was being read the riot act by Mitch Walters and some good-looking young hotshot who had flown down with him in the corporate jet to Huntsville.

"Guess if the war heated up, that would help plenty," he said softly, sinking lower in his chair.

"See if I got this right," Walters snarled, rapping a big knuckle on the table. "Two years ago, sales were 1.8 billion. Last year, they slipped to 1.2 billion. This year is sinking below a billion."

"Essentially, those are the numbers, yes. With a little luck and a strong backwind, we'll probably hit nine hundred mil."

Walters rolled his eyes and slapped the table. "That's it?"

"Mitch, this is a demand-driven business. You knew that when you acquired us three years ago. We can't make the Air Force and Navy shoot more."

Walters had dropped in for a surprise visit, then forced Dyson to spend half of a miserable hour reviewing the declining state of Globalbang's business. Thirty minutes of unanswerable questions, pierced by snarls and scowls. Dyson wasn't sure how much more he could take.

A spy at the local airport had notified Dyson the moment the big CG corporate jet touched down. He dropped everything and placed a frantic call to his wife, telling her to contact a real estate appraiser and arrange a quick sell. Mitch Walters rarely paid visits. Walters never paid friendly visits.

Walters narrowed his eyes and pinched the bridge of his nose. "Well, Dyson, that's just not likely to happen. Your numbers have been nose-diving for two years without stop."

"But we're still profitable. I've been cutting costs and laying off people like crazy."

"Not good enough."

"I've also shut down half the facility. No electricity, no water, no nightly cleanup. Half of the plant is a ghost town with big dust-balls blowing through the aisles."

Walters was staring down at one of the paper slides prepared monthly that detailed the intricacies of the company's finances. "What about this?" he demanded, thumping a finger on the page.

"What's that?" Dyson leaned forward and tried to get a better view of whatever Walters was peering at. "The supplier slide?"

"Yeah, that's right."

"What about it?"

"What have you done to squeeze them?"

"They haven't been neglected, believe me. Six months ago, we brought them all down here, turned the screws, said they'd share our pain or else."

"That's the right spirit."

"They agreed to take a ten percent revenue reduction."

"That's it? Only ten percent?" Walters growled, as if that were nothing.

"Christ, Mitch, most are in very low-margin businesses. Ten percent is crushing. It virtually wipes out any chance of profit. They're all in survival mode."

Walters peered thoughtfully at the slide for another moment. All told, there were 120 suppliers spread across six slides, but he seemed fixated on this one. "You know what you need to do?" he eventually announced, tapping his broad forehead as if the idea had just come to him.

Yeah, find a new job where I don't have to

answer to a bullying prick like you, Dyson was tempted to say but obviously didn't. "Not a clue."

"An example, that's what we need." Walters raised a finger, shut his eyes, and brought the digit down on an apparently random target. He opened his eyes and bent down. "Arvan Chemicals," he whispered slowly, as if sounding it out for the first time.

"What about it?"

"Cancel their contract. Today."

Dyson gripped the arms of his seat and recoiled backward. "I can't do that, Mitch. Just can't."

"Sure you can. It's easy."

"For one thing, it's a one-year fixed-cost contract. We'll be sued for everything we're worth."

"That right?"

"Yeah, and we won't have a prayer."

"Let me worry about that. What's two?"

"Two, Arvan is our chief chemical supplier. Without those chemicals, we're screwed. Totally shut down. Bombs and missiles don't work without high explosives."

"Is Arvan the only provider on the market?"

"No, there are two or three others. All farther away, not as cheap, not nearly as reliable."

"So what's three?"

"Three, Arvan is our best supplier. Perry Arvan runs a tight ship. I'll show you the quality control reports if you like. Perry's got the lowest defect rate of any of our suppliers. His on-time delivery is perfect."

"Is there a four?"

"Only this. If we pull the rug out from under him, Arvan will surely go bankrupt. We're Perry's biggest contract. He's signed up for sixty-three million this year after he willingly took a seven million cut from last year. It will destroy him and a very fine company."

It seemed to Dyson that Walters was biting back a smile. "You're about to make me cry, Dyson."

"Mitch, it's bad business, and a bad decision."

Walters snorted and shook his head. "Who pays you?"

Dyson took a deep swallow. "Take it easy, Mitch."

"Do I pay you to worry about other companies?"

"No."

"Remember that. In fact, you just convinced me Arvan's the ideal candidate. What a great message to send to the others. Don't tell me you don't see that."

"I don't. Explain it."

"As good a job as Arvan has done, it's not good enough. It failed to dig deeper, share more of our pain. Provide an even higher level of quality service."

Dyson felt like he was going to be sick. He couldn't believe what he was hearing — his best supplier, about to be sacked, totally without cause, all because that's where Walters's finger landed on that page. He liked and greatly admired Perry Arvan, considered him a friend, in fact. The idea of kneecapping him, out of the blue, was revolting. He glanced at the cold blue eyes of the man seated to Walters's right, hoping vainly for support, a mild nod, a squint of disapproval. Come on, his look was screaming, help me out here, tell the big jerk on your left what an outrageously stupid idea this is.

Must be one of Walters's bloodless lackeys, another of the squad of yes-men at corporate headquarters, he concluded unhappily: the man glanced away and pretended to be studying the white walls.

"You mean, execute your best soldier to make the other soldiers better?" Dyson asked, hoping Walters would see the insanity of this approach.

"Don't knock it till you've tried it. And if we drive it into bankruptcy, all the better."

"I don't understand your thinking."

" 'Cause it'll scare the crap out of the rest. The other suppliers will line up at your door begging to offer more concessions."

Dyson cleared his throat and struggled to clear his conscience. With two kids in college, and nearly two million in CG stock that wouldn't vest for two more years, there really was no choice. None at all. "Exactly what justification am I supposed to use?" he asked, an abject surrender.

Walters wrinkled his forehead and pretended to ponder this perplexing issue. His corporate counsel at headquarters had studied the contract the night before and cooked up the perfect response. "Failure to perform," Walters announced, as if the idea had just popped into his brain. "Leave it vague. No particulars, no examples. Don't give him a legal target. If he decides to sue, leave him punching in the dark."

"I see."

Walters stood, as did his younger colleague. An entire half hour, and the younger man had not said a word. Never introduced himself, never so much as acknowledged Dyson.

Walters began easing his way to the door.

"I want a call the second it's done," he barked on his way out. "Call by close of business, or don't bother coming into work tomorrow."

9

The fax arrived at 4:00 p.m. As death notices go, it was entirely lacking in warmth, detail, or civility. It read simply, "Notice effective upon receipt: For failure to perform, Globalbang hereby tenders cancellation of contract number UA124-990, said contract pertaining to all business arrangements between Globalbang and Arvan Chemicals. All future deliveries will be returned to sender, at sender's cost."

Perry's secretary, Agnes Carruthers, took one long and horrified look and with a shaking hand yanked it out of the tray before scampering in the direction of the cramped conference room where Perry was in his weekly meeting with his section chiefs.

She banged the door open and stood, breathless and terrified.

Perry stopped in midsentence. "What is it, Agnes?"

"I . . ." It suddenly struck her that perhaps

she shouldn't mention this devastating news in front of everybody. Her face was ashen, her mouth hung open. It was just so horrible. Maybe it was a mistake — yes, that's what it was, what it had to be. Or maybe somebody was playing a joke, a very rotten one. She clasped the paper to her chest and just stared at her boss, uncertain and speechless.

Perry stood and took a step in her direction. "Are you all right, Agnes?"

"Yes . . . uh, no," she stammered. "You and Mr. Belton better join me in the hall."

Agnes was old and occasionally excitable: she had been known over the years to throw the occasional outburst. Her tizzies were rare but legendary around the insular company. She looked positively unhinged, though. Mat Belton stood, and he and Perry followed her out into the hall. "You might want to shut the door," she murmured quietly.

Mat did and the three of them ended up in a tight huddle. Agnes drew a heavy breath and tried to compose herself. "This just came in," she whispered, unable to get the tremor out of her voice. She held up the fax so the terrible words could be seen.

Perry quickly read the paper. He yanked it from her hand then slowly reread it, searching line by line for a mistake or some clue that this was a joke, a forgery, a farce.

Nope: it looked dreadfully real. And quite final.

"Jesus" was all Mat could say. He repeated it, then again, and with each repetition the word grew weaker, becoming a faint whisper. If this was true, they were beyond even heavenly salvation. Mat knew what he was staring at, a certain sentence of bankruptcy.

"Failure to perform?" Perry slapped the fax in obvious disbelief. "Ridiculous. No, it's completely outrageous."

Mat insisted, "Our deliveries have always been on time. Always. Our reject rate is below a tenth of a percent. The past three years, they gave us the trophy for best supplier. This can't be right."

Perry and Mat fell silent and contemplated the ugly situation. Frankly, there was little to think about. Either they convinced Globalbang to rescind this hideous order or inside a week the banking vultures would be picking over Arvan's corpse.

Perry lurched away in the direction of his office. After a moment, Agnes and Mat scampered behind him. Perry was already on the phone when they entered, seated behind his old, scarred desk, hollering into the mouthpiece at somebody to put him through to Timothy Dyson right away.

After suffering an interminable moment on hold, an assistant coldly informed him that Mr. Dyson wasn't available at that moment, likely for weeks, maybe months, or possibly ever. At the very least, not until they stopped calling.

Perry slammed down the receiver, clasped his chest, and recoiled back into his chair.

"Are you okay?" Mat asked, moving quickly toward his boss, who appeared to be experiencing a heart attack.

"I think I'm going to be sick," Perry moaned before he lurched over and hung his head over the trash can. "We're ruined, Mat. Screwed," he mumbled.

Mat so badly wanted to contradict his boss, to offer some reprieve, some way to calm him, anything to remove the pain.

But it was simply impossible.

Indeed, they were, without question, beyond doubt, totally screwed.

The call from Jack Wiley came out of the blue at nine the next morning. Agnes tried her best to ward him off, unloading an array of contrived excuses — Perry was feeling ill, indisposed in the bathroom, expecting a conference call that would last at least an hour, and every minute of every hour of the rest of the day was overbooked.

Truth was, Perry was hiding in his office, planted firmly behind his desk, aimlessly shuffling papers and avoiding his workers, still trying to come to grips with the disaster. He had arrived at work as always at six, left strict orders not to be disturbed, and hibernated in stony silence ever since.

Agnes quietly pried open the door and poked her head in. "It's a Mr. Jack Wiley. He insists on talking with you."

"I'm busy," Perry replied. He shoved a few more papers from one place on his desk to another, anything but busy.

"He says you definitely want to talk with him, now. Says it's very important, very urgent."

"Don't know him. Tell him to call back later."

Agnes crossed her arms and studied her boss. He was in a deep funk, cranky and surly, trying stubbornly to ignore her. She wouldn't budge, though. She'd never seen him this way, and was determined to make him snap out of it. His eyes glanced up occasionally. She crossed her arms and coughed a few times.

"Oh, all right," Perry said in a reproachful tone, and lifted up the phone.

Jack quickly introduced himself. "You

might not remember me, Mr. Arvan. I was seated in the back of the conference room when you briefed my partners at Cauldron a few months back."

"I recall the meeting." He paused very briefly. "But you're right, I don't remember you."

"I thought you and I should get together. I have a business offer you'll definitely want to hear."

"I'm busy right now, Mr. Wiley."

"Please, call me Jack. I'm nearby. An hour of your time is all I ask. Sixty minutes, and if you don't find me interesting, you can leave at will."

"Well . . . what time?"

"Noon. Lunch at the Princeton Inn, my treat."

"Look, I —"

"And please bring your moneyman. Mat Belton, right? He'll want to hear this offer, too."

At noon, Perry and Mat entered the upstairs restaurant of the Princeton Inn amid a loud and rowdy crowd of locals, parents of university students, and Tiger alum, arriving early in a swirl of orange-and-black tones for the weekend game against dreaded Yale. Their mood was festive. Princeton was heavily favored by the Vegas crowd; the idea of putting it to the uppity Elis was almost intoxicating.

Perry and Mat, with their dour expressions, looked dreadfully out of place.

A cheerful young waitress awaited them at the entrance; they were promptly welcomed, then ushered straight into a small private dining room in the back. Perry and Mat had thrown blazers over their usual office apparel of tennis shirts and blue jeans. Jack, in a fine gray suit and stiffly starched shirt, was standing by a window, looking anything but casual, and gazing out at the usual midday bustle of Palmer Square. The second they entered he turned around and approached them.

Handshakes were cordially exchanged and a waiter appeared out of nowhere, hauling a tray with a scotch on the rocks for Jack, a cold beer for Mat, and a diet Pepsi for Perry.

"How did you know I like diet Pepsi?" Perry asked, narrowing his eyes, suddenly suspicious.

"A good guess," Jack said, an obvious lie. "Incidentally, I preordered. You're busy and I thought it would save time. Everybody okay with steaks?"

"Fine," said Perry, and Mat nodded.

They sat around a small table, unfolding

their napkins and studying their knives and forks. Jack barely waited until they were comfortable before he came to the point. He looked at Perry, who was sipping his Pepsi. "I hope this doesn't sound presumptuous, but I want to buy your company."

Perry choked so hard his face turned red. He pounded his chest and caught his breath. "What?"

Jack leaned back in his chair and crossed his legs. "That probably sounds a little abrupt, doesn't it?"

"Abrupt . . . no, not at all. You got it right in your opening sentence — presumptuous. Who do you think you are?"

"All right, let me explain. Until a few days ago, I was a partner at Cauldron. Like a lot of financial guys, I'm bored with investing in others, tired of watching from the sidelines. I make plenty of money, but I produce nothing. I'm ready to run my own business."

"Go on."

"I've been searching for the right opportunity for about a year."

"Have you now?" Perry asked, slightly amused.

"Yes, and after you briefed my partners, I became intrigued about Arvan Chemicals."

"Glad you find us interesting."

"So I did a little digging. You're public, and it wasn't hard. You have a fine company, Mr. Arvan, a very impressive outfit."

"We're quite proud of it."

"And you're in deep trouble."

Perry and Mat exchanged looks. How much did he know? the looks said. Maybe nothing, maybe he was throwing darts in the dark.

Straining to look relaxed and unconcerned, Mat spoke first. "There have been a few minor setbacks. Nothing we can't handle."

Jack let that incredible statement rest unchallenged on the table for a moment that felt like an hour. The silence said everything — had he screamed "bullshit" it would've been less cruel, and less revealing.

He knew a lot.

Eventually, and in a matter-of-fact tone, Jack confirmed their worst fears. "Two years ago, your sales were four hundred million. Last year sales sank to two hundred. And unless my research is flawed, the military munitions market is even slower this year." Jack's eyes shifted to Mat's face. "I assume that's what you mean by minor setbacks."

Trying hard to mask his surprise, Mat said, "Times are hard, Mr. Wiley. What's new? Survival of the fittest, and we've been around forty-five years. Believe me, we'll be standing when the dust settles."

"Don't view me as the enemy, Mat. I'm not."

"Oh, you're our friend?"

"No, but we'll get there."

"Don't bet on it, pal."

"Look, you have good people, great products, an admirable reputation. I'd like to keep it that way."

"We're not for sale," Mat insisted, scowling and trying to stare Jack down.

Perry was casually nibbling a breadroll, allowing his younger, pushier CFO to carry the battle. But in fact he did not look like there was any fight left in him, hunched down in his chair, shoulders stooped, neck flaccid. He looked ancient, spent, and for a man who was inveterately neat, slightly unkempt: unshaven, hair unwashed with a large cowlick at the back, shirt hanging out of his pants.

Mat thought his boss had aged a dozen years in the past twelve hours.

But Perry ignored the bread for a moment and commented, "You know, running a company isn't the same as investing in one."

"Believe me," Jack said, "I know that."

"Takes strong people skills. Customer relations, management expertise, technical knowledge. How much you know about chemicals, son?"

With a timid smile, Jack replied, "I took a course in college."

"And how'd you do?"

"I'm a fast study," Jack said, ducking the question. It was an inane claim anyway, speaking as he was, to a man with a doctorate in thermochemistry. "Look, I've done or participated in over a dozen corporate turnarounds. I understand business, Mr. Arvan."

"Good for you, Jack. We like to think we know a little about it, too. We're not selling insurance or breakfast muffins, though. We deal with highly volatile chemicals. One small mistake and there's a large crater in the middle of Trenton."

"We can spend all day discussing my lack of qualifications. But why don't we first focus on what I bring to the table?"

As if on cue, two waiters barged in and began laying down steaks. "Rare, right?" one asked Perry, who nodded vigorously. Evidently, Jack Wiley had done an impressive amount of research.

Perry grabbed his knife and fork, studied his plate a moment, then tore into his steak. "Go ahead with your pitch, I'm listening." He hadn't eaten since the night before and was famished.

"After fifteen years in investment banking, I can tap into plenty of deep pockets. Yours is a cyclical business, up one year, down the next. You need access to capital to get you past the rough patches."

Perry stuffed a big piece of steak between his lips. No use denying it. "True enough," he mumbled between bites. Well, what the hell, he was getting a free meal along with the lecture.

"Also I have an array of contacts." Jack went on a bit, smoothly reeling off names of companies in the industry he was confident he could appeal to for business. He recited from memory. If nothing else, he exposed an impressive mastery of the automotive and munitions industries.

Perry ate and listened.

Mat fought an urge to stand up and walk out. He was sorely tempted to say, Do you really think we haven't already banged on all those doors and begged every one of those companies for business? It's not that easy Mr. Big Shot Wall Street guy with your soul-sucking job, looking for a new hobby. You're an overconfident hustler. In fact, I'd love to give you the company for free just to watch you make a big belly flop. You'll be broke and bankrupt inside a year, and I'll laugh until my guts ache. He would have, too, at the top of his voice and with a blaring smile, except Perry placed a hand on his arm.

Jack finished up by saying, "If I might be so bold, I believe you've made a cardinal strategic blunder."

Mat by now was irritated to the point of distraction. Mr. High and Mighty, who'd never sold a nut or a bolt, was about to explain where they had screwed up so horribly. He so badly wanted to take his fork and drive it into Wiley's forehead. "And what would that be?" he asked, biting his lip.

"You've stayed independent too long, Mat. You need to partner up with somebody big who can open doors."

Mat started to object before Perry said, "Might be you're right about that, son."

"I am, Mr. Arvan. I've participated in over a dozen turnarounds, mostly companies like yours, small, independent outfits being strangled by market forces beyond their control. It takes a powerful partner to avoid being pushed around."

More looks shot between Mat and Perry. That phrase — "pushed around" — rattled around their brains. Why did he phrase it that way? Was he aware that Globalbang had just pulled the plug? How much did Wiley know? And the big question — where was this Wiley guy getting his information?

Mat scraped forward in his chair and leaned across the table. "Meaning what?" he asked, nearly a growl.

"Nothing specific, Mat. Align yourself with a powerful conglomerate and you're feared. Might makes right in the modern marketplace."

"It's an interesting proposal, but I'm not interested," Perry said, sounding very conclusive. He took another big bite of his steak. He chewed slowly for a moment, then put down his fork. "This is my company, Mr. Wiley. I built it, grew it, made it what it is today. I have no intention of giving it to some stranger."

Jack did not flinch, or indeed show any reaction at all. "Sorry to hear that," he said very slowly, very quietly. So far he had ignored his meal.

"Are you?" Mat observed. "Then why do I detect something else in your voice?"

"I am, Mat. Truly, I am very, very sorry. I was hoping we could do this friendly. Of course, I'm prepared to go the other way."

"What other way?" Mat asked.

"I want your company. I'll do whatever it takes to get it."

"Why you dumb son of —"

"Easy, Mat, settle down," Perry interrupted. He picked up his fork and resumed eating again. "What does that mean, Mr. Wiley?"

Jack crossed his arms and leaned backward. "For starters, I've contacted some of your largest investors."

"Who? Parker? Longly? Malcome?"

"Them," Jack replied, nodding, "and others."

"Doesn't worry me in the least. They've been with me a long time. They're my friends. I trust 'em."

"Two years ago, your shares were at $2.30. As of yesterday, they're at sixty-five cents. You've lost these boys a lot of cash."

"I know the share price, son."

"And so do they."

"And I've made 'em a ton of money in the past."

"Ancient history. Parker's down four million, and he's the lucky one in the group."

"Like I said, they're my friends, Mr. Wiley. I was you, I wouldn't count on 'em."

Jack twisted the knife deeper. "And the banks?"

"What about 'em?"

"They your friends, too? Do you trust them?"

"I've always paid my way."

Jack shook his head. "They're sitting on a big pile of your debt. One hundred and fifty million, last time I checked."

"They have nothing to fear," Mat huffed. From his tone, he and Perry were ready and able to write them a check for 150 million on the spot. No problem: a quick scribble and dash, the whole problem would go away.

"They are afraid, Mat, very afraid. And they're not your friends. In fact, they have hearts of ice," Jack replied, frowning tightly. "The last thing they want is to own a bankrupt chemical company."

"They won't," Mat insisted, straining and failing miserably to mask a growing dismay that Wiley seemed to know so much. Where was he getting all this information?

"You're five million in the hole on interest this year," Jack noted in a tone of absolute conviction.

Mat's mouth nearly fell open. "How do you know that?" he finally blurted. More like 5.3 million to be exact, as if anyone cared.

"Doesn't matter. Now listen closely, because here's what does: If you're overdue or short again, they're going to foreclose."

Perry's face nearly went white. The fork

slipped from his hand, and he slumped deeper into his chair and stared at the table-cloth.

And Mat was finally speechless. All his bluster and bravado had just had the floor pulled from underneath it. He had spent his entire career at Arvan, twenty-three years in which never once had he been forced to contend with the likes of a Jack Wiley. A medium-size factory in an unglamorous, blue-collar business, located in grungy, depressed Trenton, of all places, was so far off the screen that the buzzards in New York had ignored it. Oh, there'd been a few offers over the years, friendly tenders, all of them. Mostly amiable competitors anxious to grow a little the easy way, usually proposed as a merger in one form or another. A polite but firm "no thank you" and they went away.

This guy, though, just walked in out of the blue. No warning, no invitation, no sweet talk — just, Hello, I'm Jack, I'm here to rip out your guts and strangle you to death.

Mat was in the mood to fight, to tell this Wall Street pretty boy where to put his of-fer, but it was Perry's company, and out of deference he bit his lip and kept his mouth shut. His boss should have the warm privilege of telling this guy where to shove his offer.

Perry drew a few deep breaths and tried to recover his composure. "So we're clear, what are you proposing, Mr. Wiley?"

"It's fairly straightforward. My people do a quick audit, assess your value, then we decide on a fair price. I'll assume your debt, all of it. Paying it off will be my problem."

"You make it sound so easy."

"It's even easier than that, and a very good deal for you. You'll walk away with a mountain of cash. Buy a big boat, sail around the Caribbean for a year or two, and I'll inherit all your problems."

"What about my people?"

"I'll keep as many as I can. That's a promise."

"What's that mean?" demanded Mat, almost snarling.

"Some may not want to stay. I'll offer three months' severance to anybody who wants out."

"So just voluntary departures?" Mat asked, spewing distrust all over the tablecloth.

"There may be a few others. I'll try to keep as many as possible," Jack said, and you could cut the vagueness with a knife.

Perry had returned to his eating. He was

working his way through a large baked potato, slathered with butter, cutting and slicing with a vengeance. "And if I still say no?" he asked, concentrating on his potato.

"Then," Jack said very solemnly, "you face two possible scenarios."

"Please enlighten me," Perry asked, shoveling a large bite of potato through his lips.

"One, a miracle happens, an avalanche of sales fall from the sky, you satisfy the banks, and I go away." Jack conveyed this in the incredulous tone it deserved. Somehow he avoided a wicked smile, but it must've been killing him.

"What's two?"

"The banks move in. They've been preparing this eventuality for weeks, Mr. Arvan. Their lawyers are ready to launch the necessary motions. Within hours, they'll slap a lien on all your properties. You cosigned some of your corporate loans, so it's not just your company, also your home and cars."

Mat nearly fell out of his chair. Foreclosure! In all his dealings with the banks, they had given him no warning. No hints, no threats, nothing. He grabbed the edge of his seat and growled, "That's hogwash, Wiley. As you said, they don't want to own our company. They wouldn't have a clue how to run it."

"Glad you were paying attention, Mat. They don't."

"So what's different now?"

"Now they have a buyer with deep pockets in the wings. That would be me, Mat. They'll unload the company at a fire-sale price, and I'll assume the debt." Jack lifted his hands in the air and mentioned, rather casually, "Of course, it'll take a little longer, I suppose. On the other hand, it'll probably cost less."

Perry put down his fork, his plate empty but for a few fatty scraps from the steak. "You think you got it all figured out, don't you, boy?"

"I definitely do," Jack said, pushing his plate away. His face suddenly turned cold, his tone almost scornful. "Now you figure it out, Mr. Arvan. I'm offering you the chance to make some money, a little nest egg you can pass on to your children. Or you can have your life's work pulled out from beneath your feet and leave without a penny."

"You're a ruthless son of a bitch," Mat spat.

Jack coolly withdrew two business cards from his pocket and flipped them on the table. He stood and, ignoring Mat Belton, looked Perry squarely in the eye. "Call me before the banks call you," he said ominously.

Without another word, Jack walked out. He hadn't touched his meal.

Perry pulled over his plate and dug in.

10

The three men inched forward in their chairs, straining to catch every word. Walters and Bellweather, as well as Samuel Parner, the cutthroat head of CG's LBO section, were crowded in the small room in the basement to hear Jack's pitch.

The moment they heard the door close, they relaxed and exchanged smiles. As Jack had entered the Princeton Inn, one of the TFAC boys, dressed in loud orange slacks and a black turtleneck sweater, had bumped against him and pinned a state-of-the-art miniature listening device to the back of his suit coat.

The conversation in the private dining room was easily picked up by a van parked in a nearby lot, then relayed in real time to the security room in CG's basement.

Not that they had trust issues with Jack.

No issues at all. They didn't trust him, not one bit.

"Well?" Bellweather turned and asked Parner.

"He's great. Every bit as good as you claimed." Parner could barely keep the broad grin off his face. He'd heard stories about how this guy had creamed two of his best boys but never actually witnessed him in action.

"Yes, brutal, wasn't he?" Bellweather asked, proud of their new catch.

"It was brilliant. Absolutely brilliant." Walters grinned like a proud Little League dad who had just seen his son belt one over the bleachers. "I particularly liked the nice-guy act before the wolf came out."

"Wouldn't you have loved to see their faces?" Bellweather observed, pushing back from the console. "Stupid yokels, never knew what hit them."

"Did he actually contact their banks?" Parner asked. "Or was that a bluff?"

"If he says so, probably yeah. He knew all the numbers. He's thought through every detail. Our boy is full of surprises."

"I've never thought of doing that," Parner admitted, shaking his head; the envy was loud and clear.

"But they didn't say yes," Bellweather noted.

"Just a matter of time," Walters opined.

"It's a squeeze play, a perfect one. Take our money or watch the banks take it all away, and you'll walk away with nothing. Really, it's not a choice." He turned and faced Parner. "How long do you guess?"

"Let's see." He paused and did the math. Unfriendly takeovers were his specialty, and, all humility aside, he considered himself among the best at gauging the pressure points. He could smell corporate collapses from a mile away. "We're three days from the end of the month. Arvan's got payroll and a bank payment due. Probably owes some money to his suppliers, too. Plus he's got electricity, water, the usual overhead."

"Then maybe tomorrow?"

Parner nodded and grinned, the doctor about to give his verdict. "Tomorrow's a good guess. Two, maybe three days after, at the latest."

Bellweather thought about it a moment. "Should we let Wiley finish it?" he asked.

"Sure, why not?" Parner suggested, actually quite pleased at that prospect. If the deal somehow went south, it was Wiley's fault, and by extension, Bellweather and Walters would be blamed for relying on him to handle the heavy lifting. If it worked, he would stoke rumors about how he taught

Wiley the art of the deal. He couldn't lose, really.

Walters toyed with his glasses. "He's done a fine job so far. I'll tell TFAC to keep a close eye on him."

At seven o'clock, Eva Green arrived at Jack's door, wearing tight, faded jeans and a baggy white sweater that bunched and hung gloriously in all the right places and all the right ways. She arrived unannounced in a late-model red Toyota Camry with a bright smile and a lame excuse. "Hi, I'm on my way for a weekend in New York," she said, pumping a few megawatts into the smile. "I hope it's not inconvenient, but I decided to break up the trip."

They looked at each other awkwardly for a moment. Rumson was a forty-minute diversion off 95. As excuses go, it was so flimsy that she made little effort to sound convincing.

"Have you had dinner?" Jack eventually asked.

"No, and I'm famished. Let me take you out."

"You like Italian?"

"Sure."

"I'm in the middle of making spaghetti and I'd hate to waste it. Would you care to join me?"

"I'm impressed. A man who can cook."

"Don't be hasty." Jack smiled, taking her elbow and escorting her inside.

Her hair was up in a ponytail, which bounced cutely when she walked. No makeup, and she really didn't need any. She looked somehow, remarkably, even more alluring in bulky fall clothes than done up for the White House gala. She would be stunning in rags.

"Care for a drink?" Jack asked as they entered the kitchen.

"About a hundred miles ago. White wine if you have it."

Jack retrieved a bottle and a glass, and while he pried off the cork and poured her a drink, Eva leaned against the counter and eyed the kitchen. It was large, spacious, and amazingly well-equipped for a bachelor, or for that matter, even a master chef, with all the latest gadgetry and culinary accoutrements. "I've been in kitchen display stores that have less hardware."

"If you see anything I'm missing, let me know."

"You like to cook?"

"No, I like to eat."

Eva allowed a moment to pass, then said in a very forthright way, "I had a wonderful time with you at the White House."

"I had a great time, too."

"Did you? Why didn't you call me?"

"Maybe I meant to."

"But maybe you've been too busy?" she suggested, smiling coyly.

"Maybe I've been trying to work up the nerve."

"Come on, Jack. Shyness doesn't seem to be one of your attributes."

He smiled and handed her the wine with one hand and with the other stirred the spaghetti noodles. "What are your plans in New York?"

"Just a weekend fling. I have tickets to a Broadway play."

"More than one?"

"Yes, a girlfriend from college who lives in Manhattan is joining me. Last week, she was dumped by her fiancé. A month before the wedding, the cad found someone else. I'm consoling her."

"That's nice of you. And the play?"

"A musical, actually. *Grey Gardens.*"

Jack shrugged. "Is it new?"

"It is, only the first week. Two old maids live in a decrepit old mansion amid tons of garbage and a hundred cats, looking back and singing about the crumbled relation-ships that ruined their lives."

Jack laughed.

"I know." She shook her head. "What was I thinking."

Jack pulled a clump of soggy spaghetti out of the pot and pushed the noodles in her direction. "I need a judgment."

Eva carefully tugged a strand off the spoon, pursed her lips, studied it briefly, then flung it against the wall: it stuck. "Perfect." She crossed her long legs, sipped her wine, and watched him pour the noodles into a strainer.

"Tell me about yourself," Jack said.

"You first."

"You already know everything worth knowing about me."

"Do I?"

"CG's snoops have been digging through my background with a huge shovel. I've gotten calls from a dozen friends about some outfit claiming to be the FBI doing a background check. Don't tell me you didn't read a thick file on me before we went to the White House."

She looked ready to deny it but quickly decided otherwise and instead laughed.

Jack said, grinning, "You've seen mine, now show me yours."

"All right, you win. Not much to tell. Twenty-eight, single, no entanglements, no prospects."

"That's enough, you're boring me."

"Two brothers, me in the middle, lots of moving, plenty of sports, good grades, scholarship to Harvard. One of my brothers plays pro football. Maybe you've heard of him."

"Mike Green?"

"Yep."

"Left defensive tackle? The Jets, right?"

A quick nod.

"Led the league in sacks last year. And penalties. Mean Mike."

"That's Mike, but don't believe what you hear. He's a real sweetie."

"Crippled one quarterback, put two more in the hospital. What's your definition of a badass?"

"The older one, Dan. He's bigger and much meaner."

"And what's he do?"

"Pretty much whatever he wants," she said, straight-faced.

Jack chuckled.

"Dad retired ten years ago. He and Mom live in Myrtle Beach. He runs a used car lot, the Army way. Every car washed and spitshined daily. Salesmen double-time around the lot. If you don't buy a car he shoots you."

"Good technique." Jack loaded two plates with spaghetti, handed one to Eva, and then led her by the arm to the dining room. They sat at the near end of the long table. Jack placed two wine bottles between them, one white, one red.

Eva took a long sip, then looked him in the eye. "I'd like to start over."

"At least take a bite first. It's not as bad as it looks, promise."

"I mean us, you and me."

"I know what you meant."

"Well, you must admit the way we met, it was awkward . . . well, complicated."

"Was it?" he asked, forcing her to spell it out.

"I was working. I was supposed to encourage you to choose us over the competition. You figured that out, obviously."

Jack sat back and took a sip of wine. "Go on."

"So being an ambitious junior executive, I signed on."

"Shame on you," Jack said, but he was smiling. "How far were you supposed to go?"

"You're not that lucky, pal. Pleasant company was all I was asked to provide."

"I should've told them the deal was worth thirty billion."

"Thing is, you're not what I expected, Jack. Far from it."

"What were you expecting?"

"Cold, distant, and ruthless. A smiling shark, according to the dossier. The exact words were 'handsome kneecapper with a ledger.' You castrated several of our most vicious LBO boys. You were the talk of the headquarters."

"And what makes you think I'm different?"

"Are you fishing for compliments?"

"They never hurt."

She smiled and toyed with her fork for a moment. "So what do you think? Can I have a do-over?"

After a moment Jack said, "How's your spaghetti?"

They talked throughout dinner, watched a movie, and at eleven, Eva pecked him on the cheek, slipped a business card into his hand, climbed in her car, and sped off in the direction of New York City.

Before she left, they agreed they would get together the next time Jack was in Washington.

11

They would not be caught again.

Martie O'Neal fell heavily into a seat and for two full minutes steadily ignored the man seated only two feet away and directly to his right. It was the last leg of the D.C. Metro and it roared along the tracks to its final destination, a dead stop at Alexandria station.

O'Neal, who had some expertise in these matters, briefly scanned the rest of the car while Mitch Walters studied the floor and pretended to ignore him. It was midmorning, long past rush hour, more than two hours before the lunch crowd packed the cars, shoulder to shoulder. There were two old black ladies seated at the other end of the car, clutching shopping bags and bragging full bore to each other about their grandsons. A few seats away sat a young kid wearing a Georgetown sweatshirt, with his head tucked inside the hood and his nose stuffed in a thick textbook. Like all young people these days, he had earphones on, his head bobbing and weaving to the music, somehow managing to combine noise with study. He wasn't a threat.

A TFAC employee was located in each of the two adjoining cars, and after a minute, each appeared in the connecting windows with their thumbs up.

"All clear," O'Neal whispered to Walters. The absurd precautions made him feel silly, but Walters insisted.

"What have you got?" Walters asked, still staring at the floor as if they weren't speaking, feeling quite clever about his spycraft.

O'Neal carefully slid a manila folder onto his lap. "Here's everything we've gathered since last week."

"Looks pretty thin."

"Yeah, well, nothing much new on Wiley."

"That good or bad?" Walters asked, stuffing the folder in his briefcase.

"Depends on your perspective, I guess."

"Start with is he still who he says he is?"

"On the surface, yeah, everything checks out. He's smart and ambitious. He likes money. He's loyal only to himself, an opportunist. This guy bounces through firms and jobs like a revolving door. We knew all that, though."

"And below the surface?"

"Understand, I've got nothing tangible that argues otherwise."

"Yeah, but I'm paying out the nose for your instincts."

"I just don't think he adds up. Not yet. It still feels a little disconnected. I'd feel more sanguine if I found any indication that somewhere in his past he bent the rules or played dirty."

"Maybe the temptations haven't been big enough."

"That's one way of looking at it."

"For Christsakes, he stands to make a billion dollars. The deal of a lifetime, O'Neal. Every man has a price and this one would bend the pope's backbone into a soggy noodle. You thought of that?"

"Sure," O'Neal said and shrugged. In a lifetime of peeking through underwear drawers, he had earned a doctorate on human foibles and sins. The Jack engaged in this deal and the Jack from the past didn't add up.

"You're not convinced, though?"

"Look, you pay me to be paranoid, and I'm good at it. This deal you're running, it's not exactly clean, is it?"

"You could say that."

"That's what I figured. So here we got this

guy, and there's no hint in his background that he's done anything like it. Not once, never. A few of our guys went up to New York and nosed around. Everybody said the same thing. Straight shooter. Stand-up Jack. Honest Jack. I'd just like to see a little moral consistency here." He slipped a piece of gum in his mouth and began chewing hard.

"What do you suggest?"

"We gotta keep looking." A brief pause. "If we don't find anything, get the hook in him in the event he tries any funny business."

"We tried that, Martie, remember? Your clowns blew it. What a disaster. I'm not exaggerating, cost us a billion bucks."

O'Neal shifted his broad rear on the seat. "You asked my advice, and you got it." He pulled a handkerchief out of his side pocket and blew with all his force into it; then he balled it up and slipped it back into the pocket. "You're flying without a net here, Mitch. It was me, with all the money involved, I'd want a good hard grip on his balls."

Walters picked at his nose and thought about it. He bent forward and rubbed his eyes. O'Neal was obviously playing on his anxieties, making a pitch for more action, more money, a fatter contract. And though the whole board had bought into this deal, Walters had to admit that the risks for him, personally and professionally, remained enormous. If Wiley somehow managed to screw him, there was no doubt who would be out tap-dancing on the gangplank. The more he thought about it, the more uneasy he became. Jack Wiley was driving this train, juking and jiving, always a step ahead. And truthfully, Wiley had so far outsmarted the best and brightest CG had to offer. That little stunt with the burglars and Jack still stung. The way Jack had burned him, right there in front of everybody, still rankled. After a moment he said a little hesitantly, "You understand we can't get caught again?"

"Look, I know that last thing was stupid and sloppy. It —"

"Stupid?" Walters hissed. "Oh, it was more than that. It was horrible."

"Yeah, well, you said fast, and the guys went in blind. We'll put some ex-spooks on it this time. They're real good at this sort of thing."

"Don't underestimate him again. I mean it. He's very smart, and very cautious."

O'Neal bunched his shoulders and chewed harder on his gum. "We know that now."

"You know the phrase 'plausible

deniability'?"

"Hey, these guys invented that credo. There won't be a trace leading back to you. Don't worry."

"I want full approval before you do a thing."

"Naturally."

"What about Arvan?" Walters asked suddenly, changing the subject — apparently the issue with Jack was settled.

"We bugged the old man's house and got a phone intercept. Still working on gettin' one into his car."

"He suspect anything?"

"Nope. The old man believes Wiley just swooped in out of the blue. A typical Wall Street vulture, that's what the old man kept calling him."

"Is he worried?" Walters asked, barely able to conceal his excitement. He loved getting these insights. The game was so much more fun this way.

"Yeah, definitely. He and the wife stayed home last night. You'd've loved that conversation. Bickered back and forth all night. They went over the numbers again and again. It's hopeless. They're worried about the kids."

"Explain that."

"They figure they had their run. They're

old now. The company was the inheritance they were gonna pass down. It's the family piggy bank, and now it's sprung a big hole."

"And how are they leaning?"

"The old lady, she says call Wiley first thing in the morning and cut a deal. Dump this turkey before it destroys them. They're too old to recover from such a disaster. Once the banks move . . . the company, the house, their cars, they could lose everything."

"Smart lady."

"Yeah, but the old man, well, he just ain't so sure yet, Mitch."

"What's he waiting for?"

"He kept droning on about this miracle product. Says if he could just get it into the right hands in the Pentagon, all their troubles will be over."

Walters broke into a loud, satisfied chortle. "Ridiculous. It would take at least a year of tests and studies before the Pentagon showed the slightest interest. He's got a day or two, at most."

O'Neal did not join him. He inserted a fresh piece of gum through his lips and chewed hard for a moment. The old ladies in the middle of the car had moved on to a heated discussion about the price of groceries; the kid remained engrossed in his book.

O'Neal reached into the inside breast pocket of his jacket, removed what appeared to be a transcript, then flashed it in Walters's big face. "The guy ain't stupid, Mitch. He knows that."

"Oh. Well, tell me about that."

"He called his financial guy a little after midnight. Mat . . . Mat . . ." — a hurried glance at the transcript — "Mat Belton. Told him to get ready."

"What are you talking about?"

"Told him to hit the phones hard first thing in the morning. Find somebody with deep pockets, offer him a big cut of their miracle product. Belton estimates ten million will do the trick."

"What trick?"

"Bridging money, he called it. One guy is all they need — one moderately rich guy willing to stake ten million in return for fifty or a hundred million when the product comes home to roost."

Walters rocked back in his seat. He rubbed his forehead and thought about this. "He's more desperate than I thought," he concluded. But rather than look gloomy he broke into a huge smile.

"What're you smokin'?" O'Neal asked. "Sounds like a great idea to me."

"His company is publicly listed. We're

talking major SEC violations. Jailhouse stuff."

O'Neal stared back with a blank expression. Lacking a background in finance, he had no clue what the problem was.

Walters shook his head and curled his lips as if Perry Arvan's plans sickened him. "It's insider trading. Offering an outside investor confidential, inside knowledge as a lure for his money, information he hasn't even shared with his own stockholders, that's a serious crime."

"If you say so," O'Neal replied, as if to say, big deal, so what? The absurdity that they were breaking even more serious laws seemed relevant only to him.

"Also, private loans are a corporate no-no," Walters went on, now sounding very righteous. "The polymer was developed on company premises, using company employees, on company property. The shareholders own it. He can't sell off pieces or encumber them with a major debt without their express knowledge and approval."

"I think he's gotta get caught first," O'Neal noted very reasonably.

"You have this conversation on tape, right?"

"Clear as a bell."

"So there it is."

"Yeah, there it is . . . a totally inadmissible conversation."

If that minor technicality worried Walters, he gave no hint of it. With a great screech the train ground to a stop; the two black ladies got up and waddled off, followed by the student, bouncing and rocking to his iPod. Both men sat staring at the floor, neither moving.

"Send me the tape," Walters finally announced, then stood, adjusted his suit, and, looking suddenly purposeful, departed.

"No problem."

Jack was seated in his car in the middle of a large parking lot, reading a paperback novel, when the long black limousine slid up and parked less than three feet away.

Mitch Walters popped out of the back, gripping a briefcase and unloading a smug grin.

Jack stepped out of his car and they shook, rather limply. "Listen, Mitch, I don't think this is such a good idea," Jack said.

"Hey, you're right, Jack, it's a great idea." Walters spent a moment surveying the parking lot, the surrounding streets, the large collection of junkheaps parked around them; not a single BMW or Mercedes in the lot, but plenty of old pickups that seemed to be fading and rusting before his eyes. His stare stopped at the large pile of red bricks with the words "Arvan Chemicals" across the entrance.

"What a dump," Walters remarked with a sour expression. He withdrew a long cigar from his pocket, neatly clipped the end, and spent a long moment puffing and sucking to get it lit. The call he made to Jack three hours earlier had not gone well, to put it mildly. Jack had confidently asserted that he had matters well in hand, before Walters unloaded the news about Perry Arvan's hunt for a white knight willing to make a generous wager in return for a big chunk of the holy grail.

Just as he suspected it would, this news caught Jack flat-footed and momentarily baffled: it was a rare opening and Walters exploited it to insist on taking a more active role in the takeover. Jack's protestations were vehement and a total waste of breath.

Walters had his mind made up: the time had come to push Jack into the backseat; time for the Capitol Group, and for Walters himself, to take the lead. It was also the first advantage Walters had on Jack and he intended to use it for all it was worth. He ended the conversation abruptly by informing Jack that he was about to jump on the smaller corporate jet for a fast sprint to Trenton Airport, drive to the factory, and pay a nasty visit on Perry Arvan.

Jack could join him or not. His choice. Didn't matter to Walters.

"You say you have Perry on tape planning to commit a crime. Did I hear that right?" Jack asked, giving Walters a wary look.

"Yep, him and his money guy, Belton."

"What crimes?"

"Conspiracy on top of two or three major SEC violations. Dead to rights. One of my corporate lawyers listened to it and said it's lockdown stuff. And if they called across state lines, you can add interstate fraud."

"Where did you get these tapes?"

"None of your business," Walters snapped, smirking and making no effort to disguise how much he was enjoying the moment. It felt so good to be on top for a change. "You said it yourself, we're partners. I don't have to tell you a thing."

"Is it legal?"

"Who cares?"

"In other words, no."

"So what?"

"Was this the handiwork of your pals at TFAC again?"

"Just say I came into possession of a very incriminating tape. Now I intend to use it.

Arvan thinks he's found a way around you, Jack, but I'm going to stop him."

"I don't like it, Mitch."

"You're breaking my heart."

"You intend to blackmail him," Jack said, shaking his head.

"Think of it as saving him from himself. That's how I think of it."

"You'll have to explain that."

"He's about to engage in an illegal act. Several acts, actually. Like a Good Samaritan, I'm stopping him from making a bad choice."

"Very creative reasoning."

"Thanks, I'm quite proud of it."

"I suppose I can't stop you."

"Good guess. You can come along and support me or get lost."

Jack looked frustrated but tagged along.

Agnes Carruthers did not recognize the face of either of the two men who barged into her office, though the name of the younger one struck a chord from their phone conversation two days before.

"He's extremely busy," Agnes staunchly insisted, edging forward and pursing her lips. The bigger of the two men was standing two feet from her in an effort to intimidate. This was her boss, her office, her domain. "You should've called, asked for an appointment," she insisted, raising her sharp chin and staring down her nose.

Walters placed his big hands on her desk and launched forward, about three inches from her face. "Listen up, lady. I've flown up from D.C. and don't you dare tell me no."

"You listen up, buster. Mr. Arvan's got more important things going on. I'll see if I can fit you in next week."

"You won't be in business next week," Walters barked with a nasty, knowing smile. Another day or two and he would own this company. He had just made his first executive decision: he would personally fire this old hag and shove her out the door. He hoped she had a pension. He would personally assure she never got a dime. "You know who I am?" he asked.

"Sure do," Agnes replied, not backing down an inch. "You're the fella who's gonna be outta here in two seconds, or I'll call security."

Jack eased himself around Walters. "Excuse me," he said, using a hip to edge Walters aside, and putting on his best smile. "Please, if you can just tell him we're here. Let him decide, please. If he says no, we'll leave quietly."

Agnes's eyes moved back and forth between this nice-looking young man with such pleasant, respectful manners and the big, blustery windbag who was glaring back with a threatening sneer. "All right," she said to the young man, firing another withering look at the bully before she got up and disappeared into her boss's office.

She popped out a moment later, pink-faced, and ushered them in. Perry Arvan and Mat Belton were seated in chairs in the corner of the office, surrounded by stacks of spreadsheets. Between the mountainous piles of paper and their drawn expressions, they had been there all day, going over the dismal numbers and hoping for a miracle. Perfect, just perfect, Walters thought.

Jack stiffly performed the introductions, then moved against a wall and remained quiet. "What's this about?" Perry asked, dropping a sheaf of papers and edging forward in his chair.

Walters pointed at Mat Belton. "I suggest you ask him to leave."

"Why?"

"We're going to have what you might call a sensitive conversation. It would be best for all concerned to keep it confidential."

"I trust Mat."

From the wall, Jack said, "Mr. Arvan, you

220

might want to do as he says."

Perry and Mat exchanged looks. "All right," Mat said to nobody, then after a moment's hesitation, to Perry, "I'll be outside the door if you need me."

The moment he left, Perry asked Walters, "Who are you?"

"The CEO of the Capitol Group. I'm sure you've heard of us."

"Nope, sure haven't."

"We're partnering with Jack here to buy your company."

"What's that mean?"

"He brought the idea to us and we decided to back him. Provide financing. Help market the products, that sort of thing."

"I see."

"So what do you say?"

"About what, Mr. Walters?"

"The sale. You going to pull the trigger or not?"

"Pull the trigger?" Perry reclined into his seat and his fingers formed a steeple in front of his mouth. "That how you boys speak of it? You make it sound so easy, so simple. A mild squeeze and it's over."

"Answer the question."

"All right. Haven't made up my mind."

Walters sauntered over to the desk and put down his briefcase. With a theatrical gesture, he flipped it open and withdrew a small tape player, preloaded and ready to roll. Perry quietly removed his glasses as Walters punched play. The sound of Perry's voice speaking with Mat Belton came through loud and clear.

"Listen," Perry was saying in a tone garbled with excitement or perhaps relief, "I've got a great idea for saving the company . . ." and so on, as he ordered Mat to prepare a list of every wealthy investor in the company and out, rich men they would begin speed-dialing in the morning. Perry sat, wiped the lens of his glasses, and listened. Except for a small flutter around his left eye his face was entirely impassive. The call lasted three minutes and ended with him and Mat debating how far they should go to sweeten the lure — Mat argued low, Perry high — deciding in the end to offer a thousand percent return.

"How'd you get that?" Perry demanded the moment it ended.

"Why does it matter?" Walters snarled. He wasn't about to confess to Perry that his phones were bugged; it was self-evident anyway. If pushed, he would put on a show of innocence and insist that somebody — he didn't know who — had left the tape on his doorstep. An anonymous donor. Who

222

knew how he or she got it? And who cared? That the alibi was as woefully implausible as it was nebulous and impossible to disprove made it all the better.

"It matters to me," Perry insisted with a dark squint.

"It won't to the SEC when they listen to it. They'll only hear you on the tape, plotting with your CFO to break the law."

"I have ears. I know what it is."

"Oh, good. Saves me the trouble explaining all the trouble you're in. Do the words 'criminal conspiracy' mean anything to you? Old men don't fare well in prison."

Perry looked over at Jack. "You in on this too, son?"

Jack stared at the floor and refused to answer.

"So what's the deal?" Perry asked in a matter-of-fact tone, again confronting Walters.

"Glad you asked. You agree to sell the company today and this tape will disappear."

"And if I don't?"

"Bankruptcy. Prison. Disgrace. It won't be pretty. The FBI and SEC will be crawling all over this place tomorrow. They'll subpoena your phone records, see who you called, and probably arrest them, too."

Perry sank back into his chair and released a heavy sigh. "Don't leave me much choice, do you?"

"Let me make this clearer." Walters fought back a smile and mustered his most threatening snarl. "You have no choice, absolutely none."

"Okay."

The answer shot out so fast, Walters was obviously a little taken aback. He shifted his feet a moment, peered at Perry in astonishment, then recovered his balance. "Okay?"

"You got ears, too, Mr. Walters. Assuming we agree on a price, let's get this over with."

Before Walters could answer, Jack pushed off from the wall. "One hundred million dollars," he announced, loudly and distinctly, like it was a nonnegotiable figure.

"A hundred million?"

"Yes, and in return, you'll sign over all rights, all patents, all intellectual rights. All properties will be ours."

Perry popped forward in his chair, wiping his hands through his white hair, apparently stunned. "A hundred million." He gawked at Jack. "That's a very generous offer. Why so much?"

"I think you know the answer."

"The polymer."

"Yes, that's the deal. You walk away with a

hundred million and we own the polymer."

Perry stared at the wall a moment, dumbfounded. It was impossible to tell if he was angry, shocked, merely crushed, or all of the above. This was the first blunt admission of what this was really about. They didn't care a whit about his company, his employees, the chance to resuscitate the plant and turn around the business that had been in Perry's bloodstream for the better part of his life.

No, this was about only one thing: the polymer he had created with his own ingenuity and bare hands.

"How'd you learn about it?" he asked after a painfully long moment.

"I'd prefer not to say," Jack replied, avoiding Perry's eyes.

"You mean you won't say."

"All right, that, too."

"Well, if that's what you boys want, I think I'll ask for more. It's worth a fortune, probably billions. You fellas obviously think so. I'm not giving it away for a song."

Walters shifted his large bulk and said, "Maybe you missed something here, Arvan. The price is set. This isn't a used car lot. No haggling, no give. Wiley gave you our final offer."

"That sounds like a threat."

"Nice to see you're paying attention. I can use that tape and pick up the pieces afterward."

Trying to sound reasonable and restore a little amity to the conversation, Jack said, "Without the polymer you wouldn't get one million for this company. You couldn't give it away. You're a hundred and fifty million in debt, and your business is collapsing around you. Take our price. Get out now while you still can."

The bluff crumbled in Perry's lap. "Guess you're right," he said, as if he had ever contemplated otherwise.

"Then you agree to the sale?" Walters asked.

"You fellas are holding me up, but you've got a deal. Uh . . . you know, long as you're assuming the debt, too."

"That's part of the package," Jack assured him quickly, speaking for both of them. Now that they had him on the ropes, it was important to meet his demands; don't give him a chance to rethink it or back out. Jack told him, "I've already negotiated this with the banks. They're prepared to sign a new covenant tomorrow."

"And my employees?"

"Same as before. Three months' severance to any employee who wants to leave. But there is, well, one last condition."

"What's that?"

"We'd like to present this to your shareholders and employees as a friendly takeover. We don't want any complications, strife, or bad feelings. Between your shares and three other large stockholders — Parker, Longly, and Malcome — there's enough votes to lock this in. This is important, Perry. We expect you to round up their support. Tonight."

"Then you better offer the shareholders a decent price."

"Seventy cents a share. That's more than fair. About twenty percent above today's market price. There's thirty million shares outstanding. You own eight million, right?"

"Sounds about right. Mat knows a bit more about it than I do."

Mat was called back into the room, and while he and Jack fought and haggled over the details, Mitch Walters leaned against Perry's desk and dreamed about the polymer and its miraculous ability to print money. It was a remarkable coup, one Walters was quite proud of. The Capitol Group would pay Arvan $100 million in cash, hand over another $15 million to the shareholders — for less than $150 million in cash, a pittance, CG would own the most extraordinary military technological break-through of the decade. Sure, there was another $150 million in debt, and of course, the $20 million bonus promised to Jack to be factored into the equation: still, the grand total for a corporation with the size, resources, and wealth of the Capitol Group barely came to a rounding error on the annual statement.

It would not be CG's money, anyway. Not a penny of CG's capital would be at risk. Within a day he would dispatch a delegation to Russia or the Middle East and see who wanted a piece of the action. Both places were flush with billionaires hunting for profitable investments. The money would come quickly and easily, Walters was sure. Russia's growing class of fabulously wealthy were particularly anxious to park their cash overseas. And the Saudis and Kuwaitis, given the spike in oil prices, were again flush with petrodollars, a flood of cash, a venture capitalist's dream.

Two hundred million would be more than enough, but why not go for three? For that matter, why not five hundred?

What a day, what an accomplishment. He planned to get the boys in CG's publicity department to kick it into overdrive: they could work all night for all he cared. Walters wouldn't settle for less than the covers of *BusinessWeek* and *Investor's Business Daily.* That night he would make the rounds of a few business cable shows that would allow him to boast and brag to his heart's content.

A large front-page spread in the *Wall Street Journal* was something he had always dreamed of, something that now looked like a distinct possibility. He wondered if he could get a copy of the *Journal's* portrait of him as a trophy to hang on his wall. He would put it right behind his desk, just above his head, so it would be impossible to miss. What a statement that would make.

He would use the trip back to D.C. to rehearse and refine his performance. He would be tired by then, but was sure he could muster enough energy and enthusiasm for this one bold stroke, a fast-paced dash through the cable business shows.

Not overly boastful but not humble either, he told himself. Strike just the right note: tout the product and himself but don't beat it to death. Don't grandstand but also don't leave any doubt whose vision and deft hand closed the deal.

It was a chance, the first of his three years as CEO, and he intended to use it for all it was worth.

He was tired of all the former government

bigwigs around him. That oversize board filled with grandstanding political has-beens, the sinecures to former admirals and generals, and too many deputy or assistant secretaries of this or that to count. He was tired of the whole stable of Uncle Sam's former flunkies feeding at his trough. He privately loathed them. He detested their self-importance, their inflated titles, was bored with their exaggerated war stories, nearly wretched at their endless boasting about all the people they knew, the strings they could pull, and the doors they could open.

He sucked up to them, but privately seethed.

Mitch Walters was a businessman, plain and simple. A distinguished graduate of Wharton brought in to manage the exploding complexities of a corporation that had outgrown the mental nimbleness of a bunch of ex-government hacks.

During his years as CEO, he had been bullied and sneered at, treated as little more than a hired flunky, a bookkeeper to the famous clowns above him.

A bunch of condescending, windbag know-it-alls, all of them.

That was about to change.

In a year, as the miracle polymer became

the talk of the industry, as more profits poured in than they could possibly count, he would squeeze the board for a fat bonus. It would be a memorable bonus, a record payoff. He had brought home the bacon and would insist on being amply rewarded.

The start point would be seventy million — why not? — but he would settle for a mere fifty, he promised himself.

Why be greedy?

12

At nine the next morning, the assault began — an army of nosy, cold-eyed accountants, mouthy consultants, and human resources assassins descended on Arvan Chemicals. They scrambled out of four large buses and poured resolutely and quickly through the front door of the plant. All were hired locusts from an arsenal of northeastern consulting firms who would give the company a long-overdue scrubbing. In their gray and blue business suits, and by their calm but chilly demeanors, they were easy to distinguish from the workers wearing stained overalls and strained, anxious expressions.

The assault was well planned, a maneuver rehearsed and perfected countless times as the Capitol Group took over and "turned around" other companies. The consultants were all seasoned veterans. Once they hit the front door they spread out and crashed into every nook and cranny of the business, from the mixing vats to accounting, to the employee records room, to the musty shipping room, to the dreary mail room in the back.

They asked thousands of questions, scribbled notes on the clipboards, then barked more questions. They spoke one language, the workers another: the consultants peppered the workers with phrases like, What are you doing to create multiphase strategic alliances? . . . How are you enabling expanded, collaborative commerce? . . . Name the steps you are taking to create seamless, integrated, and streamlined business manners. In response, they got a chorus of shrugged shoulders, bit lips, nervous chuckles, and befuddled expressions. Work at the plant ground to a standstill.

By 9:15, the five chemists who had worked on the polymer were located and herded into the small conference room upstairs. They mustered around the long table, were sternly ordered to sit, and step two commenced.

A glowering executive from the Capitol Group stood at the head of the table and threatened to fire them on the spot unless they immediately signed thick nondisclosure agreements protecting CG's intellectual property rights. The six men looked horrified. They exchanged back-and-forth looks of confusion; Arvan Chemicals had always operated on integrity. Perry had never thought to force or even mildly encourage them to sign a vow of silence. Trust had always been good enough.

The executive, a lawyer naturally, went on a bit about what their new employer would do to anybody who refused to sign — firing would be immediate, and loaded in his briefcase was an expandable folder filled with devastating lawsuits and injunctions he would file that very day. Fill in a name and fire away. As only a lawyer can do, he threatened, cajoled, and bullied until the last terrified man scrawled his signature.

By ten, all documents pertaining to the polymer were collected in a large safe and a guard was posted.

Also by ten, Perry had signed the contract, a forty-page document loaded with legalese, clauses and subclauses, conditions piled on top of conditions. In return for his hundred million, among many other things, he agreed to relinquish all proprietary ownership rights, to abide by a strict vow of silence, and to never set foot in the factory he had built and nurtured and groomed for over

234

forty years. He vainly tried to insert a few clauses, mainly protections for his work-force, but CG's negotiators crossed their arms, scowled, and stonewalled.

Perry had already consigned himself to surrender anyway. The negotiators had been through this a hundred times, the last-minute guilt of the conquered. But why, on the cusp of victory, allow him to burden them with troublesome conditions? Just sign the agreement, they flatly insisted, just get this over with, and eventually Perry caved completely.

At eleven, four burly guards with Capitol Group patches on their thick arms helped Perry out of his chair and escorted him downstairs, then across the factory floor and out the broad double doors, straight to his car. A large group of horrified workers tried to approach him, but the guards pushed and barreled through like an NFL offensive line. The uniformed quartet stood with grim smiles and watched him climb in and start the engine. He gave one long pathetic look at the plant, one look at what had been his life's work, then slowly he eased out of the parking lot.

They watched until Perry's car dis-appeared into the streets of Trenton.

Reinforcements arrived promptly at noon.

Another bus pulled up and disgorged a squad of CG chemists and metallurgists, technical experts brought in to assess Arvan's breakthrough and decide on the fastest, most efficient way to kick it into production. They crowded into the small conference room and began studying the blueprints for the precious polymer. They had been given three principal questions to answer: How much of the polymer should be manufactured here? How much could be shifted to other plants, in other states, in order to build broader political support? How fast could it be jammed into mass production?

Meanwhile, the consultants on the shop floor began breaking the production teams into new units, breaking apart teams that had operated together for years. It was all part of the standard shock treatment. Sow confusion and fear, upend the old ways, disorient the workers, humiliate the supervisors, divide and conquer.

By close of business they would know who to lay off; by dawn the next day, a squad of guards would be posted at the doors, gripping clipboards with the names of those who would be allowed to enter and those who would be coldly sent home, permanently.

The hatchet men from human resources were given a fairly light objective: eliminate fifty percent of the workers and ninety percent of the supervisors, who were considered too set in the old ways.

Of course, not a dime would be paid to those they dismissed. Not a cent of the promised severance packages.

Of course, this would incite the usual flood of lawsuits and occasional picketing over broken promises.

And of course, CG's lawyers would employ their usual tactics to drag out the cases for years, filing motions, pushing extensions, stonewalling for all they were worth.

Eventually, CG would settle for half of three months' pay to anybody financially able or stubborn enough to cling on that long. But statistically, they knew only four out of ten employees had the resources to hire a lawyer; only one out of those four had the angry persistence to battle it out to the bitter end.

Day three, one of CG's many former senior government officials would be dispatched on a fast trip to Trenton for a pointed, one-sided chat with the mayor and city council. The economics of keeping the plant in Trenton looked dire, he would warn them with an appropriately grim and regrettable look. Poor schools, high personal and business taxes, dangerous streets. Not a good combination, he would say, frowning tightly.

The Capitol Group also happened to own another chemical company, a recently modernized plant with plenty of room for expansion, one situated in a nice, lovely, leafy community with first-rate schools and safe streets. It was located in Tennessee, where the politicians were friendly to businesses and understood the need for generosity.

The business logic of shuttering the archaic Trenton plant and shifting the entire operation to shinier Tennessee was nearly irresistible. A war was being waged back at headquarters. The accountants were well armed, loud, and pitiless. Their main concern, really their only concern, was with the numbers. The financial logic screamed for consolidation; it would reap a thousand economies and savings. The senior leaders of CG were humanists, though, and horrified at the thought of heaping more damage on an already depressed town, though they found it hard to argue against the numbers.

If, on the other hand, the city fathers could find it in their hearts to cough up a few generous tax concessions, perhaps the carnage could be avoided. The humanists needed something, a weapon to curb the hard appetites of the number crunchers.

A complete tax holiday for five years would go a long way.

Further, he would warn them, there would be some necessary personnel "dislocation" — as polite a way as possible to say mass firings — and CG expected the local politicians to ignore the complaints.

Agnes Carruthers was the first casualty. She was seated behind her desk, in the same lumpy old chair she had occupied for thirty-two years, through good times and bad, tending to her boss's every whim and need. She knew the company inside and out. She knew all the suppliers and all the customers, could nearly recite from memory the birthdate of every employee. She prided herself on being a mother figure, figuratively and literally, as all three of her children now worked at Arvan. Lawrence, her husband, had as well, before he passed ten years before, God bless him.

A courier walked in, dropped an unmarked envelope on her desk, and briskly departed. Agnes took a long sip of her tea and opened it: "You remember yesterday when I asked you, Do you know who I am? I'll tell you. I'm the new owner of this company. Collect your things and get out. You're fired."

The takeover was a godsend for Mitch Walters. For two days he was a hit on all the business shows, who were enchanted with the concept of a thin coat of paint that could deflect a rocket. Mitch was hazy on the particulars — frankly, he had no idea how the polymer worked — but huffed and bluffed his way through.

A telephonic board meeting was held four days after the takeover to confirm the purchase and plot the next steps.

Walters plunged into the call with an overly generous narrative about how his personal intervention "defanged an unexpected Hail Mary pass by Perry Arvan" and "salvaged the deal that nearly slipped out of Wiley's grip." He was vague on the details. Nobody bothered to ask him to elaborate. In Walters's case, it was better not to ask, they all knew.

He was followed up by the chief financial officer, a thickset, brainy accountant named Alex Ringold, with a serious manner and droll voice, who bluntly confessed the bad news. The wars in Iraq and Afghanistan had slowed into grinding contests. From their very profitable starts they had bottomed out into slow-motion battles of attrition that were dramatically eroding the company's earnings. Few of CG's defense companies had any upward momentum — Humvees were still selling briskly to replace those that were blown up, as were select electronic products — but the month before the Pentagon had canceled a large artillery program, as well as an order for three additional battleships. And now a big-ticket future fighter program for the flyboys was hanging in doubt. CG was the lead contractor on two of the three programs, and a healthy contributor on the third.

The loss of the artillery and the battleships alone would cost CG many billions in future revenue. The pain, though, was being felt across the board. Military munitions, contract services to the troops, maintenance contracts for tanks and Bradleys that were no longer seeing much use — all were sinking and not likely to see any improvement in the near term. The latest analysis projected only nine percent growth in profits, which incited a disgruntled chorus of angry groans and curses from the board.

One of the board members, a garrulous former secretary of state with strong Texan roots and a gargantuan ego to match, roared, "What the hell, what do we gotta do? Maybe we'll start another war. Iran could use a healthy ass-kickin'. That'd be a good war, and a long one."

This coarse strategic insight caused an onslaught of light laughter. It wasn't at all clear he was joking, though. Two months before he had authored a red-meat editorial in the *Wall Street Journal* that argued the same case, that if Iran wanted nuclear weapons so much, well, we should send them a few of ours, free of charge.

Ringold waited till the chuckling died down and said, "So as you can see, the timing of the Arvan takeover is a financial boon. The idea is to get it under contract and into production at the earliest date. Mitch, is it possible to have an impact this fiscal year?"

"That's the whole point," Walters announced, bubbling with enthusiasm. "We should see an eight to twelve billion pop, maybe as early as next year."

A nice one-two punch; it was apparent that he and the CFO had colluded on this conversation.

"You're sure that's not exaggeration?" a voice asked, a high-pitched twang they all recognized as Ryan Cantor, the son of Billy Cantor, the aging former president. The old man, they knew, was eavesdropping on another line, leaving the tawdry business negotiations to his middle child. After a long career in politics the old man had his heart set on cashing in — since leaving the presidency he had sold his name to anybody who offered, and now was doing TV pitches for Flagorex, a preventative for premature ejaculation — but had no intention of leaving his fingerprints.

It was the same way he had run his presidency; after four years there was no Cantor Doctrine, no great peace initiative, no treaties, or even a telltale title that identified his tenure. It was all so sad. His years in the Oval Office elicited little historical interest, because, frankly, aside from a devastating recession, nothing of note had been accomplished. In frustration, the president secretly paid a writer to produce a glowing biography — the only one written, complimentary or otherwise — then couldn't find a publisher willing to print it.

Walters almost chortled into the line. "Oh, no, Ryan, it's quite real. If we short-circuit the Pentagon procurement process, the cash flow should start pumping in a few months."

"I know it'll be a stretch," the CFO added, doing his part, "but our projections show that a contract inside two months would make a world of difference on the bottom line."

"How do you intend to accomplish that?" asked another voice in a strong Australian brogue. This was William Haverill, the former Australian prime minister, a charmingly manipulative man who had left office under an ugly cloud of suspicion. Procurement scams were a field in which he had considerable expertise and success. It was rumored that he and a few close chums had ripped off over two hundred million dollars.

The rumors were flagrantly false — three hundred was more like it.

Nobody could prove it, though; the money disappeared into the black hole of government programs, shuffled back and forth through a dizzying maze of appropriations until all sense of accountability was lost. The cash eventually squirted out the pipeline into a series of amorphous consulting companies, all empty shells registered under a miasma of phony names, then got washed and rewashed in a byzantine tango through countless banks. Haverill was currently living high on the hog in a large, sumptuous chateau in southern France, along with three doting mistresses. The warm weather and sultry beaches reminded him of home.

The mistresses made him glad it wasn't home.

Walters allowed that question to sit for a moment before he suggested, "I propose we put Mr. Secretary himself in charge of that. In fact Dan's perfect."

Bellweather, as Walters knew, was not on the line. He was at Walter Reed Hospital at that moment having a hemorrhoid lanced. It was an appointment he had booked only after Walters swore that the telephonic board meeting was meaningless and missable: a pro forma discussion, nothing more. The trap was laid, now the time had come to snap it shut. Walters was tired of Bellweather, tired of his "oversight," tired of the board's watchdog looking over his shoulder and second-guessing his every move.

"You think that's a good idea?" another voice asked.

"You kidding? He's a highly respected former secretary of defense. A living legend. He can —"

"Are you there, Dan? Are you listening?" another voice broke in, a provincial British accent this time; obviously the former defence minister.

"No, he's at a doctor's appointment," Walters informed the voice, swallowing the urge to unload the degrading details — at that moment Bellweather was probably bent over a metal table, howling his guts out, with his naked butt up in the air as an Army doctor stabbed and prodded at his best side.

The same voice, with typical British dryness, observed, "Well, uh, about Dan, he might not be the right sort for this job."

"No?"

"I seem to remember that he wasn't all that popular or admired when he was secretary."

"There's an understatement," another voice chimed in quite loudly, now that it was clear Bellweather wasn't listening. The boys at the top were quite competitive. "He was hated. Absolutely detested. One hundred generals threatened to resign in protest over his behavior."

"What was that about?" the former Australian prime minister asked. He loved nothing more than hearing tales of political scandal.

"Well, it wasn't any one thing. He shifted a few big Army programs to friends. Covered up several scandals, ignored billions in cost overruns, saddled the Army with some horrible programs. All deals he cooked up with old cronies on the Hill. Then in a tragic effort to refurbish his image, he got 160 soldiers killed —"

"Ah, yes, I remember that. The Albanian fiasco. That was Dan's watch?"

"Sure was. What a farce. We had to apologize to Albania for allowing our troops to bleed and die on their soil."

"Not to worry," Walters quickly reassured them all. "Today's generals and admirals were young lieutenants and captains back then. They remember nothing about those problems."

"As they say, time cures all ills," Haverill noted with a hearty chuckle — it was his favorite mantra, and they all laughed. He was ensconced in France with his mistresses and away from his wife and two children, because if he set foot in Australia he would likely be thrown in chains. But like all politicians he was an incurable optimist. With time and enough money thrown at the right public relations firms, his rumored crimes would be pasted over or forgotten. That, or the statute of limitations would run out and he could return home, the beloved old man, the prodigal son back from the lam.

"Today," Walters insisted, "Dan is a senior statesmen. Last of the old breed, that sort of thing. He can open any door he wants."

"I think he's an ideal choice," said Ryan Cantor, obviously speaking for his father. The boy had less brains than a turnip. His

247

old man wasn't much brighter, but he didn't get to be president without understanding how Washington ticked.

"Be sure to tell your father how much we admire him," Walters said, grinning. The message was received; the old man would hide behind the scenes but he would back up Bellweather, twist elbows, and make whatever calls were needed.

"What do we do about Wiley?" asked Phil Jackson, as if to say Jack had served his purpose and was outliving his usefulness.

"Easy," Walters answered. "Assign him to Bellweather's team. Lord knows, he's got as much riding on this as we do."

"But he knows nothing about Pentagon contracting," said Alan Haggar, the former deputy secretary of defense.

"Exactly."

"Oh, I see. Just get him out of the way."

"You got a better idea?"

They all laughed.

Andrew Morgan was hunched over in his booth by the window, nursing his fourth beer as he quietly admired the gallery of James Joyce photographs on the wall. It was his third straight night at Ulysses, a legendary Stone Street bar where the rich and hopefuls of Wall Street gathered after work to boast and complain.

A quick glance at his watch, 8:00 p.m. He'd been there since five, watering and watching, long enough that his ass had slipped into a coma. He waved at the waiter to haul over another beer, his fifth. One more, he promised himself. Just one, a fast one, then he'd wander back to his hotel and call it an early night.

It was now three weeks to the day since his boss, Martie O'Neal, had dispatched him to New York City to dig up all the dirt he could find on Jack Wiley. Two other associates plumbed the more traditional snoop's sources, the firms Jack had passed through on his way to a partnership at Cauldron. Morgan was assigned the more ambiguous, less promising role of hunting in less structured environments for an informal source, primarily hanging around Wall Street hangouts and watering holes, praying for a miracle.

Three weeks of long days spent in fashionable restaurants and longer nights trolling in bars. Twenty-one straight days befriending Wall Street lizards, and rewarding their tedious ego-swollen stories with free lunches and drinks. Amazing how much they could drink and eat when someone else was paying the tab.

What a steep descent from his former days in the CIA, he thought. All those years undercover in Moscow, Cairo, and Peru, ducking and dodging, trying to turn KGB agents, hunting terrorists, and harrassing narcotraffickers. All good things come to an end, but after twenty-five years of honorable work for an elite government agency he was stunned at how far he had fallen.

A complete and utter waste of time, he'd told Martie after his first week. Seven days and nights wasted on mingling with arrogant brokers and haughty investment banker types. He'd located six Wall Street boys who knew, or knew of, Jack Wiley. None knew him well. All had the same thing to say: great guy, honest as the day is long, a Boy Scout in a resplendent suit. Played squash with him once was the closest recollection he got; Jack had spotted his opponent ten points, and kicked his ass off the court. He doesn't even cheat at squash, Morgan had moaned. Stay at it, Martie had ordered. Sometimes a shot in the dark pays off. You never know.

Their client, after all, was willing to foot the rather impressive bills for a ritzy Manhattan hotel and all the expensive food and booze Morgan could guzzle. It was a big boondoggle, Morgan knew, and a very expensive one, but his interest in it had flagged weeks before.

From Morgan's experience of the past three nights, Ulysses didn't really start hopping till eight. The early starters and ambitious drunks were already there in force. But by nine the floor would be clogged up with the world's youngest millionaires, and an even larger number of motivated young ladies hunting a lifetime pass to a grand home in the Hamptons, a Maserati, all the trappings the right husband could buy.

Another hour and the place would be shoulder to shoulder with couples in lust, half for sex, the other half for money.

He was turning to study a troop of glittering young lovelies who had just entered when a man fell heavily into the seat across the booth. "I hear you're buying free drinks," the man said by way of introduction.

"I was, but I'm tired. Shove off, pal. Find yourself another table."

"Sorry." One of the business cards Morgan had been handing out by the thousands over the past three weeks landed on the middle of the table. "Thought we might have something to talk about, but okay, fine."

He was getting up and starting to leave

when Morgan reached over and grabbed his arm. "Maybe I've been hasty. What'll you have?"

"Gin and tonic." The man smiled and fell back into the seat. He picked up the card and inserted it back into his pocket.

While he signaled the waiter, Morgan used the opportunity to examine his visitor. Tall, about Wiley's age, expensive, well-tailored gray suit, dark, oiled-back hair. More or less your typical Wall Street type. The suit, though, was a thousand dollars, definitely not two; chances were he was on the mid- to lower end of the food chain. After three weeks Morgan could write a book about the denizens of Wall Street and their culinary and haberdashery tastes. The waiter arrived and Morgan ordered one for his guest, another beer for himself. "So who are you?" he asked.

"Is that important?"

"If you want the drink, yeah, it is."

"I don't come that cheap, Mr. Morgan."

Morgan leaned forward and planted his elbows on the table. "I'm not sure I hear what you're saying."

"Then listen close, pal. You're hunting for info on Jack Wiley. I have what you're look-ing for. I'm not the charitable type, though."

"I don't remember running into you before."

"You didn't. A friend gave me your card."

The drinks arrived and Morgan and his guest sank back into their seats and took their first deep sips together. Well, he was dressed and coiffed like a Wall Street type, but Morgan had a feeling he was a little out of place. Time to get the important detail out of the way. "How much?" he asked, swirling his beer in the air.

"Fifty thousand."

Morgan nearly spit his beer across the table. His elbows flew off the table, his big head pushed forward. "Who are you kidding?"

"If you knew what I have, you wouldn't ask such a stupid question."

"What makes you think anything you have is worth that much?"

"For starters, you gave my friend your card almost three weeks ago. I figure you've been here at least that long. Three weeks in a luxury double suite at the Wall Street Inn, frequenting some of our fine city's most exclusive bars and nightclubs. Somebody's footing a lot of cash to learn about Jack."

Morgan neither confirmed nor denied, just sat and tried to hide his astonishment. He was stunned. This guy knew everything:

how long he'd been in town, the places he had visited, where he was staying. Morgan had been detected, followed, and apparently watched like a two-bit novice. Mr. Former Spook, a veteran of Moscow and Cairo and Colombia, and this guy across the table had totally outfoxed him.

His guest allowed himself a slight smile. "Also, you're hired help. No offense, but that cheap off-the-rack suit doesn't help you fit in. I don't know how much a private dick costs, but three weeks of your time can't be cheap."

Morgan pointed his chin in the air and said, "So what?"

"So it's not your money, right? Why should you care what it costs?"

"Fifty thousand would have to buy some very good information."

"What do you have so far?"

"A few interesting tidbits. Some very valuable leads," Morgan lied and tried his best to make it sound sincere. In truth, he had gained ten pounds, swilled enough booze that his liver was swollen, and learned absolutely nothing remotely interesting about Jack Wiley.

"You got nothing." The smile widened. "This is Wall Street, buddy. Nobody's telling some stranger tales out of school. No angle in it."

"What about you? You're willing to break the code."

Morgan detected the first flash of anger — a slight tightening around the eyes, a jaw muscle flexing. Barely perceptible, but it was enough. "Maybe I've got reasons," the man insisted, making an obvious effort to mask his strong dislike of Jack Wiley.

"Like what?"

"It's personal. It'll cost you an additional ten grand to find out about that."

"Give me an idea what we're talking about."

"Fair enough. Here's a hint. Did you ever wonder why Jack bounced in and out of so many firms?"

"Yeah, we thought about that . . . for about two seconds, 'cause it's so obvious. Better offers, better pay. Greed. The usual motives. I figure you guys are all whores. It's all about money."

The man chuckled and sipped from his drink. "You don't know much about Wall Street."

"What part did I get wrong?"

"The only part you got right was about all of us being whores."

"Now tell me something I don't know."

"I can't believe you guys missed it. It's

right before your eyes. Jack hopped through four firms in twelve years. Four. The Street doesn't work that way. It's all about seniority, Morgan, about sticking around to get tenure. That's where the big money is."

"Then why did he leave?"

"Leave? Usually, he didn't; he was shoved."

"I asked why?"

"That's the fifty-thousand-dollar question."

"Come on, give me a little more to go on here."

"No, you have enough." The pleasant smile was replaced by a deadpan grin. "Now here's the rules. Pay attention, because if there's any mistake, you'll never see me again. The payment will be in cash. You don't have that much on you, and anyway, you're just a flunky. So tell your bosses you think I'm a good investment."

"Listen, you need —"

"No, I don't need to do anything. But you definitely do. Call by tomorrow, or don't bother," the man said, and he was on his feet. He was holding a card by the edges and he quickly flipped it on the table. "When you have permission, call this number. Ask for Charles."

"Wait . . . uh, Charles, I don't have

enough —" but before he could finish that thought the man rushed into the thick crowd and began making tracks for the exit.

It was unexpected and happened so fast, Morgan was caught flat-footed. He quickly recovered his senses, darted out of his seat, and began racing after Charles. He caught sight of a head of glistening black hair, and began dodging left and right, shoving people out of his way. Charles had about a twenty-foot lead, but Morgan was brutally clearing a path and closing fast.

Suddenly a pretty young blonde woman grabbed his arm and started howling at the top of her lungs. Morgan tried to break loose, but her grip only tightened. Her screams began to draw a world of attention. He quickly found himself hemmed in by young men, a mob of nice suits glowering at him, blocking him, and asking the young woman what he'd done to her.

"He grabbed and squeezed my ass," she roared quite loudly, her arms flailing as if he'd assaulted her.

"I did not," Morgan bellowed back in a tone filled with indignation. "I swear. Listen, I've got a wife and three daughters, for godsakes. I never touched her."

She stamped a foot and pointed a scornful finger at his face. "Pervert. You sick, disgusting pervert," she howled.

"I didn't touch you."

"Well, somebody did."

"Not me."

"I thought it was you."

"It wasn't, okay?"

The crowd around him settled down. The situation was harmless. Maybe the old guy did it, maybe he didn't; so what? Just a harmless squeeze anyway, and who cared if this old lecher indulged in a quick feel? A few of the men backed off and returned to what they were doing. Others began talking among themselves. A few chuckled.

Morgan dodged through an opening that suddenly cleared and raced as fast as his feet could carry him toward the exit. But Charles was gone, disappeared into the night.

All right, so you think you're smart, Morgan thought; the girl had obviously been a setup, the perfect diversion. He was surprised he had fallen for such a simple trick.

And he was nearly certain that the phone number he was given was connected to a disposable cell phone, probably under a false name. He could easily find out, but knew it would be a waste of time. Based upon what he'd just seen, Charles knew enough tradecraft to avoid such a stupid mistake.

Charles wasn't as smart as he thought, though.

Morgan raced back to his booth. Charles had left his glass and, by extension, a clean set of fingerprints. By the next day Morgan would know Charles's real name, where he lived, where he worked, and from there he would uncover his relationship to Jack Wiley.

When he got to the table the glass was gone. In its place was a small note: "Nice try, Morgan."

13

The appointment was at eleven, and the escorts were standing and waiting at the stately River entrance to the Pentagon, ready to get the ball rolling as the black limo rolled up.

Bellweather emerged first, followed by Alan Haggar, and Jack brought up the rear. The escorts rushed them through security, then up two flights of stairs to the office of Douglas Robinson, the current secretary of defense.

It was the Dan and Alan hour from the opening minute. Bellweather, after a brief moment surveying the office, declared, "Doug, who's your interior decorator? What an improvement over my time."

"My wife."

"Listen, be sure to give her my compliments."

"I hate it."

Bellweather laughed and squeezed his

arm. "So do I. It's god-awful."

A crew of waiters bustled in and began setting plates, glasses, and silverware on the large conference table off to the left. The secretary was busy, very busy; not a minute was to be wasted. To underscore that point, a uniformed aide popped his head in and loudly announced they had only fifteen minutes, not a minute more; the secretary apparently was due at a White House briefing of epic importance. Jack was pretty sure this was fabricated — the bureaucrat's rendition of the bum's rush. Another man, older, a scholar-looking gent of perhaps sixty, wandered in next and was introduced as Thomas Windal, the undersecretary of defense for procurement.

Jack first shook Windal's hand, then the secretary's. Windal's shake was halfhearted but firm, while Robinson's grip was limp bordering on flaccid. In truth, the secretary appeared exhausted, almost depleted: Jack thought he had aged considerably from the TV images of only a year before. He had large rings under his eyes, a dark suit that looked loose and baggy as though he had experienced a sudden weight loss, and a pale, resigned smile that suggested this meet-and-eat was at the bottom of his wish list. He'd far rather be taking a nap.

Robinson turned to Haggar, who, for a very brief period, had been his number two. "How you doing, Alan? Getting rich?"

"Working on it. That's what we're here to talk about," Alan said with a wicked smile, making no effort to disguise their purpose. They began shuffling and ambling to the table.

"So what are you guys pitching today?" Robinson asked wearily, as if they were annoying insurance salesmen.

"Would you care to guess?"

"That polymer your blowhard Walters was bragging all over TV about a while ago? Am I right?"

"Yes, and we'll get to it in a moment," Bellweather said, falling into the seat directly to the right of Robinson. "So how's the war going?" he asked, casually flapping open his napkin.

"Which one?" Robinson asked, a little sadly.

"We get a choice?"

"You do, but I don't. Iraq? Afghanistan? The war on terror?"

"Why don't we start with Iraq?"

"Just horrible. My in-box is crammed every morning with letters awaiting my signature. Condolence notes to parents about their kids that were killed. I can barely sleep. Do you know what that's like, Dan?"

Bellweather quietly nodded. He thought it best, though, not to remind Robinson that he'd gotten 160 soldiers killed on that senseless lark to Albania. Truthfully, he couldn't even remember what that was about. Albania? He must've been high or tanked when he ordered that operation.

Then again, he hadn't sent any letters or even brief notes to the families. Why should he? Death was one of the things their kids were paid for. "Thank God I was spared that fate," he replied, scrunching his face solemnly, munching on his salad. "How about Afghanistan?"

"More of the same." A brief pained pause. "Just not as bad, thankfully, at least not yet. But there's always the future not to look forward to."

With only twelve minutes left, they weren't going to waste more time or words commiserating with Robinson. Haggar, always the numbers man, worked up a concerned expression and launched in. "Do you know how many of those soldiers were killed by explosive devices?"

"Somebody, a month or two ago, showed me a chart. I don't recall the numbers exactly. I know it's a lot."

"Well, you've had 3,560 killed as of this

morning," Haggar said casually, as if they were discussing ERA stats in baseball. "Twenty percent due to accidents, disease, friendly fire, the usual cost of business." A brief pause. "Sixty-eight percent of the total were a direct result of explosives."

"Is that right?"

"Yeah, well over half. Amazing when you think about it, and ninety percent of those were roadside IEDs. Another ten percent were killed by rockets or roadside ambushes."

"Higher than I thought."

Bellweather reached across the table for the ketchup. "That's why we're here, Doug," he explained. "We want to help."

Laughable as that claim was, nobody so much as smiled.

"And you think this polymer will make a difference?" the secretary asked.

Bellweather was smacking the bottom of the bottle hard, slathering his hamburger and French fries in ketchup. "Jack, tell him about it," he ordered without looking up.

Jack quickly raced through a description of the polymer, briefly encapsulating the physics behind it, the years spent in research, the difficulty of getting it just right. He was careful to come across as factual rather than boastful. A light dissertation more than a sales pitch.

"You might want to look at this," suggested Haggar as he handed the secretary a copy of the pictorial results from the live testing done in Iraq. Robinson was barely eating, Jack noted, pushing a fork aimlessly around on his plate. He slid on a pair of reading glasses, opened the book, and began quietly flipping pages while Haggar began to prattle about the miraculous results.

After a quick pictorial tour, he removed his glasses and handed the book to Windal, his undersecretary. "Take a look at these," he said, obviously impressed. "So what do you want me to do?" he asked, ignoring Haggar and now looking at Bellweather.

"Jesus, Doug," Bellweather said, as if the question were facetious. "This screams for a fast-track, no-bid approach."

"That's a big request, Dan."

"Is it? Haggar's statistics show we're losing eight soldiers a week to bombs. It's become the insurgents' weapon of choice. Our kids are sitting ducks. That's nearly forty soldiers a month, blown apart and butchered while we look for a way to protect them. Now we have it."

Robinson turned to Windal, whose nose was still buried in the photographs. "What do you think, Tom?"

Windal shoved the book aside, shook his head, and scowled. "Damn it, I know how important this is. The generals have been screaming at me for over a year. We've thrown billions into this and it's about to pay off. There's a lot of promising programs out there right now. Uparmoring, three or four new bomb-resistant vehicles, even the use of robotics to locate the bombs and disarm them. The best minds have worked this problem and the results are coming in. It's very competitive."

"Yeah, and all of those ideas are crap. They take way too much time to make it into the field," Haggar argued, quickly and vigorously.

"Time is a consideration, but —"

"New vehicles have to be tested, refined, built, then fielded," Haggar continued, waving his arms for emphasis. "That takes years. And those programs are habitually plagued by big setbacks, maintenance glitches, and unexpected delays. The schedules aren't worth the paper they're written on. Uparmoring kits aren't much better. And when you add the weight of heavy armor on vehicles not designed for it, you pay the price in busted transmissions, collapsing frames, and faulty brake systems. You know that."

Bellweather, chewing a big bite of his hamburger, said, "He's right," as if there was any chance of disagreement.

"Everything takes time," Windal answered, almost apologetically.

"Not our polymer. Mix it, then paint it on. We could have it in mass production inside a month. Thirty days. How do those other programs stack up against that?"

"A no-bid, single-source contract is out of the question. I'm sorry."

"Why?"

"You know why, Alan. The competitors would raise hell. They have billions invested in their alternatives. A lot of their ideas are absolutely ingenious. They won't let you end-run them this way."

"Screw 'em. Lives are at stake and that's all we care about," Bellweather insisted, failing miserably to make it sound sincere.

"It's not that simple. If this polymer's as good as you say, you should be more than willing to expose it to testing and fierce competition."

"Forty lives a month, Tom. Waste another year, that's four hundred lives, minimum. Think of all those letters cluttering Doug's in-box."

"Look, I'd get raped if I caved in to your request. Your competitors are just as powerful, just as well connected as you fellas. They've got deep pockets and plenty of influential friends on the Hill."

"So that's it?"

"Yes, I'm afraid that's it."

Not looking the least frustrated or even disappointed — Jack thought, in fact, that he looked almost giddy — Bellweather pushed away from the table and got to his feet. Haggar also worked his way out of his chair. Jack had barely taken two bites of his hamburger, but taking the cue, so did he.

"Hey, I appreciate your time," Bellweather said, sounding quite gracious and sincere.

"I can't thank you enough for stopping by," the secretary of defense replied, matching his tone.

A few peremptory handshakes later, they were being hustled back down the hallway and downstairs to their limousine.

Haggar was bent over, mixing a drink from the minibar as they raced over the Memorial Bridge into D.C. proper. He handed Jack a scotch. "What did you think?"

"What am I supposed to say?"

"Anything you like. The truth."

"All right, I'm badly disappointed. Crushed. The meeting was a disaster."

"You think so?" Bellweather asked, eagerly

grabbing a bourbon on the rocks from Haggar. He took a long cool sip and relaxed back into the plush seat.

"They were totally unreceptive, Dan. You pitched a great case. Both of you did, all the reasons for jumping right into this thing. It's a no-brainer. They didn't care."

Bellweather and Haggar both enjoyed a good laugh, at Jack's expense. Could he really be that naïve? After a moment Haggar said, "They were giving us the green light."

"How do you get that?"

"We knew, and they knew, they couldn't just give us everything we asked for."

"And how is that favorable?"

"Well, Jack," Bellweather said in a condescending tone, "they just described the roadblocks. They were begging us, virtually screaming for help."

"Really?"

"Learn to listen better."

"I'm all ears now."

"A noncompetitive, no-bid deal is a certain invitation to scandal. We knew that going in. It draws reporters and muckrakers like flies. Drives them berserk."

"I don't follow."

"Robinson and Windal were giving us a road map to make this happen. Clear a few hurdles in Congress. Muzzle our competitors, make sure they don't have a chance to raise a big squawk."

"And how do you do that?"

"That's why we make the big money, Jack."

Jack stared out the window. They were passing by monuments to Washington's greats, Lincoln to their left, and off in the distance, Jefferson. Eventually he asked, "Where are we going?"

"To pay a visit on an old friend," Bellweather answered, sipping from his bourbon and staring off into the distance.

Representative Earl Belzer, the Georgia Swamp Fox to his colleagues, had spent twenty-five long years on the Hill. For the past decade he had served as the feisty, rather autocratic chairman of the House Armed Services Committee, a roost from which he ruled the Defense Department.

He had avoided military service himself, for reasons that shifted uncomfortably over the years. During the wild and woolly seventies, it was ascribed to an admirable act of youthful conscience against the perfidious Vietnam War; in the more conservative eighties it morphed to a disabling heart murmur before a competitor discovered his childhood medical records. And there was his most recent excuse — screw off, none of your business.

He was now beyond needing an excuse.

He represented a backwater district in Georgia that hosted two large military bases. Twelve years before — a few brief years before he rose to the omnipotent job of committee chairman — the Defense Department had tried to shutter both of them. They were extraneous, ill-located, contributed nothing to national defense, two sagging leftovers from the First World War that had long since become senseless money sumps. The Army was begging to have them closed. They were hot and muggy, and the training areas were brackish swamps. Aside from a few ubiquitous fast-food joints and one overworked whorehouse, there was nothing for the soldiers to do. Virtually no soldier reenlisted after a tour at either base.

But they also employed twenty percent of Earl's constituents. The federal money that funneled through the bases supported another thirty percent.

If the bases went away, his district and his political career would both become pathetic wastelands. Before he was elected, Earl had been a struggling small-time lawyer, filing deeds and scrawling wills, banging around hospitals and morgues, advertising himself on park benches and in the Yellow Pages, scraping by on $30K a year. And that was a good year. In truth, he admitted to himself, he really didn't have much talent for the law. It was a miracle he'd done that well. If he had to return home in disgrace he couldn't pay clients to give him their cases.

His appeals to his congressional colleagues elicited little sympathy and no support — the base closure list was nationwide, large, and expansive; almost two hundred bases were targeted, after all. It was every man for himself. In desperation, Earl eventually took a wild gamble; he marched over to the Pentagon and appealed directly to Secretary of Defense Daniel Bellweather.

The secretary seemed understanding. Both bases could easily be saved, Earl was informed. For the price of a small favor or two, Bellweather would take another close look at the closure list and make the alarming discovery that two posts of staggering importance in the middle of Georgia, a strategically vital state barely a stone's throw from Cuba, had sloppily slipped onto the list. America would be defenseless against Castro's hordes, he said with a wink.

What kind of favors? Earl nervously asked. Well, for instance, another House member badly wanted a new Army truck built in his district; one more vote, just one compliant lapdog to say yea, and his worthy dream would be fulfilled. Can we count on you, Earl? Bellweather asked with an ingratiating smile.

Earl thought about it a moment. The truck made even less sense than keeping his bases open — the Army had more trucks than it could drive, a whole new plant would have to be built, workers hired and trained, the cost would be mountainous, perhaps exceeding thirty billion dollars. And anyway, the Army despised the truck, a curiously idiotic vehicle, designed by a drug-addled moron, with twelve gears and twenty U-joints that was destined to become a maintenance nightmare. Earl had already come out loudly and quite forcefully against it. He had gotten a little worked up at a recent press conference where he termed it a disgraceful rip-off, an incomprehensible scandal, a mechanical insult to the taxpayers. Earl had run for office as a reformer, dedicated to root out waste and abuse. His campaign slogan was "Send a washing machine to Washington." The truck was the ideal target, and he had pounced on it with a wordy vengeance.

If he reversed himself now, his reputation

would be ruined. He would never be able to look himself in the mirror. He would be a laughingstock in the House, another pathetically corrupt pol to the press, a spineless hypocrite to the public.

"Sure, no problem," he squealed after about two seconds of indecision. The important thing was, he would be a hero to his voters.

It had been the fatal "I do" that forever changed Earl's political career. From that moment on, like a fallen woman, he had no reputation to protect, no grand cause to espouse, no principle that couldn't be fudged or bought. He threw himself into an endless succession of deals and bargains and compromises, and made the swift ascent to the chairmanship of one of the House's most powerful committees.

And he owed it all to Daniel Bellweather.

They met in a tiny, run-down Chinese restaurant three miles from the Capitol building, in a decrepit neighborhood better known for crack wars and corner hookers than meetings between the rich and powerful. Representative Earl Belzer was seated at the table and waiting when they arrived.

He was alone. No handlers. No harried-looking aides hovering over cell phones, carrying his bags, worrying about his schedule.

Said otherwise, no witnesses.

Belzer, a formerly skinny man, had packed on a world of weight, all of which seemed to have settled in his gut, which hung over his belt like a giant melon. His florid face, greased-back silver hair, and almost ludicrously elephantine ears gave him an odd resemblance to LBJ in his later years.

Together, the four of them looked sorely out of place in their expensive suits. Fortunately, few customers were around to notice — two, to be exact. One was a smelly, homeless wino enjoying a warm sanctuary from the chill, and the second a young Asian kid scribbling in a coloring book, probably the owner's daughter.

Earl leaped from his chair and immediately began a vigorous round of hand-pumps. He greeted Bellweather and Haggar like old chums. "Pleasure to meet you," he said to Jack, a little more coolly.

Bellweather quickly cleared the air. "He's with us, Earl, you can trust him."

"And the pleasure's all mine, sir," Jack said, smiling nicely.

"Call me Earl, boy."

"Okay. Earl."

"Long as we're gettin' in each other's pockets let's not be formal."

An ancient waiter appeared, they tried to order coffee, and after being told it wasn't on the menu, all switched to tea. Earl had already studied the menu and ordered four helpings of dim sum and General Tso's chicken. Nobody objected: they weren't here for the refreshments anyway.

"So, Earl, did you get the packet I sent over last week?" Bellweather dove in the instant he settled into his chair.

"Yep, sure did."

"And what did you think about our polymer?"

"That stuff really work as good as the packet says?"

"We fixed up a batch last week and tested it. Shot everything at it, rockets and bombs and missiles, then threw in the kitchen sink."

"Yeah?"

"The results were amazing. Stunning. Like wrapping yourself inside Superman's cape."

"You don't say." Earl was shoveling spoonful after spoonful of sugar in his tea. He was either double-tasking or had attention deficit issues.

"Look, this shouldn't take long," Bellweather assured him, sensing Earl's lack of engagement. "Know why we're here?"

Earl took the first sip of tea and nearly spit it out. After a moment he said, "Considerin' that you picked this out-of-the-way craphole-in-the-wall, it ain't hard to figure out." He dumped in three more spoonfuls of sugar.

"Let me spell it out for you, Earl. We've got the hottest defense product of the decade. In no time, we can paint all the Army and Marine vehicles in Iraq and Afghanistan and voilà! — they're all bomb-proof."

"That's certainly a good thing," Earl mumbled, still more interested in his tea than the polymer.

"No, it's a *great* thing, Earl, an incredible breakthrough." He smiled, then it flipped into a deep frown. "There are, however, a few issues. Start with the competitors. We'd like to know which one has the —"

"I know all about 'em," Earl burst in, making it clear he'd already done his homework. He might not be overly fascinated by the qualities of the polymer, but he'd come well armed and wanted Bellweather to know it. He took another careful sip of tea, and appeared mildly satisfied. Then he put the cup down and faced Bellweather. "GT, General Techtonics, leads the pack. They got this weird armored vehicle with a triangular underside. Carries a squad of twelve men. A real nifty idea. Deflects all the blasts away from the troop compartment."

"And what's two?"

"That would be Orion Solutions." Earl smiled. You've come to the right place, the smile said; ol' Earl's open for business and he's got all the answers. Another sip of tea and he explained, "They build this wild-ass robot. Sensors on the front sniff out the bomb, it approaches, then blows itself up. Like mutual suicide. Know what they call it?" Bellweather shook his head, and the congressman chortled, "Jimmy Durante's special."

It wasn't very funny, but they all laughed hilariously. "And those are the only two?" Bellweather asked.

A confident wink. "Only two that matter," he answered.

"You're sure? I need hard data. This is important, Earl."

"A lot of other ideas are out there, none with any traction, though. These two are well into the appropriations stage. They've been tried and tested. The generals are thrilled with 'em."

After a thoughtful pause, Bellweather asked, "Anything in the area of black programs we should worry about?"

"Nope, none that far along."

"All right, good. Now how deep are these

two into appropriations?"

"Well, GT is furthest along. Comes up for a vote next month."

"Who's pushing it?" Bellweather asked, much like a pro golfer asking his caddie about the lay of the green before he took his best putt.

Jack sat and watched them. He was obviously out of his depth, out of his milieu, out of his comfort zone, and doing nothing to mask his amazement at how the game was played. This was the chairman of the Armed Services Committee, after all. Here they all were in this filthy little wreck of a restaurant, huddled around a small, chipped linoleum table with Earl telling them everything they needed to know.

"That would be Drew Teller, from Michigan," Earl explained, scratching an itch underneath a cuff. "Acts like he's got a pocketful of GT stock, which might be he does."

"That his motive?"

"Oh, hell, Teller's got lots of incentive. Eighty percent of the vehicle will be built in his district. I'd guess about four thousand jobs at stake. He eases this through, he's a shoo-in for reelection, for life."

"I don't know him. How powerful is he?"

"Straight answer? He's not, at least not

very. A big blowhard pretty boy."

"But . . . ?"

"But he spent the past year dolin' out favors by the boatload, pandering to ever'body in reach. If you had a bill, he'd vote for it. Actually supported that nutty Rothman bill to ban Easter bunnies and Santa Clauses in department stores. Drove the Christian groups nuts. He's runnin' around now, callin' in the chips."

"Will it go through?"

A fast nod. "Appears so."

"What about Orion?"

The old waiter reappeared, hobbling and creaking, bearing a large tray loaded with five orders of food. They stopped talking while he was in earshot. Given the situation, it paid to be cautious.

Earl snatched a beef roll off a plate before the old man could set it down. His thick fingers stuffed it between his lips and he chewed loudly and enthusiastically while the old man laid out the bowls and dishes, then waddled off.

After noisily sucking the grease off his fingers, Earl picked up where they'd left off. "Hell, you know them fellas."

"Pretend I don't."

"Been stuffin' lots a pockets lately. Bank-rolled a few key elections, and they're lending their corporate jets out like it's the congressional air force."

"Have they got the guns behind them?"

"Oh, probably about six or seven former senators and congressmen in their employ. The place is like a retirement home for former Hill staffers, so they know all the tricks. Hosted three big junkets this year. London, the Riviera, Bermuda." Earl paused and awarded them a big wink. "Did Bermuda myself. Plenty of pretty women, enough champagne and caviar to sink a barge." He shook his head, apparently reminiscing about the experience.

"How far along are they?"

" 'Bout six months out, probably."

"Six months," Bellweather echoed, almost in disbelief. Six months! The boys from Orion would never know what hit them; two years spent perfecting this goofy little robot, and it was about to become an anachronism.

"Yeah," Earl rattled on, filling in the now unnecessary details. "Seems their robot's got a few awkward habits. They did this big test a few months back and invited ever'body. That crazy little robot apparently sniffed gunpowder, and began chasing one of the guards around, threatening to blow him up."

Bellweather laughed. "And did the test

have a happy ending?"

"Oh, he ran all over the place, screamin' and hollerin', for 'bout five minutes. It was real entertaining. After a while he got smart and dropped his piece, then, boom — the robot blew it to smithereens."

After a few obligatory chuckles, the table grew quiet for a moment. Jack stared into his tea. Haggar was smiling. Bellweather was thinking, calculating the odds against him.

Earl looked expectant — with one hand he was snatching and gobbling more rolled-up delicacies from the dim sum plate, while with the other he was drumming his chubby fingers on the table, impatient to hear the deal.

"Focus on GT first," Bellweather suggested. He popped something loud and crunchy in his mouth.

"Yeah, good call," Earl seconded as though he'd thought of it himself.

"We'll lay the groundwork for you."

"That's important," Earl noted. "How?"

"This vehicle . . . what's it called?"

"The GT 400."

"Right. It's . . . well . . . a great idea with fatal flaws," Bellweather said, mentally forming the idea as he spoke. "Rushed through design and development, hurried through testing. The usual sad story. Haste makes waste."

"That's the ticket," Earl said. "What flaws?"

"Well . . . uh, it's top-heavy, for one thing."

"It is?"

"Sure. A major design snafu, an all too common misstep by combat vehicle designers. They piled on so much armor it's subject to rolling. Can't keep its balance on curves. You know, unsafe at any speed."

Getting on top of the idea, Earl said, "A rolling death trap."

"Yeah, I like that. It's catchy," Bellweather said, beaming at his student. "To achieve a safe distance from underground explosions, they kept raising the chassis off the ground. Now the center of gravity is too high."

Earl had his fist stuck deep in a bowl of fried shrimp, or something that resembled shrimp. He was fishing around, hunting for the perfect mouthful. "Like that Ford SUV," he mumbled, his eyes glued to one particular shrimp. "Tippin' over all the time."

"I'll hire a couple of experts to build the case, maybe expound on it a bit to the press."

Stuffing the piece in his mouth, Earl mumbled, "There's gonna have to be some hearings, naturally."

A pat on the arm and a grave nod from

Bellweather. "Only responsible thing to do, Earl."

Earl scratched his head and said, " 'Course, I'd need ample justification. Y'know, a spark to get it rollin'."

"Don't worry, I'm sure one will come along."

"How you figure to handle that?"

Bellweather thought about it for a moment. "I have a strong premonition that somebody in Defense's procurement department is about to send you an anonymous letter. An insider, terribly bothered by the shoddiness of the testing. The vehicle was dangerously tipsy but nobody wanted to hear about it. He was brushed aside, and isn't happy about it."

Earl shook his head, dismayed by the horror of it. "Hell, that'd have to be looked into."

"I like your logic. And were you to schedule the hearing for . . . oh, say about three weeks from now, a lot of critics will be ready to raise a noisy racket about it."

Haggar, feeling like a third wheel, decided to throw in his two cents. "Make it a last-minute thing, Earl. No warning. In fact, announce an entirely different reason for the hearing."

"You mean, call it a program review,

maybe a cost overview. Something like that."

"Perfect, something totally innocuous. GT won't be expecting an ambush. They'll send over a bunch of accountants and be totally off guard."

"Great idea," Earl mumbled, already picturing it in his mind. A bunch of number crunchers armed with spreadsheets and cost analysis proposals, gawking in shock as they were being pilloried about the intricacies of vehicular physics. Get a few staffers to work up a bunch of questions that would stump Albert Einstein. How fun. They'd be frozen in their chairs, peeing in their drawers, totally clueless. "Wonderful. What then?" Earl asked, popping a shrimp between his lips and clamping down hard.

Bellweather tackled this one. "But be careful. An outright program termination would incite too much resistance. Too much heat and noise. GT and the generals will scream murder."

"Not just them," Earl observed, sucking on a dim sum roll. "Teller'll throw a real hissy fit. Don't get between that boy and a TV camera."

"So don't kill it," Bellweather advised, "delay it. Send it back for another year of rigorous testing until the safety concerns are ironed out and mollified. A good hard scrub before we waste all those billions, a reasonable pause before we expose our boys to uncertain dangers."

Like that, Bellweather stopped talking. Earl stopped eating. Haggar began scribbling something on a napkin. The meeting seemed to lurch into a new phase. Jack knew enough to keep his face expressionless, his mouth shut.

By unspoken agreement, the ball had slid to Earl's corner. He wiped his plump lips on a cheap white paper napkin and leaned back in his chair. "I believe it will work," he concluded with a small, mysterious smile.

But there was nothing at all mysterious about it to Bellweather.

The former SECDEF who had first introduced Earl to this game looked slightly annoyed. "We will of course be very appreciative," Bellweather muttered, sounding anything but. A long, awkward silence. "What do you have in mind, Earl?"

"Glad you asked, Dan."

"I'm sure you are."

"Five million for my next campaign would certainly be nice." Earl had dropped the country bumpkin and was suddenly the sharpy riverboat gambler. He was leaning across the table, eyes narrowed, gleaming with total concentration.

Bellweather threw down his napkin and nearly howled. "Christ, Earl, that's too much."

"Well . . . what's enough?"

"Three million. That's all we budgeted, all we can afford."

"See, Dan, I'm also factorin' the price of ushering this polymer of yours through the political thickets. I expect you'll be looking for a noncompetitive, fast-track deal." When nobody contradicted that, he continued, "I'm a one-stop shop, Dan, all that and a bag of chips."

"Five is still too much."

"Nah, it's a real good deal and you know it. Kill the competitors, and grease the pole for your polymer. Nobody else can handle this."

After a long, tense pause, Bellweather said, "Even you can't do it alone, Earl."

"Oh, damn, you're right. I'll need a little more to spread around. Throw another two million into my PAC."

Bellweather looked ready to argue, but he didn't have the strength. "You've learned this game too well," he whispered.

"Yeah, well, I had a good teacher," Earl said.

Martie O'Neal was happily hidden in the

third stall to the left, comfortably ensconced on the toilet, when his cell phone began bleeping and rattling. He dropped the girlie magazine, lurched over, and spent ten frantic seconds trying to dig the phone out of the pocket of the trousers gathered around his ankles. "What?" he barked.

"Martie, it's me, Morgan," said the familiar voice.

"Whatcha got?"

"Gold, maybe, or maybe fool's gold." Morgan quickly filled in the story about Charles, omitting only a few insignificant details like how Charles found him, how he escaped, and that infuriating little stunt with the note in place of the glass. Some things are better left unsaid.

Martie asked the obvious. "He worth fifty K?"

"Who knows?"

"You, Morgan. You're supposed to know."

"I can't vouch for his reliability," Morgan answered, hoping he wouldn't be called on that vague response.

"You got nothing? Fingerprints? A phone number? Anything?"

"Uh . . . he was very clever."

"You mean he outsmarted you."

"I just wasn't expecting it," Morgan stammered, trying to make it sound like no big deal.

"I don't like that."

"Me either. He was very slick. Could be a con."

"That what you think?"

"I've been here three weeks handing out business cards by the bushel. It's like a trail of breadcrumbs, an invitation to get rolled. What do you think?"

O'Neal had worked around the clock, without a day or weekend off since he got this job. The billings were great but the hours were killing him. Walters phoned nearly every day, pressuring for an update and hectoring him about the lack of results. His wife had begun bitching and moaning, about chores left undone, about dinner dates broken, about coming home too tired for conversation or sex. Jack Wiley was ruining his life.

Now the wife was threatening to have his battle-ax mother-in-law come for a long, miserable visit; things were about to go from terrible to horrible. All that hard work, effort, and expense and he had found nothing incriminating or even remotely distasteful about Jack Wiley. He was frustrated. He lay awake at night thinking about Wiley. He hated him, hated everything about him, the goody-two-shoes. He had been so confident he would find something; he had promised Walters instant results. "When are you going to meet him?" he asked Morgan, obviously committed.

Charles might be a shot in the dark, but O'Neal was past the point of caring. This was the first inkling that there might be some dark secret in Jack's past, some chink in the saintly armor. He'd be damned if he'd let it slip by. Besides, it wasn't his money.

"He said I better call today or forget it," Morgan replied.

"He'll insist on a meet tonight. Keep the initiative, limit our time to prepare. You know the game."

"Yeah, that's what I figure, too."

"I'll send two more guys up on the next flight. They'll be hauling fifty thousand in cash. Can you handle this?"

"Kid's play. Don't worry," Morgan replied, trying to sound calm and glib. In his Agency days, he'd done dozens of bagjobs like this. And all those operations were against real spies and terrorist thugs and bloodthirsty drug lords.

He'd only been fooled the first time, he reassured himself, because Charles had dropped in without warning.

They arrived fifteen minutes early for the start of the movie. His choice, Eva told him, whatever he wanted to watch. Then she raised her eyebrows over the flick he suggested — a brawling, manly epic filled with battles and slaughters — and argued for a different film, one that had received rave reviews, a blockbuster she coyly described as a warm old-fashioned western with a minor twist, called *Brokeback Mountain.*

They settled on a compromise, a forgettable romantic comedy with a pair of even more unexceptional stars. "So, how was your day?" Eva asked as they settled into their seats.

It was a weeknight. The crowd was sparse, so they had two prime seats all to themselves in the middle of the front row. They had come straight from work and met at the theater.

"Long, interesting, extremely profitable," Jack said, noisily rummaging through a large box of popcorn poised on his lap. He'd missed dinner and this would have to suffice.

"What did you do?"

"Drove around town mostly. Bellweather

has plenty of friends." Very few of which they had met at their places of work, Jack might have added, but didn't.

Bellweather and Haggar had given him an enlightening tour of the city's hole-in-the-wall restaurants, splendid places to conduct illicit business in plain sight. By day's end, Bellweather was suffering a murderous case of heartburn. Haggar twice had bolted from the table to contend with bouts of diarrhea. Making illegal deals apparently wasn't for those with weak stomachs.

"Washington is a small town, at least among those that matter."

Jack laughed. "So I'm seeing."

"You sound disenchanted."

"Then I've given you the wrong impression."

"Have you?"

"Yes, I'm having a ball. It's a side of democracy I never imagined."

This was their second date since Eva dropped by his house that first time: they were beyond the getting-to-know-you phase, not quite at the I'm-very-comfortable-in-your-presence stage. After a moment, Eva said, "The rumors around the office are that you're going to salvage our annual earnings."

"I wouldn't know about that."

"It's a very big deal, Jack. They say Bell-weather is spreading around a lot of cash to set this up."

Jack looked away. "Rumors like that are dangerous."

"Oh, you know accountants. We always need something to discuss at the water-cooler." After a moment, Eva asked, "Is it true?"

"I wouldn't know," Jack lied. It was more than a lie, it was a mountain of untruth. To the best he could tell they'd spread around promises of nearly twenty million that day — seven to Earl Belzer, five to an obnoxious, boastful, crotchety senator on the Senate Armed Services Committee, then another eight distributed judiciously among a variety of think tanks and reputed watchdog groups, in return for vigorous vows to tarnish and smear the GT 400. Jack lost count of all the promises, all of the handfuls of cash to be laundered through third parties, then doled out to the usual array of PACs and 527s, the capital city's equivalent of money laundering. Haggar, with his passion for numbers, made careful notes after each meeting.

At one point, Bellweather bragged to Jack that CG had a highly respected specialist in such matters, a magician who could make money disappear off the corporate books, then reappear in politicians' pockets without a trace of its source.

Jack was too amazed to be shocked. They made it look so easy. No, it was easy. In only a few short hours Bellweather and Haggar had bagged two of the Hill's most powerful legislators and arranged the almost certain sabotage of their most threatening competitors. At the bargain price of only twenty million bucks, they would rake in billions. So little capital for such a mammoth gain.

After a moment of tense quiet, Eva put her hand on Jack's. "If I've gotten too personal, Jack, I'm sorry."

"Don't worry about it."

"I am worried, about you."

"Why should you?"

"Because I like you."

"I mean, why worry?"

"This town is rough, maybe rougher than you think. Don't let the smiles and back-slaps lull you. You might be getting in over your head."

Jack smiled. "In New York people cross the street when they see me coming."

"Do they?"

"There are warning signs all over the city — watch out for big bad Jack. Mothers threaten their kids to be good or Jack will get you."

"Oh, you're *that* Jack." Eva pretended to recoil back in her seat. After a moment she said, "Look, I'm sure you're a terror to behold, up there. This is a different world, with different kinds of players."

"Do you think they're trying to hurt me or set me up?"

"I didn't say that. No. As long as your interests are aligned with theirs you should be fine. It's just that I care about you. I don't want to see you get hurt."

"Eva, this country prints billionaires like postage stamps. Why shouldn't I be one? Besides, this polymer will save the lives of hundreds or thousands of soldiers. If we have to cut a few corners to get it into the field, so what?"

"Be careful. That's all I'm saying."

"I'll start wearing body armor tomorrow, thank you."

"And I'm offering my services," Eva added, gripping his hand a little tighter. "I know these people, Jack. They're sharks. Confide in me and I can help."

"If I need a watchdog, you'll be the first one I call," Jack promised vaguely, but not the least bit unfriendly.

The movie was even worse than its reviews.

14

Morgan took an anxious step out of the cab and onto the curb at the corner of 10th Avenue and 53rd Street. He checked his watch — 7:20 p.m. right on time. Charles had been abrupt and very demanding on the phone. Arrive by taxi, Morgan was told in a tone that brooked no objections. Don't be a minute late. Come alone; no trailers, no wires, no funny business.

If Charles so much as suspected his instructions weren't being obeyed to the letter, Morgan could stand on the street corner till the cocks crowed. Charles swore he would disappear, not to be heard from again.

Rivers and Nickels, the TFAC reinforcements, had landed as scheduled on the four o'clock shuttle at LaGuardia. They arrived hauling a briefcase stuffed with cash as well as a stern reminder from O'Neal not to screw this up. Martinelli and Tanner, the two snoops who had spent the past three weeks trolling the Wall Street firms, were also ordered to assist.

Five men. Four highly trained former government agents to back up Morgan, four hardened pros to make sure they learned a little more about Charles and his fabulous claims.

Morgan drew up the plan. It was well thought out. There were no objections from the other four. The idea was to trail Charles after the meeting, or, barring that, get a usable fingerprint, or at the very least a few good photos. Somehow, whatever it took, they needed to learn his real identity and the nature of his relationship to Jack.

The four backups were littered around the surrounding streets in a variety of poses and disguises. They arrived an hour early and picked out their positions with exacting care. Martinelli and Tanner were parked in separate cars, idling nearby, waiting to punch the gas and follow; Rivers and Nickels would trail on foot, wherever Charles led them.

Despite the hard warning from Charles, Morgan was wired and ready to broadcast.

For two full minutes Morgan stood on the corner alone, trying to appear relaxed and guileless as he pretended to watch the traffic. Out of the blue, he felt a light tap on his back, and when he turned around Charles was there, grinning. Morgan quickly put two and two together — evidently Charles had been waiting in a nearby store, marking time and watching until Morgan showed.

"Did you come alone?" Charles asked predictably.

"Yes, just me," he lied.

"Are you wired?"

"No, I swear."

"You're lying."

"Check me if you like," Morgan offered with a smug smirk as he held out his arms and spun around. I mean it, go ahead, search as long and hard as you like, he said to himself. The bug was state of the art, very tiny, encased in a button in his coat; it wouldn't activate until he squeezed it. The newest thing, totally dormant and undetectable by a wand or any known electronic detector until he chose to turn it on. That would come later.

"Doesn't matter," Charles said with a nonchalant shrug. "Come on. Walk beside me."

"Where are we going?"

"You'll see."

"I have the money, Charles." He held up the case for inspection. "It's all here, fifty thou in cash."

"Good for you. Now we have something to talk about." Charles was already walking, so Morgan took off after him.

"Well, I'm here, so why don't you start talking now?" Morgan asked, very sociably. It was an old ploy, one taught to all the scrubs in the Agency school in Virginia — divert the prey's mind and get his attention away from the environment and the trackers. They were side by side now, moving slowly, a casual stroll. A cripple could follow them at this pace.

"Relax, Morgan. It's worth the wait, I promise you."

"I'm just wondering why you're so paranoid."

"I have my reasons. Believe me, they're good ones."

"All this secrecy and clandestine crap, why can't we talk without all this cloak-and-dagger?"

This question seemed to get on his nerves. "Maybe you don't know Jack as well as you think you do."

They turned right and headed toward the narrower streets of the theater district. The crowds were growing thicker but Charles hadn't tried any funny business yet. Morgan wore a yellow windbreaker so loud it virtually glowed in the dark, another trick he'd learned in his years as a spook. In the densest mob, in the dead of night, he'd be impossible to misplace. "Jack's harmless," Morgan insisted after a long moment. "We've seen nothing to indicate any problems."

"You checked his Army record?" Charles asked with an amused grin.

"Yeah, sure."

"Uh-huh. What did it say?"

"Clean as a whistle. War hero, loved by his troops, admired by one and all."

For some reason this brought a condescending chuckle from Charles and a nasty side glance. "You guys aren't as good as I thought."

"Look, pal, we got his official record."

"No, you got his unclassified file," Charles said sharply. "There's another record, the real one. The Army calls it a classified fiche."

Through his CIA service Morgan was familiar with them. "What was he, a special ops cowboy or something?"

"In fact Jack was Delta. Everything's smoke and mirrors with those people."

Morgan had no idea whether this was true. "Can you prove that?"

"I know it, okay? Point is, Jack can kill you with a toothpick. He can get into and out of Baghdad, in wartime, without being detected. He did that, you know."

"Uh, no, we —"

"And check his record from Panama. He hunted down Noriega. It was Jack who kept him from escaping, chased him into the Vatican embassy."

They walked and talked a little more before Morgan asked, "You got a copy of this file?"

"You're kidding, right? You asked why I'm afraid of Jack and I'm telling you. I wouldn't want him carrying a grudge against me."

"That all you've got?"

"That's barely an appetizer, Morgan," Charles said, picking up his pace a bit. "Now shut up."

Martinelli was about thirty yards behind the two men, squeezing the steering wheel as he weathered a symphony of honks and angry gestures. New Yorkers! He remembered the old joke about the tourist totally lost in the city and he stops and asks a native for directions, saying, "Aside from 'get screwed,' could you please tell me the way to the Empire State Building?"

He cursed and wished Morgan and Charles would pick up the pace. The taxi driver directly on his rear was nearly leaning on his horn. A quick glance in the rear-view mirror — the driver wore a turban and had a thick Sikh beard. Amazing how quickly even foreigners dropped their hospitable native manners and adopted the surly rudeness of this city.

To his left and right, he could see Rivers and Nickels following on foot, both on opposite sidewalks, blending in quite nicely.

Then without warning, Morgan and Charles hung a right onto a one-way street with traffic going the wrong way. Martinelli started to follow before a fusillade of horns reminded him it was one-way.

He uttered another loud curse, backed up, and began driving to the next block to try and pick them up again at the far end of the street. The Sikh was leaning outside the car window, howling obscenities, his middle finger stuck in the air.

They were on West 45th, passing theaters now. The best Morgan could tell, Charles never once glanced back, or even looked around to check if they were being tailed. Never once gazed at reflections in storefront windows, never bent down to tie his shoes and steal a furtive peek. Could he have overestimated this guy?

Morgan pressed his coat button, activated

the mike, and asked, "Where are we going?"

"Shut up."

"I just want to know."

"You'll know when we get there."

They took ten more steps when, without warning, Charles grabbed his arm and yanked him into the covered entrance of a theater. Morgan hadn't been paying attention to the overhead billboards; he hadn't a clue which theater, or which play. He kept his mouth shut as Charles smoothly handed two tickets to the doorman, and they were inside.

They had apparently arrived right on time for the start of the show. Only a few stragglers were still milling around the lobby, exchanging gossip or whatever. He saw that they were in the Gerald Schoenfeld Theatre, and according to the large poster on a stand-up easel, the night's entertainment was *A Chorus Line.* "What are we doing here?" he demanded.

For the first time Charles faced him. "You look pale, Morgan. Don't tell me you've seen *Chorus Line* before?"

"Well . . . no, I haven't."

"Good. It's sold out. I paid a fortune for these tickets. Thought you'd be more appreciative."

Morgan was pleased that he had lured

Charles into naming the play before it struck him what Charles had done and why. Who cared if the trailers knew where they were? It was sold out, so they couldn't get inside. Such a simple, obvious ploy, why had nobody thought of it?

Charles seemed to sense what he was thinking. "Worried about your friends out on the sidewalk?"

"I told you I came alone," Morgan insisted without the barest hint of conviction.

The final curtain bell was ringing and the last loiterers in the lobby began a mad hustle for their seats. Charles didn't budge. "Are we going in to watch the show or not?" Morgan asked, speaking loudly so the boys out on the street could hear.

"Come with me."

"Where?"

"The men's room."

"Why? You want me to hold it for you?"

Charles didn't smile or in any way reply to the infantile wisecrack, just began walking quickly to the men's room. They could hear the orchestra blaring the opening notes of the theme song. The restroom was empty when they entered. Charles moved toward a urinal, reached down to his front, then spun around with a .38 caliber in his right hand. "Now, we're gonna do this my way, Morgan. Don't get nervous. I won't shoot you unless you make me."

Morgan's mouth gaped open in shock. "A gun," he gasped loudly.

"I believe that's what it's called, yes."

Morgan balanced his feet and tightened his grip on the briefcase. "What's this? A two-bit holdup?"

Charles studied Morgan's face a moment. "I told you to come alone, and you've turned this into a street orgy. I warned you not to wear a wire, and you're a walking DJ. You're making me nervous, Morgan. This" — he began shaking the gun — "is to make sure you don't break any more rules."

Morgan adjusted his expression to one of resignation. "Hey, pal, I have no intention of getting myself clipped, not over fifty grand. Hell, it's not even mine. Here," he said, taking a step closer and jamming the briefcase in Charles's direction — another five feet and he'd be all over him. A quick kick in his groin, a chop across the forearm, then he'd make him eat that gun.

Charles immediately stepped backward and the gun popped into Morgan's face. "Don't. That would be very stupid." The sound of the hammer being cocked was loud and ominous.

"All right."

"Step back."

Morgan stepped back.

"Put down that case."

Morgan placed the case on the floor. Whatever the man with the gun wanted.

"Good boy. Now take off your clothes."

"What?"

"The clothes, Morgan. Remove them."

"Forget it. No. That's just not going to happen."

Charles leaned his back against the wall. "Listen to me. I offered you a deal, and I intend to honor it. But on my terms, not yours."

When Morgan did nothing, Charles leaned toward him and announced very loudly, "Listen up, fellas. Your friend Morgan is about to blow this deal. Because of his silly modesty, you're not going to learn things about Wiley you couldn't imagine. It'll cost you fifty thousand to get nothing."

"Who are you talking to?" Morgan asked. This time, not only was he not convincing, it sounded asinine.

"Jack has a nasty scandal in his past, Morgan. Very nasty. It's everything you've been hunting for, and then some. But you'll never find it without me."

Well, what the hell, Morgan thought. Charles had already made a fool of him —

twice — so what was a little more mortification? Only one thing was worse than this: after all this time, effort, and money to come back empty-handed. With a great show of reluctance he removed his jacket and tossed it to Charles. Then his shirt, his shoes, and his trousers, until he was naked but for his socks and underpants. He couldn't remember a more humiliating moment. "Get into that stall," Charles ordered, waving the gun at the far one along the wall.

Looking very aggravated, Morgan dutifully entered the stall, and Charles closed the door behind him. He could hear Charles walk around, then the sounds of him entering the adjoining stall and sitting down. "What next?" Morgan asked, wondering how it came to this.

Twenty-five years in the CIA. He had survived so many dangerous encounters, outsmarted so many bad guys, and this amateur, Charles, had the money, and he had the gun, with Morgan stripped down to his undershorts in a public bathroom. He cursed himself for turning on the mike. The entire episode had been broadcast to the boys out on the street. He knew the ribbing was going to be absolutely horrible, and he was right. "What are you doing?" he asked, after a long moment with no answer.

"Counting my money, Morgan. Since you lied, I want to be sure you haven't cheated me. Now, shut up."

"It's there, all of it," Morgan insisted with as much force as he could muster, given the circumstances. "You can trust me."

"Twenty thousand, one hundred. Twenty thousand, two hundred . . ."

The trail crew heard every word until the instant Morgan, confronting a gun, disrobed to his skivvies. They knew which theater they were in, knew it was *A Chorus Line,* they heard the request to enter the bathroom, and they heard the gun come out.

Then, silence.

After a frantic, whispered huddle, Nickels took the first shot and scrambled to the ticket window. "Please, just listen," he said to the pale, wrinkled old man smiling back from behind the thick glass divider. "I flew out all the way from Oregon."

"Oregon? That right?"

"Yes."

"Long flight. Pretty state, I hear. Never been out there myself."

"This is my life's dream."

"Yeah, good choice. Great show."

"Yes, and, well, I have to fly back tomorrow." Nickels shrugged his shoulders and produced a tragic frown. "My assistant was supposed to order tickets. The useless cow screwed it up." He held up his arms and looked perfectly crestfallen.

"No kiddin'?" the old man grunted. "Know what?"

"What?"

The old man tapped a skinny finger on the SOLD OUT sign.

"Aw, come on. You and I know you've got extra tickets back there. A few set aside for cast members, maybe, or there's always a few no-shows. Always. One is all I need, just one," he pleaded, pressing a trio of hundred-dollar bills against the window. "Nobody will know," he whispered with a sly wink. "Not a soul."

The old man took his eyes off the money and stared at Nickels. "Look up," he said.

With a befuddled expression, Nickels's eyes moved up. "That," the old man announced, pointing at the lens, "is a camera. Reason it's there is to keep jerkoffs like you from corruptin' a sweet old man like me."

Nickels looked like he wanted to say something, but couldn't think of the words.

The old man pressed his hands on the counter and bent forward. "Why don't you smile for the nice man inside before you take a hike, pal?"

Nickels had struck out, and he edged away, then walked halfway down the block, where Rivers was waiting. "Take your best shot." He added, "Be careful of the old man. A real wise guy."

Rivers nodded, then walked briskly to the window. He tapped the nightstick softly against his left leg as he walked, and with the other hand reached up and straightened his NYPD cap.

The old man looked up and offered a nice smile. "What can I do for you, Officer?"

Rivers straightened his husky shoulders. "The precinct just got a call from someone inside the theater."

"Yeah? About what?"

"About a robbery taking place inside."

The old man leaned forward on his elbows. "A stickup?"

"With a gun and everything. Go figure. I was told to check it out."

"So what? You want I should let you in?"

"What do you think? Yeah, and make it quick."

"Where's your partner?" The old man's eyes narrowed and shifted left and right. "Don't you got any backup?"

"Handling another call. Busy night." An officious-looking but slightly impatient smile. "Listen, Gramps, you gonna let me in or not?"

"Hey, I'm not givin' you no trouble. Hell, two of my kids are NYPD. The Hannigan boys, Danny and Joey. Maybe you know 'em."

"I, uh, might have heard the name. Quit gabbing. I'm in a hurry here."

"Yeah, I'll bet," he replied, shaking his head. "Hey, what precinct you with?" the old man asked, maintaining the same unhurried, casual air.

Rivers had to pause a moment. "The Fifteenth."

"Then why's that badge you're wearin' say you're with the Seventh?"

"I was just transferred. What do you care? Do I need to call the precinct? A life could be at stake."

"Reason I'm askin' is, the theater district's covered by Midtown North."

"Yeah, so?"

"Reason I know that is 'cause this little button I just pushed, it connects me directly to the precinct house. Usually takes those boys about two beats to get here."

Rivers stared back, obviously startled. "You did what?"

"You heard me. So either you can wait here and tell 'em why yer impersonatin' an officer, or you can beat it, you jerk."

Rivers pondered the situation for about half a second, then wisely chose to bolt. The old man cackled and shook as he watched him scramble down the street. He loved his job.

Charles finished counting the money, at last. "Congratulations, Morgan, it's all here," he announced.

"Told you it was."

"Yes, but you lied about so many other things, I wanted to be sure."

"It's cold in here," Morgan whined, slapping his arms for effect. "Could I have my jacket back?"

Charles laughed. "That was clumsy, Morgan. I was wondering where the bug is."

"All right. Just get on with it."

"One question before I start."

"Do I get a choice?"

"No. Who are you working for?"

"None of your business."

"Then tell me this. Do these people intend to hurt Jack?"

Morgan weighed the question before he answered. What did Charles want? Wiley hurt, or just smeared? He took a gamble and said, "They intend to mess him up good."

"Damn, that's great. Just what I was hoping," Charles said. Morgan could almost hear the smile on Charles's lips.

A notebook and pencil slid under the separation panel. "It's a long story and you might want to take notes," Charles suggested. "As you know, Jack got out of the Army in 1992, a decorated war hero, hungry to get rich. After he got his business degree, a classmate from Princeton arranged an introduction for Jack at Primo Investments. Let's, uh, let's say this guy's name was Ted."

"Ted what?"

"Just Ted," Charles replied coldly. "So Ted told Primo's CEO that our boy Jack was a stand-up guy, an all-American boy — Primo would be lucky to get him, he said. So Jack got a few interviews, and, naturally, our boy impressed everybody. The CEO started him as an associate, at 120 grand a year. He placed him in portfolio analysis, doing dreary back-office work, but a perfect place to break in a novice, to learn the nuts and bolts. And, naturally, Jack attacked his work with a vengeance and continued to make a grand impression."

"We already know about his history at Primo," Morgan interrupted.

After a brief pause, Charles asked, "And what did they tell you, Morgan? No, let me guess. They loved Jack."

"Pretty much, yeah."

"That's true. They did love Jack, in the beginning. After only six months he got a big promotion and another bump in salary. Better yet, they switched him into client accounts in the wealth management section. Understand, Morgan, that for a firm like Primo, only the best and brightest work with clients. Geeks and antisocials are hidden, kept in the back rooms. See, Primo won't touch you as a client unless you have at least a hundred million to invest and people with that kind of money aren't easily impressed. But of course Jack is a master at good impressions. In no time, he was managing about four big accounts, and he began bagging new ones. He brought in three that first year. Three! Jack, you see, was a natural . . ." Charles petered off, having made his point.

"You're wasting my time," Morgan interrupted again. "I told you, Primo said the guy was a stud."

"I know you did."

"They even threw a one million bonus in his lap the day he left. That's what I call love."

They heard the bathroom door open, the sound of footsteps, then the noises of a man emptying his bladder and humming a show tune to himself, followed by a noisy, high-powered flush. They stayed quiet until the door closed again.

"About the bonus, we'll talk about it later," Charles promised, sounding mysterious. "Anyway, in the winter of 1994, Jack was out in the Hamptons dining with a client when Edith Warbinger joined their table. Edith was eighty-three, a very pleasant but doddering old widow. Jack's client thought he was doing her a favor introducing her to Jack. She said she had no children, no close relatives, nobody to turn to. Her husband had been an early investor in IBM. His father had left him a few thousand shares, dating back to the twenties. The son was a department store manager, without a clue how the market worked, so he did the easy thing and adopted Pop's investing habit. A lifelong skinflint, he plowed in everything he had, every spare nickel and penny, and without selling a share, rode it all to the top. When he finally cashed out, even after a whopping tax bill, he was worth over three hundred million."

"We should all be so lucky."

"And like all the nouveau riche, he went on a giddy splurge. He promptly bought a big house in the Hamptons, a bigger yacht, a fleet of Mercedes, all the trappings of long-denied wealth." Charles paused for a moment then chuckled. "Two months later, an aneurysm struck, and he was dead."

"The Lord giveth, the Lord taketh away," Morgan couldn't resist saying.

"But he doesn't really look after fools and idiots. See, poor old Edith didn't understand squat about money. The hubby had handled everything. A controlling bastard, he kept her on a leash, gave her a stingy budget and watched how she spent every penny. Now suddenly the hubbie's dead and she's rolling in dough, three hundred million without a clue how to handle it, and along comes Jack. Smiling, confident Jack. Don't worry, he tells her, he'll take care of everything. Edith, naturally, succumbed to his charms and turned over her whole fortune to him."

"Spell Warbinger," was all Morgan said.

Charles did, then picked up where he left off. "So Jack sets up the standard arrangement in such cases, a paying trust. Jack oversaw the investments and handled the monthly disbursements. Edith got a monthly allowance of three hundred thou to do whatever her heart desired. The rest of the earnings, which were considerable, were plowed into more investments. Even that proved too much for her to handle.

Turns out poor Edith had Parkinson's and it was progressing fast. Soon all her bills and fiduciary responsibilities were transferred to Jack."

"She handed him the keys to the kingdom."

"That's right, Morgan. There was no lawyer, no executor, no skeptical husband or greedy children worried about their inheritances watching over his shoulder." Charles paused for a long moment. "Only Jack."

"How much did he take?" Morgan asked.

"Wrong question," Charles replied, chuckling.

"Then what's the right one?" He was taking notes as fast as his hand could scribble. The dates and names were written down in his pinched style. He was relying on his memory for the larger narrative.

"You have to understand, Morgan, a firm like Primo has airtight controls and unrelenting oversight. The firm was known for large partner paychecks, but the associates made dirt. The temptations were unbelievable and the firm knew it. Take Jack. By then he was making two hundred grand a year, a pittance in Manhattan. And he's managing several large fortunes that each number in the hundreds of millions. He drives out to their gaudy mansions in the Hamptons and Greenwich, plays golf with their brazenly spoiled kids, ogles their toys, then drives back into the city, back to his rotten little one-bedroom apartment."

Charles paused for a moment, then remarked, "Imagine how that feels, Morgan. Can you picture it?"

"Must be tough."

"And of course, he knows firsthand that they are too stupid and incompetent to manage their own fortunes."

"I got it. It was irresistible. Now tell me how much he stole."

Charles ignored his query and said, "Now here's the sweet part. All her life, Edith dreamed of a worldwide cruise. Through all those miserable decades, married to a penny-pinching prick, she dreamed of getting away, of climbing onto a boat and seeing the world. Life had passed her by. Now she was eighty-three and degrading fast. There wouldn't be another chance."

"So Jack tells her to go for it."

"Of course he does. He puts her house and cars and the yacht up for sale. He finds this lavish cruise ship, a floating barge overflowing with luxuries and extravagances. It's a great bargain, Jack tells her, but you have to buy a stateroom. For five million, it's all yours. Yours to live in, yours to enjoy, yours to sell after you're bored with the seven seas. A stately topside birth, all the gourmet meals you can eat, three years bouncing through exotic ports from Asia to South America. Know the best part? It was a Greek shipping line. It never touches a U.S. port. Can you see it now, Morgan?"

"Sure, but keep going." No, he didn't see it.

"Only one problem."

"What's that?"

"Edith's Parkinson's. At the rate she was deteriorating, odds are she'd be a total loon long before the end of the cruise. And by law, of course they have to disclose any serious health concerns to the shipping line. The ship has a doctor but he's not inclined to spend all his time administering to some drooling old broad with the shakes who can't remember to take her meds." Charles paused to allow Morgan to think about the ravages of such a cruel disease, then said, "Still, the shipping line wants Edith's millions, Edith wants to hit the high seas, and eventually a solution is found."

"Money cures all ills."

"Not a cure, it offers a manageable solution, though. A private nurse is found. For another million bucks, Edith can rent a small, less expensive room for her far belowdecks."

"Go on."

"So on April 2, 1995, Edith begins her new life. She flies to Copenhagen and checks into the Hotel d' Angleterre. Presumably she spends the next five days roaming the city, tiptoeing into her adventures as a wanderer. On April 7 she checks out, signs onto the ship, and a few hours later she embarks on the dream of her life. This much was confirmed later," Charles explained.

"Mind if I get up and stretch? My ass is falling asleep."

"If I'm boring you, we can stop now."

"My ass, not my ears. I want the full fifty thousand treatment, pal."

Charles chuckled, then continued. "Jack and Edith decided beforehand to forgo the complications of credit cards. The ship has a bank so every month Jack wires half a million into her account. It's so much easier. And every few days, like clockwork, money is withdrawn. Sometimes small amounts, sometimes large. With port calls every three or four days, this raises no suspicions. Presumably Edith is going ashore, indulging her every wish and passion. Perhaps the spending was lavish, even wildly excessive, but it was hers to waste, right?"

The door opened again. The conversation stopped until they heard the sound of it closing again. "What then?" Morgan asked, clearly engrossed in the story.

"Then, Morgan, is three long years later."

"End of the cruise, right?"

"And the beginning of the mystery. Here's what's known. On April 18, 1998, the ship docked in Piraeus. After three years at sea, it needed a dose of maintenance and refitting. Also, if Edith wished to continue playing Sinbad, she needed to ante up another two million, the nautical equivalent of a condo fee. On the evening of the eighteenth, she disembarked from the ship — just hobbled down the plank into town and jumped into a cab. That's the last they saw of her. When, two days later, she failed to return, the shipping line contacted Jack."

"And what did Jack do?" Morgan asked, collapsing back onto the toilet.

"Booted it upstairs."

"She just disappeared?" It was getting chilly in the bathroom, and he began rubbing his arms. He desperately wanted to ask Charles for his clothes, but he already knew the answer.

Charles continued. "And by now, her fortune had grown to 450 million. The stock market was roaring. You could throw darts at it and double your money, and Jack had managed her investments brilliantly."

"And it was all there, in her account?"

"All but the money Edith had gotten from the ship's bank. No suspicion of foul play at this point. An old lady afflicted by Parkinson's walked off a ship and vanished. She was eighty-six, probably half brainless, and who knows what other health issues she had. The possibilities were endless. A heart attack or stroke couldn't be ruled out. A mugging or kidnapping were both possibilities. Or maybe she was out there, in a Parkinson's haze, wandering around Greece, unable to remember how she got there, or even her own name."

"So what did they do?"

"At Jack's insistence, the CEO and CFO at Primo convened a confidential meeting to consider the situation. It presented an unusual quandary, to say the least. People with that kind of money don't just disappear without a trace. The in-house legal counsel told them Edith's fate wasn't their responsibility; she was a client, that's all. The firm wasn't her family. On the other hand, nearly half a billion of her money was in their hands."

"So?"

"It presented what you might call a heartbreaking dilemma for the firm."

"I don't get it."

"You see, Morgan, Edith left no will. No known survivors, nobody who cared about her. She was a legal orphan. But her fees to Primo by this time exceeded ten million a year." As if Morgan missed the significance, Charles pointed out, "Ten million pays a lot of partner bonuses."

"And where does Wiley come into this?"

"Well, no decision was made. Not then. The CEO and CFO said they wanted to wait a reasonable period to see if Edith showed up. As week after week passed, Jack was running around the firm loudly telling everybody how concerned he was about poor old Edith. He wanted her disappearance reported to the State Department, wanted the firm to hire a team of PIs to launch a hunt for her. The bigger the nuisance he made of himself, the more his CEO tried to ignore him."

"Why?"

"Because, legally, Morgan, a person has to be missing three years before you get a presumption of death. Then, absent a will or any known heirs, the disposition of Edith's fortune conveys to the government."

"So Jack and the partners had a little difference of opinion."

"Hardly 'little,' Morgan. Three years of billings meant thirty million, at a minimum. Throw in a little creative bookkeeping — after all, the client wasn't paying attention — and it was a license to take a lot more. Why shouldn't Primo squeeze a hundred million, or even two, out of the arrangement? Skim a bit off the top and call it a performance bonus. Who would ever know? Nobody would miss it. It was all going to disappear into the black hole of government coffers, after all."

"Doesn't sound like Jack did anything wrong."

"You're right, he looked like a perfect angel."

It took a moment for it to settle in before Morgan said, "He was supposed to, wasn't he?"

It wasn't really a question.

Charles continued. "After a month, the CEO and CFO brought Jack back into the boardroom for another confidential chat. Just shut up, they told him — come in to work every day, send Edith her monthly allowance, invest the rest of the money, pretend everything's normal. It would be well worth his while, they promised. An early partnership was a sure bet. They offered him an incredible bump in salary, as well as a piece of what they were already calling the Edith bonus." Charles paused, then added, "In their minds, they were already spending Edith's millions."

"And he said yes, right? After all, Jack's a smart boy." By now, Morgan was hanging on every word. This was better than he had ever expected, so much more than he had ever imagined. Nothing like a tale of wickedness, graft, and avarice among the rich and powerful to brighten the day. It was worth sitting half naked in a cold men's room listening to Charles drone on.

"He turned them down cold," Charles said. "They were infuriated. In the moments after he left, they talked about reassigning him, or simply firing him. Picture it, Morgan. All that stood between them and Edith's fortune was Jack."

Morgan asked, "Then why didn't they fire him?"

"Did I fail to mention the inconvenient stipulation in Edith's contract?"

"I think you did."

"Jack was her adviser and investment manager." He emphasized, "Not the firm, just Jack. To move a dime of Edith's money, his personal signature was required."

"Sounds like Wiley had them by the short hairs."

"You think so?"

"Sure. He could've held them up for millions."

"You know what? The CEO and CFO thought so, too, and wondered why Jack didn't do just that. It was a sure thing. Better yet, on the face of it, it broke no laws. It may have blurred every ethical boundary, but in theory at least, it would appear legal."

"So why didn't he?" Morgan asked.

After a moment, Charles asked, "What do you think?"

"He didn't need it."

"Okay, why not?"

"A good chunk of her money was already in his pocket."

"You're getting warmer."

Morgan thought about it a moment longer. "No, that still doesn't make sense."

"Great. Why not?"

"Because they were offering him more money. More is always better."

"Think harder, Morgan. Why not score a few more million? Better yet, why not join a scam that also incriminated his bosses?"

"Yeah, I see that. Even if they found out Jack was already stealing cookies from the jar, they couldn't rat him out, because he would rat back on them, right?"

"It would be beautiful."

"Then I don't know." After a moment he growled, "And I'm tired of playing this game."

"You're still not thinking like a thief. Put yourself in Jack's shoes."

"Because Jack had persuaded the old lady, Edith, to leave everything to him," Morgan guessed.

Charles chuckled. "Jack wasn't *that* charming."

A long pause as Morgan considered more possibilities. The option that Jack was simply too moral and upright to engage in such unethical behavior had already been discarded. Why would he walk away from more millions? Then it hit him and Morgan almost squealed, "Wow."

"That's right, Morgan. Jack had a much more serious crime to worry about."

"Murder."

"Yes, murder. A much more dreadful secret to conceal. In fact, Edith never set foot on the boat. The real Edith disappeared three years earlier."

Morgan began smiling to himself. "The nurse, right?"

"Definitely her," Charles said very softly. "Before the cruise, you see, nobody on the ship had ever seen Edith in person. The business transactions had all been handled by Jack. They knew only what he told them. Edith was old, ill, wealthy, a widow. The nurse also happened to be quite old, white-haired, moderately educated. Any skilled forger could easily prepare the necessary documents, a passport, driver's license, social security card. Lord knows, it was a simple impersonation to pull off. So, for three years the nurse doddered around the boat, pretended to be mildly senile, withdrew money by the armful, and lived the life."

"Then one day she walked off the boat and skipped with almost twenty million in cash."

"So it appeared."

"Quite the scheme."

"Yes, it was brilliant," Charles said, sounding awed by the cleverness of it all. "A foolproof way to get around the firm's very thorough safeguards."

"So what did the firm do?"

"They had no choice. Jack was calling the shots."

"What's that mean?"

"They notified the American embassy about Edith's disappearance and hired a Greek private detective agency to look into the situation."

Charles paused for a moment to allow

Morgan to catch up. It was a lot to absorb and he could almost hear Morgan's circuits whirring.

"Know what I don't get?" Morgan eventually said. "Why would Wiley want it looked into?"

"Think about it. It had to be done that way. She had to disappear and it had to look real. Then, by insisting on the investigation, Jack looked pure."

"Yeah, that's smart."

"Too smart, in fact. He overlooked one thing. His partners got greedy."

"They didn't believe him, did they?"

"Nope, because they thought like crooks," Charles said in an amused tone. "They found it impossible to believe anyone could be so saintly. How's that for irony?"

"So what did they do?"

"Behind Jack's back, they told the Greek PIs it smelled like an inside job. Based on that tip, the PIs worked backward. The plan only worked as long as everybody assumed it was Edith on that boat, Edith withdrawing the cash, Edith disappearing."

"And somebody had to create that assumption."

"And the author had to be Jack."

"What happened to Edith?"

"Who knows. She was never found. Her

corpse was never found, either. The PIs scoured Piraeus and Copenhagen. They checked morgue records, talked with the police, turned over every rock, and got nothing. Their guess was that she was cremated, then her ashes were dumped at sea."

"Yeah, that's how I'd do it."

"Only one problem. Nobody could prove how the nurse got hired. Jack claimed he didn't know — maybe the shipping line arranged it, maybe Edith found her on her own. The shipping line said it had no record or memory of it, but it's not the kind of thing they typically do. They considered it doubtful."

"And Edith, of course, wasn't around to speak."

"As they say, sometimes the best witness is a dead one."

"What about the nurse? Surely they had a photo of her."

"After a lot of work, they found an old couple a few suites away with a picture of her seated at their table for dinner. It was a waste of time. She looked identical to a billion other old grandmothers on the planet."

"Fingerprints?"

"A few were collected from the suite."

"And?"

"Could've been hers, or any of the countless maids who cleaned the suite over the years. The crews on those boats turn over as regularly as fast-food joints. The prints weren't on record, anyway. Another dead end."

"Probably one of the qualifications for the job," Morgan gamely concluded.

"Probably so. Here's how the PIs figured it. Jack and the nurse, they opened up one or two Swiss accounts before the cruise. Over the years, she withdrew from Edith's account, went ashore, and dumped it into theirs."

"How much did Jack get?"

"If it was fifty-fifty, Jack cleared about ten million."

"Yeah, but odds are, Jack being the mastermind and all, he bagged more."

"I'd say that's a good guess. Probably at least fifteen million, tax-free, salted away in a Swiss vault," Charles said.

Morgan now was into the second-guessing game, and he suggested the obvious. "But nobody could prove it, could they?"

"Nothing could be proved. Nobody could prove Edith was dead. Nobody could prove the nurse was hired by Jack. Nobody knew where the money went. I told you, it was brilliant."

"What did they do?"

"Understand that the last thing Primo wanted was for this to go public. The firm's reputation would be ruined. Rich people don't entrust their millions to crooks, or to investment firms too incompetent to protect against internal corruption."

"But they fired him, right?"

Charles laughed. "Not a chance."

"Why not?"

"They had a suspicion, Morgan, nothing more."

"Yeah, but it was pretty damned —"

"And Jack could always sue them. Plus the CEO and CFO had that filthy little discussion with Jack they now wished to keep under the rug — the one about ripping off more of Edith's fortune. Jack, you see, had them by the balls."

"It's hard not to admire it," Morgan said, almost smacking his lips. Regardless how immoral it was, Jack had pulled off a stunningly beautiful swindle, and Morgan spent a moment contemplating its elegance. It was the scam of a lifetime. Jack was a very talented boy. "So what'd they do?" he asked.

"You're not going to believe it."

"I'm beginning to believe anything about this guy."

"They paid Jack one million to go away. A

bonus, they called it, and both sides signed mutual nondisclosure agreements. One million and neither party could ever whisper a word about the other."

"A bribe to keep his mouth shut."

"Welcome to Wall Street. It's a long, hallowed tradition."

Morgan could hear Charles stand, then shuffle his feet for a moment. "Wait a minute," Morgan yelled.

"That's more than fifty thousand worth," Charles replied. "Admit it, Morgan. I didn't cheat you."

"No, you're forgetting something. Proof."

"Find it yourself, Morgan. It's out there, if you look hard enough." The stall door opened and Charles stepped out. "Follow the trails and you'll find it."

"No, wait," Morgan yelled, and the noise bounced around the walls but nobody answered. He pushed open the stall door, leaned out, and peered into the men's room. Empty.

He stepped out, then opened the door to the stall so recently occupied by Charles. The metal briefcase that contained the money sat on the floor. Morgan lurched forward and opened it — also empty except for a small note: "Keep the case and the locating beacon tucked inside. Once again,

Morgan, nice try."

Then a fresh thought struck Morgan. He began a mad scramble around the men's room, a desperate hunt for his clothes. They weren't in any of the stalls. Not in the big trash can, not in any of the nooks or corners.

He cursed, kicked over the trash can, then made a mad dash for the door.

He emerged just in time to meet the crush of theatergoers pouring into the lobby for the intermission.

15

The assault on General Techtonics began quietly and slowly. On October 12, in a small page seven article in the *Defense News* concerning the GT 400, an anonymous source expressed some generalized dismay about the speed of the testing and vehicle safety. Two days later, *Defense Acquisition Review Journal* printed a letter to the editor with a more pointed complaint about the GT 400's rush to production and the possibility of safety lapses. Nothing too specific; just an overheated rant about the dangers of moving too fast.

Earl's hearings were scheduled for October 30. By the week before, nasty quotes in articles and disturbing rumors were appearing with disturbing regularity.

On October 28, only two days before Earl's hearing, and with brilliant timing, the Capitol Group put on the first public live display of the miracle polymer.

The demonstration was held at Fort Belvoir, a sprawling base located close to the capital, thus a convenient location for the viewers CG was most concerned with. A slew of senior generals, every member of the House and Senate armed services committees, and a small army of senior Pentagon officials were offered free rides to and from the demonstration. They'd heard rumors about the polymer, curiosity ran high, and they came in droves. The press also arrived in force. A high-class caterer was on hand and guests were treated to a magnificent spread of exotic munchies. The reporters flocked to the table and began stuffing themselves.

An array of armored vehicles were positioned in a large open field — four targets coated in polymer, eight without. While guests grazed on foie gras and pickled herring, a galaxy of firepower was unleashed on the targets. For ten minutes, explosive devices, rockets, and missiles rained on the cluster of vehicles. Nothing could survive such a beating. A dense cloud of smoke hung over the field, interspersed with bright flashes as the shooters kept blasting away. When the crescendo of violence finally stopped and the smoke cleared, eight ruined wrecks were burning brightly. The four polymer-coated vehicles were amazingly intact.

Next the guests wandered in small gaggles over to the next field where an old M-113 armored personnel carrier was positioned about three hundred yards away from a large reviewing stand. The venerable 113 was a staple of the old Army, since relegated to the status of a relic. It was built of aluminum, thus very burnable, a relatively thin-skinned vehicle that had become a death trap on the modern, more lethal battlefield. Once again, a terrifying array of missiles, rockets, and bombs pelted the vehicle.

After three minutes of splendid violence, the shooting stopped and the M-113 sat there without a dent, much less a hole.

The guests were stunned. Before they could recover, Bellweather nearly bounced to a microphone on a small stage. He offered a few explanatory remarks about the extensive testing already done in the authentic laboratory of Iraq, but said little about the polymer's amazing qualities. Why should he? They had witnessed it with their own eyes. The demonstration was like nothing anybody had seen before. An old cold war antique had been dragged out the graveyard, plastered in polymer, and survived everything they could throw at it.

Then, in a memorable moment that had been carefully planned, with Bellweather still standing on the stage, jawboning the crowd, the rear ramp of the M-113 clanked down and ten men marched glibly out of the back. Unknown to the crowd, of course, as a precaution, the inside of the 113 had been triple-lined with tons of Kevlar. Bellweather beamed as the crowd gasped.

He was tempted to play the huckster and say, Yes, that's right folks, CG is so confident in its polymer that we're willing to risk real lives! He held his fire, though; the big surprise was about to come.

One of the ten men separated from the pack and walked confidently toward the bleachers. As he drew closer they recognized the beaming face of Mitch Walters, CEO of the company that produced this incredible miracle.

After the cheers and clapping died down, Mitch stepped to the microphone and informed the crowd that CG intended to go for a no-bid, noncompetitive contract — not for itself, not for profit, certainly not for any selfish motive, but for our gallant boys in battle. Thousands of lives were at stake. The whole calculus of the Iraq war would be upended by this new battlefield contraceptive. The insurgents with their lethal bombs and rockets would be frustrated to no end. You saw it here, folks, the chance to win this war. The chance to make horrendous weapons no more useful than slingshots firing pebbles. He asked for their support and was confident he would get it.

Then, without taking any questions, Walters ducked into the back of a long black limousine and sped away.

The limo rushed him straight to the hospital. Walters clasped his head, and howled and moaned the whole way. Despite the plugs in his ears, his left eardrum was severely damaged. The tinnitus in his right ear didn't clear up for three days.

Eva's trips to New York were becoming frequent. The reasons varied — an old friend in the city needed her counsel, an accounting seminar, a meeting with a bank, and so forth.

She dropped in to see Jack every time. Jack himself, after a few weeks of furious activity in D.C., began spending more of his time at home in New Jersey. He explained to Eva that Bellweather and Haggar and Walters had matters well in hand. The Washington tango wasn't his dance. He was comfortable leaving it in the hands of the pros.

The night watcher from TFAC was poised down the street in his usual hiding place, lurking in the driveway of an empty house, when Eva turned into Jack's driveway and parked. He jotted the car model and license number in his log, then settled back and watched closer. From the car model he knew it was her; just as it had been her three other times when he was on shift.

"Rich guys got all the luck," he bitched into his radio.

"Her again?" the man parked in the base van two blocks down asked.

"Yeah, yeah, her."

"What's she wearin' this time?"

"Who cares?"

A quick laugh. "Yeah, you're right. Wanta bet about tonight?"

"I say she stays. I say Jack gives it to her good. She'll crawl out to her car in the mornin'."

"You're on," the base station manager said. "Twenty bucks." It had become a fun game among the watchers, these frequent arrivals of Eva, a few hours inside, then a quick kiss at the door before Eva climbed back into her car for the drive to New York. No overnighters. To the best they could tell, no sex at all, unless Jack and Eva were into slam-bam-thank-you-ma'ams.

The binoculars popped out and he placed them against his eyes. Eva, to his delight, was dressed to the nines in a short skirt, very short, that showed off her very excellent legs and great tush, and a tight upper bodice that illustrated her very ample bosom. He watched her bend over, stretch, and reach into the car for something. "Oh, that's it, girl, bend further . . . oh please, a little more," he mumbled out loud to himself, straining for a good peek. The moment dragged on and the watcher enjoyed every second of it.

Next a short, confident walk to the door. Jack was obviously expecting her, they brushed lips, and she entered hauling two boxes of pizza and a small overnight bag. Mushrooms and cheese for her, meat lover's delight for him. They moved straight to the dining room, where, no doubt, a few bottles of wine were already uncorked. That should help set the right mood.

"Guess what she's carrying?" the watcher informed the man inside the van.

"What?

"A suitcase."

"Yeah?"

"Black overnight bag. The money's mine.

She and Jack are gonna do the bedsheet tango."

"I'll stick with my bet."

"Thank you," he said and laughed.

Two hours later, the door opened and Eva stepped out, suitcase in hand. The watcher was now crouched in a clump of thick bushes only fifty feet from the door. He mumbled a curse and listened.

Eva was saying to Jack, "Are you sure? My meeting's not until late morning."

After a long moment, Jack said, "I'm sure."

"Why, Jack? I'm not used to throwing myself at men. I'm definitely not used to being turned down."

"Sorry. I'm just not ready."

The watcher couldn't see it, but could almost picture Eva's face. She was looking up into Jack's eyes, he was sure, with an expression that registered between hurt and embarrassment. "I deserve a better explanation than that," she remarked, now with a distinct chill in her voice.

"I don't have one."

"You can do better than that, Jack."

"Okay, I'll try. I've rushed into things a few times in the past and regretted it."

"I'm not the past, Jack."

"I know that."

342

"I won't offer again."

"I don't blame you," Jack said. "When the time comes, I'll be willing to fight for it."

Then for a long moment, silence. It struck the lurker in the bushes that Eva was wavering between telling Jack to kiss off or breaking down in tears. Tell him he's a hopeless idiot, he wanted to scream. Kick, spit, and scream how much you hate him. He suddenly loathed Jack. Poor, poor Eva. How could he do this to her? Really, how could any man turn down such a fine piece of tail?

He watched Eva spin around and stomp to her car, heels making loud angry clacks on the concrete the whole way. She climbed in, slammed the door, and burned rubber all the way down the street.

Jack stared down the street after her, then stepped inside and closed his door.

The meeting was short and to the point. Walters was sitting behind his desk, idly playing with a paperweight. Bellweather, with his arms crossed tightly against his chest, was hunched against the far wall.

O'Neal and Morgan stood before the desk and wrapped up the final details about the meeting with Charles in New York, and his astounding revelations. They had been speaking for fifteen fascinating minutes. Mr.

Big Shot Walters never invited them to sit.

"He killed her?" Walters asked, coming forward in his chair.

"That's what Charles claimed," Morgan answered.

"And you believe it?"

"I see no reason not to," Morgan said. "The story was so elaborate, so detailed. Hard to believe it was fabricated."

"It was considerably more than we expected to learn," O'Neal offered, a loud understatement, though somewhat short of an endorsement.

The room fell quiet as the men considered the full import of Jack's past. A con artist, a thief, *and* a murderer. Two of three they had hoped for, maybe even expected; the murder gave them pause.

"Well, he was Delta," Bellweather remarked, as if that explained everything. "Purebred killers. Jack certainly had the ability and experience to pull it off." But he still wasn't sure he believed it himself. Could Jack Wiley really be a murderer? Did he really kill an old lady? Could the smooth, aloof Jack they all knew be that viciously cold-blooded?

Walters looked at the wall for a moment until he found the good news. "If it's true," he said, "it gives us the edge we've been looking for. If he steps out of bounds, we've got all the ammunition we need to yank him back."

"Except evidence," O'Neal answered, injecting a bit of reality.

Walters fixed him with a hard stare. "Do you believe it?"

"Maybe. But we don't know the identity of the source. This guy Charles is a blank slate. We got nothing that proves whether it's true or not."

Morgan felt the need to throw his two cents in and said, "I'm convinced Charles was telling the truth."

"Are you?"

"In fact, if I had to guess, Charles was Ted."

"Who?" Walters asked. He did not enjoy talking with this common investigator and made no effort to hide it. He was the CEO, after all; it was beneath his station.

"Ted," Morgan repeated. "The friend from Princeton who introduced Jack at the firm. Ted vouched for him. Ted was responsible for Wiley getting the job. After Jack walked with the old lady's money and a million-dollar buy-off, Ted was left holding the bag."

"What makes you think that?"

"I don't know. A hunch."

"We don't pay you for guesses," Walters snapped.

"There just was something in the way he told that part of the story. A pause, a hesitation, an intonation. I dunno, something. He's Ted. I'm sure of it."

Walters leaned back in his chair and unleashed a skeptical frown. "Anything else?" he asked. "I mean anything factual?"

"Yeah. He had names, dates, plenty of details. Only one thing explains that. He was in the firm same time as Jack."

"That it?" Walters asked. He now had his hands clasped behind his big head with his feet on the desk, pretending to be bored. It was his favorite managerial stunt, making them sweat, intimidating his underlings with indifference, forcing them to say more than they intended.

"Only this," Morgan said, looking Walters directly in the eye without blinking. Morgan had never met him before but he'd certainly heard the rumors; a tough-guy wannabe in Gucci loafers. Seemed about right to him. "He asked if you guys intended to hurt Jack or just humiliate him. This is important to him."

"And what did you say?"

"That you're gonna bring a world of pain on Jack. He liked that, Mr. Walters. Liked it very much," Morgan said. "Charles, or Ted, or whoever, is carrying a real nasty grudge."

Walters paused and glanced at Bellweather. "What do you think?" he asked, unsure he wanted to hear the answer. The accusation of murder was a new factor, one with a world of troublesome ramifications, but they were in too deep with Jack to walk away at this point. Jack had that damned contract that bound them together. And he had been with them almost every step, dodging and bribing their way through Washington.

After a moment, Bellweather surmised, "Jack might be more than we bargained on. Depending on your perspective, we either over- or underestimated him."

"Tell me something I don't know."

"Question is, do we have anything to worry about?" Bellweather pushed off the wall and began pacing around the office as he talked. "If true, Jack is sly, deceptive, and very dangerous."

"Yeah, but if we can prove it, he'll be a lot less dangerous."

O'Neal and Morgan studied their shoetips as Bellweather and Walters went back and forth, bickering over the pros and cons of getting the goods on Jack. Both did their best to appear bored and ambivalent as they bit back nasty smiles. It was a waste of their time, but they would bill CG for every second of this meeting, so who cared? Really, what was there to debate?

Of course Bellweather and Walters were going to go for it — they'd throw a fortune at the hunt for evidence, if that's what it took. This tale was simply too good to ignore.

Walters, the expert in human behavior, would be the first to figure out the big possibility, O'Neal was sure. Bellweather might be more ruthless, but age and success had dulled his edge. Walters was all that, plus he was hungry and ambitious. He'd clawed and backstabbed and stepped over a hundred bodies on his way up to CEO. He would yank out his mother's fingernails if it would gain him another inch of advantage. He was actually surprised it was taking Walters this long to figure out the enormity of the incredible break that just landed in his lap.

They had uncovered Jack's dirty little secret; now, if they could prove it, Walters had the weapon he needed to drive Wiley out of the deal. Here's a blast from your past, Jack — evidence that you whacked an old lady, evidence you stole her money, evidence you blackmailed your firm into shoving it under a rug. Proof of just one of those charges would drive Jack to his knees. Sign over your shares, forgo a billion in profit, and it'll remain our nasty little secret.

Eventually Bellweather and Walters stopped talking. Walters stood and walked around his desk. "Do you think you can get proof?" he asked, directing a finger at O'Neal. "Something that would stand up in court?"

"Probably," Martie answered, making the word sound more like "absolutely, no big deal." It was, however, not merely a big deal, but a huge one. He'd bill the Capitol Group for millions. He'd throw a dozen people at it, work them around the clock, invoice triple for overtime, and bill his client for every paper clip and wasted photograph. "Charles left us plenty of leads," he continued, listing his reasons. "We know the victim. We now have it narrowed down to one firm. We'll get the names of everyone in Primo during those years. Somebody will know something. Someone'll talk."

"I want it done fast."

"I'll put my best people on it." Dozens of them at inflated costs.

"Don't get caught."

"Not a chance. A good cover and he'll never know a thing. Anyway, we're still watching his house. We'll add a few more men, watch him everywhere he goes."

"What are you waiting for?"

O'Neal and Morgan backed away and fled from the office. The moment the door closed, Bellweather put his rear end on the corner of Walters's desk. "Good call," he said.

"I know." Walters walked back behind the desk and collapsed into his chair. He picked up the picture that O'Neal had left in the middle of the blotter.

It was taken by one of the trailers following Morgan and Charles that night. A color, blown up to ten-by-twelve, showing Charles meeting Morgan on the street corner. He pinched the bridge of his nose and studied it closely. The mystery man was maybe five inches taller than Morgan, thin, well dressed, wearing an expensive blue cashmere topcoat. The shot was blurry and mildly out of focus but showed that Charles had dark features, dark, swept-back hair, a large beak, and shrewd eyes. "Know who this guy is?" he asked without looking up.

"Not a clue. Who?"

"The billion-dollar man."

16

The hearing was everything they had paid for. And every bit as entertaining as they'd hoped.

Four GT executives showed up — three accountants and a smooth-looking, unctuous lapdog from GT's congressional relations branch, brought along to appear friendly and ride herd on the number nerds. The executives arrived ten minutes early and seated themselves at the long witness table. They came armed with spreadsheets, which they spent five minutes meticulously arranging on the table. They came fully prepared to answer the most vexing questions about the cost of the GT 400.

The two previous days, the three accountants had spent long hours in front of murder boards exhaustively preparing for the hearing. A team of inquisitors bellowed questions at them, contradicted, argued, and browbeat until the three never blanched at the most egregious assault. The hearing was only a pro forma cost review. A mundane event, nothing more. But given the egos in Congress, there was always the risk of some loudmouthed representative trying to grandstand at their expense. They were ready. They had all the answers. They sat quietly and tried to hide their cockiness.

Thirty-five members of the congressional subcommittee were in attendance — an unexpectedly large turnout for such a tedious hearing. All were seated on the large podium, already looking bored out of their minds. All thirty-five had tried to squirm out of it, but Earl had bent elbows and traded favors in an effort to arrange a large audience. In addition, a small cluster of reporters, including one from the *Washington Post* and one from the *New York Times,* were on hand, seated in the empty rows of chairs reserved for guests. They'd been lured to the hearing by telephonic tips from a sneaky member of Earl's staff he often used to plant stories or leaks. The reporters had been told to expect a big story and plenty of fireworks. A pair of C-SPAN cameras were rolling, a common sight these days, nothing to be alarmed about. Three bright-looking staffers were hunched in their seats directly behind the empty chairman's chair, exchanging notes, smirking at each other, eager for the fun to begin.

The air of boredom broke with three minutes left to begin. The door in the rear cracked open and a new visitor stepped inside, an attractive female dressed in a flattering red business suit that nicely accented her dark brunette hair, long legs, and slender figure. She had large green eyes, a small, upturned nose, high cheekbones, and a wide, generous mouth. The thirty men on the podium sat up and took notice. A few male reporters noisily shifted seats to make room for her.

She looked around for a moment before the Capitol cop on duty rushed over and offered to help her find a seat. They wished they were him: oh, for an excuse to engage her in a conversation. They all watched as she shook her head — her long hair flipped back and forth, her features crinkled so beautifully. She chose her own seat, an aisle chair far in the back, where she was by herself. They watched as she sat, and they peeked and stared as her skirt rose and showed a little more leg. Great legs. Long legs. Legs that seemed to go all the way to the ceiling.

One of the reporters, tall and lanky, with a well-groomed fashionable three-day stubble, who obviously thought of himself as a cocksman, spun around in his seat and unloaded a flash of teeth. "Hey, babe, what paper you with?"

"I'm not."

"I'm with the *Journal*," he said, as if that meant something.

She said nothing. It meant nothing.

"My name is Rex," he tried again. "Rex Smith. So why're you here?"

By now every eye in the room was on her and Rex. Rex had had the nerve to do what they all wanted to.

The universal hope was that he failed miserably.

"I work in the Department of Defense," she said. "I was having lunch nearby. Thought I'd drop by and watch."

"You have a name?"

"Doesn't everybody?" In other words, get lost.

"What's yours?"

"Mia," she said. No last name, just Mia. She began digging through her briefcase, visibly trying to ignore him.

Spurred on by all the stares he was attracting, Rex wasn't about to back down. He couldn't think of anything intelligent to say, so he offered the lame compliment, "Nice name." Another smile and he asked,

"So, what do you do in the Department of Defense?"

"Well, Rex, I'm a lawyer," she answered without looking up.

"A lawyer."

She finally met his stare. "Yes," she said very calmly, very coldly. "I specialize in suing reporters for lying, defamation, or deliberate falsification."

"Oh."

"So I suggest you turn around and pay close attention to the hearing, Rex. Get every detail right. I'll be watching."

Rex stared blankly at her for a long moment, then turned around; he suddenly became preoccupied with his reporter's pad. A few chuckles broke out among the other reporters. It was a brutal putdown. They admired her delivery.

Mia ignored the stares and chuckles and went back to digging something out of her briefcase.

As chairman, Earl entered five minutes late, fell gingerly into his chair, pulled his pants out of his crotch, offered the witnesses a pleasant, hospitable smile as if they were old chums, welcomed them to the hearing, then led off with a few empty peremptory remarks about the great importance of protecting our troops, buying them the very best equipment, and the role of this committee in oversight.

Then he fixed his bleary eyes on the three accountants. In his most homespun tone, he asked, "So you three fellas are all executive vice presidents?"

The older, plumper one in the middle answered, "Actually, sir, I'm a senior VP." He motioned at the men to his left and right. "Rollins and Baggio here are executive VPs. They work for me."

Earl nodded. "A senior VP, huh? Guess that makes you pretty high up over there."

Edward Hamilton, the senior VP, offered a quick smile in response. This was so easy. "I'm one of only ten senior VPs in the company," he announced as if he were a finalist for Miss America. Any second he'd be blathering about world peace.

"So we got the right folks up here to talk about this GT 400?"

"Yes, you could say that."

"And we should expect you to know a lot."

"I think that's a fair assumption, sir," Hamilton answered with a loud, confident smile.

"Good, good. I was hoping GT didn't send a coupla dunces up here."

Hamilton chuckled. He decided a little more explanation might be helpful. "Rollins, Baggio, and I have been overseeing the GT 400 from its birth, you might say. I'd venture to say we know as much as anybody." He smiled brightly. He should've said about the finances, but why waste words?

"Well, then, I'm surely delighted you're here," Earl announced, smiling tightly as one of his aides leaned forward and handed him a piece of paper. He adjusted his glasses and squinted at the paper for a moment. He cleared his throat, leaned into the microphone, and asked very softly, almost pleasantly, "Can any of you gentlemen tell me when you first became aware of the rollover problem?"

"I'm sorry." Hamilton hesitated, then asked, "What problem?"

"I'm sure you heard me. The rollover problem."

"I'm, uh, I have no idea what you're talking about."

"You don't, huh?" Earl asked. He leaned his big bulk forward in his chair, planted his elbows, and asked, "Do you think a company that wants to sell the military a multibillion-dollar product has a responsibility to thoroughly test it?"

Hamilton by now was completely flustered. He glanced at the stooge from congressional relations for help, for advice, for a signal, anything. The stooge couldn't seem to take his eyes off the floor. "I, uh, well —"

"This is one of those easy questions, Mr. Hamilton. Answer it."

"Uh . . . why, yes. Yes, of course."

"Thank you. Now, that didn't hurt, did it?"

A nervous smile. "No, sir."

"Now, if, during the course of this testing, a problem surfaces, what should the company do?"

Again Hamilton glanced anxiously down the row at the weasel from congressional relations. He was looking away; the walls of the chamber now seemed to hold his interest. After a long pause Hamilton said, "To be frank, this isn't my area of —"

"Look at me, not him," Earl barked. "This is my hearing after all. Do I need to repeat the question?"

"No." Hamilton drew a deep breath and fingered a few spreadsheets. What was going on here? "I suppose it should report the problems."

"You suppose?"

"Uh . . . yes, I believe it has that legal responsibility."

Earl nodded. "So why didn't you?" he asked in a very reasonable tone.

Unsure what this was about, Hamilton

said, "I wasn't at the testing."

It was the wrong answer and Earl made him pay dearly for it. He lifted up a thick binder and waved it in the air like a thunderbolt he was about to stuff down the witness's throat. "Have you seen this report?"

The question was spurious; no, of course he hadn't seen it. Other than Earl, nobody in the room had laid eyes on it. The report — a thick compendium of charts and graphs and diagrams and tables — had only been compiled late the night before. It had been placed in Earl's hands only that morning.

The man who prepared it, formerly a research analyst at the Insurance Institute for Highway Safety, now a hired whore at a local think tank, had labored around the clock for two weeks trying to get it right. To his dismay, the GT 400, it turned out, had an almost impossibly low center of gravity. He was forced to tinker with the computer models until a ninety-degree turn performed at 140 mph did, in fact, produce a mild tipover.

The best-designed European race car would be hurtling toward Mars long before that speed. As for the GT 400, it couldn't surpass 60 mph if it had three rocket engines strapped to its ass.

Hamilton was squinting, trying to see

what Earl was waving around. "I have no idea what you're talking about."

"Yeah, well, I expected you'd say that," Earl said, rolling his eyes and glaring with contempt at this pathetic attempt to lie. "This here's an expert report showing that the GT 400 is subject to rollover."

Hamilton exhaled a deep breath. "I find that hard to believe." He had no idea whether it was true or not.

"You calling me a liar, son?"

The reporters perked up and began scribbling notes — the promised entertainment had arrived.

"No, sir. It's just I find that report —"

But Earl was already furiously waving another paper in the air. "And what about this?" he demanded, now sounding quite aggrieved. "I received this here letter from somebody in the Defense procurement office. Know why? He became incensed by what he called a big whitewash during the GT 400's shoddy testing." Earl was wired and on a roll; he'd managed to squeeze "incensed," "whitewash," and "shoddy testing" into the same sentence.

"That's absurd."

Another aide bent forward and handed Earl a thick stack of clippings. He grabbed them and began flinging them, one by one, on the floor in the direction of the witness table. "Know what these are?" he yelled. "Newspaper and magazine reports from the past few weeks. They detail the shoddy testing and deplorable effort by your company to hide the rollover problem."

Hamilton's mouth hung open. His face was red and forming the first drops of sweat; he could not stop tugging at his shirt collar. He felt as though he were suffocating. This was just so atrociously awful, so unfair. If Earl wanted to know about amortization rates or outyear repair costs, fine. But Hamilton wasn't a vehicular engineer. Hell, aside from a few glossy photos in the company brochures, he'd never even seen a real GT 400. He tried two or three times to make that point, but Earl talked right over him as he kept flinging those damning articles in his direction like bullets.

When Earl's hands were finally empty, he yelled, "I can't believe you'd come in here and ask us to spend forty billion dollars on a rolling death trap." He paused, wanting to be sure the reporters captured his pet phrase. "Forty billion. For a rolling death trap," he repeated, again, more deliberately this time, as though the more slowly the words were pronounced, the more lethal they became.

"I'm sure we can explain those reports and that letter," Hamilton sputtered lamely.

"Explain now. I'm listening."

"Well . . . I —" This was all so humiliating; he hated Earl Belzer.

"Do you know we are at war, sir?"

"I read the papers, yes." That glib response just popped out of his lips. He instantly regretted it.

Earl carefully removed his reading glasses and placed them on the table. "Was that crack meant to be funny?" he sneered.

"Uh, well, no," Hamilton stammered, visibly squirming in his seat. The murderboard sessions were a limp badminton game compared to this.

" 'Cause let me tell you something, boy. Over three thousand of our fine boys and girls have died over there. Three thousand sons and daughters slaughtered by Muslim fanatics and weirdos. Maybe that's funny to you and your company, but not up here, Mr. Big Shot executive."

The other thirty-four committee members were now wide awake and watching intently. Most were old pros at this game, and until this moment had reserved a fair amount of pity for poor Hamilton trapped behind that big witness table. It was all about power. Earl was both a player and the ref, free to make his own rules, free to barrage his witness with unanswerable questions, free to interrupt at will.

Hamilton never stood a chance. He was a bit player in a long, hallowed congressional prerogative to hold lopsided hearings, scold and browbeat witnesses, and never allow anyone but the members to deliver a complete or coherent thought. It was ridiculously unfair, of course. Still, Hamilton was expected to adhere to the proper decorum — behave like a slaughtered lamb, lie down, and be gracefully butchered.

A row of deepening scowls were now glaring down at the witnesses. Rollins and Baggio began quietly inching their chairs away from Hamilton, avoiding the line of fire, trying to dodge a stray bullet from Earl, who looked like he wanted to pull out a gun and blast away.

Hamilton wanted to get up and bolt, but his feet felt like concrete. "I'm sorry," he mumbled as contritely as he could the moment Earl seemed to be finished.

The aides hunched in the seats behind Earl launched into giggles as they fingered the large stacks of papers positioned on their laps. Hamilton couldn't take his eyes off them — what would they hand Earl next? What other loathsome crime was this awful man going to accuse him of? What fresh claim was going to appear, without warning, out of thin air?

He needn't have worried. Earl was out of ammunition — the remaining papers were a harmless collection of office memos and take-out menus carelessly added to the mix — but his aides had been ordered to appear ready to drown the witnesses in damning reports.

Earl fixed him with another nasty frown, then said, "I won't waste any more time reviewing the vast hoard of material I've received" — he waved a dismissive hand through the air as though his aides had three trucks full of reports and terrible claims and dreadful assertions that, out of generosity, Earl would not rub in his face — "and I don't know whether all these reports and complaints and technical analyses are true or not. I'm no expert in such things. But my daddy always used to say, where there's smoke, there's somethin' burnin'."

Hamilton knew he had to do something. He took a deep swallow and said, "I'm sure we can satisfy your curiosity on these rumors." He paused and tried to look hopeful. "Now, uh, now that we know your specific concerns, I feel sure that —"

"Are you proposin' another hearing?"

"Yes," Hamilton said, exuding relief at the thought of someone else taking this awful beating. "That's exactly what I meant."

Earl stared at him in disbelief. "Do I work for you, Mr. Hamilton?"

"Uh . . . no."

"That's right, Mr. Big Shot. You might find this hard to believe, but this committee stays fairly busy with the people's business."

"I didn't mean to imply —"

"Excuse me, sir," Earl bellowed with a ferocious finger pointed at Hamilton's face. "This is my committee. I set the rules. You speak only after you are asked a question. Do you understand that?"

Hamilton could barely produce a limp nod. If he had a gun he'd shoot Earl; he'd shoot himself, too.

"So, since we have all these reports and vile accusations of vehicle deficiencies" — Earl paused to steal a glance at his notes to be sure he got the words just right — "and since I'm sure you gentlemen from General Techtonics want the very safest equipment for our soldiers in battle, I'm gonna do you a big favor. I propose to this committee that we give you six more months to extensively test your vehicle."

Hamilton was rubbing his temples. His bosses were going to kill him. A six-month delay would be financially devastating. More tests could cost billions. "Am I allowed to register a protest?"

"You certainly may. We live in a democracy."

"How?"

"Write your congressman."

Earl asked for a hand vote. Without objection or comment, he quickly got thirty-five in favor. Twenty of those yeas had recently received mysterious donations to their reelection committees; three had been promised assistance or support on various pet bills or pork requests; two new members were simply trying to garner favor with the committee chairman.

Amazingly, Earl had pulled this off with only one million dollars; the other million contributed by CG to his buying spree, of course, ended up in his pockets. Democracy at its best.

He slammed the gavel and the hearing immediately broke up. Mia ignored the noisy exodus of chattering congressmen, staffers, and reporters and stayed glued to her seat, pretending to read a memo, until the last member quietly closed the door behind him.

She got up and approached one of the C-SPAN cameramen, a large man with a big belly, awkwardly bent over gathering his equipment, preparing to move on.

"Sorry to bother you," she said to his back. "Would it be possible to get a copy of your tape?"

He was playing with a machine on the floor. He never looked up. "Sorry, no."

"Try yes instead."

"Not mine to give, lady. Belongs to C-SPAN."

"Would it help if I showed you this?" she asked, flashing a card at his back. He turned around and stared at it: Mia Jenson, Investigator, Defense Criminal Investigative Service. Then out popped her DCIS shield, which he glanced at also for another moment. "It's quite real," Mia assured him. "I'm a federal agent."

"What's this about?" he asked, now staring at her,

"That's none of your business." She glanced at the identity card hanging around his neck. "Listen, Carl, I'm asking politely now. I could just as easily come back with a subpoena."

"Look, I'm not trying to be a pain."

She gave him a slight smile. It seemed apologetic. "Oh, what the hell. Between you and me, Carl, we're looking into a few irregularities in the GT 400."

"I see."

"Probably nothing. Chasing rumors. My bosses ordered me to come back with the tape."

"Why don't we bring this to my bosses?"

"I'd rather not."

His forehead was wrinkled with suspicion. "Is there a reason why?"

"It's a confidential investigation at this point. That's how we're treating it. Like I said, it's merely exploratory and we'd rather not have GT learn we're looking." Her features wrinkled with disgust. "They'll throw a battalion of lawyers at us, and hide anything incriminating. The investigation will be dead before it gets started."

"Okay."

"Make me a copy. Nobody'll know. Please, Carl."

"Sure. No problem." Carl happened to have a high-speed tape copying machine, and two minutes later he handed her the tape.

Mia thanked him and disappeared.

They walked at a fast clip through the elegant lobby of the Madison Hotel until they were met by a duet of burly men; East Europeans of some variety, both of them. They looked like bookends, spectacularly muscled, fierce-looking, and no doubt armed to the teeth. Neither spoke a word of English. They greeted Bellweather and Walters with respectful grunts, escorted them to the elevators, then stood stiffly and quietly in the corner while the elevator whisked them to the ninth floor.

Next, a brisk walk down the long hallway to the very end, where one of the Madison's most opulent and expensive suites was located. Another pair of brutish bookends was planted beside the door. After quick nods and more courteous grunts, they ushered the Americans inside. No pat-downs, no questions. They were expected, obviously. And they were welcome.

The large suite they stepped into had been transformed from standard American luxury fare into an Arabian fantasy. The floors were plastered wall to wall with thick, handwoven oriental carpets. Shimmering silk fabrics and tapestries hung from the ceilings. The sofas and chairs had been replaced with enough oversize floor cushions to seat a hundred. The temperature was set at a sweltering ninety degrees. All the discomforts of home.

Two gentlemen in white robes with bright gold edging sat cross-legged in the middle of the floor. They were sharing a silver hookah pipe and munching from a large bowl of dates.

The one on the left offered a faint smile. "Ah, Daniel, nice of you to arrive on time."

"Your highness," Bellweather said, and bowed slightly. The exaggerated and entirely phony formality brought smiles to both their faces.

"Won't you be seated," Prince Ali bin Tariq requested with a commanding flourish of his right hand. Ali was the forty-third son of the Saudi king, formerly, and for an amazingly long eighteen years, the Saudi ambassador to the United States. Educated at Harvard and Oxford, he was highly westernized, an accomplished diplomat, a drunk, a womanizer, and a flamboyant rascal who had once treated D.C. as his own playground.

During his long tenure as ambassador he had helped fix three presidential elections, bought enough congressmen and senators to stuff two Rolodexes, fathered countless illegitimate children, purchased six fabulous homes from Palm Beach to Vail, along with three luxury jets to shuttle him around his real estate empire, and along the way became the senior and most esteemed member of Washington's diplomatic corps.

Eighteen years away from his stuffed-shirt kingdom, eighteen years of sin and frolic, and all the pleasures and contentment unlimited wealth could buy.

During many of those years, Bellweather had been his frequent partner in bar-hopping and whoring around town. They shared women, they drank an ocean of booze, and on one amazing occasion they christened Ali's newest Boeing 737 with a wild, fantasy, around-the-world orgy. Just Bellweather and Ali, and thirty women chosen for their physical variety and amorous skills.

That exhausting but remarkable trip had been the cause of Bellweather's second divorce, the ugliest of the three. Definitely the most enthusiastic and sexually imaginative of the ladies, it turned out, was a very determined PI hired by his wife. The PI returned from the trip with a thick photo album showing Daniel in an assortment of insane poses.

After one glance at the album, he offered wife two a swift, uncontested divorce with a "fair settlement." When she then mentioned her ambition to open a public photo gallery, he collapsed completely; whatever she wanted, she could have it. She took him at his word and looted him for all he was worth. The house, the cars, all of his cash that she knew about.

It was worth every penny. The thought of those terrifying photos in the public eye was nauseating.

Then, three years ago, after a series of media articles about the prince's outrageous lifestyle became too ugly to ignore, his father called him home. It was one thing for a Saudi prince to bribe, corrupt, fix, and blackmail in a foreign land. Infidels, after all, were born incorrigibly corrupted; what was wrong with squirting a little more fuel on the fire?

His father, however, drew the line over a photograph of Ali in *Entertainment Weekly,* a leering smile on his lips, a bubbling flute of champagne in one hand, the other planted firmly on the rather skinny fanny of one of Hollywood's most celebrated sluts, which said something. The girl was only sixteen. Worse, she was made up to look only thirteen. Ali was crushed. For eighteen years he had lived the life of dreams. The idea of returning home, to a hot, sandy, dry country, to give up his American mansions, his powerful dedication to scotch, to live in a barren land without booze or blonde women — he'd developed a particular longing for golden hair — sickened him. He sent a long letter home, an elegantly worded missive telling his father to screw off.

But after the king threatened to cut off not only his inheritance and lifestyle emoluments, but also his head, Ali decided his affection for his family was calling him.

Bellweather and Walters had by now fallen onto their rear ends. Emitting a series of loud grunts, they were trying their damnedest to wrench their legs and knees into the same cross-legged stance as the Saudis.

His features twisted with pain, Bellweather asked, "You got a call from President Cantor?"

"Yes, yes," Ali said with a quick wave. "Billy mentioned you have something interesting for us. Something quite lucrative."

The moment Ali returned home, he had begged his father for a position in the Kingdom's Ministry of Finance. High, low, didn't matter. With his contacts and unscrupulous friends, he swore he could do a world of good for Saudi investments overseas. The king had a different idea and instead threw him in a Wahhabi-run rehab facility to dry out. A prison would've been more merciful, and less dreadful. Ali found himself in a small, unadorned room with only a bed and prayer mat, trapped in the middle of the desert with nobody but other spoiled and depraved reprobates for company.

He nearly went mad. It was such a steep drop from his former life. After a long, horrible two years of staring at white walls, of interminable sermons on faith and abstinence, of prostrating himself in prayer throughout the day, while he secretly dreamed of booze and blondes, Ali finally got his chance. He wrote a long rambling letter to his father swearing he was cured. A newly purified servant of Allah, he was now anxious to get out and make serious amends for his many sins. His timing couldn't have been better. With oil prices shooting through the ceiling, the royal family was suddenly awash with cash. Gobs of it, many, many billions of Western money, was flooding the small kingdom. Black stuff was pumped out, rivers of green stuff flowed in.

Finding safe places to park all that cash had become a mammoth problem.

But at long last, after two horrible years of unmitigated misery, his father gave Ali the chance he had dreamed of, an opportunity to escape and make frequent trips to the West.

Over the wretched course of those two pathetic years, the only thing that had kept Ali from hanging himself in his cell were all the wild fantasies he stored in his head and replayed over and over. He developed a mental catalog; things he had done, things he would like to do again, new things he'd like to try. The time had come, at last, to indulge every last one of his preserved fantasies.

However, the man seated to Ali's right, Bellweather knew, was a former imam and an iron-willed zealot, dispatched by the king to keep a tight rein on his forty-third son and be sure he didn't lapse back into his nasty old habits. The temptations of the West were strong, and Ali obviously had a few willpower issues.

"How much did Cantor tell you?" Bellweather asked.

"A little. Something about a liquid you will squirt on your tanks and jeeps."

"He told you what the polymer does?"

"More or less."

"Are you interested?"

"More or less," he repeated in that maddeningly opaque Middle Eastern way. In Arabland, apparently the words "yes" and "no" would draw a lightning bolt from the heavens.

"Then let me update you," Bellweather suggested. He quickly proceeded through an energetic explanation of the polymer, a hilarious story about the dashed hopes of the GT 400, and the state of play in getting

375

a defense contract. He made it sound like a gold mine — which it was — and a sure thing — which was drawing closer to reality every day.

Ali and his watchdog made loud slurping noises as they pulled tokes from the hookah. Ali listened politely but appeared only mildly interested.

Walters sat quietly and let Bellweather handle the pitch. Walters secretly loathed Arabs. His family name had been Wallerstein before he got it legally changed. He had aunts and uncles in Israel. A few cousins in the IDF. He wanted nothing to do with these Bedouin schlemiels, except for their money; about that he had absolutely no qualms.

"So now you want to sell us a piece," Ali suggested the moment Bellweather finished.

"That's the general idea, yes." No fuller explanation was asked for, or indeed necessary. CG never put its own money on the line. They developed a project or takeover target, then quickly invited others to share the financial burden and gains. The financial term was "leverage," shorthand for accumulating capital and spreading the risks of failure across multiple parties. In this case it meant buying all the influence that CG's powerful group of insiders and power-peddlers could muster in the hunt for profit.

CG, however, carried it to absurd lengths. This was the secret to its success, the basic principle its founders had always preached. No matter how enticing the gamble, do it with other people's money. They took funds from New York, Geneva, Frankfurt, Mumbai, Taipei, Moscow, really from anyone with deep pockets and the willingness to accept their stark terms. The source of the money made no difference. But the Saudis had long been their most frequent investor.

There was good reason for this. Billy Cantor, the former president and now CG board member, had during his time in office done the Saudis a few quiet favors. He had squelched several embarrassing inquiries that ranged from bribing American officials to some fairly egregious SEC violations. When several of the Saudi royals visited Las Vegas, and engaged in a wild bash that led to allegations they had kidnapped ten showgirls and treated them like a private harem, he had signed a secret order allowing them to jump on planes and flee home.

Then, after sixty American soldiers were butchered in a horrifying terrorist bombing at a U.S. air base outside Riyadh, with strong hints of government involvement, he had ordered the FBI and CIA to bring home their investigators and call it quits.

He did these favors not out of love for the Saudis. Truthfully, Arabs, Pakistanis, Indians — all those semi-dark people looked so much alike to him. He was well aware, though, that his long life in politics was grinding to a sad close. He had so little to show for it.

He'd been such a miserable president, with so few accomplishments to write or brag about afterward. No, he wasn't likely to get rich off speeches and books, like the others of his ilk. With his heavy lisp and oversize tongue, he'd never been a good orator anyway. Even Nixon — Nixon! — had made a large fortune peddling books.

Sadly, the sum total of Billy's insights and ruminations about statecraft or good governance could barely fill a two-page article. And after his regrettable attempt at reelection prompted a record landslide for the other side, it was clear the nation just wanted to forget him. So he'd spent his last months in office stuffing in as many favors to rich, unpopular countries and greedy defense contractors as he could get away with.

Now those old favors were paying back a thousandfold. The Saudi royal family came when Bill Cantor called. They had few fans in America, and a president, even a former one, even one with such a lackluster record and astounding level of unpopularity, was worth whatever he cost.

"This sounds interesting," Ali murmured before he took a long draw on the hookah. After holding it for a long period he exhaled a large cloud in Walters's direction. Walters nearly fell over. The smell was oddly pungent and seemed familiar. After a moment of careful sniffing, it came to him. Cannabis. Ali and his watchdog were sharing a huge doobie.

Well, what the hell. Maybe Allah had a thing against alcohol but not weed.

Ali selected a nice plump date from the bowl and studied it. "How much have you laid out so far?" he asked.

"About 128 million, between the purchase of the company and a fee to the finder. Then twenty million or so, for . . . well, let's call it marketing expenses."

Ali's eyebrows shot up. "Twenty million?"

"Yeah, I know."

"The price has gone up, Daniel."

"Everything's going up. The price of buying an election. The price of holding the seat. The bastards pass on these costs to us, their customers." Bellweather leaned back and stretched his legs. The effort to twist his old body to mimic Ali's contorted position was killing him. "Their greed is astonishing."

"So all told, what, nearly 150 million?"

"More or less. We project another 250 million for production costs and assorted odds and ends. Raw materials, factory upgrades, new equipment, that sort of thing."

"How much will you charge the government?" Ali asked.

"Impossible to say at this point. Depends how many vehicles they want coated. And how fast."

"Yes, yes," Ali said in a knowing tone. "Cut the bullshit, Daniel, it's me. How much?"

Bellweather considered a bluff or a lie, but this was Ali bin Tariq; he was better wired in this town than the CIA and FBI combined. Finding it impossible to hide the proud smile, he said, "Conservatively, eight billion the first year."

Without missing a beat, Ali said, "A sixteenfold markup. You're talking almost a two thousand percent return."

Bellweather attempted a humble shrug that quickly turned into a loud smirk. It was impossible to act humble about this. "Yes, it's a beautiful thing, isn't it?"

"My God." Ali's eyes lit up. He had to take another deep draw from the hookah. Walters was getting high off the exhaust.

"We're at the stage now of turning this into a joint venture," Bellweather informed him, suddenly very businesslike. "The risks are minuscule at this point. No, they're negligible. But we like to take care of our friends."

"How much can we get in for?" Ali asked without hesitation. His eyes looked like smokeholes but his instinct for business was perfectly lucid. Bellweather wasn't at all surprised. In the old days, Ali could have sex all night long, slug down two bottles of scotch for breakfast, and still pilot his plane from Florida to Vail. His stamina was legendary.

"Depends," said Bellweather.

"On what, Daniel?"

"The buy-in's five hundred million."

"What a coincidence. All your up-front and production costs."

"Yes, and that's not the least bit unreasonable. All the risks were up-front. It's in the bag now."

"And suppose we are interested — I'm not saying we are — what's our percentage?"

Bellweather paused for a moment. "Well,

we're structuring it differently this time, Ali. It's unique. We're not offering a stake in equity."

"I don't understand."

"This is a high-profile project. It's likely to generate a lot of attention. Having foreigners out front might create a bit of a problem. The money will be carried on the books as dummy accounts. It has to be invisible."

Left unsaid though certainly understood was that the Saudis could not funnel money to Sunni insurgents in Iraq with one hand and be seen reaping financial benefits from the American war effort with the other. They couldn't simultaneously fund bombers and their bombs, and reap profits from protecting against those explosives — at least not publicly.

"So what do we get?" Ali asked, glossing over the obvious conflict of interest.

"A guaranteed return, and that's more than enough," Bellweather insisted. "Double your money in one year, with no risks. Think of it like a short-term loan with a spectacular return. It'll make your father very happy, Ali. Five hundred million into one billion, almost overnight."

"I don't like it." Ali threw down the hookah pipe and drew back into a sullen slump. "Ownership is important to us. You know this, Daniel. A piece of the pie, something long-term."

"Too bad for you," Bellweather snarled. He pushed off his hands and started to get up. "You're about to make our Taiwanese friends very happy. They want in, and they're not placing any stupid, picky conditions."

"Wait."

Bellweather collapsed back on his ass. No effort, this time, to contort himself into a sitting pretzel. His left knee was killing him.

Ali sat for a moment puffing away, contemplating the deal. After a moment he suggested, "It would only be possible if a Saudi was present as adviser. Five hundred million is a great deal of money, Daniel." He shared a quiet look with Bellweather his watchdog wasn't meant to catch.

A moment passed before Bellweather figured out the nature of this odd request. "You know what?" he said. "That would be helpful. But it would have to be someone seasoned, someone Washington-savvy."

Ali's face wrinkled with disappointment. He sighed as though a terrible burden was being placed on his shoulders. "And I suppose this adviser would be forced to spend a great deal of time here, in Washington?"

"I'm afraid that's absolutely necessary."

"It would require constant trips back and forth."

"Nearly continuous," Bellweather said, scowling. "And long stays."

"He would need an apartment," Ali announced.

In addition to providing the imam watchdog for company, Ali's father was keeping an iron fist on his wallet. Sin, particularly in America, was expensive.

"Perhaps he would agree to use our luxury condominium. Large and sumptuous, three bedrooms, an indoor sauna, great view of the Potomac."

"Your hospitality is overwhelming."

"We'll do our best to make his stays as comfortable as possible."

Ali tried his best to hide the boisterous smile as they shook.

17

On December 2 the House of Representatives met to vote on HR 3708, a discretionary appropriations bill to authorize two years of payments for CG's amazing polymer. It had been sent to Congress off-cycle, which was not unusual in the crush of war. The originating request had come out of the Pentagon. It was a short, direct plea for a fast-track, noncompetitive authorization, another common feature of a chaotic war. The needs and safety of the troops did not adhere to inconvenient schedules.

The floor debate was brief and uneventful. A few lonely voices tried to raise a squawk, but the tally was decisive: 415 in favor, 20 against.

The measure had popped out of the House Armed Services Committee only a few days before, and after Earl rubbed a few elbows in the Speaker's office, it sped to the larger body for a floor vote.

Representative Drew Teller of Michigan, reeling under intense pressure from General Techtonics, made a spirited attempt at opposition. The committee vote to push back the GT 400 had caught him completely flat-footed, and put him miserably behind in the race to capture all those Pentagon dollars. Obviously it had been an ambush. And just as obviously, it was a creation orchestrated and skillfully executed by Earl Belzer. In the days afterward, the executives of General Techtonics and representatives from the many loudmouthed lobbying firms in its employ flooded Teller's office with calls and visits to get to the bottom of this.

Money and favors were leaking out of Earl's office like lava from a volcano, their sources informed them. Big money. The kind of dough that could only mean big corporate backing, but by who? Where was Earl getting the juice from? And why?

The answers to those questions became crystal clear when the legislation authorizing the Capitol Group's polymer sprinted through Earl's committee, got greased on a fast track through the Speaker's office, and in almost record time ended up on the floor for a full vote.

It was a classic rush job: notice of the House vote came with less than twenty-four hours' warning. Poor Teller did his best to rally the troops. He called in every favor. He made more promises than he could begin to meet. He called and begged and cried to everyone in reach trying to muster opposition. It was Drew's finest hour. He worked tirelessly throughout the night, working the phones, leaving no stone unturned, fighting this measure like an all-out war. The result was as pathetic as it was predictable.

Drew was no competition for Earl Belzer. He could not begin to match Earl in tenure or legislative acumen; nor, try as he might, in sleaziness. He was a pretty-boy second-termer from a small, insignificant Michigan district that was choking to death on closed factories. His lone claim to fame was his marriage to the daughter of a former governor, a rather homely girl with few prospects. In return for taking the ugly cow off his hands, the governor fixed his election.

On his own, in fact, Teller was only able to collect serious commitments for a paltry two votes against. One was a scoundrel facing a certain indictment for graft, who wanted to go out with his middle finger waving in the air. The other was a boisterous, pony-tailed radical from San Francisco who, as a matter of firm liberal principle, opposed any defense spending.

Aside from this pair of notorious oddballs, nobody wanted to be seen voting against a measure to protect the troops, much less one that had been the object of so much favorable press in recent days.

Earl, in a particularly nasty tactic, arranged for the vote to occur at midday, then persuaded his friends in C-SPAN to air it repetitively into the night. He bused in a small army of military wives and parents. They arrived at dawn and stood on the steps of the Capitol building, handing out a slick brochure filled with before-and-after shots of soldiers wounded and killed by IEDs and terrorists' bombs. The brochure was bluntly titled *Let's See Who Cares About the Troops,* and closed with a dire warning that America was watching.

At the last moment, though, Earl had second thoughts. A total shellacking might raise suspicions of a fix, so he ordered seventeen of his friends to vote against. Not an impressive amount of opposition, but a respectable showing. All were either in safe districts or doomed to certain defeat in the upcoming election. Their votes were meaningless and harmless.

Afterward, Teller sent him a short note of thanks for absolving him from a total humiliation.

That same afternoon, members of the House and Senate met in conference and compared bills, the usual procedure when considering a massive splurge of taxpayer money. The meeting was cordial and went smoothly. Oddly enough, their committee bills regarding the polymer were almost identically worded, as if they'd been written by the same hand.

By late evening, via a hasty voice vote, the authorization for two years of spending on the polymer was approved by both the House and the Senate.

Jack was seated in Walters's big office, along with Bellweather, Haggar, and a ragtag gaggle of the boys from the LBO section, waiting for the call to come. They had gathered together at five, after receiving the welcome news about the House vote. Now they were awaiting confirmation by both the House and Senate. Though the outcome was nearly certain at this point, the tension in the room was thick as grease. A few were smoking. The head of LBO couldn't stop pacing from wall to wall. Bellweather repeatedly mumbled dire warnings about nothing being certain in love or politics; on both counts, he should know. Every five minutes,

Walters speed-dialed somebody on the Hill and demanded an update.

Jack leaned against a wall, arms crossed, and said little. Though he had brought them this breakthrough product, he was obviously an outsider, and even more obviously, he was now seen as the guest who had stayed at the party long past his welcome.

The call didn't come until seven. Though Jack couldn't hear the voice on the other end, he was sure it was Earl himself calling to take credit.

Walters held the receiver to his ear. Very gradually, acquiring velocity with each word he heard, he broke into a huge grin. "Uh, okay," he muttered. Another pause, then, "Listen, we can't thank you enough."

Another brief pause to listen, then, "No, that doesn't mean we intend to offer you a bonus."

He closed his eyes and, without looking, hung up. A table was positioned in the corner of his office. Six ice buckets sat there holding enough chilled bottles of Dom Perignon to inebriate a herd of horses. All eyes were on his face.

Finally, ever so slowly, the eyes cracked open and Walters whispered, "Break out the champagne."

The loud cheer was followed by a mad

dash to the corner table. The sound of corks being popped occupied the next thirty seconds. After fifteen minutes of loudly toasting and congratulating one another, the meeting began to break up. The LBO boys needed to rush back downstairs. Time to get back to their unending hunt for more targets, more takeovers, more ways to increase the ballooning wealth of the behemoth known as the Capitol Group.

Jack and Bellweather ended up alone with Walters. Mitch had his feet up on the desk, guzzling champagne straight from the bottle, like it came out of a firehose. His shirtfront was drenched, he was gulping it down so fast. Walters pulled the bottle away from his lips just long enough to ask Bellweather, "Ever seen a deal come together so beautifully?"

"Never, not once. From concept to legislation in two months. I'm sure it's a record. How much did Earl say they authorized?" he asked.

"You're gonna love this."

"Spill it."

"We asked for sixteen billion spread over two years."

"I know. I did the asking."

"On his own, Earl added another four billion."

"Twenty billion," Bellweather said, almost unable to believe it himself. Twenty! CG had produced some sweet deals in its run, but nothing remotely comparable to this.

Jack was still sipping from his first glass of bubbly and he broke up their mutual congratulations, saying in a tone of clear admiration, "I have to admit I never imagined this could happen so fast."

"You came to the right place," Walters boasted. "Didn't we tell you that at the beginning?"

"I never doubted you for a minute. I just thought . . ." Jack shrugged and let that thought trail off.

Walters was uncorking another bottle with his big hands. "You thought what?"

"I thought there'd be more testing, for one thing."

"Already done." The cork popped out and a big gusher flowed over the sides of the bottle into Walters's lap. "Remember? You gave us the results."

"Yeah, but those were done by private contractors, not Defense people."

"So what?" Walters bent forward and splashed champagne into his goblet. Half of it spilled onto his desk. Between the victory and the bubbly he was giddy. "The tests were done in Iraq, in real-life, authentic conditions. We're in a war and time is a definite consideration. The Pentagon chief of research, development, testing, and evaluation was also at that big demonstration we threw out at Belvoir. He saw the results firsthand."

"And that was enough?"

"Apparently so."

"What about production and quality control reviews?"

"What about 'em?"

"Look, I'm no expert in defense contracting," Jack said, almost apologetically. "I read some of the regulations, though. There are a lot of hoops, multiple stages, a regular maze. An evaluation stage, cost analysis, production control restraints, establishing oversight systems."

"We *are* experts in defense contracting, Jack."

"I know you are. I'm just asking how it works."

"They were willing to cut a few corners for us, okay? Why not? We're a certified contractor with a long record. Besides, we're leapfrogging this program on our contract for uparmoring Humvees. It's a long-established program, already in country. The same crews and facilities will be used to apply the polymer."

"I want to be sure you're not getting me into any trouble. Tell me you're not."

Walters just stared back. After learning about Jack and the dirty games he had played at Primo, the decision had been made to cut him out of the loop as much as possible. For starters, they now had a few serious trust issues; Jack, after all, might be a killer, a swindler, and a blackmailer.

For another, as soon as TFAC came back with the goods, Jack was history. The partnership contract was going into the trash. His ass was going to be out on the street.

At this point, the less he knew, the better.

"Don't worry about it," Walters snapped, as though Jack were an ingrate. They'd just turned him into a potential billionaire, after all, and here he was, yapping about the details. "Just be damned glad this happened so fast."

"I'm so happy I can barely express myself. But as your partner, I thought I had a right to know." Jack leaned on his desk and looked him in the eye. "I am still your partner, aren't I?"

"Oh, sure." Walters and Bellweather locked eyes in a way that Jack wasn't meant to catch. "We always honor our contracts," Bellweather said very solemnly.

"Glad to hear it." Jack put down his

champagne flute and backed off.

"You have nothing to worry about," Walters lied. "We'll definitely take care of you," he promised with a rubbery smile.

Andrew Morgan had begun to feel he was chasing ghosts. He easily got his hands on a complete personnel roster for Primo Investments, circa 1998, the year Jack departed the firm for calmer waters.

The CEO that year was one Terrence Kyle II, graduate of Yale and the highly esteemed Wharton School of Business. His CFO was Gordon Sullivan, Harvard undergrad, Harvard Business. They were the two who caught Jack, the same two who tried to enlist him in another scheme, and then, eventually, the two who cooked up the questionable deal to pay him a million bucks to go away.

A quick search through Nexis revealed that Terrence and Gordon died in a tragic plane crash less than a year later. A little more digging revealed the circumstances.

In December of that year, six months after they parted ways with Jack, they rented a small private jet and flew to a glitzy investors' conference in Vail. After three days of mingling with their fellow financial pirates, of partying and boozing and hitting the slopes, they took off in a snowstorm and promptly flew into a mountainside. The jet was instantly obliterated. All aboard were lost. The bodies were atomized by the collision and/or the ensuing fire. The National Transportation Safety Board conducted the investigation.

The private jet had been leased from a small firm that catered to the rich and famous. That firm had an excellent safety record. The pilot and copilot were both former military — both in good health, both had extensive flying careers, both had flawless records. The controllers in the tower testified that the storm had let up enough to allow a safe takeoff, and in their view weather wasn't a factor. The cause of the crash was listed as pilot error, a conclusion based on nothing particularly definitive. It was the catchall phrase the NTSB often used when no specific cause could be found.

Nothing strange about this. An aviation expert Morgan tracked down informed him that NTSB investigations involving private aircraft sometimes weren't all that thorough or extensive. In a typical year, the NTSB investigated several hundred accidents. It was a small agency, overworked, bouncing from one disaster to another. Unless an accident involved a commercial airline, a high-profile celebrity death, an excessive death toll, or there was cause for unusual suspicion, the investigators tended not to probe too deeply.

But factored in with Charles's tale about Edith Warbinger, Morgan couldn't avoid feeling that the timely deaths of Kyle and Sullivan were terribly convenient for Jack. A mysterious airplane crash that wiped out the two men who knew the most about Jack and Edith — was it too convenient?

When further research revealed that three board members from those years also were dead, under interesting circumstances, Morgan had a strong sense he was on to something. Were they all part of a cabal to get Edith's money? He had to consider the possibility that Jack might have been clearing up the loose ends, eliminating any witnesses he left behind. If he could kill an old lady in cold blood, after all, what was the harm in killing a few more? Jack might be much naughtier than they thought.

First up was Paul Nussman, banged by a car as he bicycled through Manhattan. The collision was so violent that Nussman flew sixty feet before he was impaled on a fire hydrant. A hit-and-run, midday, yet no witnesses, no pictures. The killer was never found.

Bernard Kohlman fell off a ladder and broke his neck as he cleaned the gutter of his Greenwich home. He was sixty-two, a severe acrophobe, arthritic, overweight, lazy, with no history as a handyman. His wife told the police she didn't even know they owned a ladder.

And Phillip Grossman committed suicide; his body was discovered hanging from the balcony in a gay movie theater. He was a closet homosexual, and though his secret was well-known, he went to great lengths to conceal his lifestyle. A public death in such an incriminating manner and place seemed spectacularly out of character.

Apparently those were not healthy years to be a senior executive or a board member at Primo.

The first living survivor of the firm Morgan decided to track down was Marigold Anders, executive assistant to Terrence Kyle II, the now deceased CEO. Assistants were always a fount of inside dirt; they tended to be gabby, too.

Anders, it turned out, lived on Long Island, in the quaint town of Montauk, as far east as you could travel before you dropped into the ocean. He called and identified himself as a federal officer performing a routine background check on Jack. The standard spiel.

Marigold said yes, of course she remembered Jack. When he invited himself out for an interview that afternoon, she said she had nothing better to do, then hung up. He took that as permission to drop by.

After a long, traffic-choked drive on the LIE, Morgan rolled into her dirt driveway at five in the evening. Marigold lived outside the town in a small clapboard house surrounded by flat potato fields and the occasional picturesque winery. It seemed as far from New York City as she could get, physically and spiritually.

He spent a moment taking in the house as he parked. The outside screamed for a thorough painting, there were missing shingles on the roof, the yard was wildly unkempt, and the car in the driveway was a model so old he didn't recognize it. With a cracked windshield, missing hubcaps, a patchwork of oxidized paint, the heap should've been junked ten years ago. After ringing the bell twice — he doubted it worked — he wound his way around the house to the back.

He found Marigold there, hunched over in a rusted green lounge chair, puffing a cigarette and staring into the distance.

He introduced himself and produced the shiny badge O'Neal had issued him.

"Have a seat," she said, casually pointing at another rusted wreck about five feet away from her chair.

He eased carefully into the chair — one of the four legs was barely holding on by a thin strip of rusted metal — and studied her a moment. Probably a looker in her day, but age and wrinkles of bitterness had taken a steep toll. Late sixties, he guessed, with the leathery skin and deep rasp of a lifelong smoker. It was a cold late December evening, and she wore a ratty blue overcoat that, like her, was well past its prime.

He yanked out a notebook and assumed a professional demeanor. "You said you used to work with Jack Wiley. Mind if I ask a few questions?"

"You the one who called this morning?"

"Yes, ma'am."

"You drove all the way out here, didn't you?"

Oh, great, Morgan thought. Getting anything out of this sour old prune was going to be worse than a Sunday afternoon with his wife's church group. But he'd made the long drive and was determined to come back with something.

"How well did you know Jack?" he asked.

"Not very. I was the CEO's executive assistant. He was just a lowly associate."

Morgan pretended to read from a list of questions in his notebook. "Did you have a good impression of him?"

"Sure, he was cute." She waved her cigarette in the air and cackled. "Nice ass, too."

"Do you believe him to be trustworthy, to possess good qualities and character?"

"Well, I wouldn't know about that, would I?"

"Wouldn't you?"

"Wasn't like I did any work with him. I was a glorified secretary, for godsakes."

He made a brief entry in his notebook before he launched another official-sounding question. "How long did your time at Primo overlap?"

"Oh, I don't know." Marigold sucked a deep cloud of smoke into her lungs as she thought about that a moment. "Two . . . no, I think, more like three years."

Morgan decided to edge gently into this. "Did you ever know Jack to get into any trouble with the authorities?"

"You mean cops?"

"Them, or any other legal authorities."

"If he did, I sure as hell didn't know about it."

"Did Jack have any problems at the firm?

You worked for the CEO. Anything that came to his attention?"

Marigold frowned at him. "That sort of stuff was always treated real confidential. You know, kept behind closed doors."

"But did you ever hear about anything? A stray comment from your boss? Watercooler rumor, that sort of thing?"

"Why? He in trouble or something?"

"Not at all, no. Just a background check." Morgan worked up his most reassuring grin. The old hag was a nosy pain in the ass. "Sorry if I'm wasting your time, ma'am. I'm required to ask these questions."

"Well, I don't know nothin' about any of that."

"The name Edith Warbinger mean anything to you?"

"Nope. Should it?"

"Jack handled her investments back then. A large account, a mountain of money."

"I told you, I never heard of her."

"Okay, you're doing fine. Can you tell me what happened to your boss?"

"Why?"

"We're trying to track him down. Can't seem to locate him anywhere."

"Are you Feds always this incompetent?"

"What do you mean?"

"Well, ain't like he moved anywhere in a

decade," she said with a dismissive smile. "Check Flushing Cemetery."

"He's dead?"

"No, he bought a condo there. 'Course he's dead, you idiot. Bastard bought it back in '98." There was a slight slur to her diction. Morgan was sure she'd been drinking.

"No kidding," Morgan said, acting surprised. "Heart attack, stroke, what?"

"Plane crash. Too bad, too."

"Yes, it's always sad. So young, such a promising life cut short."

"No, you fool, I was always hoping he'd die slow and agonizing. Maybe catch some exotic disease, some particularly nasty, lingering kind of cancer. Guess he got lucky."

"You didn't like him?"

"He was a lousy, rotten crook. Real bastard to work for." She crushed out a butt on the ground and immediately fired up another.

Morgan pretended to make another small notation in his notebook, casually mentioning, "I'm surprised we missed it. A plane wreck, huh?"

"Yeah, him and that so-called CFO. Another real creep. They got stir-fried together against a mountainside."

"Accident?"

"Why? You thinkin' I did it?" She stopped and cackled, then it quickly developed into a nasty smoker's hack.

He waited till the wracking noise stopped, then said, "Just, you know, it's a little weird. We've tried to track down several of Primo's board members from those years. Three of them — Nussman, Kohlman, Grossman — they're all dead."

"Are they?"

"Very."

"Too bad." Didn't sound that way, though.

"Unhealthy place to work, huh?"

"Are you through?" she asked, stirring in her chair.

So far he had nothing. She was wearing her affection for Jack on her sleeve. Nothing interesting was going to come from the old hag unless he played it a little smarter. He gave her a hard, menacing stare as if he already knew the truth. "Thing is, a few sources told us there were serious tensions between Jack and your boss."

"What sources?"

"I'm afraid I can't divulge that."

"You need to talk to better people, bud. As I remember, Jack was too canny to get caught in Kyle's crosshairs. Real smart boy, that one." She stood and brushed a few ashes off her coat.

"Then maybe you can help me here. Do you remember any of Jack's close friends in the firm?"

A quick shrug. "He was an associate, I was the boss's assistant. Wasn't like we went out for drinks every night. I was too old for him anyways." She finished off her cigarette and lazily tossed it into a clump of wild bushes.

"Please, this could be helpful. A few people dumped on Jack. Personally, I like him. I'd just like to balance the ledger a bit."

Marigold thought about it a moment. She obviously didn't trust him, but wanted to do Jack as much good as she could. "This is all I'll tell ya. Talk to his assistant."

"You have a name?"

"Yeah. Su Young . . . something. Chinese, maybe Korean."

"How about an address?"

By now she had her back turned and was walking back to the house. "Lazy government bastards," she remarked over her shoulder. "Go find her yourself."

18

The Pentagon office of the Defense Criminal Investigative Service was located in room 5E322, on the fifth floor, almost midway on the outermost ring, indisputably the least desirable location in a building known for its lack of pleasant accommodations. The fortified doors hid a windowless warren of cubicles, in essence a large walk-in safe due to the sensitive nature of the work done inside these walls.

The room was designed for no more than twenty. Currently, forty investigators and assistants were crammed and pigeonholed into the space, at risk of suffocation.

Nicholas Garner, chief of the financial crimes division, cursed as he banged a shin on a stray chair, and fought and squeezed his way through the terrible sprawl of office furniture. He finally reached the seventh cubicle on the left, where he dropped an armful of papers on the desk. "I need you to plow through this."

"When?"

"Today, Mia."

Mia pushed away what she was doing and looked up. "What is it?"

"Mendelson Refineries."

"Is this a quiz?"

"Midsize refining outfit. Located in Louisiana. Place called Garyville."

"Is there some particular suspicion I'm supposed to hunt down?"

"You tell me."

She picked up the thick stack of papers and began riffling through the pages. It was a chaotic mess — financial spreadsheets, billings, invoices, payment slips. Nicky had apparently ordered one of the overworked assistants to make a mad dash through the procurement directorate and dredge up every piece of paper dealing with Mendelson Refineries. It would take hours to go through it all. Then many more hours to separate the wheat from the chaff in a frenzied hunt for real evidence, if indeed any existed inside this mass of garbage. "Another inside tip?" she asked, sounding annoyed.

A quick nod. "Hotline, again. Male voice, anonymous, the usual. He swore up and down Mendelson's cheating us blind."

Mia sipped a Diet Coke and rolled her eyes.

Garner offered a stiff, apologetic smile. "I know, and I'm sorry. We did get a trace this time."

"And where did it originate?"

"Pay phone outside Garyville. Maybe another prank, might be real. Standard rule applies — you don't check, you don't know."

The hotline was a great idea that was rapidly souring into a dispiriting disaster. Sources were supposed to call the hotline number to report abuse or financial shenanigans, and this would trigger an investigation. The ratline, it was called. All tips were confidential and this was the beauty of it. No names, just blame.

The past few months, however, the hotline had been inundated with a suspiciously large number of reports of abuse or thievery. The callers were nearly all anonymous. All the calls had to be painstakingly looked into; very few panned out.

The heads of the DCIS now suspected that the industries that did business with the military were adding a new wrinkle to their never-ending ways to screw the government — send the investigators chasing after a flood of false leads and empty claims, and they would become too busy to watch and catch the real crooks. It seemed to be working, unfortunately. The room was full of bloodshot eyes. Sick days were shooting through the ceiling. Morale was sinking. Worse, since the calls picked up, overall convictions were down thirty percent.

Mia stared back in mock frustration. "Why me again, Nicky?"

Garner ignored the look and the comment. "The source claimed Mendelson's undercutting deliveries by two percent. Last year, the Navy bought a hundred million in jet fuel from the company. All told, about two million in fraud."

"Wonderful." At thirty-one, Mia Jenson had four years of practicing law in the private sector, and now two hard years under her belt laboring in the trenches of the DCIS. It was a small agency with big responsibilities.

And by almost every measure, Mia Jenson was its most bizarre member.

A graduate of Dickinson College, early, compacting four years into three, then she attended Harvard Law, where she shot to the top of the class. Not number one, but an incredibly close number two, and had she not overloaded on securities courses, number one would've eaten her dust. She concentrated on corporate and contracts;

two of her case studies made the law journal. She was associate editor of the law review her final year.

Beautiful, brilliant, fluent in two languages, she was courted and offered an associate job by twenty top firms. Almost all offered six figures with a dizzying array of perks.

She interviewed them. She spurned all offers to visit their firms; she insisted they come to her, peppered them with questions, and made it clear she was picky.

They didn't mind, or at least they pretended not to. She was hot, she was in demand. They wanted her.

She turned down the top fourteen offers and settled eventually on a small, quirky boutique firm in D.C., at half the salary of her top offer, but the promise of a fast track to partnership. The money meant nothing to her, she insisted. The challenge and the nature of the work were all that mattered.

That firm, Wendly and Wexer, specialized in cutting-edge corporate legal issues. Mainly its clients were oil companies, big communications firms, sports stars, and entertainment — all areas where laws, regulations, and contracts were constantly shifting.

For four years, Mia worked the twenty-hour days demanded of eager young associates with dreams of an early partnership rattling around their heads. Eventually the firm billed her out at $450 per hour — amazingly, a rate equaling that billed by full partners in many top firms.

One of her victories forced the FCC to change a long-standing law after she discovered a loophole and drove a truck through it.

The early partnership was hinted at, and she had no reason to doubt it.

Then out of the blue, one day, she walked into the office of the managing partner and politely handed him her resignation. He was stunned — his most promising associate, such a bright future, a billing machine, and she wanted to walk away.

Worse, she was a woman in a firm that was painfully overdue for a partner who wore lipstick. Also, like nearly every male in the firm, he secretly nursed a big crush on her.

He begged her to reconsider. She wouldn't, she said, with an expression that indicated she meant it. Did you get a better offer, he asked; come on, give us a chance to match it. Nope, not that, but she offered no other reason. Better partners to work with? A firm shake of the head; they've all been wonderful, absolutely great. A bigger office, better perks, nicer view, shorter hours? How about a one-year sabbatical to unwind and enjoy life?

No, no, no, to all of the above.

One week later, Mia entered nineteen weeks of rigorous training at the Basic Agent Course held at the Federal Law Enforcement Training Center. Then ten weeks bouncing around various Army bases where she mastered the byzantine world of the military procurement and contracting system.

A federal law enforcement agency, the Defense Criminal Investigative Service works under the Department of Defense's inspector general. The IG is the Pentagon watchdog, and DCIS is the IG's hammer, filled with boys and girls who carry real guns and nice gold shields. They investigate waste, fraud, terrorism, and theft, and they execute real warrants and make real arrests.

Based presumably on her background, Mia made a strong plea to be assigned to the financial crimes unit in the Pentagon, and that request landed on the desk of Nicky Garner. His office was ridiculously understaffed and scandalously overworked. With two wars raging and a defense budget ballooning out of sight, corporate graft was a huge growth business. It was as if a big sign hung outside the Pentagon — "Here's the jackpot, boys, come and grab it." A tenfold increase in investigators wouldn't have a prayer of keeping up. Almost any warm body would do.

Still, Nicky didn't know what to make of her.

For one thing, she was absurdly overqualified for a starter agent. Besides, how could anybody trade the fat paychecks and enviable perks of corporate law for a lowly starting government salary of $36,000? The best anybody could recall, no Harvard Law grad had ever worked as a special agent. Not one, ever.

Was she an eccentric, a power freak, or just plain nuts?

Nicky decided to initiate her in charge card fraud. It was menial, low-level work, busting small-time hustlers and crooks; it was also a perfect excuse to keep her under close scrutiny for a while. See if she had a screw loose, or scary aggression issues, or ran naked through the halls — it had all happened before.

When, after only three months, she surpassed the office record for arrests leading to prosecutions, Nicky changed his mind. She seemed perfectly normal, whatever the hell that meant these days. She was efficient, hardworking, and with her impressive background in law, a magician at building airtight cases. Nicky piled the work on her. She was already handling triple the caseload of a typical DCIS grunt.

The only peculiarity was that she preferred to work alone, with a curious tendency to be slightly secretive; she wasn't snobby or standoffish, though. She was a welcome addition at the Friday night happy hours when the investigators unwound from a long week of weeding out crooks and busting perps.

The past eleven months, she had been chasing the big-time white-collar crooks at the corporate level. And whatever doubts Nicky once harbored were a thing of the past.

"What else are you working on today?" Nicky asked, very reasonably, as though this was negotiable. It wasn't.

"A meeting with the prosecutors on the Boeing case. Case goes to court next week. Also, I need to take some depositions on the Phillips Aviation case." She waved a hand at the stack he had just placed on her desk, almost lost among all the other stacks. She was very neat and tidy but the profusion of paper was too much for such a small desk. "Don't worry, Nicky, I'll do it."

"Yes, you will. But thanks." Nicky turned around and began the torturous journey back to his office.

The moment he was out of sight, Mia pushed aside the documents dealing with Mendelson Refineries. She pulled out the stack she had hidden beneath another stack when Nicky surprised her and returned to the documents she had been reading.

In her right hand was the Senate bill providing funding for CG's polymer, in her left the House version of the same bill. She was halfway through the two pieces of legislation, meticulously comparing them line by line. They were identical, so far; even the periods and commas were identically placed.

Mendelson Refineries, even if the tip panned out, was worth, at best, only $2 million in fraud. She would study it later, only after she finished her own project.

A much bigger fish was in her sights.

It took Morgan a full day to track down Su Young O'Malley in a small, untidy row house in Queens, about midway on a long block of eerily identical homes. He'd wasted nearly a week locating her. The name change threw him for a full five days. After she left Primo, it turned out, she had married an

NYPD cop, produced four kids, and now lived the harried existence of stay-at-home mom.

Morgan could hear small kids squalling in the background when she came to the door. He withdrew his phony badge and gave her the usual cooked-up story about a routine background check.

She explained that she was alone with the kids, and quite busy. He assured her that he didn't mind; he would fit his questions in between diaper changes and feedings.

After a moment of indecision she caved and invited him in. The home was small and cramped, the floor covered with toys and child pens and enough kiddy bric-a-brac to outfit a Kids-R-Us superstore. Su Young immediately dashed over to a crib where a tiny runt in PJs was howling and flailing his arms.

She lifted him out, planted him firmly on a shoulder, and began to weave back and forth. After about fifteen seconds, the kid shut up. "What do you want to know?" she asked with a strong Brooklyn accent.

Morgan quickly took her through his repertoire of soft opening questions, the same ones he had tried out on Marigold Anders — was Jack a good boss, was he honest, forthright, a true red-white-and-blue American, and so forth.

Yes, all the above.

Then came an unwelcome break while she dashed into the kitchen for some mysterious purpose. He sat and listened to her banging around. She emerged a few minutes later, her hands loaded with feeding bottles. She tossed one at him. "Pick any kid you want and get to work," she ordered.

He chose the one who looked almost catatonic, put him on his lap, and stuffed the bottle between his lips. "You're not working anymore?" he asked, an attempt to be friendly.

"Nope."

"All these kids, I guess. Good call."

"No, I quit before the kids."

"Why?"

"Working for Jack was a ball. After he left, I got stuck with a slimy jerk. One of those guys with a fetish for Asian girls. Know what I mean? Always touching me, always making lewd comments. 'Hey, open my zipper and read your fortune, cookie. Why don't you chop on my stick?' And those were his best lines. I got creeped out and quit."

"Should've reported him."

"Hah! Good luck. It's Wall Street. Boys will be boys."

Morgan paused for a moment. Who cared?

"Do you remember a client named Edith Warbinger?"

For a moment she looked confused, and he was ready to end it there. But she popped a palm off her forehead. "Oh, you mean Mrs. Warbitcher."

"Yeah, I guess. How much do you remember about her?"

"A lot. Too much. Our most high-maintenance account."

"I heard from someone that she had Parkinson's."

"Only later. She was just very, well, let's say demanding."

This didn't match what Charles had told him, about a sweet, naïve old lady who had entrusted Jack with everything. Maybe it was a matter of perspective. "In what ways?" he inched forward and asked.

"What way wasn't she? She thought that bundle of dough gave her the right to be that way. She'd had a miserable life, and after the money came in, took it out on everybody. Drove Jack and me crazy."

"I heard she went on a long cruise."

"Oh that." Su Young laughed. "What a relief. For us, I mean. I'm sure it was miserable for the cruise line."

"Then she disappeared, right?"

"Someplace in Greece, I think."

"Any idea what happened to her?"

"My guess would be the crew tossed her overboard. I hate to speak ill of the dead, but she really was a demanding bitch."

"That bad, huh?"

"I could tell you stories for an hour."

"What did Jack do when she disappeared?" he asked, before the stories could start.

"He, or maybe the firm, hired some private detectives. For good or bad, she was our client. Jack insisted on it."

"Was she ever found?" Morgan asked.

"What's this got to do with Jack's background check?" She was staring at him with growing suspicion now.

"Just following up on something somebody mentioned. Please bear with me."

"No, she wasn't found."

"And this was right around the time Jack left the firm?"

"I suppose it was around then."

"Why did Jack leave?"

"Why don't you ask him?"

"We did. I'm corroborating. Please answer."

Su Young pondered this for a moment, as though she had never considered the question. "You know what I thought? I don't think he was *ever* happy there."

"Wanted to make more money, huh?"

"No. I mean, I guess who doesn't, right? Just, well, it wasn't a nice place to work. Cutthroat, dog-eat-dog. Plenty of backstabbing and unhappy people."

"Did Jack have any problems with the CEO?"

"You mean Kyle?"

A quick nod. "I heard they were at each other's throats."

"No, he . . . well, they all loved Jack. He brought in so much money, the big shots pretty much left him alone. Even gave him a million-dollar bonus when he walked out the door. Should've been a lot more, given what he did for them, you ask me."

Morgan had a long list of questions left to ask but it would be a waste of time to prolong this. Jack's more questionable activities evidently did not make it down to the secretarial level, which came as no surprise. Morgan put down the baby and stood. He straightened his jacket, then slapped his head. "Oh, one last question."

Su Young was already out of her chair and moving for the child he had just put down. The kid was making fast tracks for the hot radiator in the corner, but she snatched him off the floor just in time.

As nonchalantly as possible, Morgan

asked, "Do you remember who introduced Jack to the firm? They must've been close. Another Princeton grad, I think."

"Tough question." She paused for a moment. "All the Wall Street firms are loaded with Ivy studs. But Jack was always pretty close with Lew Wallerman. I think they knew each other before."

Morgan thanked her, then walked out and closed the door quietly behind him. He stopped for a moment on the porch, withdrew the copy of Primo's personnel chart, and began running his finger down the page, scanning for Wallerman.

The thirtieth line down, there he was, listed as working in wealth management, just like Jack.

"You're Charles, and I got you," he said out loud, and laughed.

19

By the second week of January, polymer-coated vehicles of all sorts were flying off the line. Humvees, Bradleys, M1 tanks, even the newest addition to the combat fleet, the Stryker, were lined up bumper-to-bumper to get a lifesaving face-lift. Fights broke out between the crews as they jockeyed to be next in line; the alternative was a long wait in a country where bombing had become the national sport.

FOB Falcon; Camp Graceland; Rasheed Airbase; Camp Cuervo; Engineer Base Anvil; Camp Whitford; Camp Whitehouse, FOB Rustamiyah, Baghdad — all had painting facilities that were beehives of activity. Converting the same crews who had been armor-plating the vehicles into painting teams proved to be kid's play.

Even after spreading the chemical production around five different facilities located in five different states, the frenetic effort to supply sufficient quantities of the polymer fell abysmally short. Five or six large batches arrived in Iraq improperly mixed and had to be dumped, late at night, into nearby Iraqi rivers. Every other day, it seemed, the painting in Iraq ground to a halt. Quality control was another problem. Complaints poured back to the Pentagon about slipped schedules, shoddy workmanship, and the slapdash, miserably managed nature of the entire operation.

The leaders of CG weathered the storm of criticism the same way they had withstood the old chorus of complaints about its uparmoring program, a program that had also experienced notable problems. They ignored it. Frankly, it came as little surprise. The same inept managers oversaw the polymer application, the same lackadaisical crews worked three-hour shifts, stole off for long lunch breaks, and retreated to their air-conditioned trailers by three every afternoon for prolonged happy hours.

CG fell back on the tried-and-tested excuse that it was hard to hire good people for long-term duty in a scary war zone. What they wouldn't admit was the bigger truth: in an effort to pump up profits, at the pitiful wages they were offering, nobody with half a brain would consider working for CG in Iraq.

After a while, once the noise grew too loud, CG shipped over a few new bodies and added night crews who quickly adopted the local work habits and managed to produce only a minor improvement.

But the results were spectacular, if you ignored the occasional blemish. In the first month, out of twenty attacks, only three coated vehicles were destroyed by roadside bombs. In each case, as investigations later revealed, the cause was faulty workmanship; CG's coating crews had somehow, incredibly, overlooked the need to paint the whole vehicle.

To manage the finances of this exploding new company, CG assigned a veteran CFO, a carefully chosen executive well seasoned in defense contracts, who promptly handpicked a team of cutthroats with similar backgrounds. Military contracting officials were notoriously overworked and outnumbered, and often were far less skilled than their private-sector counterparts. CG's team knew all the tricks, and took them to the max.

They padded the hours, added hundreds of ghost workers on the ground, jacked the cost of materials and production facilities through the ceiling, and double-billed as often as they thought they could get away with. And why not? The risks were almost inconsequential; in the unlikely event they were caught, a light slap on the wrist was the worst they could expect. The polymer was far too vital for the Pentagon to even consider anything as drastic as a punitive cancellation.

But if the incredible happened, and the Pentagon caught on, CG would express contrition, reassign its managers, pay a small penalty, and bring in a new team of clever shysters who would start over with the same tricks.

Eva continued to drop in at Jack's like clockwork, every week. Their relationship seemed to be going nowhere fast, but she persisted. After all these months, they still hadn't slept together, still hadn't shared anything more passionate than a breezy peck on the cheek.

Jack's visits to D.C. had tapered off to a predictable routine. Once a week, he made a quick drop-by visit to his small office in CG's headquarters to make the rounds and get updates on the polymer. Even those trips had turned into a waste of his time. The executives who had been so open and communicative in the early stages seemed to have developed collective lockjaw. Nobody would admit it, but somebody had put out the word to ignore him.

A month before, Mitch Walters had coldly informed him of a new requirement: if he wanted to meet with the CEO, an appointment booked at least two weeks in advance was required. No problem, fine by him, Jack replied.

He had yet to call for an appointment. For over a month, he had not spoken with either Bellweather or Walters. They could cold-shoulder and shove him aside as much as they liked, as far as Jack was concerned; he had something they couldn't ignore in that big contract, after all.

He owned a quarter of the polymer and its earnings.

By the way the cherry red Camry corkscrewed into Jack's driveway, mowing down three bushes before it squealed to a grinding stop, the TFAC watcher wondered whether she was drunk, furious, or both. After five months of observing Jack's home the watcher couldn't wait for this job to end. He was bored and miserable. The excitement Eva's visits once prompted was a thing of the past. The betting game had long since been discarded; there were no longer any odds on whether Jack and Eva would or wouldn't.

Jack, for whatever reason — and many had been deliciously debated over the months — simply had no intention of letting Eva into his sack.

They admired his humbling willpower, and detested his indifference.

The TFAC man watched Eva stumble out the car and weave her way precariously to Jack's front door. "She's both," he blurted into the microphone connecting him to the man parked in the van at the end of the block.

"What are you talking about?"

"Eva. She's back, rotten drunk, and pissed enough to throw a punch. Old Jack's about to get an earful." He rolled down his window and listened. What fun. He was parked nearby, across the street, in the driveway of a young couple who were off on a European safari for a month. He could hear everything.

Eva pounded loudly on Jack's door and stood there, swaying back and forth. "Jack, you bastard, come to the door. Come on, open up, I know you're there." She was bellowing loud enough for the whole neighborhood to hear, nearly the whole county. Lights began popping on in bedrooms. A few faces crowded up to windows.

After about a minute of her hollering and banging, the door opened. Jack stood there in his bathrobe. He invited her inside but she refused. "I'd rather have it out, here, buster. I want the whole neighborhood to hear this," she announced at the top of her lungs. She was definitely getting her wish.

"If that's what you want, fine," Jack said, remarkably smooth and patient. He crossed his arms and leaned against the doorjamb. "What's this about, Eva? What's the matter?"

"You just shut up, 'cause this is my show. I'll do the asking." Her speech was slurred; the s's came out with h's, and the t's virtually disappeared. She was totally, utterly smashed.

Jack shrugged.

"How long have I known you?" Eva demanded.

"Seven months, more or less."

"Am I ugly?"

"No. You're very, very beautiful."

"You got a problem? Some fetish I don't satisfy? Whatsa matter with me, Jack? Boobs too small? Butt not big enough? Too easy, not easy enough, what?"

He smiled and tried to get her to relax. When she didn't smile back he said, "It's cold, come inside."

She leaned forward and gave Jack a strong blast of whiskey breath.

"You're drunk, Eva. You're making a fool of yourself."

"What if I said I'm in love with you, Jack?"

"That's nice. I like you, too. I just don't like to be rushed."

She swayed drunkenly from side to side. She was beautiful. Even drunk, with messy hair and slack, boozy features, she was still beautiful, and sexy. When she nearly toppled over, Jack reached out and grabbed her arm. She brushed it off. "Why haven't you ever kissed me?"

"Maybe I'm too busy to get involved right now. Maybe the timing's not right. Listen, you drove all the way up here, you've been drinking, and you're unsafe on the roads at any speed. Come inside. Let me put some food in your stomach."

The watcher nearly slammed a fist on the dashboard. Food in her stomach? Wrong combination, you jerk. A stunning woman is standing outside your door, she's inebriated and loose, and desperately wanting something more than polite conversation and a light kiss. Come on, Jack, he felt like jumping up and screaming — be a man. All these months of frustration, give her a night to remember. Just do it out of pity.

Suddenly the air seemed to go out of Eva. Her shoulders slumped and she sagged against the doorjamb. "Can I spend the night?" she asked, sounding suddenly both tired and meek.

"I think you'd better."

"With you?"

"Don't push it."

The watcher could hear her sobbing as she stepped inside.

Definitely, Lew Wallerman was not Charles.

He was short and very, very black, for one thing. Morgan wondered how a black man ended up with a name like Wallerman, but was afraid to ask.

He wore decrepit clothes that were loud evidence of indescribably awful taste — brown checkered suit that would be hard to push at a Goodwill sale, blue-and-white polka-dot tie, and thickly striped shirt that was a mass of wrinkles and stains. His scuffed black shoes were at least ten years old and hadn't smelled polish in years.

Lew Wallerman had loser written all over him.

They were seated in a small, shabby pub in Manhattan. It was midday but Wallerman had insisted they meet at this bar. He lost no time showing Morgan why. The place was rowdy, and seemed to attract the model crowd, meaning a small tribe of cadaverous young skeletons in petite skirts and enough leering men to make it worth their while. Wallerman had barely fallen into his seat before he ordered two beers with a scotch chaser. He was on his lunch break, he'd told Morgan. He ate out of a glass.

"So what's this about?" he asked Morgan.

"Jack Wiley."

The name struck an immediate chord. He bent forward and placed his elbows on the table. "Jack, huh? What trouble is he in this time?"

Morgan's heart skipped three beats. He swallowed hard and tried to keep his voice normal, his expression only vaguely interested. "What makes you think that?"

"It's Jack. Always just a matter of time with old Jack."

"Tell me about that."

"You know Jack? Ever met him?"

"Not really," Morgan confessed.

The elbows came off the table. Wallerman offered a smug, knowing smile. "Just say that Jack's always working some sleazy angle or another. A smooth operator with a million shady ideas."

This sounded so good, but Morgan decided to inch into it. "You knew him in college?"

"Yeah, I knew him." He launched into a tiresome spiel about their relationship, from beginning to end. They were separated by a year, and pursued different majors, but were both in the same eating club, Princeton's peculiar variation on a fraternity. Both were always busy and caught up in separate pursuits, Jack with classes and lacrosse, Wallerman struggling just to get through the academic load. They occasionally ate together. They double-dated once or twice. Attended all the eating club rituals together. Friends but not particularly close ones, Wallerman admitted. They drifted apart after graduation, Jack heading into the Army, Wallerman, dreaming of big bucks, shooting straight to Wall Street and the fast action. They met again at Primo Investments.

"The very years I'm looking into," Morgan replied, smiling broadly now, finding it impossible to conceal his excitement. He could smell the jackpot, at last. The drinks were being delivered. Wallerman snatched a large frosty stein out of the waiter's hand and it shot straight to his lips. Not sips, big gulps.

With the back of his hand, he wiped the

beer froth off his upper lip. "Yeah, I figured that," he said, smiling back. "You heard about Edith, I guess."

"A few things, sure. Rumors, mostly."

"Let me tell you, whatever you heard is probably true. Jack walked away with a boatload of cash. Millions, many millions. He struck the mother lode with that old broad."

"You think he had her killed?"

"You know what they say?"

"No, remind me."

"The definition of a perfect murder is on the high seas. No corpse, no evidence, impossible to prove." He was staring now at a hot young thing with a jewelry store attached to her lower lip. She was standing by herself, not drinking, not eating, just begging to be admired. "Jack knew that, of course."

"But you think he did it?"

"Oh, sure he did it."

Morgan seemed to smile and frown at the same time. "Say I could find evidence that implicates him, would you be willing to testify to that effect?"

Wallerman had been in the middle of guzzling his second beer. The drinking stopped and the mug slammed down on the table. "Are you crazy?" he yelled.

A few people at nearby tables turned and gawked. Attention was the last thing Morgan wanted.

"Quiet down," he whispered gravely. He waited a moment until the stares went away and Wallerman put the beer back where it belonged, at his lips. Another long guzzle slid down his throat. The tension melted from his face — Morgan was amazed at how fast a shot of booze calmed him. He leaned forward and asked Lew, in a low voice, "My guess is we're talking because you have a grudge against Jack, right?"

"We didn't part on the best of terms."

"Be more specific."

"He walked off with all that money, and I stayed in a lousy, crumbling firm. Less than a year later, the CEO and CFO died, and all the air went out of the place. I was stuck in a dead end with no way out."

Morgan stroked his chin and thought about that. He took a stab and asked, "You think Jack had anything to do with their deaths, too?"

It didn't seem like a question Wallerman had considered before. It did seem to intrigue him, though. "You think he arranged the plane crash?"

"Just an idea I'm throwing out."

"I don't know anything about that."

"From what I hear, Kyle and Sullivan suspected him. They put a PI firm in Europe on his ass. Their deaths were awfully convenient for Jack."

"It does sound like Jack's style. He's meticulous that way. But like I said, I don't know anything about it."

"Did you ask Jack to cut you in?"

The slits of Wallerman's eyes grew narrow. After a hesitation he admitted, "We might've had a conversation along those lines."

"And he refused, right?"

"Basically, and not politely either." Another long gulp of beer, then he smacked his lips. "He told me to screw myself. It was very big money and I would've been content with only one or two million. He could afford it. It was no way to treat a friend."

"Don't you want to pay him back?"

"We're still talking aren't we?"

"Okay, look, it's simple. I need proof Jack did it. If you could —"

"And I need cash," Wallerman interrupted before Morgan could complete that thought. Screw the details, let's talk money his face was saying. The second stein of beer now sat on the table, empty. Lew was leaning back in his seat, arms crossed tightly across his chest.

"How much?" Morgan asked, his eyebrows pinching together.

"It won't be cheap. There's a lot to consider."

"For instance?"

"For one, Jack's a dangerous man. There's his history to consider. Delta, war hero, and he obviously killed Edith. He's not squeamish about erasing problems."

"How much?" Morgan repeated.

"I'd have to quit my job and run. It would mean the end of a lucrative, quite promising career. I'd need enough to live on."

Morgan strangled the urge to burst out laughing. Whatever had become of Wallerman's career, profitable or promising didn't enter the picture. He was a sorry lush and a loser. He didn't even have enough money to purchase a decent suit. The best thing that could happen to him was to scrap it all and start over. Morgan should charge him for the opportunity.

"Just tell me how much," he repeated, more insistently.

"Only two million," Wallerman answered, making it sound like an extraordinary bargain.

"Bad joke. How much?"

"I'm not budging. Know why? There is no evidence, zilch, nada, none. Jack is smart.

436

After he left, I went through everything. The records of his transactions with Edith, bank transfers, everything. I even went through the hard drive of his old computer one night after everyone went home. You won't find a thing, Morgan, not without me."

"So what are you offering?"

Wallerman's eyes were glued on a skinny little thing with a cocktail in her hand, leaning against the bar. Morgan forced himself to look twice before he believed she was real. Long, bony legs on full display, a ridiculously purple pageboy haircut, a thick tattoo of barbed wire around her neck, wearing an outfit that looked like it was designed by a sociopath.

She looked barely old enough to be potty-trained, much less purchase alcohol.

Wallerman finally tore his eyes away from her and stared hard at Morgan. "Let's cut the crap, okay? My guess is you're not a federal agent, you're a hired thug. You're being paid to burn Jack, and you need help."

This was stated quite factually and Morgan weighed for a moment whether it was worth trying to bluff or lie his way through.

As though reading his mind, Wallerman added, "But if I'm wrong, and you are, as you claim, a Fed, two million is way over your head. Then it's *sayonara,* pal."

"No, you're right, I'm a thug. I work for some people who want the goods on Wiley."

"What people?"

"None of your damned business. Here's all you need to know. They're big and extremely powerful. Put the right material in their hands, they'll destroy Wiley."

"Then I'm your man. We have a deal?"

"Not until it's clear what you're offering. The money's not mine and I'll need to explain what it buys."

"Use your imagination, Morgan."

"I'm, what, how do they say it these days? . . . imagination-deprived."

"And I'm the ugly skeleton from Jack's past. I can approach him and ask for extortion money, or I know enough to make him jump a plane and flee for Brazil. He'll disappear into a deep, dark jungle, and you'll never worry about him again."

"Are you willing to wear a wire?" Morgan asked, apparently with a different plan in mind.

"I love an audience. Sure, why not?"

"Do you think you can get Jack, on tape, to admit he killed Edith?"

"Of course."

"Don't give me that confidence act. How?"

"Might be that I have a few things I

haven't told you about. Things I won't tell you about because I'm not an idiot and I don't want to be cut out of the money."

They spent a moment ignoring each other. Wallerman was letting his offer and terms sink in. Morgan was wondering if this thing was the real deal, or was Wallerman only a blowhard trying to lie and finagle his way to a big payday. But he had brought up Edith without prompting and he certainly seemed to know what he was talking about. And unlike Charles, Lew Wallerman had gone to no trouble to conceal his real identity or cover his tracks. If he screwed Morgan, TFAC could and would find him. The punishment would be severe. In this business, this was the definition of an insurance policy.

"What if it doesn't work?" asked Morgan.

"Then I only get half. Up-front of course. If it succeeds, and it will, fork over the other million."

"Let me make a call," Morgan said. He got up, walked outside to the sidewalk, and, using his cell, called Martie O'Neal at headquarters.

As Morgan expected, the two million price tag prompted a long string of foul curses, but eventually the curses lapsed into quiet gags and groans, then Martie got over the sticker shock and the talk turned serious. Sure, it was a lot of dough. But after all these months of looking they still had nothing. Charles had given them a promising lead, but the son of a bitch had been too smart to allow the conversation to be taped. It was all hearsay from an anonymous source. Legally speaking, it was worthless.

Mitch Walters was now all over O'Neal's ass. Walters was tired of empty promises, tired of lame excuses, tired of false leads that turned into disappointing dead ends, tired of throwing good money after bad. Worse, he was growing tired of TFAC. He was threatening to take his business elsewhere.

The two million wasn't really an issue. A drop in the bucket for CG. Yes, Walters would approve it, O'Neal was sure. Oh, he'd bitch and curse up a storm, call O'Neal an array of filthy names, and unload a fresh vow to take his business elsewhere. But he'd pay.

With a cool billion at stake, Walters would pay any amount at this point.

The guard briefly gawked at the badge, then waved her by. After she passed and stepped into an empty elevator, once he knew she wasn't looking, he grabbed the phone and punched the hotline. "A DCIS agent just came in," he said into the phone.

"Headed where?" the shift boss asked.

"Upstairs. She just got in the elevator."

"What floor, moron?"

He jumped out of his seat and made a mad dash to the elevator bank, in time to see it stop on the number 6, then he raced back to the phone. "Sixth floor," he said, breathing heavily.

"Describe her."

"Nice, red dress and short heels. Brunette, medium height, fine-looking . . . hot, actually."

By the time Mia Jenson stepped off onto the sixth floor and spent a long moment waiting for the receptionist of the LBO section to get off her phone and pay attention to the shield jammed in her face, a lawyer from CG's legal counsel's office and a large uniformed guard were already standing behind her.

"What can we do to help you?" the lawyer asked. He was young and handsome in his superbly tailored, dandy dark suit; he carried himself like he knew it.

Mia turned around. Her smile was forced and stingy. "Agent Jenson, DCIS." She held up her shield and allowed him a moment to examine it. "I'm here to meet with some of your people in the LBO section."

"Do you have an appointment?"

"I don't need one." She waved the shield in front of his face.

"To meet with them about what?"

"To ask a few questions about the polymer."

"You're on the wrong floor, then. If it's another complaint about the production in Iraq you need to talk to our business partnership group. Second floor."

He took her arm to guide her to the elevator, but Mia forcefully plucked his hands off. "Touch me again without my permission, and I'll slap your ass in cuffs."

The hands dropped, and the lawyer took a fast step backward and reassessed the situation. The lady was young, beautiful, and definitely vicious.

"I choose who I want to speak with," she said coldly. "What's your name?" she asked with a notable edge.

"Thomas Warrington, from legal counsel. You'll have to explain why you want to talk to our people."

"Well, a moment ago, it was a friendly visit to ask about some of our contracting people. Why, do you have something to hide, Mr. Warrington?"

"No. Absolutely not."

"Because if I suspect you do," Mia threatened, as if he hadn't said anything, "I'll return with a subpoena and a few of my more curious associates and turn your company upside down."

Warrington looked at her; from his expression he didn't know what to do, how to handle this snarling lady with a shield. Did she mean it? Could she get a subpoena? He had already painfully underestimated her once; he wasn't about to make the same mistake twice.

"Drop the ugly threats, Agent Jenson. We're very open around here. I'll accompany you if you don't mind." He tried out his best smile.

"And if I do?" She wasn't smiling back.

"I'll still accompany you."

"Suit yourself. Who in your LBO section handled the takeover of Arvan Chemicals?"

The lawyer was unfamiliar with the details of the Arvan deal but wasn't about to admit it. Not to her anyway. The receptionist and guard were staring at him, trying to suppress their amusement; he could feel the blood rushing to his face. "I'll tell you when we get there." He started to grab her arm, but quickly remembered what happened last time. The hand dropped to his side as if he had just touched a flame.

"Follow me," he mumbled.

His first stop was the office of Samuel
Parner, head of the LBO section. He ordered Mia to wait in the anteroom while he
slipped into Parner's office for a quiet,
confidential chat.

What does she want? Parner whispered as
if she might have her ear pressed against his
door. She was vague but mentioned something about some contracting people in the
Pentagon, and now the Arvan takeover, but
that doesn't make sense, does it? the lawyer
answered. Nope, not if she wants to gab
about the Arvan deal, so I'd better handle
her myself, Parner insisted. Do we have
anything to worry about? the lawyer asked.
Not a thing, absolutely not, Parner assured
him with a confident grin.

Don't let the good looks fool you, the
lawyer warned him; my balls are rolling
around the floor by your receptionist's desk.

Warrington stepped out and ushered Mia
into the office. With a show of affected
calmness, he offered her a seat. She fell into
the rotating chair across from Parner's big
desk and carefully crossed her legs. Parner
stayed in his chair, feet planted on the desk,
and studied her with a pugnacious smirk. If
she wanted to play macho games, she had

come to the right place, the right guy. No introductions were offered, no handshakes extended. The lawyer moved to a corner, where he stood stiffly and tried his best to look threatening.

"What's this about?" Parner demanded forcefully, switching his expression to a deep scowl.

"I'll ask the questions," Mia answered, not the least bit friendly or intimidated.

"Then I may not answer," Parner shot back. He was not about to be pushed around by some pip squeak with a shield, no matter how great her legs — and they were indeed perfect, far as he could tell.

The lawyer quietly nodded his approval at Parner — that's it, this is your turf, your office, and your rules, his nod said.

For a moment Mia said nothing. She also turned her eyes to the lawyer in the corner and, speaking at Parner, asked, "Did I read you your Miranda warning?"

"Not that I remember."

"Because if I had," she continued in a cool professional tone, "you would have the right to be silent, the right to have a lawyer present, and I have the right to use anything you say against you in a court of law."

"I watch television. I know my rights."

"Always nice to have an educated public.

Surely you also know, then, that in the absence of that warning, Mr. Parner, you have no right to be silent. Since I'm a federal officer pursuing an official investigation, in fact, you have the obligation to answer my questions. Do you understand that?"

Parner glanced at the corner and the lawyer nodded again, not quickly this time, almost glacially. His specialty was corporate law, but best as he could recall, it sounded like a pretty good rendering of con law 101. He wished now he had paid more attention in class. He wished even more that some other lawyer from the office had been sent to handle this banshee.

Parner said, somewhat reluctantly, "I think I understand."

"Let me help you understand better. I can ask you these questions here, in the comfort of your office, or I can come back with a warrant, drag you out in cuffs, and ask you in less comfortable surroundings. Do you understand that?"

Parner nodded again, without any more silly glances at Warrington. The fancy mouthpiece in the corner was slowly shaking his head, not in disagreement, but in amazement. This agent had raced from a friendly little drop-in visit to flinging around vile threats in nothing flat. Parner's feet were off the desk now. He was shifting in his seat, playing with a paperweight, struggling to conceal his growing anxiety.

Parner managed a very weak, "You can do that?"

She offered him a bitchy smile. "Amazing how much power and authority the Supreme Court grants me, don't you think?"

"Very amazing," Parner agreed, and he meant it.

"Question one," she announced, getting right down to business. "How did Arvan Chemicals come to your attention?"

"I don't understand the question."

Mia uncrossed her legs and edged forward in her seat. "You boys wait here, and I'll be back in an hour." She stood and began straightening her dress.

"Wait!" Parner yelled, and it was nearly a scream.

"Why should I? You're wasting my time."

"All right, I'll answer your questions." He paused, drew a few deep breaths, and tried to compose himself. "We have nothing to hide. The Arvan deal was brought to us by a New York investor."

"Name?"

"Uh . . . I don't remember."

"See if this helps. Jack Wiley?"

Parner and the lawyer exchanged looks she wasn't supposed to see. How did she know that? More important, how much else did she know? After a momentary hesitation — what would it hurt to answer truthfully? — Parner managed to produce a slow nod. "I think that's the correct name."

"And what did Wiley offer you?"

"I wasn't present at the initial meeting," he offered truthfully. "So I have no idea," he lied. He had listened to that horrible tape of Jack running circles around his underlings at least half a dozen times, but was confident she had no way of knowing such a tape even existed.

"Was it a takeover?"

"Something like that."

"Would you describe it as a friendly takeover, or an unfriendly one?"

"Friendly . . . definitely friendly, Agent Jenson," he said, regaining his confidence. "Mr. Arvan developed a wonderful product that showed remarkable promise. But he was way over his head, and he knew it. He wanted to get it into the hands of a bigger company that could get into the field fast. I'm happy to say he chose us. We felt honored. He was handsomely paid."

"How was it tested?"

"Thoroughly. And under the most authentic, arduous conditions."

"I asked how, Mr. Parner, not how well."

After another moment's hesitation, Parner said, "Uh, I wouldn't know, not exactly, anyway. I head LBOs, not test and evaluation."

"I know who I'm talking to." Then very calmly she asked, "Did your company contribute any money to Congressman Earl Belzer, of Georgia?"

"What?"

"It's not complicated. Did you bribe Belzer, yes or no?"

Parner wasn't about to answer that. No way. Not truthfully, anyway, and he was saved the trouble of having to tell another big whopper by Warrington, who somehow worked up his nerve, took a big step forward, and planted himself firmly in the middle of the discussion. "We're through answering questions without a subpoena. This company has done nothing wrong, and I don't like your questions."

"You don't have to."

"Uh . . . are we under investigation, and if so, for what?" It was the question he should've asked the moment he laid eyes on her. He knew he was on dangerous ground, but wasn't exactly sure why. "What's your purpose for coming over here?" he demanded, continuing his feeble attempt to turn the tables.

Now Mia looked amused. "I came to introduce myself."

"Introduce yourself?"

"Since you'll be seeing plenty of me, I thought we should become acquainted."

She was on her feet and out the door before they could ask her what she meant by that vague threat.

20

The meeting convened in the expansive office of Mitch Walters. The pen-and-ink portrait of his head from the *Wall Street Journal* now hung, front and center, in the place of honor on his wall of fame. Only a select few were invited — Walters himself, Daniel Bellweather, Alan Haggar, and Phil Jackson, the steering committee for the polymer. It was an emergency meeting. It was also a tense one.

Jackson was the legal cutthroat whose judgment would mean the most, and from the beginning he proceeded to take charge.

It opened with a hard, fast-paced interrogation of Thomas Warrington, the baby-faced lawyer from the general counsel's office who had had the dismaying misfortune to meet Mia. Jackson treated him with all the cold contempt he reserved for a rookie attorney who had gotten his pants pulled down. "So you just let her waltz into our

LBO section," Jackson taunted, as if to say Warrington had stood aside and let her pillage the company safe.

"She had a shield," Warrington answered, plainly terrified. "And she was very assertive."

"But you failed to force her to explain why?"

"She never gave me the opportunity."

"Idiot. Of course she didn't."

He winced. "I tried to get it out of her," he complained, painfully aware of how pathetic that sounded.

"Beat it, get out of here. I never want to see your face again," Jackson barked with a threatening glare. Warrington nearly scorched the carpet he moved so fast.

The other three men were all staring with deep intensity at Jackson's face.

"What do you think?" Bellweather was first to ask.

The glare melted into his more typical expression of bored condescension. "My guess? She's fishing. She smells something, but she's got nothing. Not yet."

"I don't like the questions she asked Parner," Walters complained. Then, as if anybody needed to hear it recounted, "About the takeover, about the testing, about the money to Belzer. They were too close to home. Why would she be interested in those areas?"

"Could be she was firing shots in the dark," Haggar suggested. "Everything she asked could be gleaned from the newspapers. Everyone knows we bought Arvan — hell, Mitch shot his mouth off to every TV network and newspaper that would give him a second of attention. And everyone knows defense products are tested. Also, it's fairly obvious to any observer that Belzer hammered the polymer through Congress."

This provided a reassuringly harmless explanation that was comfortably plausible, of course. And it satisfied nobody, including Haggar, who had suggested it in the first place. He produced a slight shrug to show he wasn't buying it himself.

"What do we know about this Agent Jenson?" Jackson asked, shifting his black eyes across their faces.

Haggar leaned forward. "I called a source in the IG's office. Guy who used to work for me. He didn't know her, but he pulled her file."

"What's it say?"

"Harvard Law, second in her class. Don't ask me why she's working in DCIS, it makes no sense, but there it is. Worse, she's good at her work. Last year she earned two awards for excellence. Quite impressive for a rookie agent."

"So she's an eager beaver," Bellweather said, trying to sound dismissive, as if that made any difference.

"Does your source say we're being investigated?" Walters asked Haggar.

"No. He knows nothing about it. A lot of investigations, though, especially sensitive ones, are kept compartmentalized until the last minute. It's possible he's out of the loop. I told him to nose around, see if he can find anything out."

"Sounds like we have nothing to worry about," Walters said, relaxing back into his seat.

Ever the lawyer, Jackson snapped, "You're a fool, Walters. You're paid to worry. It sounds like she just came over to rattle our chains, but you can bet she's not through. She was sending us a message."

They discussed the perplexing problem of Mia Jenson till they were tired of talking. The meeting lasted forty minutes, long beyond the point where the conversation was at all useful. In the end, after much bickering and arguing, they decided no action was warranted. They would do nothing and watch, for now. They would prepare a few options in the event Mia Jenson developed into a bigger problem, but the ball was in her court.

Jackson, the expert in scandals, took the seasoned legal view that she was attempting to provoke them into doing something stupid. A classic cop's ploy. She had good intuition, a strong hunch, and absolutely no evidence. She was hunting and bluffing, precisely because she lacked legitimate grounds to ramp up an official investigation: without that authority her options were severely constrained.

"So don't do her any favors," Jackson cautioned, staring pointedly at Walters, the hothead.

Bellweather said, "But we do have one loose end to worry about."

"Jack Wiley, I know," Jackson said. "I'll pay him a visit."

The shiny black Town Car rolled up to Jack's house at five. Jackson had called ahead. Jack was waiting for him.

No warm hands were proffered, no phony pleasantries exchanged. Jack led Jackson to his big family room, where they fell into a pair of comfortable burgundy leather chairs and spent a moment getting settled.

Finally Jack asked, "What's this about?"

"Have you been contacted by any DCIS

agents?"

"What's DCIS?"

Jackson briefly explained, then said, "An agent stopped by the headquarters this morning. She has nothing remotely concrete, but she's nosing around."

"About our polymer?"

"What else."

"If she has nothing, why's she nosing around?"

"We're not worried at this point. You shouldn't, either. It's actually predictable. The polymer is a very large, no-bid, single-source contract. That sends up warning flags and suspicions. I'm sure she's just poking around."

"So it's harmless?" Jack asked. His elbows were planted on the armrests, his fingers formed a steeple in front of his lips. He could've been a cocky college professor in the faculty lounge quizzing a hapless freshman. His posture and the skeptical tone of his questions were getting on Jackson's nerves.

"I told you, I'm confident that it's just exploratory. As long as nobody gives her cause, she'll realize it's a waste of her time and quit wasting ours."

"And that's why you're here?"

"Glad to see you're paying attention, Jack."

"You're worried about me. How touching."

The slitty little eyes tightened and the narrow face squeezed into a lawyerly frown. "You don't like me, do you, Wiley?"

"You're perceptive."

"I don't like you either, but it doesn't matter. I'm warning you that we're all in this. You, us, we all sink or swim together. We've all blurred a few ethical boundaries, including you, Wiley."

"Interesting choice of words, Jackson. Don't you mean, broken a few serious laws?"

"Who cares what I mean. Assure me you're on board."

"Or what?"

Jackson came far forward in his chair, a hard lurch, until their faces were inches apart. His features crumpled into a tight mass of wrinkles; his jaws clenched tight, his eyes bulged. The expression was one he used, nearly always to great effect, to bully and intimidate powerful committee chairmen, grizzled judges, and hardened lawyers. He was quite proud of it.

"I'm not a man you want to cross, Wiley," he hissed. "And in case you haven't heard,

CG's not a group you want to tangle with. We've got more firepower and resources than you can handle."

He allowed this portentous threat to fester; he watched Jack's face for the typical reaction, a sudden collapse into resignation, a tremble around the lips, at the very least a quick shifting of the eyes.

Jack didn't blink. Instead he leaned back into his chair, crossed his legs, and smiled. "With billions of dollars on the line, why would I want to screw it up, Jackson?"

Jackson continued to examine Jack's face. The cool response bothered him. Not that he expected Jack to cry or bawl or choke or anything, but neither had he expected the cold amusement in his eyes.

Then again, he reminded himself, the face he was studying belonged to a hardened murderer and a thief. Between his years in Delta, then his involvement in the murder of Edith, and possibly his former CEO and CFO, and the mysterious deaths of three board members, how many had he killed? No surprise that Jack had ice water in his veins.

Well, Jackson could be just as pitiless and coldhearted. After maintaining the hard stare for an interminable moment, he told him, "Her name's Mia Jenson. A lawyer,

458

and a smart one. She knew your name. I have a strong premonition she'll find an excuse to have a word with you."

"Is she cute?"

"Keep it simple, Wiley. Don't get smart. The takeover was friendly. You know nothing about how Defense got interested in our product. You know even less about how the DOD contract came about. Your arrangement with us is a limited liability partnership, and your role was very, very limited."

"Should I take notes?"

"Don't mess with me, boy. You're out of your league."

"You done?"

"Yeah, I'm done."

"Then it's my turn," Jack said, slowly and deliberately, still comfortably ensconced in his chair as if he had not a care in the world. "You and the rest of the Capitol Group are trying to edge me out of this deal. I'm not stupid, Jackson. Now you need me again. Don't cheat me out of a single penny, or else."

"Or else what?"

"Use your imagination."

Nicky Garner was loitering beside her desk when Mia came into work the next morning. "Got time for a few words?" he asked.

"For you, always, Nicky."

"In my office, now." He looked grim and unhappy. Nicky led as they made their way through the cluttered maze to the small room in the back corner. As section chief, Nicky was the only one to even have an office, a questionable privilege, if it could even be called that; a closet would've been more comfortable.

Nicky tried to set a good example in neatness, but it was hopeless. Files and legal manuals were strewn everywhere. Stacks of paper were piled against the wall, in corners, anywhere he could find room. Enough Post-it notes were plastered to his desk and walls to make the room look like it was painted yellow.

Nicky quietly shoved the door closed, stepped over a few piles, and walked to his desk. He leaned his hip against it and asked, "What the hell were you doing at the Capitol Group yesterday?"

"How did you learn I was there?"

"I was called up to the IG's office last night, after you left. Hanrady, an assistant to the IG, said you raised hell at CG, ruffled a few feathers, and he got a call. He asked me what's up."

"What did you tell him?"

"The truth, as embarrassing as it is. I have

460

no damned idea. Wanta tell me about it?"

"Relax, Nicky. Nothing to tell, really. Just following up on some complaints passed to me by some friends in contracting. You know about CG's polymer?"

"Sure, I know. They say that stuff's better than Miracle Glue."

"It may be, but the application operation in Iraq is a horrible mess. Remember all the complaints about CG's uparmoring program? Guess what? They're up to the same tricks."

"That kinda thing gets worked out between contracting officials," Nicky said, now looking suspicious.

"I know. But our folks are frustrated. They asked me to put a scare into CG. The last thing they want is a repeat of the past few years where CG blew off all the complaints. People are getting killed over there."

"What did you say?"

"I'm not stupid, I colored between the lines. I asked a few simple questions. If they're nervous, that's exactly how I want them."

As good as Mia was, Nicky reminded himself, she was still a junior agent prone to making rookie mistakes. He pushed off the desk and said, "The Capitol Group is not some penny-ante outfit, Mia. They define

461

the word clout. They are the big league. You don't just go over on a whim and stick a finger in their eye."

"I know who they are. They have everybody but God on their board," Mia answered. "But they work for us, last time I checked. They take our money, don't they?"

Nicky stared hard at her face, as if trying to see if he was missing anything. His phone rang and he picked it up.

"I've got work to do," Mia said, and she shot out the door.

21

The plan was simple.

A few nights every week, Jack grew tired of his own cooking and slipped out to a local eatery. All local places, so he could enjoy a cocktail with his meal without being overly concerned about picking up a DUI on the trip home. Thursday's usual was McLoone's Rum Runner, a restaurant in Sea Bright with good seafood, great river views, dark wood paneling, a roaring fireplace, and a sailing ambience.

Thursday, and as usual, Jack was out the door at seven. By seven-thirty, he was comfortably seated in McLoone's, at his customary table for two beside the roaring fireplace. Without a menu, he ordered the house favorite, stuffed shrimp, and his usual cocktail. The glass of scotch on the rocks was being delivered when a familiar figure passed by his table.

The figure came to a dead halt. "My God,

Jack . . . Jack Wiley. That is you, isn't it?" the man asked, feigning confusion.

Jack put down his scotch and looked up. "Hello, Lew."

Wallerman took two steps closer, right beside the table. "What are you doing here?"

"I live nearby."

Wallerman looked around for a moment, then back at Jack. "I'm here alone. Mind if I join you?"

"I'm expecting somebody," Jack lied, glancing at the door as if somebody would walk through any second.

"Then, I'll just join you for a quick drink. Catch up on old times. The moment your guest arrives, I'll get lost." Without waiting for an answer he slipped into the seat across from Jack and held a hand up for the waitress. "So what are you doing these days?" he asked ever so casually.

"A little of this, a little of that. Nothing interesting."

The waitress arrived. Wallerman ordered two gin and tonics, and make it fast. He reached into his pocket, dug out his cell phone, and carefully positioned it on its backside in the center of the table. "I'm expecting an important business call. No rest for the greedy."

The phone had been loaned to him only

an hour before by Morgan, who at that moment was hunched over in a black Dodge van outside in the parking lot, overhearing every word. The phone had been recently reconfigured by TFAC's tech department — the insides had been gutted and replaced by two wide-angle lenses facing apart, and a digital microphone so sensitive it could hear a fly fart. TFAC was quite proud of it. This was the first time the newest marvel would see use in a real-life setting.

Morgan, munching popcorn in the van, had his eyes glued to the side-by-side video monitors. Jack's face appeared on the left screen; Wallerman's on the right. He slapped the console and blurted out, "Ha, got you now, you bastard."

Jack was staring straight ahead at Wallerman. "You seem to be doing well, Lew." His tone was edged with surprise.

Immaculately dressed as he was, in a brand-new, two-thousand-dollar blue suit bought by the TFAC boys, he looked like he was doing better than well. His nails were neatly buffed, his hair smartly trimmed by a two-hundred-dollar stylist. Even his teeth had been whitened and varnished to a high sheen. It took a lot of time and money, but he looked exactly like what he wasn't: a Wall Street fat cat loaded with cash ready to pitch a deal worth millions, or billions.

"I have to admit I'm doing better than I ever expected," Wallerman offered, trying to capture just the right dose of humility. No answer from Jack, and it was clear he didn't want to talk. "So, you married yet?" Wallerman asked in an effort to keep the conversation flowing.

"No. You?"

"Tried it once. That was one more than enough. Caught her red-handed in bed with this guy I was doing a hundred million deal with. I didn't mind losing her, really. I married her because she put out. Turned out she put out for everybody. The hundred million broke my heart."

Jack laughed, politely at best. Rich-boy humor.

Wallerman let a moment pass, then admitted very softly, "Truth is, Jack, I expected to find you here."

His eyes glued to the screen, Morgan studied Jack's face for a response to this interesting confession. He was instantly rewarded by a dramatic change in expression — stage fright might be a good word to describe it. "What's this about?" Jack asked, unable to hide his concern.

"Let's talk about Edith Warbinger first," Lew insisted. "Long time ago, I know, but surely you remember her."

"Oh, that." Jack leaned back in his chair, a clumsy attempt to look indifferent. "Too bad what happened to the old girl. But you're right, it's ancient history."

"She's gone but not forgotten, Jack."

"What do you mean?"

"Remember when I asked you to cut me in? If I recall your exact words, you told me to screw myself. I needed the money back then. Needed it badly. It would've changed my life, Jack. You really hurt my feelings. An old pal from college, I introduced you to the firm and even vouched for you. How could you blow me off that way?"

Jack sat stiffly in his chair and listened; he said nothing. He definitely looked rattled, though, in Morgan's view. His lips were pursed. The skin seemed to tighten on his face. A pair of long creases appeared between his eyes.

Morgan edged closer to the screen and couldn't stop himself — he laughed. Ha — thought it was all behind you, didn't you, you slick bastard. The perfect crime, perfectly executed, perfectly forgotten. Boo! Here comes Edith clawing her way out of a watery grave, come to exact her revenge.

Wallerman was spinning a table knife on the tablecloth, a fitful effort at smothering his euphoria. All those years spent dreaming of getting back at Jack, years of digging and hoping and waiting, finally the moment was here. Morgan admired the way Wallerman dragged this out; the impulse to blurt everything, to stuff it all in Jack's face had to be killing him. Hold on to it as long as you can, he wanted to say; let Jack contemplate all the ugly possibilities. Let him stuffer and stew.

Eventually, Lew informed Jack, "After you left, I went through everything. Your files, your computer records, your client statements. You were good, Jack. You left nothing behind."

Jack seemed to relax. "Too bad, you wasted your time. You always were a jerk."

"Well, almost nothing," Wallerman continued, still spinning the knife, still ignoring Jack's face, but carefully dropping one little note of concern. "A few months later I was sitting in an investing conference, bored out of my mind, when I got a fresh idea."

"Oh, come on, Lew. You cheated your way through Princeton and stole investing ideas at Primo. You wouldn't know a fresh idea if it sat on your lap."

Wallerman smiled at the insult. "Is there anything Jack might've forgotten? Anything he overlooked? You see, you had become a fixation for me. I couldn't get you out of my mind — you ran with all those millions and left me in a lousy firm filled with greedy scum, backstabbers, and liars."

"Think about this, Lew. Maybe you belonged there."

Again, Wallerman seemed to enjoy the insult. This was his moment of triumph, and he wasn't about to let Jack spoil the fun. "Then it hit me."

"This is fascinating. Tell me what you think I forgot."

"Your travel records. The second the conference ended I raced back to the firm travel office. I scoured the records for hours. You made plenty of overseas trips during those years old Edith was supposed to be on that boat."

"Now you're boring me." He didn't sound bored, though.

"You went to Copenhagen the week before Edith arrived. In fact, you stayed in the same hotel she later checked into. You even billed it to the firm. What were you doing there, Jack?"

"Good customer relations. Making arrangements for Edith's trip."

"How thoughtful. You sure burned through a pile of cash on your charge cards. Over twenty thousand on women's clothing, another five thousand for luxury luggage. I've got copies of the receipts, in case you're interested."

"I'm not. Are you through?"

"Hardly. See, I asked myself, why would Jack be buying all those clothes and luggage for an old broad with all that dough? Then I answered myself — you weren't."

"Now you're speculating, Lew."

"The nurse you hired to take Edith's place, she needed to look the part. She had to show up in fine clothes, hauling fancy luggage, looking like she could buy the damn boat."

Jack managed to produce a nonchalant shrug. It was unconvincing. He never dreamed he'd be hearing these words.

"Then, about twice a year, you continued to make trips to a variety of locales spread around Europe and Asia. I'll admit, Jack, I didn't get it. Not until I plotted all those locations on maps did it make sense. They were all seaports."

"I like seafood and sunshine. Are you through now?"

"Almost, Jack, almost. Next, I contacted Vermillion Shipping Lines, the company that owned Edith's cruise ship. They were kind enough to check the log. You know what?" He paused to stare at Jack's face, as if searching for a true answer. "Yeah, I guess you know. The dates and locations of your trips were an exact match to the days Edith's ship visited those ports."

Out in the parking lot, Morgan couldn't tear his eyes from Jack's face. Not for a second; he didn't want to miss a single grimace, a single erratic shift of the eyes, a single pained mood swing. He was stuffing popcorn into his mouth, chewing violently, enjoying himself immensely. Jack seemed to sink lower in his chair. He began rubbing his temples, as if his head was splitting. He had nowhere to run, nowhere to hide. Mr. Cool and Calm was wilting before Morgan's eyes, every twitch and pregnant pause being recorded in digital, high-definition color by the tiny cameras hidden in plain sight in the center of the table. Wallerman was masterful. Morgan greatly admired the performance.

Lew paused for a deep gulp of gin and tonic. A little dribbled out the corner of his mouth, and he sloppily wiped it on a sleeve of his new two-thousand-dollar suit. "You just had to be sure your imposter was playing you straight, didn't you?"

Morgan now was watching the flames from the fireplace play across Jack's face. Hooded eyes, lips drawn tight — perhaps it

471

was the flickering light, but he looked almost saturnine. "Is that all you have?" he asked Lew in a low, menacing voice.

"You wish, Jack. Once you know the basics, the whole fraud comes apart. I have a mountain of evidence. Did you know there's no statute of limitations on murder?"

The waitress arrived to take Wallerman's dinner order. "Get lost," Jack barked at her, very rudely. One quick glance at his face and she scuttled away from their table. "What do you want?" Jack growled.

"What does any man want?"

"You tell me. That's why you're here, after all."

"World peace. A rich, beautiful nymphomaniac who owns a beer factory. A billion dollars in the bank of my choice. Can you give me those things?"

"Out of my price range. What do you want from me?"

"Well, you see, Jack, I haven't made up my mind yet."

Jack leaned across the table. His face was inches from Wallerman's. "Indecision can be an unhealthy thing, Lew."

Wallerman replied with a quick smile, "Look over in that corner." He pointed gleefully to the far end of the room and Jack spun around and looked. Two men in dark suits smirked at him. One flipped the bird; the other settled for a sarcastic wave. It was their debut and they hammed it up for all it was worth.

Wallerman wouldn't agree to this meeting without a safety blanket, and TFAC had obliged, providing the pair of happy thugs now smiling and glowering at Jack.

"In case you're wondering," Lew mentioned — now all bravado — "the Rottweilers are mine, and armed to the teeth. Don't dream of doing anything stupid."

Jack collapsed back into his seat. Staring at the tablecloth, he pleaded, "We can work this out, Lew. Just tell me what you want."

Wallerman stood, picked up the cell phone off the table, stuffed it in a pocket, and walked around until he stood beside Jack, who seemed frozen to his chair. He bent over and, about two inches from Jack's ear, whispered, "I'll be in touch, pal."

The meeting would be brief and unnoticed, as usual. Harvey Crintz waited till the yellow cab rolled to a stop by the curb, peeked inside to be sure it was the right one, then scurried to the rear door and hopped in.

"How're you doing?" the driver asked without turning around.

Crintz spent a moment getting comfortable. He pulled his pants out of his crotch and sat back. "Glad you got my message," he said. The cab began rolling.

The driver, Tim Paley, peeked at Crintz's face in the rearview mirror. Paley was a midlevel flunky in CG's government contracts division. He was ambitious, hungry, and more than willing to do a little dirty work if it furthered his professional advancement.

Crintz was an old friend, one who for the past five years had been bought and paid for by a special slush fund — a hidden pile of cash created for the worthy purpose of buying CG friendships in a city filled with underpaid midlevel bureaucrats.

But Crintz, a Christian of the born-again variety and a dedicated family man, would never take cash to fix a contract or favor a bid. That would be a gross violation of his professional ethics and the law. He provided inside scoops and tips, nothing more — also a breach of the law, just not as serious.

Five thousand a month in the Bahamian bank of your choice only bought you so much loyalty.

"So what's this about?" Paley asked.

"I'm not sure. Are you people under investigation over the polymer?"

"Don't think so. Why?"

"Because someone's getting real interested in it, and you."

"Be more specific."

"DCIS. Agent named Jenson. She's been crawling all over our contracting office the past few weeks."

Crintz held a low-level position in the office of the Pentagon's inspector general, an obscure job but one that gave him a bird's-eye view of everything. He had started his career in procurement, and after gaining considerable expertise in contracts and accounting made a midcareer shift to oversight of his old activities. His insights were invaluable, worth vastly more than $60K a year to CG.

True to his background as a contracting agent for Uncle Sam, he was being flagrantly ripped off and was too stupid to demand more.

"What's she asking about?"

"Hasn't asked anything," Crintz answered. "She demanded all existing files on the contract. Everything."

"All right, what do you think she's interested in?"

"Hard to tell. She hauls the files upstairs, I guess to make copies. She returns them a few hours later."

Paley remained quiet and thought about

it a moment. "Who handled the contracting process for the polymer?"

"You know her, I think. Sally Gramble. Johnson and Hughes assisted, but they're both new and very junior. You probably already know this, but they weren't the driving force. Mostly they did what they were told by people upstairs. Everything was top-down on that contract. I doubt you have anything to worry about from any of those folks."

Paley gripped the steering wheel and thought about it a minute more. "I'm not sure it's a problem anyway. The contracts are pretty clean, aren't they?"

"Strictly boilerplate. Form contracts with a few alterations to tailor them to the requirement."

"Then what does she want with them?"

"That's what I'm asking you."

They were on the GW Parkway now, headed toward the McLean exit, stuck in the right lane and driving slowly, with traffic whizzing by on their left.

"I'm not worried, it's probably nothing," Paley repeated. "What do you think?"

"I think DCIS agents don't collect hundreds of pages of contracts for light reading. I think anytime a DCIS agent is interested in you, it's bad news. I'd worry, if I were you boys."

"I'll pass the word," Paley assured him with another glance in the mirror. "You want to go anywhere special?"

"Back to the Pentagon, and step on it. I'm hungry and this is my lunch break."

An hour later, Paley was standing, grim-faced, in his boss's office relaying Crintz's report. His boss immediately picked up the phone and called the CEO.

22

Phil Jackson was right.

Mia Jenson showed up on Jack's doorstep shortly after nine on a dark Tuesday night. Ernie and Howie, the TFAC crew on duty, saw her pull up in a strange car then park, in Jack's driveway. They immediately ran her plate via a deal they had with the local cops; ten seconds later, they had her name and address in D.C. Thirty seconds after that, they had her identity as a federal law enforcement officer.

This hurried research was handled by Howie, the man inside the van. Ernie, the on-site watcher, was parked at a curb, two houses down. Ernie had poor hearing so he whipped out his bionic ear and sound booster, jammed the earphones over his head, stuck the amplifier out his car window, scooted down in his seat, and listened.

Mia walked directly to the front stoop, pushed the doorbell, and waited. He could hear her breathing, the sound booster was that good.

The front light popped on, and a moment later Jack opened the door. "Are you selling Girl Scout cookies?" he asked. A real wise guy.

"Not quite, Mr. Wiley." Mia shoved her shield in his face. "I'm a federal agent with the Defense Criminal Investigative Service. I have a few questions."

Jack didn't look surprised in the least. "Should I get my lawyer?"

"That won't be necessary."

"What's your name?"

"Jenson. Why don't you invite me inside?"

"I'd rather talk here. You won't be staying long."

"Is that the way you want it, Mr. Wiley?"

"Look, Miss . . . What's your first name?"

"Agent. Special Agent, if you prefer to be formal."

"Lovely name."

"Thanks, I'm quite proud of it."

"What's this about?"

"Do you know a man named Perry Arvan?"

"Yes, so what?"

"Did you approach the Capitol Group with a proposal to take over his company, Arvan Chemicals?"

"I might have."

"How did you learn about the polymer Arvan developed?"

"How did you learn that I learned about it?" Jack countered, smiling nicely.

"None of your business." No smile in return.

"Okay, it's none of yours either."

Ernie pulled a sandwich out of a greasy brown paper bag and turned up the volume full blast. His wife had made him this snack, pastrami on rye, his favorite. He took his first large bite and chewed slowly. This was getting fun.

"Why did you choose the Capitol Group as your partner?"

"Is that a question?"

"Didn't it sound like a question?"

"No, it was too stupid for a question. The Capitol Group's one of the richest, most powerful corporations on the planet. The polymer's right down their alley. I considered four other companies and settled on them. Call it a no-brainer."

Then, out of the blue, she asked, "Do you know Representative Earl Belzer?"

Ernie had no idea who Belzer was, wasn't sure why she asked, but had enough common sense to know she was hedging at something important. He put down the sandwich and listened closely.

After a moment's hesitation, Jack said, "Can't really say I do. Why?"

"What if I told you I have pictures of you and Belzer together?"

"I'd say you're a liar," Jack told her cheerfully.

"Do you like Chinese food, Mr. Wiley? You barely touched the dim sum, so I'm curious."

After a long moment, Jack said, "I think we're done talking." Any hint of nonchalance or bluster evaporated from his voice.

Mia quickly shoved a hand against the door before he could close it in her face. "We're finished when I say we're finished. Listen close, because I'll only make this offer once. I'm going to bust up this nice little racket you boys are running. I've got a barrelful of evidence already. I collect more every day. It might take another week, or a few more months, but I'm going to come down on you and your pals at CG. It'll be one of the biggest busts ever."

"If you're so confident, why haven't you moved yet?"

"It's going to happen soon enough, believe me. When I do, you and plenty of others are going to jail. Not some federal country club, but a real prison with the worst scum we scraped off the streets. They adore spoiled rich men in prison, Mr. Wiley. Do I need to explain what happens in those places? You watch movies. Surely you have the picture. A big good-looking Princetonian, you'll be a big hit in the shower room."

"Very funny. Do I look frightened?"

"Oh, it won't be a comedy, Mr. Wiley. Only one or two of you will get a chance to avoid that fate. One or two of you will get smart, cut a deal, and turn state's evidence. I'm offering you that opportunity, Mr. Wiley, the rare chance to be the first on your block. If not you, it'll be somebody else. In this game, believe me, it's not fun to be near the end of the line."

"Get lost," Jack said, sounding very final, and he slammed the door. Mia stood there a moment, eyeing the doorknob in the darkness, then got back in her car and sped away.

Ernie got on the radio and called Howie. "Wow. You got all that on tape?" he asked.

"All of it," Howie answered.

"Better get it down to Martie, real quick. Sounds like big trouble."

"No kiddin'," said Howie. Within five minutes he was playing the tape over the phone to Martie O'Neal.

Mitch Walters was out of pocket and unreachable, in Bermuda, at what was billed as a CEO convention, a thin pretext for a bunch of chubby rich white men to sneak off and hit the links in a glorious setting.

Phil Jackson was deep in a legal conference with a tearful U.S. senator who had just been caught red-handed by the FBI with half a million in cash stuffed in the deep freezer in his basement. The moment the Fibbies swung open the freezer door, the senator's thoughts turned to one man, a Washington legend; if anyone could save him from becoming political roadkill, Jackson was the guy. While the FBI ransacked his house, he snuck into a bathroom, called Phil, and begged for help.

He had no legal excuse for how the money got there, but had been smart enough to keep his mouth shut when the Feds showed up flashing their warrants and badges. Now, with a press conference looming in an hour, Jackson had his cell phone turned off so he and the terrified senator could bang their heads together and construct an alibi without being disturbed. This was it — his long, storied political career, his reputation, possibly his freedom on the line, with one good shot at explaining how such a big bundle of money mysteriously materialized in his freezer.

In a stroke of good fortune, the senator's wife had passed away only two months before, from cancer — a loving and loyal mate, a caring, doting mother to his two teenage children. Jackson was brutally candid about the price of freedom. After thirty minutes of tearful bickering, of swearing up and down that he would never soil his dead wife's memory, the senator at last succumbed to the inevitable — trashing her was his best and maybe his only chance. He and his lawyer had their heads together now, plotting how to blame it all on her.

That left only Daniel Bellweather, who at that moment was also slightly preoccupied. He was half clothed and rolling around the floor with Prince Ali and five naked call girls. All blondes, of course, and at a thousand per for a night of unrestrained frolicking, quite expensive entertainment. They were reliving their rowdy old times on the small living room floor of CG's lavish riverside corporate condominium.

The watchdog imam dispatched by Ali's daddy to keep an eye on his son had a tumbler of gin in one hand, a big-breasted blonde in the other. Ali's enthusiasms had proved too infectious for the iron-willed zealot. After three weeks together, the imam was drunk or high more often than sober.

Though he generally considered cell phones a nuisance, Bellweather was glad he had brought his along this time. He shoved an anorexic blonde off his lap, pushed the receive button, and heard Martie say, "Listen to this."

For three minutes he sat there, ignoring Ali, ignoring the bevy of blonde lovelies, ignoring everything but the sounds of Mia's brief interrogation and the ugly echo of her threats.

The moment it ended, Martie asked, "What's this picture she mentioned to Wiley? Anything to worry about?"

Hell, yes, it was something to worry about — since no doubt Bellweather's smiling face was plastered front and center in the photograph, it was a disaster — but Bellweather was still too stunned to speak. So she knew about the luncheon with Earl. How much else did she know? How long had she been watching? How closely? How much other evidence did she have? The questions came fast and rattled around his head.

Phil Jackson's confident assurance that she was just an overambitious busybody, blindly fishing, obviously missed the mark. She was the firm's worst nightmare, a shield with the goods.

"Yeah," he told Martie, after he got his

heart out of his mouth, "it's a big damn worry."

"Who is she?"

"She was a mild nuisance, yesterday. Today she's poison." He felt an almost irresistible urge to call Wiley and warn him he'd better stand fast, or else. Unfortunately that would give away that CG was having him watched and tailed.

"Want us to check her out?"

"Yes, but don't get caught. Don't even come close to getting caught, understand?"

"She's a federal agent. I definitely understand."

At nine the next morning, Mia entered Nicky's office, quietly closed the door, and delicately eased herself into the lone chair, a worn, crumbling antique that looked old enough to predate the Pentagon. Nicky was on the phone, chewing out some hapless agent for blowing a promising lead in an important investigation. He cursed a few times, unusual for him.

Mia cradled a folder on her lap and waited. "I'm busy, what do ya got?" Nicky barked the moment he hung up. It was only Wednesday. He looked worn out and exhausted already. Two dozen fresh cases were piled up in his in-box. His mood was foul.

"We have to talk, Nicky."

"Okay, what is it?"

"Remember when you asked me about the Capitol Group?"

"Yeah, and you jerked me off."

Mia squirmed in her seat a moment. She certainly had, though she wasn't about to confess it. "Here's the deal. Just between us. I want your word that you'll keep this confidential."

"No, you don't have my word."

"Nicky, this is big."

"I don't horse-trade with my own agents. If you got something, tell me."

Mia got up and shoved the folder in his face. Nicky splayed it open. He read it slowly. "Jesus, where'd you get this?"

"A source."

"An inside source, obviously."

"Good guess. And I'm not going to disclose the name. Not for now, not even to you, Nicky."

"For godsakes, you're a federal agent, not a reporter. There's no damned First Amendment in this office."

There was a long pause as they glared at each other across the desk. Nicky used his fiercest glower to try to back her down. A waste of time. Mia had her jaw set, her arms crossed.

This was the one big problem with a brilliant agent with a Harvard Law degree, he quickly concluded with no small amount of annoyance. She had a world of good options outside the service. She could tell him to screw himself and mean it. It was amazing that she took this thankless job in the first place; any day, she could catch a dose of sanity and shove off for greener pastures.

"I suppose you have a good reason," he said with a weak nod.

"The best. I gave my word. And it's the only way my source will continue to cooperate. A lot's at stake here, twenty billion excellent reasons to keep my source talking. I'm not saying it's going to happen, but people get killed or seriously hurt over a lot less. For now, the less who know my source's identity, the better. That includes you."

Nicky didn't agree, but neither did he raise an objection. What would be the point? "This for real?" he asked, holding up the folder, pinching it between his fingers as if it were a ticking bomb.

"Quite real."

"You know what it means?"

"I think I do. CG's polymer wasn't adequately tested. It means we have to call an immediate, drastic halt to the entire coating operation. Then a major fraud investigation against one of the most powerful and influential companies in Washington. Have I missed anything important?"

"How about a major scandal that will rock the capital?"

"Okay, we'll add that to the list."

Inside the folder Nicky was holding like a contaminated vial of germs were the summary pages of a report prepared by a company called Summit Testing — the final results of a privately financed study, contracted and paid for by a company called Arvan Chemicals.

The report claimed that after four months, the polymer's miraculous protective qualities somehow broke down, eventually dissipating to nothing.

One day the polymer could defeat nearly any bomb on the planet; the next it could barely stand up to a mild breeze.

"When did they start the coating operation over there?" Nicky asked. He was catching on quickly.

"About three and a half months ago. They're shamefully behind schedule. But many hundreds of vehicles are now coated and vulnerable. The soldiers call them polyplus roadies."

"You know what it means to try to stop this?"

"Think what it means not to, Nicky."

"Why don't you help me think about that?"

"Thousands of soldiers are now rolling around Iraqi streets, thinking they're impervious to the worst the jihadis can throw at them. They're taking risks they would never contemplate otherwise. One morning they wake up and get a very nasty surprise."

Nicky waved the report in the air. "How do I know this is reliable?"

"Yesterday I had a chat with the president of Summit Testing. The company's credible. Its reputation within the industry is impeccable. They were hired, almost two years ago, by Perry Arvan to conduct a field test in Iraq. A private defense contractor agreed to serve as the guinea pig. Dozens of its vehicles were coated and sent into the most violent streets in Baghdad. For four months, no problems, everything worked great. Then one day the polymer broke down completely."

"How?" Nicky asked. "Why?"

"They have a hunch. They aren't entirely sure it's right, though."

"Let's hear the hunch."

"The reactive explosives in the polymer are nitrogen-based. It's a rare occurrence, but they suspect ultraviolet rays from the sun break down the reactive qualities. Starts out gradually, then accelerates quickly. Physicists could explain it better than me, but apparently it's known to happen."

It was suddenly clear to Nicky how volatile the summary in his hand was about to become. Senior people in the Defense Department had pressed hard for a quick, noncompetitive contract for CG. Nicky had heard rumors about shortcuts and favors. All big defense contracts generated plenty of nasty gossip, often spawned by jealous competitors, but in the strain of running a building that spends five hundred billion dollars a year, they were usually ignored as long as they weren't too serious or perceptibly credible. This one just became all too credible.

Nicky swiped a hand through the gray stubble on his scalp. "So you're asking me to take this upstairs based on a guess? To stop the biggest, most publicized defense breakthrough of the decade because of a hunch?"

"It's no hunch that the polymer breaks down, Nicky. Let's not argue, okay? You've got the report. It's a stone-cold fact. The only uncertainty is what causes it."

Nicky collapsed back against his desk. He pretended to read the file again and think about it. He wasn't squeamish, nor was he cowered by CG's reputation and power. In twenty years in this racket, he'd seen it all. He'd been involved in taking down some of the biggest giants in industry, been cursed at and threatened, once had bricks thrown through his car window. No, he wasn't worried about the fallout.

What bothered him was Mia.

He'd been getting pestering calls for days, asking what she was up to. As large and fragmented as the Pentagon was, it had a small-town culture with gossips and nosy busybodies on every hallway. She was hassling CG, and vacuuming up contracts and background material from the procurement people. She was doing this all on her own. The question was, why? He considered three or four reasons and liked none of them.

But it really didn't matter. He had no choice. None at all. Nicky finally said with clear reluctance, "All right, I'll bring this upstairs to the director. But I'm not happy, Mia. I don't like being the caboose."

"You're doing the right thing," Mia said, making an obvious effort to sound reassuring. "I'll tell you everything when the time's right."

23

It took only six hours for the summary Mia put in Nicky's hands to work its way up the chain to the very top. Three hours to be read, confirmed, and painfully contemplated by the director of the DCIS. An hour and a half to be viewed with undisguised horror by the undersecretary for procurement. Then another hour and a half for the director of test and evaluation to dream up a few lame excuses, none even remotely credible, before the procession of deeply addled senior officials marched into the office of the secretary of defense with the alarming news.

The president of Summit Testing fielded calls from every level. At one point, he even gathered the evaluation team that had spent six long months in Iraq. On the speakerphone, they defended their scientific judgment and recited their impressive résumés — two PhDs in molecular chemistry from

MIT, three master's degrees from a series of other distinguished academic institutions — and recounted how they arrived at the incontrovertible conclusion that the polymer was a star that quickly fizzled into a flop.

They explained that the study and pictures CG had bandied around town to such terrific effect in fact represented only their preliminary results. For three months and twenty-nine days the polymer had worked like magic. In jubilation they had prepared their report and labeled it as the final; the polymer was the thing dreams are made of, with an album of astonishing pictures to prove it.

Only a few days after the "final" report was finished, and only two days before the crew was scheduled to climb on a freedom bird and fly home, did the word "final" turn into "disastrously premature." The first bad news hit. Two coated vehicles were destroyed by roadside bombs.

The wrecks were hauled back to the compound and rigorously inspected. The remarkable defensive qualities were entirely and mysteriously gone. History. The polymer was now nothing but a ridiculously expensive paint job. Over the ensuing weeks, as more of the polymer-coated test vehicles became casualties, the examinations continued. More wrecks hauled into their yard, more head-scratching, more disappointment as the team realized all those months were a waste. You see, they said, not all the vehicles deteriorated at the same pace, or even the same way.

There were variations. Some coated vehicles degraded quickly; a few lingered months longer. Some vehicles exhibited a patchwork, a quilt of polymer with all its amazing qualities intact, intermixed with large dead spaces. Others seemed to turn off uniformly as if flipped by a big switch. Why remained a mystery. The answer was complicated and elusive. There were too many variables, too many unanswerable questions: how long a vehicle remained under cover from the sun; how thick the coatings were; how the intensity of the sun fluctuated with the seasons.

All these things could be factors, or maybe none of them at all. It was impossible to say.

The team remained in Iraq another two months, until the last of the coated fleet was completely defenseless. There were no visible signs of degradation, they said; the polymer gave up no clues as to its virility. Worse, there was no safe way to test for the degradation of the polymer they were aware of.

Aside from flinging an explosive against the vehicle and watching it either burst into a fireball or shrug it off, you couldn't tell whether the polymer was effective or not. A vehicle could survive the worst you throw at it one minute, and be a death trap ten seconds later.

That troubling unpredictability meant the polymer was dead on arrival.

The old, now disproved "final" report was stuffed in a drawer, never meant to see the light of day. Few copies had been produced. Distribution was strictly controlled. Aside from Summit's own file copies, only Perry Arvan had received, or even laid eyes on, the fool's gold, to the best of their knowledge.

And no, nobody from the Capitol Group had ever called Summit to discuss or confirm the results.

All attempts to locate Perry Arvan proved disappointing. His telephone service was disconnected. Ditto for his water and electricity and heating oil. His home was vacant and had been for a long time. According to New Jersey's DMV, his cars had been sold off months before. There had been no use of his charge cards or his local bank for nearly five months.

Eventually his oldest son was located, in Pennington, New Jersey, where he lived with his wife and three children. Yep, Dad's been gone for months, he confirmed — right after the company was sold, he and Mom flew south, leased a nice yacht with a small crew, and vowed not to set foot back on American soil until they walked every lovely beach on every neglected island in the Caribbean Sea. Last time they called, they were in Saint Martin, inching their way south toward Trinidad and Tobago. Dad was fine, Mom slightly sunburned but having a blast; his father hinted that this was likely his last call for a long while.

Oh, yes, he could definitely see how his father's long jaunt seemed a little peculiar, Perry's son offered, very agreeably. Then again, Dad had the company he spent forty-five years building stolen under his feet by some big greedy corporation in D.C. If he wanted to vanish for a while, to put it all behind him, who could blame him? Plus, after forty-five years of unrelenting work and crushing responsibilities, why not steal away for a prolonged, sun-soaked hiatus where the most pressing issue was which rum to try next?

Do you happen to know the name of the

boat? the head of DCIS asked with a grave edge. Nope, they never mentioned it. Where did they rent the boat from? You know what, they never mentioned that either.

As they spoke, the son silently congratulated his father on whatever it was he had pulled off. Three Pentagon bigwigs were on the phone line, peppering him with questions. Perry's son wasn't naïve. Their voices crackled with apprehension and accusation.

A scam of some sort, and whatever it was, it had to be huge.

Run, Dad, run, he thought to himself.

The call came at the worst possible moment. After two prolonged days of nearly constant drinking and occasional golf under the baking Bermudan sun, Mitch Walters's back was killing him. He had valiantly teed off that morning, but after the fourth hole he gave up and limped off the course, kneading his lumbar, heading straight to the hotel's massage parlor. A large black masseuse with fingers like power drills was just working his way down the lower vertebrae. Two other CEO types were getting the kinks worked out on nearby tables. To his right was Paul Merrill, the thirty-two-year-old, hyper-brilliant founder of a software firm, now on the *Forbes* list as one of

America's ten richest men. On his left, Carl Jorgenson, a hedge fund guru, also worth billions, just not as many as Merrill, was groaning quietly.

Briefly wondering who might be calling, he positioned the phone to his left ear and grunted, "Mitch Walters" into the receiver.

"This is Thomas Windal." Very abrupt — no hello, no warm greetings.

It took a moment before Walters registered that this was the Pentagon's undersecretary of procurement. "Uh, hi, Tom. How's everything up there?"

"Bad. Awful, Mr. Walters. This call represents your official notification."

Mr. Walters, not Mitch, he noted.

Walters slapped away the hand of the masseuse and sat up. "About what?"

"As of this moment, the polymer contract is suspended. We now enter a thirty-day period. That's how much time you have to show that the polymer is effective or the suspension becomes permanent."

Windal's tone was flat, distant, cold, and officious. In part this was because he was getting his distance from what looked like an impending disaster, and from its author. In larger part, the head of the DCIS and two stone-faced senior agents were standing three feet from Windal's desk, ensuring the legal niceties were strictly adhered to.

Walters felt like somebody had just driven a nine-iron into his groin. "Jesus, Tom, what's this about?" he roared into the phone.

"A courier will drop off the official notification before close of business, Mr. Walters. The details will be noted in the notification. We'll talk through our lawyers from now on," Windal coldly announced before he hung up.

Walters's chubby legs now were swinging off the side of the massage table. His mouth hung open; he couldn't seem to close it. He couldn't seem to put down the cell phone either. The sound of twenty billion dollars slipping away left him too lightheaded to do anything but gawk. Half a minute later, it was still parked at his ear as if Windal was chatting away on the other end.

For some reason, the only thing he could think about was the lobster bisque he had eaten for lunch. Two oversize bowls of the stuff, delicious going down, now threatening to be harsh and bitter on the way back up.

Merrill and Jorgenson were peeking at him with knowing smiles. Nothing so amuses the rich and successful than the sight of a fellow titan crashing and burning. Walters thought about cursing them, or maybe slapping the infuriating smirks off their smug faces. Instead he tried to manufacture a look of deep contentment as he mumbled into the phone, "Yes, yes, and of course, thanks. For a ten billion contract we'll try our best to please."

The other two weren't fooled. They chuckled and shared snickers across the room. As a matter of form, Walters was always invited to these events. That didn't mean they had to like him.

He jumped off the table and scampered to the bathroom. It turned out he was right — the lobster bisque tasted hideous second time around.

He skipped the shower and, still wearing his sweaty golf clothes, bolted for the airport, hopped on the big corporate jet, and raced back to D.C.

Martie O'Neal treated it like an all-out crisis. By Thursday morning he had managed to produce a fairly reasonable sketch of the source of all this trouble: Mia Jenson.

Single, born and bred in Chicago, youngest child, one older sister, three older brothers, father an insurance salesman, mother a stay-at-home type. The Jenson kids all went to college, but Mia was the undisputed star. She excelled at Dickinson but really blossomed at Harvard Law, where the accolades piled up. Nothing in her background or childhood raised any red flags.

But also, nothing yet explained, or so much as hinted at, why she had dumped such a promising, lucrative career for a miserly paycheck in law enforcement. O'Neal's snooping instincts were screaming that this was an important mystery that needed to be answered. Perhaps the most important question.

She lived in a small yet elegant house in D.C., across the busy road from American University in a decent neighborhood of older, modest homes. She had paid cash. No mortgage, no debts at all; just a charge card balance she diligently disposed of at the end of every month. Total savings in the neighborhood of $700K, no doubt the result of her lucrative years in a private firm. She lived prudently and dressed frugally. With her looks, she could wear rags and stop traffic. No expensive habits, good or bad.

Given her lifestyle, and that she had willingly dumped a $400K salary, with a virtual guarantee of doubling that in a few short years, for a paltry $36K a year, Martie doubted she could be bought off for any price.

He decided to call an old chum in his former office in the FBI background unit and eventually was put through to the agent who had performed Mia's check for a secret clearance. A welcome shortcut, but the agent's best efforts proved wretchedly disappointing.

He turned up nothing of any particular interest. She dated occasionally, but nothing serious — not now, not ever. Apparently her beauty, brains, and self-confidence scared off a lot of men. A moderate drinker, there was no evidence of drugs or other nasty addictions. She liked to jog. She was Catholic, though not overly devout. She had plenty of friends, nearly all of whom had swell things to say about her. The striking exception was a classmate from law school, a male, who claimed she was a rabid lesbian feminist, an antisocial, sexually frustrated dyke. The evidence suggested otherwise and that claim was discounted. A bruised and frustrated suitor, most likely.

O'Neal was browsing his notes as he recounted these unhopeful facts to Bellweather and Walters. He had collected a lot more information but sifted out the useless clutter. Who cared what brand of shoe she preferred, or the name of her childhood dog? The two men across from him were grim and tense, and their mood was impatient. It was only six in the morning, still dark outside. Aside from the guards trolling the hallways, they were the only ones in the building. Walters had called him at midnight and insisted he rush in with whatever he had. "So you have nothing we can use against her?" Walters prodded the second he wrapped up, looking like he just got hit by a bus.

"No. Not really. But this is just preliminary. A little more time, I'll find something. Always do."

He didn't feel it necessary to remind them that he had finally nailed their boy Jack. Not that they had congratulated or even thanked him. Then again, in Wiley's case, a little more time had meant four long months with millions in billings.

"We don't have more time," Bellweather snapped. He rubbed his eyes and slid back his chair.

He and Walters looked exhausted. Both were unshowered and unshaven, wearing yesterday's wrinkled clothes — in Walters's case a golf shirt that showed off his over-hanging gut and shorts that displayed his sunburned, hairy legs. Neither man had slept the night before, O'Neal concluded. Walters had developed a nervous twitch that made his left eye flutter. Bellweather seemed cooler and somewhat more collected, but the competition was light.

"Look, you warned me to be careful," O'Neal complained. "That limits my options."

"All right, what's next?" Bellweather asked.

"Haven't gone into her home yet. Who knows what could turn up there, or what nasty surprise we could leave. We could try to infiltrate her family. They always know more dirt than anybody."

"Can you get into her office?" asked Walters, looking hopeful for the first time.

"It's a secure facility," O'Neal replied, wincing as if to underscore how tough it would be. "But yeah, probably. It'll take a little creativity, though. You want to see how much she's got on you, right?"

"That would be nice," Bellweather observed. A wicked smile broke out, his first of the morning.

"But if that doesn't work," Walters snapped, playing the tough guy and pounding a hand on his desk, "it's time to consider other measures. Something more extreme."

"Extreme" was a vague and interesting

word. It could mean blackmail, extortion, or perhaps something considerably more drastic.

O'Neal did not warm to this idea, nor did he ask for clarification. He was more than willing to bend and break a few laws for these people — or, more accurately, their money. No way, though, was he going to snap legs or waste anybody on their behalf. It was a stupid, desperate suggestion anyway.

After a respectful moment meant to suggest he was being thoughtful about it, O'Neal said, "Forget it, Mitch. Christsakes, she's a federal agent."

"So what?" Mitch was suddenly enjoying the thought of her dead.

"Settle down and think. Maybe a week ago you coulda tried something like that. Not now. Not after she popped this bomb on you. Something happens to her now, if she slips and falls on ice, Feds will be crawling up your ass."

"But —"

"Shut up, Mitch," Bellweather snapped with a mean scowl. He turned back to O'Neal. "What about Wiley?"

"What about him? I'm not sure what you want me to do at this point. We're keeping this guy Wallerman on ice, for now."

"Where?"

"Holed up in a luxury suite at the Waldorf-Astoria in New York. Room's four grand a day, he's ordering takeout from Atelier's and Alain Ducasse's, insists on going to a Broadway play every night. He's got us by the balls and knows it. He's costing you boys a bundle. He's two million in the bag on us already, and now he's making noise about more. A lot more."

Bellweather and Walters exchanged looks.

"What does that mean?" Bellweather asked.

"Says he's already accomplished everything we asked. We already got all the help two million will buy."

"How much is he asking?" Walters asked.

"An additional five."

"Five what?"

"What do you think? Five million, or he swears he's through."

"Greedy bastard."

"Thing is, at these prices you should make a decision about Wiley fast. I know you fellas can afford it, but he's getting expensive."

"Well, it's touchy at this point," Bellweather moaned, sounding uncharacteristically uncertain. "Consider the possibility that Wiley conned us. Somebody did, and there are only two candidates. Wiley or Arvan."

"Or maybe both," Walters commented.

"Yeah, but Wiley's done something like this before," O'Neal argued, and the insinuation was clear. "Once that we know of."

An uncomfortable silence hung in the air a moment. They had reached the real purpose of the meeting. Everything was coming unglued so fast: first, Mia's terrifying hint to Jack about that incriminating picture with Earl Belzer; then that horrible bitch getting their precious polymer stopped in its tracks; now the disastrous news that the report that had drawn them to the polymer in the first place was a hangman's noose.

The jackhammers just kept striking. What was next?

It was all happening so fast. They needed to get in front of this thing, get control. This was no time to lash out blindly; neither could they afford to sit tight and do nothing.

"I called Phil last night," Bellweather said softly. "We played with the possibilities until four this morning. Somebody's taking us on a ride."

"Where's Arvan?" Walters asked. He'd given some thought to this as well, and had formed his own suspicions about who might be behind this catastrophe.

"Nobody knows. The Pentagon tried for hours to locate him. He's disappeared, been gone for months. He took our money and fled to Central America." When nobody responded to that revelation, he suggested, "He might've done this alone, or at the least he was Wiley's accomplice."

"Wiley's not our boy," Walters countered, hefting a paperweight in his hand and looking quite sure of himself.

"I suppose you have a reason for that blind opinion."

"Sure, plenty of them. Because Wiley owns a quarter of the polymer. Because he thinks he'll make billions on this deal. So why feed us a poisoned chalice? Why flush a fortune down the toilet? Doesn't make sense. Also, he's still in plain sight, right where we can reach out and touch him."

"Maybe he's not as smart as we thought," O'Neal offered.

"Or he's smarter than we thought," Bellweather snarled, still under the influence of his long, rambling discussion with Jackson the night before. The lawyer never liked Wiley; he certainly never trusted him. Perhaps it was an emotional bias, but he was strongly inclined to believe Wiley was the driving force behind this fiasco. Bellweather badly wished Jackson were here in the room with them now, applying his aloof logic to the situation.

Unfortunately, at a well-attended press conference the night before, the crooked senator Jackson was representing had made a crass stab at pinning the rap on his dead wife. The attempt bombed badly. The senator's teenage children became incensed at all the mean things he said about their mom and hastily rushed out to the parking lot where they convened a fascinating press conference of their own.

The kids confessed they were lurking in a dark corner of the basement, pushing a little coke up their noses, when Dad came bounding down the stairs happily hauling a big sack. Peeking around a bunch of old boxes, they watched their old man pack the dough in the freezer. Took him twenty minutes to cram it all in.

Jackson was with the senator now, at the federal court where he was being arraigned. Jackson had shifted his strategy; now the senator was being framed by his own kids, a bunch of selfish, rotten, ungrateful thugs who got the money pushing drugs to rich classmates at their elite private school. The senator was probably a lost cause, but Phil Jackson never left a client in a lurch, especially when it was such a public spectacle and Jackson could preen and glower in front of the cameras. It was good for business.

"Let's bring Wiley down for a talk," Bell-weather suggested. "Send up the jet. We'll get this straightened out this afternoon."

"Good idea," O'Neal said, having nothing better to offer. "He has no idea you're behind Wallerman. It'll be a big, nasty surprise," he said, only wishing he could be there for the show.

"Any chance you can locate Perry Arvan?" Walters asked, directing a look at O'Neal. He still had his doubts about Wiley. Perhaps it was stupid pride, but he just couldn't believe Jack had outsmarted him.

"I doubt it. I got no people in the Caribbean. I could hire some locals, but nobody I trust. Besides he could be hiding on a boat in the middle of a grove on some out-of-the-way island. Or he might be on the other side of the world. We got only what his kid said. The kid might be wrong, or he might be covering for his old man. Let the Pentagon look for him. They have a much higher chance."

Walters nodded. Made sense.

For now they would concentrate on the bird in hand, Jack Wiley.

24

It turned out Jack had left his car in D.C. after his last visit. Some sort of vacuum lock developed in his brakes, he left the car at a repair shop, and took the train and taxi home. The car now sat in the CG parking lot, fit and ready to roll, but clearly some other means of transportation needed to be devised.

So Bill Feist was sent up with the smaller jet to fetch Jack. No need to pretend to be pleasant this time, and it was a point of pride with Feist to suck up only when he had to. From the opening moment, he was cold and distant. Jack came along willingly. He kept to himself. He folded his long frame in the seat and read a trashy paperback novel on the way down.

Feist sipped gin by himself and stared out the window at the ground whizzing by below.

An hour later, they landed at Reagan

National and glided up to the private terminal. Thirty minutes after that, following a fast sprint in a corporate limo through D.C. traffic, they were standing outside the CG conference room.

Jackson had finally torn himself away from the senator's road show and the warm glare of the rolling cameras. After arranging bail, stealing a quick shower, then spending five minutes alone with Lew Wallerman, he quickly decided he liked what Lew had to show him. In the right hands — his hands — it would be devastating. He grabbed the evidence and brusquely ordered Wallerman to wait in a side room until called.

Jack came into the room and fell into the same chair he had occupied all those months before, when he and Walters had scrawled their names on that now regrettable contract.

As before, the steering committee was arraigned on the opposite side, but this time deep frowns replaced the greedy smiles. No refreshments on the side table. No warm greetings. Nobody jumped up to pump his hand and tell him how swell it was for him to be there.

Now Jack was the enemy.

A tape recorder was gently whirring somewhere in the background, feeding the whole session to the secret room in the basement. The tape would be carefully doctored afterward. Certain parts would be omitted, but they were confident they would coerce or dupe Jack into making a few incriminating admissions. A few was all they needed.

"We have some questions," Jackson opened with a severe glare. "Have you heard the news about the polymer?"

"What news?" Jack asked. He looked around the table, genuinely curious.

"Our contract's been suspended. The report you gave us was a phony, an interim report that was overcome by events and supposed to be shelved. The precious polymer you led us to has a short half-life. That's a big problem for us." Jackson bent forward. "So the first question is, where did you get that report, Jack?"

They watched his face to see how this horrible update registered. Jack pulled on an earlobe and stared at the table. "This is news to me."

"Is it?"

"Yes, and I'm sorry. Can we fix it?"

"We're not here to answer your questions. Where did you get that report?"

Jack took his eyes off the table. "I'm getting tired of that question, Phil. It's still none of your damned business."

"It's very much our damned business. We're confronting the possibility of a major fraud investigation as a result of that report. You're implicated as well, Wiley. Now, where did you get it?"

"You have your facts wrong, Phil."

"Do I?"

"It wasn't me who used that report to persuade the Pentagon to buy the polymer. I questioned Mitch and Dan about short-cutting the Pentagon testing requirements. I was sure it was a bad idea. Both assured me it was no problem."

Jackson swung and examined the faces of Bellweather and Walters. "Is he telling the truth?"

"No, he's lying," Walters insisted in a rush of words — of course it was true.

Bellweather affirmed the bald lie with a hard nod.

"Where'd you get that damned report?" Jackson demanded, more loudly and slamming a fist on the table.

"You must enjoy the same answer. None of your business."

The four men on the other side of the table exchanged quick glances; without a word they decided to jettison the friendly approach, which really was never that friendly anyway.

Bellweather pushed forward in his chair and tried to look sad. "Sorry, Jack, you're making us do this," he said, trying to make it sound deeply lamentable. His hand reached out and punched a button on the table.

A few seconds later, the door swung open and Lew Wallerman entered. He swaggered to the head of the table and stood, smiling at Jack, smiling at them, smiling at the walls — he couldn't stop smiling.

A look of what could only be called shock registered on Jack's face. He tried to recover but it was hopeless. "Lew, what are you doing here?" he asked limply.

Lew was enjoying his moment in the limelight. He was thrilled to be here, and happier still to see the terror on Jack's face. He was happiest of all, though, over the five million bucks wired only an hour before to the bank of his choice. That five now sat with the other two million chilling in a Bahamian vault. Lew was suddenly a rich man. "I'm friends with these boys here," he boasted, directing an arm at the right side of the table, where the steering committee sat intently watching Jack's face.

Jack said nothing. No wisecracks or grating taunts for once. His lips were stapled shut. He was staring at Wallerman as though

Jeffrey Dahmer had just joined him at the dinner table.

"Hey, pal, don't look so surprised," Lew said, leering back. "I warned you we'd get together again."

"This is crazy, Lew. We can work this out."

"Can we?"

"Let's have a word, just you and me, outside." Jack began pushing himself out of the chair.

"Forget it, Jack."

Jack collapsed back into the chair.

It was Jackson's turn, and he shoved a large green file box toward the middle of the shiny conference table. "Know what this is?" he asked with a sadistic grin. He patted the top of the box fondly.

Jack gaped at it. After a short moment that seemed to stretch forever, he muttered, "I can guess."

"I wouldn't want you to guess wrong."

"I'm sure you'll enjoy educating me."

"You're right. I'll enjoy it immensely. Inside is a long and incriminating report from a Greek detective agency about the disappearance of Edith Warbinger. Also plane tickets, charge card receipts, and hotel billings that shed a great deal of light on an old mystery. More than enough light, Jack, to resurrect a murder investigation."

Jack couldn't tear his eyes off that damned box.

"It might be somewhat circumstantial," Jackson continued in a maddeningly calm tone. "But in my view, it's enough for a conviction. Murder, grand theft, graft, those are just a few of the high points."

He fell silent and allowed Jack a generously long moment to consider this news.

"This is blackmail," Jack stammered.

"Well . . . yes," Walters chimed in from the side with a dark smile. "You got us in this mess, Wiley. And you're going to help us out of it, or we're going to destroy you. You'll go away for life, believe me."

"We regret we had to do this," Bellweather said gravely, trying to look and act like the good cop amid a roomful of horrible cops. It wasn't convincing. "You left us little choice, Jack."

"I can see it's breaking your hearts. Tell me what you want."

"For starters, where did you get that report?" Jackson demanded for the fifth time.

"Where do you think I got it?"

"Perry Arvan."

"Good guess."

"Did you know it was a false representation? Who was behind this scam?"

Jack sat up and rubbed his temples. "Why don't you ask Perry?"

"He's gone. Disappeared into the Caribbean. Hasn't been seen in months."

Walters complained, "He took our hundred million, saddled us with this pig in lipstick, and went on the lam."

"Good for him," Jack mumbled. He was back to staring down at the table.

"If you think that's funny, it's not," Jackson roared. Incredibly, he thought he saw the hint of a smile beginning to form on Jack's lips.

Jack stood up. He looked at the faces across the table. A change seemed to come over him. "You know what?" He paused and appeared to make up his mind. "I'm tired of your stupid questions."

"No you're not. Sit down and finish or I'll shove this evidence up your ass."

"I don't think you will. For a lawyer you're painfully inept, Jackson."

"What?"

"You know the phrase Mexican standoff? Maybe mutually assured destruction works better. The moment I'm arrested, I'll start singing. I'll have nothing to lose. I'll cut the best deal I can get, and tell everything I know, which is considerable. We'll all hang together."

Before anybody could answer, Jack faced Wallerman and suggested, "Go screw yourself, Lew."

He ducked out the door before any of the stunned men could think up a reply.

Mitch Walters shut and locked his office door. He walked back to his desk, trying to avoid the harsh stares from Bellweather, Jackson, and Haggar, who were sitting stiffly in the chairs splayed around the office.

They were still stunned by Wiley's response. They had been so sure he would collapse in fear and meet their every demand. They were going to force him to take the fall over this. The rest of his life in prison for murder, or a far shorter term for confessing to authoring this scam. That was the deal they were prepared to offer him. There really was no choice for Jack. That was the script they had cobbled together that morning; unfortunately, the lead in their nasty little play totally blew his lines.

Jack had a good point, though. They were pointing loaded guns at each other's heads. Their finely honed plan was now in shreds. Somebody should've seen it coming. If they all weren't so exhausted and under such miserable strain, they would've seen the flaw in their plan.

Nobody was ready to propose a new one.

Walters could sense the coldness from the others. Three sets of mean eyes watching him. He knew they were going to hang this on him if he gave them half a chance.

"Has anybody briefed the board about this yet?" Jackson asked.

Walters glanced at his watch and said nothing. The name of the game had just switched to damage control. That meant three big questions: How screwed were they? What steps did they need to take to squirm out of it? And how much was this going to cost?

"Not yet," Bellweather answered, sounding miserable. "They'll have to be told today, I suppose."

They all knew it was going to be ugly. It was nearly impossible to assess the carnage at this point. So much hung on the immense profitability of the polymer. In a year of sorely depressed earnings, the polymer was going to be the golden fountain that spewed out such immense profits, the savior that covered up so many sins and weaknesses. It had promised so much.

The directors were going to throw a noisy fit. They would cry and howl and wail, and eventually they would demand heads.

What to do about the impending legal

situation was a different matter, a far touchier one. Handled properly, it would be mildly embarrassing, but they were confident they could contain the damage and avoid a major scandal. They would do the usual: stonewall, bury the evidence, and pull all the right strings. In this town, the right favors in the right circles, enough money tucked in the right pockets, and who knew — maybe, just maybe, they could limit this to a minor humiliation.

Thank God they weren't a public company and didn't have to concern themselves with all those complications. There would be no stockholders' revolt, no hammering of their stock, no antagonistic directors screaming for a bloody purge. Fortunately, no big concerns from the SEC either.

"How are we going to manage this?" Haggar asked, getting to the point.

Jackson jumped in. "First thing we're going to do is destroy all the files." He glanced at Walters. "No subpoenas have been issued. Not yet. Get rid of everything, incriminating or otherwise."

"Got it. A big, indiscriminate bonfire before close of business."

"Is there anybody in the firm who knows enough to do us harm?"

"A few folks, probably. I'll have to think

about it."

"Make a list and gather them together. Be liberal, don't overlook anybody. Have legal counsel remind them about their legal obligations to the firm, then offer a strong recommendation about the right to remain silent."

"Easy enough."

"You might want to consider a few quick overseas transfers. Anybody who looks like trouble, send them to the other side of the moon. Tomorrow wouldn't be too fast."

Walters nodded. What a relief to have the expert in scandals here, offering his sage advice.

Jackson rubbed his jaw and looked thoughtful. "Here's the only happy news. Nobody was killed or harmed as a result of the polymer. At least we don't have to worry about our exposure to lawsuits from distraught families." He seemed to be rattling down a mental checklist titled "How screwed am I?"

"Right," Walters said.

"However, the Pentagon might launch a big suit to recover its expenditures. It's worst-case, but we need to consider it. How much have they paid out to date?"

Walters squirmed in his seat. He suddenly looked like his hemorrhoids were killing him. His eyebrows bunched together, and his lips felt rubbery. This was the one question he had hoped to avoid. He had lain awake the night before, sweating and contemplating the numbers.

He briefly weighed lying, or just fudging a bit. What would be the point, though? "Roughly three billion as of a month ago," he mumbled, garbling his words, hoping they couldn't hear him. "Might be another billion since then. Hard to say. A lot of big costs were front-loaded."

Jackson heard him only too well and seemed to choke. "Four billion?"

"Or maybe five," he admitted, looking away. Actually five and a half, he well knew. "What's the difference?" His eyes shifted back to their faces. "I didn't hear anybody complain when it was pouring in."

Jackson began asking questions hard and fast, forcing Walters to disclose the full and complete possible financial damage. Walters tried his best to dodge and weave and trim, but Jackson was brutally relentless.

It began to sink in what a terrible finanicial disaster this could be; it was far worse than anybody had imagined. There was a bad case and a worst case; the difference between them was almost insignificant.

The bottom line was possibly six billion in

direct losses — one promised to the Saudis, five to the Pentagon — plus many more hundreds of millions in sunk expenses — the hundred million paid to Perry Arvan, thirty-six million more to Arvan's stockholders, twenty million to Wiley for his finder's bonus, another twenty million spent on the influence-buying spree around Washington. Another three million frittered away to get the goods on Jack, money billed by TFAC, and over seven million in bribes paid to Charles and Wallerman, none of which would see the light of day on any corporate ledger.

Then, whatever had been wasted on upgrading factories, hiring workers, raw materials, etc., etc. Throw in another two or three hundred million there, Walters guessed — the numbers were already dizzying.

Nobody had worried about the costs when the polymer looked like a fountainhead of profit. Money had been spent profligately with little regard to the risks. They had been so sure of themselves, so optimistic about their amazing product, so quick to commit a hundred million here, five hundred million there. Chump change when the dream promised to produce tens of billions in profit.

When you're robbing a bank you don't

stop to count the change.

Coming back as losses, the numbers fell like artillery shells.

Their moods sank from bad to nearly suicidal.

There also was the ancillary financial damage to be factored into the heartbreaking total. Globalbang, which Walters had coerced into canceling Arvan's chemical contract, had never recovered. After the other suppliers witnessed Globalbang pulling the plug on Arvan, nearly all of them sprinted for the exits the moment their contracts expired. No way were they going to bank their economic survival on a firm that behaved so arbitrarily, so dishonorably, so cruelly.

Suddenly denied the materials to manufacture its rockets and bombs, after several months of desperate efforts, Globalbang strangled to death on a last series of futile cost cuts. It went bankrupt and out of business.

The Capitol Group had paid a whopping three billion for Globalbang back in the opening year of the Iraq war, when it seemed that buying any defense company was a license to print money. According to the general accounting principles, that stupendous write-off would have to go on this year's annual earnings. Yet another casualty of the cursed polymer.

Walters tried to make the feeble argument that the steep losses offered a tax offset, as if that was a solace. It wasn't, not at all. It was dawning on everyone in the room that, for the first time in the Capitol Group's storied history, there would be no annual profit to be taxed.

Jackson was scribbling numbers on a legal pad as fast as his ears and fingers could keep up. The creaming was worse than he ever imagined. As best he could tell, the loss could total a whopping ten billion. Ten billion!

Once Jackson mumbled that number out loud, the magnitude began sinking in with Walters. His face went pale, his chest ached, he was having trouble breathing.

The fat bonus he had planned on demanding, and had already mentally spent, was laughable. The three-million-dollar renovation of his Great Falls estate would have to stop. He'd have to withdraw the offer he made two weeks before for the lovely lodge in Aspen. He would be lucky to hold on to his job.

Jackson and Bellweather looked almost as miserable. Both had vast fortunes already, enough and more to live in grand style for the rest of their lives. But like many rich men, it was never enough. In a city increasingly sprinkled with billionaires, both were nothing more than run-of-the-mill millionaires. Sadly, millionaires just didn't get the respect they once enjoyed. A billion bought much better invitations, better access, vastly more people sucking up to you. And the word "billionaire" just sounded so much better; it had such a charming ring when the lips pursed to spit that lovely word.

The polymer had been their ticket from the M-word to the B-ranks.

Haggar wasn't nearly as depressed about the numbers as the other three. They, as well as the other directors, all had big, expensive mansions, fleets of cars, vacation homes, yachts, greedy ex-wives, even a smattering of private jets to worry about. Big lifestyles required big profits.

After a long, impoverishing career in stingy public service, Haggar had yet to cash in and had relatively little money. His lifestyle remained modest. He had few expenses — a fair-sized town house in Springfield, one kid so disgruntled, dumb, and lazy he was lucky to be attending an inexpensive community college. Plus he was still married to his first wife, the same college sweetheart he'd been hitched to the past thirty years, through good times and bad, sickness and health, and all that. In truth, they could barely stand the sight of each other. They slept in different beds, used different bathrooms, avoided each other as much as possible. But both, for their own selfish reasons, had seen his job in the Capitol Group as a reason to tough it out.

Haggar planned on waiting till he made a bundle before cashing her in for his dream, a younger trophy, somebody with uplifted boobs, slimmer thighs, less wrinkles. Someone always ready and willing for a little sex.

Her plan was to wait till he was rich enough to be worth divorcing.

Well, what the hell, Haggar figured. After ten years of sleeping in separate beds, the dream could wait for another few years.

25

They picked up Jack the moment he rushed out of the big cylinder that housed CG's headquarters, jumped into his car, and sped away. Following him was too easy. Months before, they had planted a tracking device on the undercarriage of his Lincoln. Though he spent much of his time at home, they liked the cool assurance of knowing he couldn't slip away.

They stayed at a safe distance, usually at least three cars back. The risk of being spotted was much higher than any chance of letting him slip, which was essentially zero. The tracking device was the newest thing, tethered to a satellite thousands of miles overhead; he could be driving in Europe and they'd know which street, to within ten inches. They followed at a leisurely pace, as Jack shot across the Memorial Bridge, then ground his way through the thick, midday D.C. traffic. Once or twice he got a few headlights ahead, but the TFAC trackers remained calm.

They had expected him to jump on 95 and bolt north, directly toward Jersey and his big house. Apparently he had business in D.C. to accomplish before he made the long drive home.

They were stuck at a red light when Jack made an abrupt left turn and sprinted into the busier streets of a shopping section. Every inch of his progress was followed carefully and closely on their screen. They were only mildly concerned when he made another quick turn, then his Lincoln stopped for a moment, then picked up speed again and began doing slow circles on their screen.

"Better kick it up a notch," the passenger ordered the driver. He glanced at his watch, then buried his face back in the tracking screen.

"What is it?"

"I dunno. Target's doing small circles." He thought about it a few seconds. "Maybe a parking garage."

The driver tried edging around the cars directly to his front but it was no use. He pounded the horn a few times and was coldly ignored. D.C. drivers.

He finally turned left, then followed the

tracker's orders straight to a large parking garage on 18th Northwest. "Should we go in?" he asked.

"No, pull over. Let's see when he comes out."

By his calculation, Jack's car had entered the garage only two minutes before. He watched the garage entrance for a moment before he saw people getting out of their cars, and attendants climbing in to park them.

"Damn it, it's full-service," he complained, banging a hand off the dash.

"We lost him," the driver said, voicing the obvious.

"Don't sweat it, we'll find him. Cruise around. Keep your eyes peeled on the shops and local buildings. He can't be far."

Wrong guess, because Jack at that moment was seated in the rear of a taxi speeding toward Union Station. He had called for the cab from his cell phone, and dodged into the back a moment after the attendant handed him a parking ticket for his car. Thirty thousand dollars in large bills were stuffed in his pocket. Another pocket held his Amtrak ticket for an afternoon run to New York City. A rental car arranged by somebody else awaited him there.

This was his plan, the getaway meticulously plotted and prepared so many months before. It was always inevitable that CG would begin putting things together, eventually. Once they got an inkling of what he had done, things would turn dangerous. He knew his house was being watched, knew about the trailers who followed him everywhere.

It was time to dump the watchers and trackers and disappear for a while. Time to go underground, time to see how things developed and make his next moves from there.

Everything would be handled with cash. A complete set of papers sat in the bottom of his briefcase, under a different name, a passport, charge cards, driver's license. His money, almost fifty million in cash, was at that moment electronically careening through various overseas banks. It would not stop moving for hours, until all possible trace was lost.

A trusted friend with long experience in these matters was handling the transactions. By six, the money would be cooling its heels in an impenetrable Swiss bank, undetectable to anyone hunting for Jack.

He pulled out a cell phone and placed a quick call to his lawyer. The conversation was short and to the point. The second he finished, he ditched the cell phone with a quick toss out the window. Ten more disposable cell phones were stashed in the rental car in New York. Can't be too careful, he reminded himself as the Capitol dome flashed by to his right.

Things were about to turn really interesting.

The neighborhood was dark and almost spookily quiet. The skies were thick with clouds that hid the moon, and that made them happy. They were parked in a narrow alleyway up on a hill less than a block behind her house. They could look down and see everything.

She got home from work later than the past three nights, at eight, and launched into her usual ritual. After seven days of watching and peeking, they could almost predict what she'd do next. They made a game of it and tried, but it was too easy to be fun. They quickly lost interest.

It was a small house with large windows — women had such a thing for light — and they could observe her every move with a pair of good German-made binoculars. First, thirty minutes in the kitchen cooking roast beef and potatoes. Chicken the night before, now she was in the mood for beef.

She carried her plate into her den, sat down on the couch, and settled in to catch the evening news as she nibbled from her plate. At nine she switched channels, started to watch a movie, quickly became bored, dumped the plate in the kitchen, and shifted to the bedroom.

She undressed and changed in her bathroom, emerging fifteen minutes later with her teeth and hair brushed, in a stingy teddy they all admired immensely. Nice long legs, broad shoulders, wonderful athletic build, they agreed. They laughed and shared a few lewd comments to illuminate the extent of their veneration. After fifteen minutes of reading, the bedside light flipped off. Nighty-night, Mia, one of them crooned.

That was three hours before. "Time to go, boys," Castile, the boss, hissed at the others. The moon had just dodged behind some thick clouds, the lights were off in the surrounding homes. It was perfect.

They eased out of the car and crept through the small, well-kept yards of the two houses directly behind hers. Three men in all, scooting along in dark pants, black sweatshirts, and running shoes, and each had a balaclava hood rolled on his head, which they tugged down the moment before they entered her home.

Castile, the expert at locks, did the honors. He had it picked in less than a minute, he eased the door open, and one by one they snuck inside. The house was pitch-dark but for a few night-lights sprinkled in strategic locations. Just right. Jones hauled in the bag filled with the evidence it was his task to plant in some suitable location. Phillips crept swiftly and silently through the kitchen, through the tiny living room, straight to her bedroom door, which was closed tight, as they knew it would be. He hefted the baseball bat in his right hand and waited. He was the security hack. If the door opened, if she peeked out, he would bean her, hard, and they would bolt into the dark night.

Castile tiptoed to the den. He flicked on his pencil flashlight with a concentrated directional beam and surveyed the surroundings for a moment. A small room, nothing much here. Two bookcases packed with thick legal volumes and a few novels. A short wooden filing case in the corner. A desk against the far wall — a wooden double-pedestal model with three locked drawers on the right side.

After deciding to tackle the desk first, he bent over and got to work on the locks.

Jones, in the interim, had found the back

stairs and worked his way down to the basement, which was pitch-dark. His flashlight came on and he began nosing around to select the perfect place. The basement had recently been refinished and was nicely done in his view — a fifty-inch flat-panel hanging on the wall, with a pair of thick leather couches arrayed for a great view. There were two doors, and Jones eased open the nearest one first. A small bathroom that definitely wouldn't do, and he quickly moved on. He opened the other door, and voilà — a storage room cluttered with boxes, oversize luggage, and unwanted furniture. Perfect, just ideal. He hauled in the bag and got to work, unpacking the contents and stashing bits and pieces in various places that weren't too obvious, but not too inconspicuous either.

It was at that moment that the lights flashed on. He would remember that distinctly, for whatever it was worth. They emanated from outside and seemed to pour through every window in the house, accompanied by the loud sounds of both the front and side doors crashing open at once.

Then what seemed like an army of cops swarmed inside, hollering and flashing their guns. As though they had X-ray eyes, they spread out and lunged straight for the three men inside.

Phillips was still standing beside the door, hefting his bat, when three cops showed up, pointing big mean pistols in his face, one screaming, "Drop the bat, asshole, or you're dead."

Phillips cursed, closed his eyes, and dropped the bat.

Castile was caught just as he pried open the second drawer. He wasn't ordered to do anything — two cops jumped on top of him, forcefully wrestled his arms behind his back, and slapped on a tight pair of cuffs.

Jones had just removed another brick of heroin from the sack when his turn came. Two cops pounded down the stairs and burst in, at exactly the wrong moment as far as Jones was concerned. They smiled as he dropped the brick and tried desperately to look innocent.

In less than a minute all three burglars were standing in the living room wearing matching pairs of cuffs. They were efficiently patted down by a mountain of a cop, who observed to the others that none of the three were carrying identification. The matching dark clothes, the lack of ID — the cops understood immediately. They were dealing with pros. "Keep your mouths shut," a plainclothes officer barked in their faces every time they tried to speak.

The front door flew open and Mia Jenson, dressed in dark jeans and a dark overcoat, stepped inside. A gun was holstered to her waist; a pissed-off frown was holstered to her face. "Well, well, what are you boys up to?"

The breath seemed to escape from their lungs at the shock of seeing her. How did she get outside? They had seen her in bed, with the lights out. How did she get dressed, and what was she doing with all these cops?

The idea that they'd been set up dawned on them like a bad dream. One of the cops began blasting their rights into their stunned faces; they shuffled their feet and stood dumbly taking them in.

But they were all professionals and had a well-rehearsed routine in the event something like this happened. Well, not exactly like this, not with ten cops staring down their throats in a trap they had blundered right into. And definitely not with the homeowner standing with her hands on her hips, a pistol strapped to her waist and a knowing look in her eyes.

Castile owned the lead role, and plunged in with a high-pitched squeal: "I don't get it. What's going on here?" he demanded. "What are you doin' in my cousin's house?"

"Your cousin?" Mia asked, cocking her head.

"Yeah, Juanita Alvarez. She asked us to do a little favor." A perplexed expression popped onto his narrow face. "Wait a minute, don't tell me we got the wrong address."

Mia seemed to smile. "What kind of favor would that be?"

"She had some stuff in the basement she wanted picked up. Important papers in her office, too. The drawers were locked, so you know, I had to jimmy 'em open."

Mia searched the faces of the other two men. "Is he telling the truth?"

"Absolutely," Jones rushed to say.

"Definitely true," Phillips echoed quite fervently.

The faces of the three men now looked aggrieved and flabbergasted at the shocking injustice of the situation. We're good guys, their faces screamed, just doing a family favor, and how could this mean lady misinterpret the purity of our motives?

"What's the bat for?" Mia asked Phillips.

"Uh . . . Juanita said the place had rats. I hate rats."

She faced Jones. "And what's in the bag?"

"Rat poison," Jones said, smiling at his pals.

"And I suppose you lost the house keys Juanita gave you?" Mia asked, again facing Castile.

"Must've put 'em in the wrong pants," he acknowledged, shrugging his skinny shoulders. They were sounding and looking quite cocky now.

Mia crossed her arms and stood back a minute. "What a creative alibi," she said, heavy on the sarcasm. "If it weren't for the pictures, and all we already know about you boys, I might let you walk out the door."

"What pictures?" Castile asked. This didn't sound good.

It wasn't. A helpful cop quickly shoved a clutch of ten-by-twelve black-and-white photographs into Mia's hand. Each was helpfully date and time-stamped. Mia flashed them up, one by one, long enough for all three men to enjoy a long gape. There was Jones picking his nose while seated in a nondescript gray car parked across the street from her house, taken a week before. Then Castile with his skinny, bony ass stuck up in the air, bent over, inspecting the lock of her side door in bright daylight only two days before — the time stamp said it was two in the afternoon. Mia was at work, and he wanted to be sure he brought the right pick for the break-in.

Then more shots of all three men taken at various times and in an assortment of angles and poses over the past week, observing her house, casing it, preparing the break-in.

The pictures were irrevocably damning. The alibi suddenly sounded stupid.

It struck Castile that this might be a good time to shut his mouth.

Mia said, very cool, very indifferent, "Breaking and entering, that's good for seven years, minimum. But the bat's a deadly weapon, and that has to be considered. I'd say at least another five." She pointed at the bag by Jones's feet. "I'm betting those ugly brown bricks are pure heroin. Looking at it, I'd say it's about ten pounds' worth, probably good for another thirty years. All told, that's forty years, give or take a few. What do you think, Lieutenant?"

"A little on the cheap side," the cop in plainclothes opined. He scratched his big nose and looked thoughtful. "Conspiracy, too. You forgot that."

"Oh, damn. Add another five."

They let that sink in a moment, then the lieutenant shifted his feet and said, "But I'm guessing the guy without the bat or drugs will cut a deal and rat out the other two. The guy with the bat, well, he could avoid the thirty for the dope, so probably he'll squeal, too. That leaves bozo here" — he pointed a thick finger in Jones's face — "my money's on him. He's doing the long stretch."

Poor Marvin Jones suddenly couldn't breathe. He closed his eyes and nearly passed out. This was so unfair.

"Sucker's bet," Mia announced, playing along. "Definitely, he's the lifer."

"We ain't talking," Castile sneered, looking more at Jones than anybody else. "In fact, we want our lawyers."

The lieutenant, a rough-looking type with a pot gut, edged forward. He got up in their faces. "I suspect you guys already know how this game works. Still, here's a few tips. Cops hate lawyers. Know what I mean? They suck all the generosity out of the room. Sure, you can have your damn mouthpieces, any damn time you want, but the deals won't be nearly as sweet."

"Let's separate them and see who's willing to volunteer statements now," Mia suggested. She pointed a manicured fingernail at Castile and Phillips. "Take them into separate rooms. See who wants to talk."

Castile and Phillips were hustled out of the room. Castile disappeared into her bedroom, Phillips stumbled into the compact kitchen.

Mia and a uniformed cop with an evident affection for the weight room, along with a sulky-looking Jones, were left standing alone in the small living room. Nobody spoke. Not a word, not a whisper. Jones couldn't seem to tear his eyes off the pattern of the Indian carpet on the floor. His chest was pounding. Sweat was forming a puddle in the small of his back.

After an interminable three minutes, Mia asked Jones, "Would you care to guess what they're saying in there?"

He shuffled his feet a moment, then said, "My buddies would never screw me."

"Jonesy, you're an idiot if you really believe you're worth thirty-five more years in prison to them. Could it be you're even stupider than you look?"

His name. She knew his name, and that really shook him. Only one way that could happen, somebody was already talking, already ratting. In fact, as he thought about it, somebody had tipped her off about the break-in. How else could they have been caught in this setup? His body began shaking. He never imagined they would get caught. And nobody ever mentioned that the idiot hauling the dope got the booby prize.

"Thing is," Mia continued, still very factual, "I should be very pissed at you. I'm betting that dope was meant to frame me, a federal agent."

Another nail in the coffin. Was it worse when you tried to frame a *federal agent?* Jones bit his lip and stared harder at the carpet. How much more did that tack on to his sentence?

"Odd, I know, but now I just feel sorry for you," Mia said, and she sounded very genuine.

At least they had something in common. Jones was definitely feeling sorry for himself, too. Were it he in one of the other rooms, he wouldn't hesitate a moment; without the slightest qualm he'd cut the fastest deal he could get, and begin shoving the blame at the idiot carrying the bag. The dope charge terrorized him. It was twelve pounds, not ten — not that the additional two made any difference. The sentencing guidelines for twelve pounds of heroin were brutal.

And they'd caught him fair and square, in the basement, holding a Hefty bag filled with junk in his right hand, with a big brick in his left hand.

"But there might be a way you can help yourself, Mr. Jones," Mia offered, with only a hint of reservation.

Jones saw a ray of hope, for the first time. "Tell me. What is it?"

"You want to talk about TFAC? If you have anything helpful, I'll do my best to get you a little slack."

So she knew about TFAC, too. What didn't she know? A lot, he hoped, because he suddenly felt an irrepressible urge to tell her anything she was interested in. Names, dates, his wife's embarrassing incontinence issues — name it, and he'd talk her ear off. "What's it worth and what do you want to know?" Jones asked, trying his damnedest to sound like he still had a choice in this matter.

"I'll try to get twenty knocked off. That leaves twenty, max. Behave like a model citizen, you'll cut that in half."

The nods were so fierce he nearly broke his neck. Ten years suddenly sounded like a short holiday.

"TFAC hired you to do this job, right?" Mia suggested.

"Yeah, sorta. We're contractors. TFAC brings us in for the occasional job."

"Who brings you in? Give me a name."

He thought about the twenty years knocked off his sentence — "O'Neal. Martie O'Neal." The name couldn't come out fast enough.

"What were you asked to do?"

"Look for dirt. Plant bugs in your phones. Leave a little gift somewhere in your home."

"The heroin. To set me up, right?"

"I guess. What happens afterward, I don't know." He tried desperately to sound convincing. He would never knowingly try to hurt the nice lady with twenty years of his life in her hands.

"Who's TFAC's client for this job?"

"I dunno. I swear I don't. They never tell us. I'd tell you if I knew, I just can't."

"Have you done a job like this before?"

"Yeah, coupla times."

"When was the last time?"

"Seven, maybe eight months ago."

"Who? Where?"

"Some rich guy. Up in Jersey."

"Name?"

"Wiley. Uh, Jack, or John, I think."

Mia seemed to be out of questions for the moment. The instant they got him to the station, he would spend hours being grilled on tape and filmed. Now that he was already squealing and on record with a few big admissions, the hardest part would be getting him to shut up.

She turned to the uniform. "Get him the hell out of my house and book him. Make sure he's kept away from the others."

Jones was led out the door, tears rolling down his cheeks, as he stumbled over his own feet. Castile and Phillips were also singing their hearts out, answering any question thrown their way. All three were small fry, almost insignificant in the big scheme, though. Mia didn't really care how many years they got, if indeed they got any at all.

As long as they spilled their secrets, as long as everything was on record and legally admissible.

As long as they helped her bag the big fish.

The same night, a Pentagon spokesperson, anonymously of course, leaked to the press that the $20 billion polymer contract was suspended, pending a careful review to determine its ultimate efficacy.

The decision to drop the news this way, so lacking in richness or detail or attribution, came straight from the top. The Secretary of Defense was understandably furious, but controlled. There was, as yet, no definitive evidence that the polymer failed after four months — nothing but a musty old report done years before by some private company.

In another week or two, assuming the original tests were correct, the first polymer coatings might start failing and they would know for sure about the polymer's fleeting qualities. Until then at least, he wanted this handled without any grandstanding.

But the secretary's patience with all the dirty scandals emerging from the Iraq war was exhausted. There had been so many. The greedy contracting officer who took kickbacks. The tortures committed in military prisons. The sleazy oil deals made quietly under the table. The massive arms shipment that was mysteriously misplaced and ended up in the hands of Iraqi insurgents. And too many other disgraceful memories, large and small.

So much of his limited time had been spent fending off congressional inquiries or wrestling with nosy, ambitious journalists who just wouldn't get off it.

Big wars involved big money; a little bit of profiteering was to be expected. Wars spawned greed, what's new? Deplorable certainly, but human nature didn't take a holiday just because the bullets were flying.

This, though, was different, involving as it did one of America's largest, most prestigious private equity firms. CG was a powerhouse, widely feared, vaguely admired, and uniformly envied in the corridors of power. A former American president, former secretary of state, ex–secretary of defense, all those impressive, famous foreign leaders, and countless lesser officials — barring a footlocker full of the most damning evidence, CG was not to be trifled with. The secretary definitely didn't want to jump the gun, half-cocked. A single misstep at this stage and CG would pull out all the stops and make him pay dearly.

So whatever was done had to be accomplished quietly, respectfully, and fast. No big public announcement, no fanfare was the order of the day. Word was passed down, through the deputy secretary, then the undersecretaries, then the assistants, and deputy assistants to the assistants, to all the grandly titled minions, that the only leaks on this affair would come through the secretary himself, or else.

Naturally, long before his stern warning made it halfway down the chain, the nosy Pentagon press learned all about his gag order. And predictably, they launched into an all-out frenzy. They began working the corridors, jawboning their favorite snitches, fighting to be the first to get the scoop, vacuuming for all they were worth.

To their immense surprise, there was remarkably little to learn. The stop order on the polymer had grown out of a vague warning from the Defense Criminal Investigative

Service. Few knew the details, including anybody they talked to. No nasty charges had been preferred, no big investigation initiated.

It certainly smelled like a big story, rife with the promise of a loud and embarrassing scandal. The secretary's information crackdown hinted at fear, and in their world, where there's fear, there's the possibility of a Pulitzer.

But with so little to go on, they were forced to hold their fire until, as inevitably happened, they found the crack in the ice.

In military parlance, the scandal light was lit. The reporters smuggled in booze and videos and sleeping bags, continued to work the corridors, huddled in small packs to share the latest scuttlebutt, and hunkered down in their cramped office carrels for the wait.

26

Rufus Clark was a two-bit Chicago private investigator with a less than promising practice. Nasty divorces, property disputes, and missing cats and dogs were his usual fare. Two thousand in a good month, and those were rare. He was thirty-two years old, single, with two illegitimate children, and still lived with his mother.

His lone claim to fame, pitiful as it happened to be, but one he proudly inflated to his clients, was one brief year he spent in the FBI, before being caught smoking a little weed and sleeping with some whores provided by a local crime lord whose questionable activities the Bureau was looking into. For once in his sorry life, Rufus got lucky. Too little evidence existed to do anything but show him the door.

Given his questionable background and severely limited policing experience, Rufus tended to jump at any work he could get without any serious consideration about its legality. So when Martie O'Neal called with a generous offer of $10K for only one day's work, Rufus dove in.

He held the small photograph two inches from his nose and again studied the man across the lobby. Oh yeah, definitely him, he decided, taking a few steps closer.

Martie had e-mailed him the name, work address, this old DMV photo, a few instructive background notes, and a brief list of questions for Rufus to get answered.

His target was tall and thin, wearing a nice blue suit and holding a battered old briefcase as he stood by the elevator doors and waited. Rufus edged a little closer, within striking distance, just not enough to attract attention.

The elevator door opened and Rufus closed the distance fast and darted in before the door could close. Then it was just Rufus and his target standing side by side. His target was too busy watching the numbers as the elevator climbed to notice him.

"Excuse me," Rufus blurted, producing a quizzical expression. "Don't I know you?"

Weak, but the best he could do on such short notice. O'Neal had recommended the old tried-and-true government background check story, but in Rufus's professional judgment, his target knew too much about Mia for that to hold any water. He was improvising and hoping it worked.

The target was staring at Rufus now. "Sorry, no."

"You sure?"

"Yes, I'm sure I've never seen you before."

Rufus's chubby face scrunched up as he examined the man's eyes. "Wait, you're . . . John, right? John Jenson, I'm positive it's you."

A look of surprise registered on John's face. "That's right."

"You don't remember me, do you?"

"Afraid I don't. Sorry."

"I went to Lincoln Park High, like you. Few years behind you, though. Same class as your little sister."

"Which one?"

"Mia, but she probably wouldn't remember me either. Her being real smart, and me sort of struggling. A National Merit Scholar or something, wasn't she?"

"That's right. We were very proud of her."

"So where is ol' Mia these days? Probably married, surrounded by a boatload of kids." Rufus paused to offer a wink and smile. "Between you and me, I had a big crush on her."

The elevator stopped on the eleventh floor

and John abruptly stepped out. Rufus took a short hop and joined him. "Same floor, what a coincidence," he announced with a big grin. "You work on this floor, or what?" he asked.

John pointed down the hallway to his right. "My accounting firm's here."

"Right. I've got an appointment down the other way." He pointed a lying finger down the opposite hall. "So where'd Mia end up, anyway?"

"D.C. Went to law school at Harvard then landed in a firm there." He said this with considerable pride.

"Yeah? One of those monster firms you always read about? Long hours, grinding away, no life."

"Not anymore, no. She tried that for a while. After the loss, though, she left her firm and switched to government service."

Rufus couldn't think of a better way so he came right out with it. "What loss was that, John?"

"I'm sorry. I didn't catch your name."

"Dennis," he lied without any hesitation. "Dennis Miller."

John's eyes narrowed and he began inspecting Rufus more closely, roving from his scuffed black running shoes up his worn sweatpants, stopping at the torn T-shirt.

Naming himself after a famous comedian was probably a mistake, but he'd seen him on TV the night before and it was the first and only thing that popped into his mind. Plus it might've been a good idea to dress a little fancier, Rufus realized, a little belatedly. He looked like exactly what he was, street scum looking to make a fast score.

"Sorry," John said, sounding very final. "I don't discuss family business with strangers."

Rufus could hear, could almost feel the ten grand slipping out of his fingers. "Hey, it's not like that, John. I'm no stranger. See, Mia and me, well, we were real close. I was just, you know, wondering what she lost."

"Who are you meeting with down the hall?"

"Uh . . . my lawyer."

John leaned forward and suddenly grabbed him firmly by the shirt collar. "You're lying. There are no lawyers on this floor."

"Hey, let me go. I don't know what you're talking about."

The grip tightened and Rufus ended up on his tiptoes. "Who are you and what's this about?" John hissed, showing his teeth.

It was time to scrap Plan A. Only Rufus didn't have a Plan B. He shoved John as hard as he could and made a mad dash for the stairwell. He never looked back, never even glanced as he bolted eleven floors back down to ground level, then slipped out a side entrance of the building.

After three hours of riffling through old files in the city morgue, and another two in the library scrounging through death notices in the local papers, Rufus placed a call to O'Neal in D.C.

He quickly summarized his encounter with Mia's oldest brother, as if the day had been an unmitigated success, worth the whole ten grand, if not more. Then he said, "Point is, something happened. Some severe loss that drove her out of her big firm and into government service."

"So you figure she was looking for a new purpose in life. Serving some higher cause, that kind of gushy crap?"

"That's what I heard in his voice, yeah."

"What kind of loss would do that? She was making damn good dough."

Rufus pondered the question. Probably a ninety percent cut in pay — why would anybody even consider something so damaging, so stupid? Made no sense to him. "Hell, I dunno," he admitted emphatically.

"And you found nothing at the morgue?"

"Nope. Her parents are still kicking, all the brothers and a sister are still sucking oxygen. You sure she was never married, right? No kids, not even a bastard."

"Never," O'Neal answered, sounding deeply unsettled.

There was something here, O'Neal was sure, and he was even more desperate to find it. He was being paid for his instincts in these matters — and right now his gut was screaming that the key to Mia Jenson was that mysterious loss, whatever it was.

He wished he had more time to think about it, but things were coming unhinged fast. The morning had become a nightmare. Castile was supposed to call in about the break-in to Jenson's house, but the call never came. Repeated attempts to reach Castile, both at his house and on his cell, went unanswered.

O'Neal had a team out now trying to hunt down the missing burglars; unfortunately, it was a ridiculously small team, two men, a pair of sad losers he ordinarily wouldn't have dispatched to the deli for a sandwich.

Problem was, O'Neal had everybody with the slightest tinge of competence working overdrive to find someone much more important.

Jack Wiley had fallen off the face of the earth.

O'Neal hadn't yet informed Walters that Wiley had slipped his net.

He prayed he would never have to.

Martie's prayer went unanswered. The call he dreaded came at six that evening in the form of Mitch Walters in a foul mood, demanding an update.

He started with Mia. Martie explained about the meeting with her big brother in Chicago, about the mysterious "loss," and reassured Walters that TFAC was deploying as many resources as possible to unearth the story. In this case, "as many resources as possible" equaled a sorry louse whose total PI experience was hunting down lost cats and peeking into bedrooms. But he didn't admit that, of course.

"What about her home?" Walters asked. "Your boys pay her a visit yet?"

"Last night," O'Neal answered, hoping that was the end of it.

"Did they leave her a little gift?"

"I think so."

"You *think?*"

"We're, uh, having a slight glitch getting in contact with our contractors."

"A glitch?"

"Nothing to worry about, Mitch. They went in last night and disappeared for a while. These boys are pros. They don't bring no ID, they don't bring cell phones. We'll get it sorted out. Like I said, don't worry."

He almost laughed with relief when Walters asked, "What about Jenson's office?"

"Working on it. I warned you it would take preparation and time. Won't be long," he promised.

There was a pause. Martie closed his eyes and hoped Walters was finished.

Finally Walters asked the question O'Neal desperately didn't want to hear. "Where's Wiley right now?"

"Why do you ask?"

"Just say that Wiley wasn't as cooperative as we hoped. We're worried about Jenson making contact with him again. Tell me you're keeping a good eye on him."

Another long pause, this one on O'Neal's part. He pinched his nose and confessed, "He, uh, well, he seems to have slipped away."

"Tell me I didn't hear that."

"Sorry, Mitch. Yesterday, after he left your building, he went downtown, parked in a public garage, and disappeared."

"This better be a joke, O'Neal. But I'm

not laughing."

"No, it's quite true, Mitch." He paused and struggled to keep his voice level. "Seemed innocent at the time, a momentary slip-up in coverage. But we reconsidered. Wiley obviously planned this escape a while ago."

"How do you know that?"

"It's not complicated. We have his charge card numbers, his phone accounts, his bank account numbers, all of which we acquired seven months ago. He's not using any of them. His bank accounts were electronically emptied out yesterday. He's gone totally underground."

Walters began cursing at O'Neal, unleashing a world of anger and fury. O'Neal held the phone away from his ear until Walters's well ran dry. It took a while.

"That's not helping anything," he said to Walters.

"You're fired," Walters replied back.

"Don't be stupid, Mitch. You can't fire me right now. You need me more than ever, to put this thing back together."

He could hear Walters breathing heavily on the other end. A few more scattered curses and threats flew across the line, but they lacked any semblance of conviction, just empty shots fired after the surrender to

561

an ugly reality. "Find Wiley," he barked in his most menacing tone. "Do whatever it takes, find him."

"That's not so easy. He's a smart guy, and like I said, he prepared for this. But I have a suggestion."

"What is it?"

O'Neal explained his plan — it was a great idea — and Walters quickly agreed to do his part.

It was impossible to sleep or nap.

Jack had his feet up on the coffee table and his eyes glued to the television in his hotel room, watching as William Pederson, a smooth-talking lizard in an Armani suit, stood outside the big cylinder that was home to CG's headquarters, issuing his firm's first response to the nasty rumors roaring about the city.

Pederson was enjoying himself immensely, juking and jiving into the forest of microphones jammed in his face. "No, we really have no idea what prompted the secretary's shutdown order. We're investigating now."

"Is it true the polymer wears off?" one reporter yelled.

"I won't say it's possible and I won't say it isn't. We're running tests now."

"Why wasn't it tested before?" bellowed

another.

"Who said it wasn't? I assure you it was, quite vigorously."

After that wonderfully vague and obviously self-conflicting answer, Pederson's eyes shifted to a reporter in the back of the mob wearing a conspicuously nice suit; an obvious plant. "Sir," the "reporter" screamed on cue, "wasn't the polymer invented by somebody else?"

Pederson acted as though the question annoyed him. His eyebrows knitted together. He stared down at one particular microphone. He tried his best to impart the impression that he was only answering under duress. "Yes, that's right," he said gravely. "Among the possibilities we're exploring is that somebody ran a scam on us."

The mob of reporters fell silent.

The same "reporter" in the back, a swarthy man with a big nose, asked, "You said it was a scam?"

"Well, let's say it's possible somebody committed a few indiscretions. Some of the documents we were given during the purchase of the company that discovered the polymer now appear, well, questionable."

"You mean doctored or falsified?"

"We're seeking two men, Jack Wiley and

Perry Arvan, in our effort to get to the bottom of this."

"Are you saying you were defrauded?"

"I'm saying no such thing." A brief, well-timed pause — could he say it any clearer? He was screaming it from the rooftops to any idiot who would listen. "I'm saying that we're seeking these two men to help clarify a few questionable matters. In fact, it's so important to us that we're offering five million dollars to anyone who helps locate them. Again, Jack Wiley and Perry Arvan are the names. Their photos are posted on our corporate website for anyone interested in the five million reward."

Jack had an urge to laugh that was quickly tempered by an even stronger compulsion to hop the next flight out of the country and flee to Brazil, or anywhere, really. Anywhere, that is, where there was a thick, impenetrable jungle, accommodating legal authorities, and the possibility of disappearing forever.

Instead he picked a phone from his stack of cell phones, dialed a number, and had another quick conversation with his lawyer.

27

It was thought that Daniel Bellweather had the best chance to pull it off; if not him, there was no hope. He had once shared the same job, the same onerous responsibilities, the same pressure-cooker office, after all. And when he set his mind to it, he could be fairly charming in a brusque, uncompromising way.

The secretary of defense's office had politely but insistently rebuffed the many requests by CG to meet in private about the polymer. CG had pulled out all the stops, even the big gun. Former president Billy Cantor had called, twice. He was politely but firmly told to take a hike.

An additional twenty billion of CG's annual revenue was tied up in other defense contracts. Losing the polymer was a disaster, but things could get worse. The last thing CG could afford was an all-out scandal with the ensuing possibility of being blacklisted by the Pentagon's procurement corps. For the first time in the company's immensely profitable history, the unthinkable was on the horizon — bankruptcy, or at least a dramatic shrinkage, selling off profitable enterprises, booting half the executives, and cutting the partner and director earnings to squat.

So at the last minute CG dished out $400K for a table at the annual Gridiron Club dinner, a big bash held for Washington's glitterati to gather together in a supposedly friendly atmosphere, where they set aside the partisan bickering and lampooned themselves.

The normal price for a table was $200K, but CG was taking no chances. It had a few very important stipulations.

The large black limo dumped Bellweather and a colorless assortment of lesser executives at the handsome entrance of the Capital Hilton. They stepped out onto the curb and raced inside to hobnob and be seen mixing it up with anybody who mattered in the current administration. The lobby was packed with media rock stars, politicians, influence peddlers, celebrities, diplomats, cabinet members, all jostling to look and act more important than the others.

A large retinue of reporters congregated outside trying to catch a glimpse of the rich, famous, and powerful, or maybe overhear some tidbit of priceless information.

Unfortunately, juicy rumors about the possible scandal had preceded the boys from CG. Bellweather quickly grew tired of the cold shoulders and speedy brush-offs. Only a week before, he would've been mobbed by aspiring government officials sucking up to arrange a pleasant nest in their next life. The brush-offs quickly became pathetically predictable — "Look, there's Jim and I really must say hi," or "My bladder's killing me. Gotta run and drain the lizard" — as he watched them race off.

When the waiters began pouring through the lobby and announcing dinner, Bellweather stood in a lonely corner, nursing a drink, and waited till he was the last one left. He dodged through the dining room doors just before they shut.

He worked his way to his table slightly below the dais where the president and vice president sat, straining to look pleasant and affable, despite being surrounded by all the slimy media clowns both men detested to their cores. He passed tables stuffed with men and women who couldn't stand the sight of one another — Democrats hating

Republicans, politicians hating the press, who in turn viewed anybody in office like child molesters — everybody acting phony and smiling through gritted teeth.

The temporary truce was tenuous at best. It was a miracle nobody smuggled guns or poison into the room.

Douglas Robinson, the secretary of defense, nearly turned white when Bellweather suddenly materialized at his side. The timing was exquisite — everybody was standing by their seats, waiting for the festivities to begin. "Always nice to see you, Doug," Bellweather announced, jamming out his hand.

"Get lost," Robinson whispered with a snarl. He ignored the hand.

"Can't. It's my table." Bellweather let the hand drop.

Robinson glanced down at the name placard in front of Bellweather's seat. It clearly read Arnold Smith. "That's definitely not your seat," he told Bellweather, with a look meant to say, You're a crook and a rotten thief — I'd rather French-kiss Osama bin Laden than sit next to a lying snake like you.

"No, no mistake," Bellweather said, smiling pleasantly. "Smith bowed out at the last minute and deeded me his seat."

A cardinal in brilliant red robes at the head table began saying grace. Robinson used the excuse to ignore Bellweather. He bowed his head, closed his eyes, and swore to himself he was going to fire somebody first thing in the morning. His people were supposed to check these things.

Bellweather dutifully bowed his head and smiled. On top of the $200K price of admission, it had cost CG an additional $200K to get around Robinson's security arrangements: $100K for this specific seat, and $100K for the phony name subterfuge. And it was worth every penny.

The cardinal said amen and both men fell into their chairs. Robinson reached out and found the scotch he'd carried in from the lobby. He drained the glass in a single gulp.

"Guess you're pretty mad at me and my company," Bellweather said very reasonably.

"If I had a gun, I'd blow you all to hell."

"Can't say I blame you. That phony report makes us look terrible."

"Terrible? Oh, no, that's an understatement. We're talking soldiers' lives. You cheated your country."

"I know it looks that way, and believe me, I know how it feels."

"You people, if anybody, should be ashamed of yourselves." Robinson crossed his arms across his chest and stared hard at the tablecloth. Far as he was concerned, the conversation had just ended. He intended to spend the rest of the evening chatting about the weather with the heavy grand dame to his right, a notorious bore and a horrible prospect, but a necessary one. He turned his shoulder to Bellweather and assumed a posture that screamed, Talk all you want, pal, I'm not listening.

"You see, Doug," Bellweather continued in the same reasonable tone, "the reason I know is because that's exactly what happened to us. Same thing. We were taken in. Fooled, conned, cheated. Call it whatever you want but we fell for it."

Robinson began rearranging his silverware. He'd stuff his fingers in his ears if it didn't look so asinine, and if there weren't so many prying media buzzards around to witness it.

Bellweather inched his seat closer to Robinson. "I think we were too anxious to find a solution for our boys over there. All these years, you know, seeing those awful images of kids being mangled and slaughtered. It got inside our soul. Hell, I'm not ashamed to admit it, Doug. We were so ready to believe the first person who offered a magic formula for saving our kids. Too ready, I guess."

Robinson had turned his chair and now had his back turned to Bellweather. Inside his head he was singing an old college football song, trying to drown out the noise coming from Bellweather's mouth — "Boolah, Boolah, fight, fight, fight . . ."

"Christ, Doug, you came out of the defense industry. We all did. It's one big revolving door, because that's the only way it'll work. You become a defense expert, then spend your career bouncing between defense companies and government service. It's not bad, and it's not good, just the way it is. But that doesn't make us all crooked or bent. Hell, we both wanted the same thing, our kids to stop being blown apart by bombs."

If that short speech had any effect, Robinson didn't show it. His lips were now mouthing the words "Tackle them . . . beat them down . . . victory at all costs . . ."

Bellweather grabbed his arm. "Look, you felt the same way, I know you did. I saw it on your face that first visit when we talked about the polymer. Like us, you were ready to jump on anything that protected our kids."

Unable to ignore him any longer, Robinson faced him for the first time. "What are you saying?"

"Like you were, Doug, we were taken in," said Bellweather, now feigning an expression of deep anger. "Two men, Jack Wiley and Perry Arvan, concocted this scheme. They're liars and cheats, both of them."

"Never heard of them."

"Doesn't matter. Point is, we jumped the gun, Doug. You, us, we all did."

Bellweather could see on Robinson's face that he was making headway. A slight loosening around the lips, a slackening of the eyes, the beginning of doubt — but it was enough.

He went on, "Today we offered five million bucks to anybody who helps us find those two bastards. They took the money and ran, Doug, both of 'em. By cheating us, they cheated you. Believe me, nobody wants to get to the bottom of this more than us. We want to restore the good name of our firm."

The secretary squirmed in his seat a moment. "Say this is true, what can I do?" he asked in a rather caustic tone.

"There are a few things," Bellweather mumbled, almost a whisper.

"Spit it out, Dan. And speak up, dammit!" His eyes darted around the room; the last thing he could afford was being seen in a confidential conversation with this crooked jerk. No doubt one of these sneaky media clowns had smuggled in a camera and it would look great splashed across the front page of the morning *Post,* a picture of Bellweather whispering in his ear about God knows what. He adjusted his expression to a deeper frown and tried to look like he wasn't listening.

"For one, help us find these two," Bellweather requested.

"How?"

"You've got the resources at your fingertips. Your own investigative services, for one thing. The FBI and CIA will do whatever you ask. Use them."

"What else?"

Bellweather took a deep breath, then said, "Agent Mia Jenson."

"Who's she?"

"The DCIS investigator who provided the tip about the phony report."

"What about her?"

"She's biased."

"What's that supposed to mean?"

"She hates us. She's been to our headquarters several times, throwing around nasty threats, hassling our people. It's personal for her. She has a deep grudge, a vendetta. Don't ask me why, she just does."

"That's a damned serious charge."

"I know it is."

"So what do you want me to do about it?"

"Nothing serious, just reassign her. We're requesting a fair shake, that's all. Put somebody fresh on the case. Somebody impartial, somebody harboring no emotional baggage. We want a fair process, that's all."

"I'll think about it. Anything else?"

"No, I'm finished."

"Then will you please shut up? Let me enjoy what's left of my evening."

Nicky was waiting at her desk when Mia rolled into work the next morning. He didn't invite her into his office this time.

"You pissed somebody off," he told her with his head shaking.

"Always nice to hear," she said and actually smiled. "What gave you the clue, Nicky?"

"You're off the polymer case. That's straight from the director's lips. I had the impression she was just relaying the order herself. I think this came from the very top."

"I wasn't aware I was ever on the polymer case," Mia noted.

"Neither was I. Is this a problem for you?"

Mia's smile seemed to grow. "No, I expected it. I'd be hugely disappointed if it didn't happen in fact. Do me a favor, put it in writing."

"If you insist, I will."

"I do insist."

She took it so well that Nicky couldn't hide his expression of relief.

"Of course now I have to appoint somebody to actually look into this thing," he told her.

"Who you thinking of?"

"Clete Jamison."

Mia offered a satisfied nod. "Good choice," she said. "Clete's thorough and tough."

"He is, and he's coming into this with an empty tank. It would help if you gave him some background."

"My pleasure," she said and seemed to mean it.

After a brief pause, Nicky added hopefully, "It would help even more if he knew the name of your source."

Mia placed her things on her desk and sat down. "Forget it, Nicky. My source will only deal with me. That's the stipulation. It's a matter of trust."

Nicky tore off his glasses with an air of impatience. "Look, I know there's a lot going on here you're not telling me." He examined her face for a response — there was no response. "How bad is this going to get?"

"For the Capitol Group, very bad."

"Your source is telling you other things?"

Mia shrugged and rearranged some papers on her crowded desk. The answer was yes.

"What's your source's motive? You can tell me that."

"Truth, justice, the American way. Do the right thing. I know what a rare and unbelievable motive that is these days, and in this city, but that's it."

Nicky played with his tie a moment. He'd never had an agent pull something like this. It pissed him off, confused him, made him want to stab a finger in her face and demand answers, but frankly he wasn't sure how to handle it. "Mia, an order from the director taking you off this case is a serious step. If you're caught dabbling in what is now an official investigation, I can't protect you."

"Thanks for the warning."

"It's a promise."

"I'm a big girl, Nicky. I know the rules."

"You better be sure you do. This can get real ugly."

"I'm terrified. Send me back to a half-million-a-year job in any of a dozen firms that would take me in a heartbeat. Throw some more threats at me, Nicky."

By noon, the day after the Capitol Group's spokesman offered five million bucks to anyone who helped find Jack Wiley or Perry Arvan, CG's corporate website had received thirty million hits. The announcement was like the shot that started the land rush, a reasonable analogy in this case. Three hours after the promise was issued, so many users logged on, the site crashed. It took a team of programmers two hours, working furiously in the middle of the night, to get it back up, before the flood of hits resumed.

Several big newspapers glommed onto the story and, free of charge, printed pictures of Jack and Perry along with a speculative, fascinating synopsis of CG's claims and the ensuing manhunt. By nine that morning, cable news rushed into the act and began flashing the pictures and discussing the big bounty. The faces of Jack and Perry were studied and memorized by countless more millions of citizens interested in snatching a cool five million.

O'Neal, by then, had a large call center set up, employing twenty of TFAC's people and a large, shifting clutch of executives bused over from CG. The calls went to CG's switch and were smoothly rerouted to

TFAC's call center.

By noon it was a disaster center. O'Neal had never tried this before, and it showed. He was thoroughly ill-prepared to handle the unceasing bombardment of information pouring in. Neither his own people nor CG's hapless execs were trained for this sport. They lacked the expertise to filter the good from the bad, the plainly false tips from the seemingly accurate, the fruitcakes and loonies from the moderately sane.

Jack was spotted in too many places to count. He was seen seated on the rear deck of a big yacht in Miami, knocking back mai tais, surrounded by big-breasted girls in string bikinis. Thirty seconds later, he was huddled in an igloo in Alaska munching on whale meat. At the same instant he was spotted in a movie theater in Akron, partying on the slopes at Aspen, sleeping in a gutter in Seattle, and robbing a bank in Atlanta.

Perry, also, was everywhere and nowhere.

Each call station had a large stack of tip sheets to fill out. It seemed so easy, so organized, so infallible. In theory, it was. Every time a call arrived the information was jotted on a tip sheet, then deposited inside the in-box of one of three former Fibbies who would scrutinize the material and decide upon the action to be taken. By ten that morning, all three had found the time to curse at O'Neal and tell him what an ill-conceived crock this whole plan was. Their in-boxes had overflowed hours before. Every time Fox News or CNN or MSNBC flashed up pictures of Jack and Perry, a fresh deluge arrived and the chaos grew.

Martie made the rounds, pacing, barking, exhorting, trying to keep morale up and his system functioning. It was hopeless and he knew it. The only prayer of finding Jack or Perry was the Department of Defense. It had the full and remorseless resources of the federal government to pursue Jack wherever he led them.

No matter how smart Jack was, it was just a matter of time. He would be found.

Jack, at that moment, was running hard and fast. Sweat was dripping off his head. His shirt was soaked, his breath coming out in heavy gusts. Ten minutes before he had kicked up the treadmill to seven miles per hour, a final sprint before he finished his habitual morning exercise.

He had entered the apartment in the early hours of the morning, before CG's manhunt gained traction. The day he'd ditched TFAC's watchers, he took the train to New

York, then jumped in the rental car and headed south, right back to D.C. Using a false name and paying with a fistful of cash, he had checked into a Best Western on the city outskirts, watched the news, slept off and on, and waited.

At three that morning, he ditched the rental at a local vendor and dropped the keys in a night box. Nobody saw him. He walked two blocks to a dark street corner where he was met by a friend who drove him here. The tall apartment complex was directly across the street from CG's headquarters, and the apartment was located on the twelfth floor with a commanding view of everything that happened street side. It had been rented under a false name almost a year before. The day before Jack made his dash for freedom, a friend had restocked it with enough fresh food and supplies to last a month, if need be.

The apartment was large, with three bedrooms, two of which now were filled with stacked boxes, all carefully labeled and organized.

Jack switched off the treadmill and, grabbing a towel to wipe off his sweat, walked to the big console by the window. The curtains and shades were drawn tight. All lights in the living room had been disconnected months before to minimize any chance of a silhouette in the window. He sat at the big console and played with the dials for a few minutes before he found something interesting to listen to.

A team of four men under Jack's employ had manned this console around the clock for over seven months now. They sat, eating, smoking countless cigarettes, sipping coffee by the gallon, listening, recording, filtering, and discarding the rubbish. They preserved only what was worth listening to. Not only the bedrooms, but a storage container three blocks away were loaded with tapes, the plentiful fruits of this long and exhausting effort.

Jack turned up the volume and listened attentively to the distinctive voice of Mitch Walters conversing with Phil Jackson. They were chatting in Mitch's office, according to the console light. Walters had a hard, deep voice, but it sounded hoarse and raspy, the result of little sleep and too much yelling and hollering at his beleaguered employees. Jackson's voice was unchanged, flat, insinuating, condescending. The feed was crystal clear; Jack could have been seated in the office. He closed his eyes and could almost picture them — Walters behind his big desk with his feet up, perhaps hefting a paperweight in his beefy hand, Jackson lounging in a chair, studying the CEO with his mean, slitty eyes.

"Sufficient evidence is still the problem," Jackson was saying, not nicely.

"How many times are you gonna tell me that? I'm working on it."

"Then work faster. Wiley could be found at any minute. You better have something good and legally compelling when he turns up."

"You said yourself Wiley won't be a problem. His old pal Wallerman will bury his credibility. He ripped off an old lady, then murdered her. Anything he says will be neutralized by his ugly past." A brief pause, then, "He was a crook then, he's still a rotten crook. Nobody believes a murderer."

"You're not listening, idiot."

Jack could picture Walters's face flushing with anger. His fists would be clenched, his shoulders bunched, his broad, pugnacious face puckered and red.

Jackson said very slowly, very deliberately, "You need to give me something I can work with. You, Bellweather, and Haggar get together and concoct your story. Wiley conned us, and here's how. Got it? Details, Walters, plenty of details, all believable. The three of you rehearse until you sound like a barbershop quartet. And it would certainly be nice if you produced a little paper or even a tape that backs you up. Fabricate it, if necessary. Understand?"

"All right. I got it."

Jack could hear the sound of a chair being pushed back.

"You better," Jackson said, a parting shot. "You'll only get one chance."

28

Mia slipped out of the office late that afternoon for what she told Nicky was a long-overdue dental appointment. A molar had been aching for a month; she couldn't sleep and she'd put it off too long already.

Harvey Crintz was lurking nearby, about ten doors down the hallway, where he had an excellent view of the locked entrance to DCIS's Pentagon office. He'd been there for hours, gulping coffee, chatting on his cell, watching and waiting.

Mia had stepped out a few times, but only to pick up food or hit the ladies' room, because she returned within minutes.

Crintz had been called two days before by somebody in an outfit called TFAC, who claimed that Harvey had been referred by some mutual friends over at the Capitol Group. At first Harvey had turned white and gagged. Fearful that CG had ratted him out about his cash-for-inside-tips game, he claimed he had never heard of the Capitol Group, never heard of these friends. Deny, deny, deny. They must've confused his name for somebody else, he insisted and nearly hung up.

When the words "one hundred thousand dollars" somehow found their way into the conversation, Harvey's memory improved and his listening turned razor-sharp. It was only a small favor, after all, the voice told him; nothing more serious or dangerous than what he'd done dozens of times in the past. As a member in good standing of the Inspector General's office, it wouldn't be at all unusual for Crintz to visit the DCIS office. And should he happen to, say, browse for a moment around Mia Jenson's desk, and maybe, perhaps, by chance, find something interesting and relevant to her vendetta against CG, maybe he could find a way to smuggle it out.

Crintz lost a lot of sleep the previous two days as he considered and debated the offer. The pros and cons rattled around his brain. This was more than he'd ever been asked to do, but technically only slightly more. No, on second thought, a little inside information was one thing; this was burglary and the punishment was much more severe. It *was* also one hundred grand, though. A hundred thousand dollars! His to do whatever he wanted with, his to spend, his to waste however he wished. The Mercury Sable in his driveway was old and tired, the paint was peeling, and he could hear the transmission grinding to death; he'd love to replace it with something fancier, say a racing green Jaguar, and the decision was made. Mia was about to buy him a car.

Crintz waited five full minutes until it was clear that Mia's absence was something more than a bathroom stop. He walked quickly to the door and pushed the buzzer. A voice came over the intercom and he knew it was an assistant. "Can I help you?"

"I'm Crintz with the IG's office, here to see Andy Kasprisan," he said into the speaker, identifying an agent he knew who worked in the office.

There was an irritating buzzing noise as the thick door unlocked and he quickly pushed it open. The assistant's desk was directly in front of the door, and he made sure to give her a good long glance at the Pentagon badge attached to his shirtfront as he passed. "Thanks," he told her.

"He's way in the back," she mumbled, then pushed her nose into some papers on her blotter.

"Oh," he said, an afterthought. "Is Agent

Jenson in?"

"Nope." The assistant never even looked up. "Dental appointment. Just missed her." She pointed a casual finger at the sign-in board on the wall. Crintz glanced at it and sighed with relief. Under ETR — estimated time of return — Mia had penciled in a time three hours away.

Crintz wandered around the maze of carrels for a few minutes until he located the one with Agent Jenson on the placard. The office was noisy, busy, and messy. Phones ringing, agents talking, all hotly engaged in the pursuit of waste, fraud, and abuse. Nobody paid the slightest bit of attention to him.

An agent with his nose buried in a memo was seated two carrels away from Jenson's, and Crintz smiled at him, and said, "I'm with the IG's office. Mia left something for me on her desk."

"Suit yourself," the guy said without looking up. He picked up his telephone and began making a call.

Crintz edged inside Mia's carrel and settled quietly into her seat. The gray fabric walls blocked anyone from observing what he was doing. Unlike all the other carrels he'd seen in this congested dump, everything was neat and tidy, the papers arranged in orderly stacks. Even her phone slips were lined up like battleships awaiting inspection.

He pulled out a pen and his little green notebook, then began jotting notes. The phone slips first. The voice on the phone hadn't been all that specific about what to look for, so Crintz figured he'd just snatch as much information as looked useful to justify his $100K. As fast as he could, he jotted the names and numbers in his pad. Then he moved to the stacks of files and papers on her desk, but nothing there looked all that interesting. She had a big caseload, and he was quickly lost in the stacks of testimonies, financial reports, depositions, etc.

He glanced at his watch. Seven minutes already, and he began to worry. At the rear of Mia's carrel sat a large gray metal stand-up safe with four drawers — the same model found in nearly every carrel in a building that manufactured secrets. Regulations required the safe to be locked anytime the owner stepped away, but like nearly everybody except the most fanatic security loons, Mia was planning on returning and had left hers unlocked with the drawers slightly ajar.

Crintz got up and quietly slid open the

top drawer. The files were neat and superbly organized, apparently like everything in Jenson's life. They were alphabetized, too, though he found no Capitol Group files under C. He thought he knew why, smiled to himself, and pushed the drawer back the way he'd found it. He bent down to the bottom drawer where the W's would be found, quietly eased it open, took one long peek, and struck gold.

There were about thirty thin files with titles beginning with W, then ten or fifteen thick green files labeled "Capitol Group," but he didn't know where to begin. It looked like at least a thousand pages. Far too much to read, much less memorize, and copying a pile of this size was out of the question.

And stealing all of it was definitely not an option, Crintz thought.

He got down on his creaky knees and began riffling through files as fast as he could, hoping he'd get lucky. Maybe he'd find some golden nugget that would warrant the hundred-thousand-dollar payoff. Jenson, he quickly realized, after scanning enough files, had been watching and tracking CG for months, if not far longer. She had the firm's financial reports going back three years. As a private firm, CG wasn't legally obligated to file with the SEC, but it did have to submit the material to the Pentagon procurement office every time it bid on a contract.

But Mia had so much more than that: the names and biographical data of all the key players; transcripts of all congressional hearings dealing with the polymer; a lot of background material on some company called Arvan Chemicals; and so on and so forth. From long experience in the Inspector General's office he recognized what he was looking at; she was laboriously and studiously plotting a giant case.

Then a small, thin file tucked in the rear of the drawer caught his attention. It was in the back, hidden from view for good reason, he suspected. He had to strain to reach it but eventually got a firm grip with his thick fingers. It was labeled "Source One," a mysterious title that quickly became clear.

Mia had an insider; source one was a squealing rat. Someone deep inside, he realized, as he glanced through the material. Whoever it was, had detailed the trail of events that led CG to take over Arvan Chemicals, then how CG bought, pressured, and finagled the Pentagon and Congress into arranging the sweet deal for a no-bid, single-source $20 billion contract.

The disclosures were verbal. Mia had treated their discussions like depositions and meticulously transcribed the results. By his estimate, there were at least forty pages of conversation in the form of questions and answers that he plowed through as fast as his eyes could move.

On December 29 the year before, there was this one:

Question: "Describe how the Capitol Group persuaded Representative Earl Belzer to help with the polymer."

Reply: "Well, it wasn't hard. Belzer has his hand out to anyone willing to kick in some dough. CG has a, well, what would you call it? A slush fund — I guess that's the appropriate term. And, um, this money is secret, a hidden pot of gold for buying favors. And, well, I guess you can say Earl wasn't reluctant. He dug his fist in deep." (She laughed.)

Question: "Did CG pay him money for a promise of support?"

Reply: "Yeah, but you'd never find it. See, we have this guy, an accountant. He specializes in this stuff. He comes into the office once or twice a week. A little runt with big glasses, very unfriendly, never says a word to anybody. The magician, that's what we call him."

Question: "And what does this magician do?"

Reply: "Runs the slush fund. Makes money magically appear in people's pockets. If it's a politician, he finds ways to get it into PACs, you know, political action committees, or reelection accounts. He's got thousands of tricks. False-front corporations, phony names, straw donors, he's very creative. We're a global company, and most of the fund is hidden overseas. He's good, incredibly good. You'll never catch him."

Crintz paused a second. He realized she was talking about his paymaster, the little gnome who made sure he got his monthly bribes. He went back to reading.

Question: "And how much went to Belzer?"

Reply: "I don't know the exact amount. Only the magician and the senior execs upstairs who cut the deals know that. A lot, though. We're all in accounting, and, well, you know how we are. We thrive on rumors. I heard seven million."

Suddenly Crintz heard a collection of loud voices nearby. His heart nearly jumped out of his chest. He removed the papers he was reading, stuffed the rest of the file back in the rear, closed the safe drawer, and got back to his feet.

He took a good look around. Nobody was paying him any attention, but he was through taking risks.

He walked out quickly the same way he came in. His knees were weak with fear and excitement. On his way back down to his office, he made a firm decision. A hundred thousand was too little. It was time for a serious renegotiation. That little slush fund was loaded with cash. Some third-rate political peckerwood got seven million. Seven million!

Hell, the information in his fist was worth at least a million, possibly two. Crintz tightened his grip. The clutch of papers in his fist was his early retirement to a beautiful Florida resort, a glorious golf course, a boat, young girls in bikinis flaunting bronzed bodies, his life's dream.

He relished the moment, and by the time he got back to his desk he was ready to hop on the Internet and begin the search for a nice little Florida condo, somewhere near the bars and the ocean.

The meeting opened with Walters and Bellweather thrashing and badgering Martie O'Neal, holding back no punches. Jack and

Old Man Arvan were still missing, they yelled. Why in the hell was CG paying a fortune to TFAC, an incompetent firm filled with losers, bunglers, and hacks? TFAC was sloppy and stupid; its mistakes were costing the Capitol Group billions. O'Neal relaxed against a far wall and let Walters and Bellweather vent and spew and fume till they were tired of hearing themselves talk.

A few hours before, Walters had authorized one million dollars to buy Harvey Crintz's goods; the permission was grudging and attended by another of Walters's crude tantrums.

O'Neal now held the product of that million dollars in his hand. He weathered their curses and threats with good humor, and endured their abuse with the gratifying knowledge that the moment they finished, he would make them eat their words. Go ahead, boys, he wanted to yell. Call me an asshole again. Burst a few blood vessels, scream till you're hoarse.

But they didn't seem to grow tired of abusing him, so he pushed off the wall and approached Walters's desk. "Guess what I got?" he sneered.

Walters sneered back, twice as nasty. "Don't play games with us."

"All right. I found your leak. You got a

rodent problem in this building. A snitch, someone feeding loads of incriminating info to Jenson."

O'Neal tossed the papers onto Walters's desk, then stood back and allowed the other two to read for themselves. Walters had forgotten his glasses and had to jam his face about three inches from the pages. Bellweather stood slightly behind him and leaned over his shoulder. O'Neal enjoyed the looks of growing horror on their faces.

"Jesus," Bellweather blurted after he finished. "She knows about the slush fund."

Walters was too stunned to say anything for a moment. He collapsed into his chair, gripping the armrests like a life raft.

"Relax, fellas. Not all is lost," O'Neal announced, too happy to be the irreplaceable lackey once again.

"What's that supposed to mean?" Bellweather demanded.

"Remember, I was in the FBI. Those statements are nothing but paper. Unless they're backed up by the living witness who made those claims, they're worthless."

"Worthless?" Walters managed to croak, still shell-shocked.

"Yeah, Mitch. In court, without that witness, it's all inadmissible hearsay. God bless the Supreme Court. The accused has the right to cross-examine, and you can't do that with pieces of paper."

"What are you suggesting?" Bellweather asked.

"Isn't it obvious, Dan?" Walters answered him with a sly smile, "Once we know who's talking to Jenson, we take care of the problem. No witness, no evidence — no case."

"You mean kill her?" Bellweather asked.

"Nothing that drastic is necessary," O'Neal replied, smirking with pretended innocence. "There's plenty of ways to make a source disappear. Money can cause a memory lapse. Enough money can even buy a complete reversal of old testimony. Maybe the source can just vanish for a while, take a long trip to a wonderfully remote place."

Bellweather quickly said, "Don't even mention murder in this office, Mitch. Or kidnapping either. We're businessmen. We have reputations to protect. We don't behave that way."

The three men studied each other's faces for a moment. The message was clear; nobody needed to say it. O'Neal had no famous reputation to protect, nor was he a "businessman" with a limited imagination. How O'Neal took care of the "rat" problem was up to him. Bellweather didn't need to, or want to, know about it.

"So who is she?" Walters asked. The source was referred to as "she" three different times in Jenson's papers.

"Consider what we know," O'Neal, the investigator, began. "She works in accounting. She's in the loop about the polymer. Here's some other stuff Crintz got." He planted Crintz's little green book in front of Walters. The three of them bent forward and examined it together.

Walters's eyes stopped cold on the phone messages. Three messages in particular, three different callbacks Jenson was supposed to make to the same name.

Bellweather caught his reaction. "That her?" he asked, pointing at the name as though Walters had missed it.

O'Neal leaned closer. "Eva Green. Does she work here?"

"In accounting," Walters admitted, but nothing more.

"That's where the leaks are coming from." Bellweather bent forward and studied the name more closely. "I don't know her."

O'Neal, standing with his arms crossed and watching Walters's distressed face, asked in an insinuating tone, "Who is she, Mitch?"

Mitch looked like someone had just

stuffed a fat golf ball down his throat. His face was red. He couldn't seem to find his voice, and when he did, he yelled, "Bullshit. That's impossible."

"Why is it impossible?"

"It can't be Eva. She's been working for me."

"Meaning what?"

"I sent her up with Feist last summer to escort Wiley to the White House shindig. Feist said Wiley seemed impressed with her, so we worked out an arrangement."

"Describe this arrangement," O'Neal asked, rolling his eyes. He hated amateurs dabbling in his field, getting in over their heads.

"Eva's one of those hyperambitious Harvard B-School types, always willing to go the extra mile to get ahead. She kept an eye on Wiley for me. We wanted to find out more about him and she filled in a few details. It was easy and cheap."

"Easy, cheap? What're you talking about?" Bellweather bellowed, slamming a hand against the wall. Whatever plot this idiot had hatched up now seemed to be biting them all in the ass.

"Nothing complicated, Dan. All she had to do was drop in. Visit him occasionally. Go out on a few dates. Build trust, get Wiley to confide in her."

"She was a mole?" O'Neal asked. This idiot didn't even know the nomenclature of the trade.

"Sort of, yeah, I guess. Update me on what Wiley was doing and thinking. If something more developed, I promised her a fifty grand bonus."

"And did it . . . uh, did she?" Bellweather asked, tiptoeing into the rich, lurid details.

Walters bunched his shoulders and shrugged. "Not really. He treated her like a sister. The arrangement ended months back. Eva had a sort of breakdown. Seemed like a good idea to end it."

Bellweather traded a quick glance with Martie. "Sounds like she was a double agent," he suggested.

That's exactly what it sounded like, but Walters refused to believe it. "Look," he said defensively, "I'll bring her in. Hit her up with a few questions and get to the bottom of this. If it's her, I know we can cut a deal. If it's not —"

O'Neal finished his thought — "Then we're back at square one."

"And you just wasted another million bucks," Bellweather said.

Jack was finding it hard not to burst out in

laughter as he sat at the console and listened. The arrogance of these people was appalling, their stupidity worse. They had no compunction about delving into his life, sneaking into his home, bugging his phones, and paying people to destroy his reputation and his life. Yet they had no idea, not even a suspicion, that the same things could be done back. He had tapes going back seven months of Eva huddled in Mitch's office, making her reports and seeking fresh instructions. He particularly enjoyed listening to Mitch offering her tips on how to seduce Jack.

He removed the tape, carefully affixed the date, time, location, and names of the subjects, then placed it on top of his growing stack. He inserted a fresh tape, stretched his back, then went to the kitchen to make supper.

Best to call his lawyer on a full stomach.

The time had come for him to make his move.

29

Less than twenty-four short hours after Harvey Crintz committed his first burglary, the gang of FBI agents showed up in his office. Three in all, grim-faced men in a mixture of nice blue and gray suits, holding a warrant and arresting Harvey in front of his coworkers. The agents weren't in a conversational mood.

Harvey's supervisor rushed out of his cubbyhole and began barking questions but got no answers. They flashed the warrant, pinned Harvey's arms behind his back, slapped him in cuffs, and marched him out. Harvey tried making noise about calling his lawyer and was rudely told to shut up. He had no right to a lawyer until he was booked, charged, and processed, they told him with menacing frowns. In any event, he was informed, he didn't need a lawyer, he needed a priest.

An hour later, after the three agents gave

Harvey a glimpse of the ten photographs displaying his face and his body rifling through Mia Jenson's safe — apparently it had been wired and connected to a tiny camera of some sort, a camera he had triggered in his clumsy search the day before — he agreed with them.

A priest was his only hope.

At almost the same instant, another group of Feds conducted a much larger raid on the offices of TFAC. They burst through the entrance, waving subpoenas and warrants, barking at employees to line up against walls and spread them.

Accompanying them was a large forensics team that raced upstairs and jumped on the firm's computers and preserved everything on the hard drives. After another few minutes, the moving men with boxes showed up and began hauling out loads of papers, spy equipment, virtually anything not nailed to the walls and floors.

Martie O'Neal was hiding in his office when Special Agent Danny Ryan, an old pal from Bureau days, burst through the door.

"Hey, Danny, what's up?" he asked, trying to stifle his shock. He was leaning back in his chair, legs crossed on his desk, trying hard to look and act cool rather than terrified.

"How ya doin', Martie?" Ryan answered as if they were regular golf partners. Ryan's eyes shifted around the office — what a dump.

"You tell me."

"I'd say not well, buddy."

"I'm assuming you got a warrant or a subpoena to justify this unwarranted intrusion into private premises. I wanta be sure I sue the right folks."

"Can the big threats, Martie. Makes you sound silly."

"Like that, huh?"

Ryan nodded. "You're so totally screwed I wouldn't know where to begin."

"Oh."

"You remember the procedures or do I need to explain them?"

O'Neal slowly eased out of his chair. In his early days in the Bureau he'd been a field hand; how many times had it been him on the other end of this process, watching the weird mixture of emotions on their faces, often wondering how he'd react in their place. He placed his hands on his desk and bent forward with his legs spread apart. He made a silent vow to himself that he would remain calm and unaffected. There would be no cracks in the hard veneer. He would show his old Bureau buddies how a real badass behaved. "Yeah, yeah," he said, "I got the right to remain silent, blah, blah, blah. Should I call my mouthpiece now?"

"It'd be a waste of time."

"Can I least call my wife and tell her I won't be home for dinner?"

"She knows, Martie. Another van of agents is at your house with a search warrant. I'm sure she gets the message."

Martie was suddenly fighting back an almost unstoppable urge to cry. His knees went weak, his voice thick and whiny. He squeezed his eyes shut and muttered, "When will I get home for dinner?"

Ryan understood the question. "Assuming sterling behavior and an Emmy performance in front of three absolute chumps on a parole board, about twenty years. Sorry, Martie, no deals. Don't need 'em. We got the burglars who hit Jenson's home. They all talked. We got Crintz and he'll talk, too. We got a burglary in a private home up in Jersey seven months ago, and . . . hell, truth is, we got more evidence and charges than we know what to do with. You've been a very bad boy."

As Ryan patted him down, it was dawning on Martie that he had been sucker-punched.

All these months, somebody had been pulling the strings, jerking him around like a fool dancing at the end of a long, tight noose.

"At least tell me who turned you on to me," he asked, almost a croak.

"If I knew the whole story, I still wouldn't tell. But you definitely screwed with the wrong people. Now shut up and let me finish."

When the senior agent in charge of the FBI's Washington field office sends an invitation, even the Pentagon's inspector general and the director of the DCIS respect the summons.

The meeting was set for five, the witching hour. Both senior Pentagon officials, along with a small retinue of aides, arrived five minutes early in a matched pair of black government sedans at the downtown Judiciary Square field office. A junior flunkie was at the curb and escorted them through security, then up a short flight of stairs to the SAC's domain.

Special Agent Mia Jenson and a tall man who looked vaguely familiar but none of them recognized were waiting in the hallway. Mia walked directly up to Margaret Harper, director of the DCIS. "Agent Mia Jenson," she said by way of introduction. "I work for you."

The eyebrows lowered with curiosity. "I've heard your name," Harper offered, shorthand for, because I recently booted you off the Capitol Group case.

Without hesitation or further explanation, Mia handed her a piece of paper. One page, neatly typed and signed. "My resignation," she announced without elaboration.

"I don't understand."

"It's effective immediately. Approve it and it's done."

"What's this about?"

"You'll find out in a few minutes. Any possible questions will be answered, I promise. For now, it's strongly in your interest that you approve this resignation."

"I'll do no such thing, Jenson. I don't know how long your obligation is, or what sort of trouble you're in."

"I'm not in any trouble, and my obligation's irrelevant. I'm about to hand you the biggest case of the decade. Release me, or I can't."

The crowd around them was now listening in to this fascinating conversation. Harper pondered this strange request for a minute, then replied, "I don't make deals with my own agents."

"That's the whole point. Release me and I'll hand you the biggest case you've ever seen. Otherwise, forget it."

"What's that supposed to mean?"

"Think about where we're meeting. I'll hand it off to a different investigative agency and you'll stand on the sidelines with mud on your face and watch the action. Trust me, it's strongly in your interest to avoid that."

Harper shuffled her feet and looked uncertain. "How about this?" she offered. "I'll grant a temporary resignation, hear what you have to say, then decide whether to make it permanent or rescind it."

Mia thought about it a second. "All right, that works for me."

A moment later they marched into a big conference room.

Marcus Graves, the SAC, and three senior agents were already there, seated with serious expressions at the large conference table. "Coffee and tea in the corner," Graves hospitably announced, pointing in the direction of two matching tables. One held two big urns and some cups, the other a portable tape player hooked to two large speakers.

Nobody wanted. Instead they quickly hustled around both sides of the conference table and took seats. Mia and her friend sat in the middle, side by side, with grim but relaxed expressions.

Notepads came out, pens were propped, the chairs stopped scraping the floors. The moment everybody looked ready and attentive, Mia offered them all a pleasant good evening and thanked them for coming. She continued, "My name's Mia Jenson. I'm a law school grad, granted the right to practice law in D.C. by the district bar. The past two years I've been an agent with the DCIS, but effective two minutes ago, I'm retired and back to practicing law."

Thomas Rutherford II, the Pentagon's inspector general, an older gentleman, but also a lawyer, looked at Graves, and gruffly asked, "If she works for us, why are we meeting here?"

"Why don't you let her explain it?"

"I'd rather hear your explanation first."

It was a reasonable request and Graves decided to be friendly and cooperative. "Mia came to us about seven months ago. She was looking into possible crimes by a big defense contractor. She became worried about her safety, with good reason, it turned out. Over the past few days, we busted a large criminal ring. Her home was broken into, her office burgled, unsavory people began looking into her background. Now I suggest you listen to what she has to say."

The inspector general's hands folded on the table and he stared at Mia. His expression conveyed more confusion than anger, though it was clear he was unhappy having to hear about this on foreign turf. Harper's look conveyed no confusion, just anger; a junior agent doesn't carry the dirt outside.

Mia met their stares with a firm expression. "I'd like to introduce my client, Jack Wiley. Until eight months ago, Jack was a partner in Cauldron, a private equity Wall Street firm. It was Jack who brought the deal to buy Arvan Chemicals, with its polymer and patents, to the Capitol Group."

Jack's introduction electrified the room. All eyes shifted to his face; more than a few eyes narrowed and the frowns deepened a few notches. Over the past twenty-four hours everybody in the room had learned his name. A few had seen his face on TV or splashed on the front page of their morning paper. He was the subject of a nationwide manhunt, the smiling face on a five-million-dollar wanted poster, and, quite possibly, the culprit behind a twenty-billion-dollar swindle. A few thought how he barely resembled the photo on TV — he seemed so much taller, thinner, less tanned. Jack smiled and nodded pleasantly, visibly unconcerned to be in the midst of so many law enforcement authorities.

Mia waited long enough for the shock to wear off. "On Jack's behalf, here's the deal we're offering," she continued. "Jack will come forward and offer testimony on one condition. He's a whistleblower. I'm sure we're all familiar with the program, but it won't hurt to review a few important stipulations. Last year the federal government spent over $2.5 trillion. Considering that at least ten percent of that was lost or stolen due to waste, fraud, or abuse, the Congress in its wisdom passed a whistleblower act granting a reward of up to twenty-five percent of whatever the government collects against cheating companies. Now the good news. Jack's not greedy. He wants a mere ten percent of whatever he saves."

"Or we can just arrest him," Harper threatened. "Throw him in our nastiest, most vicious federal prison and see how long he holds out before he talks."

"You don't have the grounds," Mia said, very cold, very lawyerlike.

"How about graft? Theft, bribery, falsification of documents. I'm sure we'll think up more charges. We can be very creative. Something will stick."

"Jack's done nothing wrong. He's innocent. And we have the evidence to back that up."

"And that's the first time I've ever heard a defense lawyer make that claim," Harper snapped back, baring her teeth.

Mia opened her mouth to argue, then abruptly changed her mind. "I'd like you to listen to this tape," she suggested with a swift nod at one of the agents seated beside Graves. The agent dutifully got to his feet, went to the corner, and pushed play on the tape machine.

During the short interval before the tape kicked in, Mia quickly mentioned, "The first voice belongs to Mitch Walters, CEO of the Capitol Group. He's talking to Daniel Bellweather."

Those intriguing names brought everyone forward in their seats.

Walters: "So how did it go last night?"

Bellweather: "Splendid. You should've seen Robinson's face when he learned I had the seat beside him."

Walters: "He's a dumb jerk. Always was. Any administration that would make him secretary of defense is blind or stupid. They really scraped the bottom of the barrel with that clown."

Bellweather (after a short, derisive laugh):

"True enough, but don't piss in a gift horse's mouth, Mitch."

Walters: "Think he buys it?"

Bellweather: "Beginning to. We're not quite there yet. Probably halfway, though."

Walters: "What's he doing about Jenson?"

Bellweather: "She's toast. He'll get her off our ass in the morning."

Walters: "Jesus, that's great. Just great. You really played him."

Bellweather (sounding quite boastful): "Yeah, isn't it? What did you do for the cause last night?"

Walters (sounding annoyed and whiny): "Jackson had me slaving all night. Destroying evidence, concocting stuff to pin this mess on Wiley."

Mia waved a hand and the agent abruptly shut off the tape.

If there were doubts about what Jack was offering, they instantly disappeared, but those doubts gave way to a thousand questions and suspicions.

Mia's old boss demanded, "Where did you get that?"

"We don't answer anything until we have a deal. But you're probably wondering, so I'll tell you. It's a sampler, a small taste from a huge banquet. Jack has thousands of them. He's unearthed one of the biggest frauds in history, and has a fabulous library to prove it."

Rutherford II unfolded his veiny hands and began rubbing his jaw. "How do we know your client didn't commit any criminal activity?"

"He didn't, but you don't. It doesn't matter. Jack gets all the immunity the whistleblower act affords. He's free from prosecution for anything related to this case."

"It may be the law, but that's ridiculous."

"And it's nonnegotiable," Mia shot back. "No immunity, no deal."

The inspector general was a lawyer himself, he knew a smart lawyer when he saw one, and Mia was certainly very smart. And smart lawyers always have a backup. He took a stab and asked, "And if we say no?"

"This is only hypothetical and should by no means be construed as a threat," Mia responded quickly, obviously prepared for that challenge.

The faces on the other side of the table grew uneasy — of course she was about to threaten them.

"But I imagine," Mia continued, "that my client has already made arrangements to ship all his files and tapes to some very reputable news organizations. The *New York Times* and *Washington Post* come to mind.

As you know, both adore big government scandals."

She paused to inspect the faces across the table. They hadn't accepted their defeat yet, but they definitely didn't like what they were hearing.

Mia cleared her throat and turned up the heat a little more. "Again, I don't want to be too specific at this point, but the tapes will sound even more dramatic on TV. Think of a full hour of *60 Minutes*. A three-hour special in prime time isn't out of the question, or maybe six weeks of one-hour specials. There's so much to cover, so many embarrassing avenues to go down. Believe me, everyone in this room has an incentive not to let that happen."

"Like what?" Margaret Harper asked.

"For instance, you might not like to be blamed for failing to stick up for an honest, hardworking agent when you ordered her off this case." Harper suddenly looked away. In light of the tape she just heard, she suddenly felt ill. How would that look splashed across the front page? Did Mia mention *60 minutes*? Mia redirected her eyes at Rutherford II. "Or here's another bomb. The office of the inspector general was thoroughly infiltrated by the Capitol Group. Only this afternoon one of your employees was arrested for pilfering my files and providing certain very sensitive papers to a private investigating firm working for the Capitol Group. And he wasn't their only paid plant. Would you care to hear more specifics?" Mia asked very nicely.

Nobody wanted to hear more.

"Believe me," Mia continued, "I've listened to less than a tenth of the tapes. Half the Pentagon directory gets mentioned in one way or another, none flattering."

"Oh, man." The inspector general was now rubbing his eyes. A migraine that seemed to have come out of nowhere was splitting his head open. "How bad is it?"

"Nixon and Watergate come off like a bunch of kids playing with matches in the woods compared to this."

"Who's implicated?"

"Who isn't? A lot of people sound absolutely terrible. But at worst most were only stupid, gullible, and careless, not crooked. There's plenty of those, too, but you know the press and the great American public. They might not be discriminate in their judgments."

The faces on the other side of the table conveyed a mixture of terror, shock, and disbelief.

Mia decided to push them across the

brink and said, "The congressional inquisitions alone will last months. Enough of their own members and staffers are implicated, they'll need to put on a large public lynching just to tamp down the outrage. And I'm afraid it's not just the polymer. The Capitol Group has dozens of other Pentagon contracts. Jack's tapes picked up lots of nasty tidbits about corruption related to other deals." She paused for a moment to underscore her client's generosity. "He's throwing those in free of charge."

The inspector general asked, "Why are you bringing this to us? Why not your FBI friends here?"

Graves pushed forward in his chair. "It was part of the original bargain when she first came to see us," he announced from the end of the table, evidently very much on her side. "She fed us a few cases that were important to us. That investigating firm she mentioned, it employs about a dozen Bureau alumni. All retired or otherwise separated, but it's somewhat embarrassing for us."

"And the rest is for us?" Harper asked, her eyes moving from Mia to Graves. They were down to bargaining the particulars now.

"She was very demanding on that point,"

Graves admitted. "Mia insisted on a clear division of spoils. You're going to need plenty of perp walks of your own to counter your humiliation."

"That's what she said?"

"More or less. Remember, she was a DCIS agent at that time. I've heard a few of those tapes. She's not bluffing. It's uglier than you can imagine."

"So the deal is, we get to clean our dirty laundry, you get to launder yours?" Rutherford II asked, suddenly warming to the subject.

"The esteemed members of Congress belong to us, too," Graves insisted with an uncompromising look.

"Sure, no problem," answered Rutherford II quickly, actually more than happy to concede that point. Congress funded the Pentagon and Rutherford admitted, "We have no interest in pissing off any of our congressional supporters." Then the two officials swiftly broke into a comfortable negotiation about indictments and courts and jurisdiction and other legal matters.

It didn't escape the notice of either Harper or Rutherford II how generous Graves was being. The big foot of the FBI was growing soft, they thought before the truth dawned on them — as Graves said, he had already listened to a bunch of the tapes. The spirit of intragovernmental generosity had nothing to do with this. There were more than enough indictments to keep everybody busy for a very long time, enough that he was worried about overload at this point.

"So we have a deal?" Mia asked at the first pause in their conversation.

Harper and the inspector general exchanged looks. The looks weren't all that hard to read, the decision not at all hard to make.

Mia calmly placed a paper on the table and slid it across to the inspector general. Rutherford II lifted it up and Harper leaned over his arm; they read it together, a short, precisely worded agreement that listed all of Mia's conditions, from the ten percent reward, to Jack's amnesty, to Mia's permanent separation from the DCIS. The IG scrawled his signature and handed the agreement back across the table.

Mia tucked it in her briefcase, then said, "Now I think it's time to hear from Jack what you're buying."

30

Jack opened with a smiling invitation. "Feel free to interrupt anytime you like. Do you have any questions to start?"

"Plenty," Harper fired back, unamused. "But let's hear your tale first."

"Sure. As Mia mentioned, I was a partner at a private equity firm in New York. About twelve months ago, I met Perry Arvan. He was hunting for capital to get his company through a rough patch. A midsize chemical company bleeding cash didn't fit our investment profile and my firm wasn't interested. Neither was anyone else Perry approached. I spoke with him after his pitch. He was quite dispirited, facing the prospect of bankruptcy at that point. I offered to find a buyer or a major investor willing to stake cash for a slice of ownership. A fairly common arrangement on Wall Street."

"And that's what brought you to the

Capitol Group?" one of the DCIS aides asked.

"That and my good-faith belief that Arvan Chemicals fit squarely into CG's portfolio of turnaround prospects. A few months later I approached the Capitol Group, but from the beginning CG was most interested in the polymer Perry invented. Actually, that was all that seemed to interest them. To be frank, I did little to discourage that interest. Why should I? My job was to represent the interests of my client Perry Arvan. So I shared the results of a study completed a year before that put the polymer in the best light."

Harper pointed an accusatory finger at Jack. "You mean you deceived them?"

"I meant what I said," Jack answered and seemed to smile. "Understand, ladies and gentlemen, the Capitol Group is in the takeover business. They're not novices. They're one of the most experienced firms in that line of business. They make their fortunes gobbling up companies and chewing them up. They had time and more than enough opportunity to conduct a thorough due diligence before they moved in." Jack paused, then said, "Had they ever asked me if there was another report on the polymer, I certainly would've shared the final report with them."

Yeah, yeah, right, Jack, the looks from across the table were saying.

"Why didn't they?" another aide asked.

"Greed, fear, impatience. They were afraid another big firm might get interested. They didn't want to lose Arvan, and I suppose they didn't want a bidding war that drove up the price. So Mitch Walters and a few others decided to launch a quick, dirty, very unfriendly takeover."

Jack paused and looked around for more questions. None, not yet, though there were plenty of skeptical expressions across the table.

"I was very opposed to this and told them so," Jack explained with a sad look. "Then Mitch Walters called me. He had a tape, the fruits of an illegal wiretap, of Perry making a phone call and discussing plans to call some private investors and sell off partial ownership of the polymer in exchange for cash. Perry was looking for a white knight to fend off CG's takeover, Mitch told me. It was an opportunity, and he didn't want to let it go by."

"An opportunity?" Harper asked.

"As a public company, this would be a serious violation of various securities laws. It was Mitch's intention to, in his words,

621

grab Perry's balls and force a quick, non-negotiable sell."

"You're saying it was extortion?"

"Yes, and I strongly advised him not to do it. I wore a wire, incidentally, and have that conversation on tape. He invited me to a private meeting with Perry where he dropped the hammer. He gave Perry no choice — prison or sell — and Perry caved in to every demand immediately. He sold the company and the polymer for a hundred million."

"Then he fled," Harper mentioned to anybody in the room not in the loop on this story, which frankly was nobody. "He took the money, rented a big boat, and went into hiding in the Caribbean."

Jack immediately corrected her. "That's not exactly right."

"Then where is he?"

"Nowhere near the Caribbean. Never was. Try New Mexico with his wife, in a beautiful rented lodge in Taos. Perry's wife gets seasick. He hates the sun, loves the mountains. He's living under a false identity until this gets cleared up."

"Oh, spare me. An innocent man has nothing to fear," Harper insisted, shooting Jack another condemning expression. All these evasions and double-talk, she wasn't buying a word of it. Jack and his coconspirator, Perry Arvan, had committed serious crimes and were now trying to squirm out of it. "And innocent men don't hide behind false names," she threw in, lowering her bifocals and looking down her nose at Jack.

Jack looked amused. "Something I failed to mention. A few weeks before that meeting my house was broken into. While I was down in D.C. being wined and dined and courted by CG, a group of hired thugs picked the locks, entered, spent three hours searching, and left a few gifts in their wake. All this is on film. They left bugs in my phones and hid about five pounds of marijuana they could use to blackmail me in the event I didn't hand CG the sale."

The faces across the table showed their surprise. Suddenly this was more than a simple case of graft. It was burglary and blackmail, and Lord knew what else.

Jack shrugged and continued, "My private security firm discovered all of this, thank goodness. You can imagine my surprise, so of course I contacted my client and warned him there was a chance his phone and home might also be bugged."

The Fibbies at the end of the table broke into loud chortles of laughter. Jack gave them an innocent look and the laughter grew louder. The sound bounced around the room a moment. They already knew the broad outline of the story. The details, though, were priceless. It was impossible to keep a straight face.

"You're saying Arvan never called any private investors?" Harper asked when the laughter died down.

"I'm saying Perry might've discussed a vague intention to do so, but he never had the slightest intention to follow through."

"But —"

"Forget the buts. If someone was illegally eavesdropping on his private phone calls and was misled, then committed an illegal act based on this information, where is Perry's crime?"

Mia, ever the helpful lawyer, noted, "I've researched the statutes, so I'll save you the trouble. No laws were violated, none."

"Arvan still committed fraud."

"How?" Jack asked, still with that pleasant smile.

"He withheld the final report. He deliberately misled CG about the polymer."

"He was never asked about the final report. Nor was he ever given the opportunity to provide it. Once CG forced him to sell, he was goose-stepped off the premises and barred from ever returning."

It was dawning on everyone in the room what an amazing tale they were listening to. It further dawned on them that Jack here was a very clever boy. So far, he had confessed to no wrongdoing, but he had certainly shadow-danced right up to the line.

"You see," Jack continued, "CG jumped into the sale more or less without looking." He held up his arms and shook his head from side to side as if it had been painful for him to witness. "They were so greedy and arrogant, no serious due diligence was done. They fired most of the workers, booted out the executives, and immediately kicked the polymer into production."

Mia helpfully added, "Perry set aside thirty million of his cut to pay bonuses to the fired workers after the Capitol Group promised them severance but reneged."

"And what did you get out of it?" Harper asked, looking at Jack.

"I was a limited partner. I got twenty million in cash as a finder's fee, and twenty-five percent ownership of the company that produced the polymer." He proudly waved a paper in the air they all assumed was the contract he had signed with the Capitol Group.

"Whose idea was the twenty-five percent?" the IG asked.

"Mine," Jack confessed without embarrassment. "I insisted on a big piece of the action. I fought damned hard for it."

Nobody asked why. The answer was obnoxiously obvious. The role of a confidence man is just to do that — to build confidence in the sucker. By battling hard for a big stake of ownership, Jack was conveying that the polymer was a sure thing. The idea that he had outsmarted the best brains in the Capitol Group was immensely entertaining, though nobody smiled.

"How did you get the tapes?" Rutherford II asked, almost incredulously.

"Well, by then I had . . . let's call them serious trust issues with my new partners. They had burgled my home and obviously weren't above blackmail and extortion, and God knows what else. As part of the contract, I had an office in CG's headquarters — a small, out-of-the-way cubbyhole on the second floor. It afforded me a building pass and an opportunity. These people showed no compunction about breaking laws; I decided to protect myself. I wore a wire almost every time I talked to them. I recorded all phone conversations."

"And that's the source of all these tapes?"

"A handful of them," Jack admitted.

"And the rest?"

"Almost every time I made my rounds around the headquarters I sprinkled listening devices around. I placed four in Mitch Walters's office. Another three in each of the firm's conference rooms, including the one on the top floor where the senior executive and board meetings are held. Believe me, those are some of the more captivating tapes."

"And how did you monitor those bugs?" asked one of the FBI agents, making no effort to disguise his admiration. An irrelevant technical question, and the Feds at the end of the table already knew the answer, but they wanted the Defense people to share their amazement at Jack's scheme.

Jack turned to him and said, "I had rented an apartment across the street. The devices have a range of one mile. My apartment was only a hundred yards away. I'd built a console with five noise-activated taping machines, and hired a crew to monitor the action around the clock."

For the first time it really began to dawn on everybody what a truly remarkable find Jack Wiley was.

Harper bent forward. "How many tapes did you make?"

"A lot. Too many thousands of hours to be worth listening to. I didn't want to overburden you, so my crew and I sifted through them. We disposed of anything too mundane or irrelevant, and preserved only those conversations that show legal culpability."

"Give us an example."

"Okay. For example, you won't hear Dan Bellweather ordering five whores from a D.C. call girl service, but you will hear him arranging payments to senators and congressmen to shove the authorization for the polymer through with two speedy votes. You'll also hear how he paid a certain House member to assassinate the GT 400, the only real competition. Mia incidentally got a taped copy of that hearing. It's very entertaining in a rather vulgar way."

Jack paused and searched their faces. "If I'm boring you, stop me," he said facetiously. "Or to take another example, you will hear Mitch Walters illegally offering post-administration jobs to several top assistant secretaries, and you will very clearly hear him arranging the cover-up on the polymer."

Nobody looked the least bit bored.

"Anything else?" the IG asked, clearly rattled.

"Yes, plenty," Jack assured him, no longer smiling, now looking quite grim. "Understand, I didn't go into this with the intention of uncovering such a large scandal. But the more I saw, the more I heard, the more I learned, the more horrified I became. I realized that I was way over my head. I became frightened. The power of the Capitol Group is overwhelming. They could destroy me as easily as a tank could crush a bug."

The people across the table weren't buying this, not one bit. But they also suspected that they would never be able to prove Jack was lying. Any man who could pull off such a staggering swindle wasn't likely to leave sloppy evidence around. Whatever they thought of, he had undoubtedly thought of first.

Mia stood up and announced, "My client is tired. It's been a very exhausting few days. You can ask all the questions you want later."

"Where are these tapes and when can we have them?" Harper asked with a gleam in her eye.

"Tonight. They're in a moving van shuttling around the streets of northern Virginia. Frankly, I'd like to get them off my hands. Tell me where you want them delivered."

Harper finally raised the point Mia and Jack had been anticipating from the beginning, the most important point. "What about legal admissibility? These tapes were made without the permission of both parties."

Graves glanced at Mia and, by unspoken agreement, he handled this. "When Mia first came to us she mentioned she had an inside source. She provided us with the film showing Jack's home being burgled and the crude attempt to frame him. In her view he was still at risk, and so was she."

"Then what?" Harper asked.

"Well, it looked serious, so I took that film to Justice. They went to a federal judge for permission to tape all Jack's phone conversations and plant bugs in CG's headquarters."

"On what grounds?"

"Conspiracy, burglary, attempting to fix a federal bid. You might even say Jack was acting as our agent. The bugs and tapes were legally authorized. The fruits are quite admissible in any court in the land."

Harper and Rutherford II showed no hint of surprise at this astounding revelation. Nothing Jack did surprised them any longer. Of course he got a judge to authorize his actions. Of course he had the FBI in his pocket. If the president walked in the room and kissed Jack's ass, they wouldn't bat a lash.

And though they knew they'd never be able to prove it, they were sure Jack had this whole thing planned out before he ever made that first call to the Capitol Group.

"Will Mr. Wiley testify?" Rutherford II asked Mia. In his mind he was already plotting the next move.

"In two days, you will have six hours to conduct a lengthy deposition. I suggest you film it. A lot of trials will come out of this, and Jack doesn't intend to spend the rest of his life bouncing through witness chairs. He promises to appear in court, to verify the accuracy of his filmed testimony and get it entered into evidence. That should be sufficient to use it as many times as you like. Name the time and place, Jack and I will be there. He'll swear to the provenance of the tapes, and he'll detail the story he just told."

"I'll call as soon as it's arranged," Harper said.

"Just so we're clear," Mia mentioned, as if it was an afterthought, a niggling little last-minute detail, "Jack just saved the Department of Defense from a twenty-billion-dollar scam."

For the first time, their brains concentrated on how much this was going to cost.

The math was done quickly inside their heads and the sum was staggering. The howls were immediate and loud. "We're not about to pay out two billion dollars," Rutherford II shouted adamantly.

"You already signed the contract," Mia reminded him.

If Mia took the lawyer's standard one-third cut, her share would be in the neighborhood of six hundred million dollars.

No wonder she had resigned, Harper realized with a shock.

Mia looked at their faces. "You know the old cliché — think how much you're saving, rather than spending."

"The answer's still hell, no."

"You don't want the tapes?"

"At that price, forget it. You've told us enough anyway. We'll find other ways to pursue the case," he answered smugly.

"I'd be interested to learn how."

"We'll take your client to court and sue. Or, if we want to play hardball, we'll have Mr. Wiley here detained as an uncooperative material witness, or charge him as a coconspirator. You're not the only lawyer in this room, young lady."

"Maybe I failed to mention that every tape was copied three times. Two other moving vans are cutting fairy circles around the

Beltway at this moment, one for our friends in the printed press, one for the TV news stations."

They searched Mia's face to see if she was bluffing. Not a wrinkle of doubt or uncertainty. She looked quite cool and confident.

"Are you threatening blackmail?"

"Aren't you? Lawsuits, prison? But let's not think of it that way."

"What would you call it?"

"Lawyer talk. I thought we were just discussing alternative scenarios."

"I know a threat when I hear one."

"Then call it a polite reminder."

"Ripping the government off of two billion dollars is anything but polite."

"Honor the contract, Mr. Rutherford. You'll get the tapes either way, I promise. My client wants this scam exposed. Fine with us if comes out in dribs and drabs as the story's fed over the news wire, dissected and discussed by every talking head in TV land."

Rutherford II paused for a moment, then tried a fresh tack. "Are you aware of the highest amount ever paid to a whistleblower? How unreasonable this is?" he asked.

"One hundred million. Believe me, I've studied the act in great detail. Two billion, or we'll finish this discussion in court." She waved the contract like a loaded gun.

There was a long pause as Harper and Rutherford unhappily put two and two together. Jack had not just become Mia's client; the pair had been in this together from the start. It explained so much, from Mia's earlier discovery of the report detailing the polymer's fatal flaw to what was happening here now. She had had many months to think this through, and she had used that edge to sucker them into this deal.

Oh, what they would give if only they could go back ten minutes in time, a do-over.

Suddenly Jack leaned up against Mia and whispered in her ear. She said, "Excuse us a minute," then they both got up and carried the private conversation to the far corner of the room. All eyes remained on their faces. Mia whispered something at Jack, a hiss more than a whisper. Jack leaned closer and whispered more fervently, and they went back and forth awhile. Their discussion, while quiet, was obviously an intense argument. Eventually, Mia produced a sulky nod, then backed away from Jack. They returned to the table and fell into their chairs.

Mia looked upset for a few seconds, and

it required a considerable effort to collect herself. "Oddly enough, Jack agrees two billion is a shocking sum. Too shocking."

"Thank God somebody's being reasonable."

She gave Jack a dirty look, then faced Rutherford II again. "He'll settle for one billion. Our final offer. A pitiful five percent of what the Capitol Group would've stolen were it not for Jack."

"That's still ridiculous."

"Then I'll see you in court for the full two billion."

Now it was their turn to whisper. Harper and Rutherford II got up and moved to a different corner, where they murmured back and forth at a furious pace. What are our chances if we refuse to back down and go to court, Harper asked Rutherford, the lawyer. An uncertain shrug — a contract's a contract, he whispered unhappily. He and Harper both would have to admit incredible stupidity, they'd have to argue that they had no idea what they were signing, a humiliating and feeble assertion coming from the mouths of an experienced lawyer and a senior law enforcement official. Then pray for a cheapskate judge and a long-shot verdict.

Two billion was so far over the top, it

could happen.

And what if we concede to one billion, she asked, and they began chewing over that option. Well, at least half that cost would be recouped in the penalties they would impose on CG. They would also sue to claw back the $5.5 billion already paid into CG's coffers. Clawbacks typically got back only a modest fraction of the total spent, but if these tapes were half as compelling as Mia and Jack claimed, they stood an excellent chance of getting far more; three-quarters wasn't out of the realm of possibility. A one billion investment that offered a return of possibly four, or even five billion dollars. Considered in that light, it wasn't a bad deal; in fact, it was a great deal. And when the secretary of defense heard that taped conversation of Bellweather and Walters talking about him, Harper noted, he'd want to hammer them into bankruptcy, or as close as they could get.

For one billion, they'd buy the tapes, they'd buy Jack, they'd buy control of this thing, and they'd get back billions.

Harper didn't mention the billions in embarrassment they would save. She didn't need to.

Rutherford II returned to the table. He took off his glasses and spent a moment wiping the lenses on his necktie. "All right," he finally groaned. "One billion. But you won't see a penny until we have the tapes and see for ourselves that they're everything you've promised."

Mia smiled at him.

Jack thanked them.

Graves leaned back in his chair and tried, unsuccessfully, to stifle a loud laugh. They were certainly an amazing couple. Mia had warned him only an hour before that he would be shocked by the size of the reward. How much? he had asked.

One billion, she'd predicted.

31

For two weeks, the Capitol Group was the talk of the town and the sole and abiding concern in newsworld. The cable talk shows could squawk about little else. Talk radio went on a rabid tear. Every day, more arrests were made, adding more oxygen to the bonfire that threatened to become an endless flame. Three congressmen and two senators were charged, fifteen staffers also, and nobody believed it would end there. A mood of heavy despair hung over the Capitol building like a thick mist. Four more congressmen and two senators announced they were stepping down at the end of their terms, sparking wide suspicions that they had cut deals to avoid indictments.

The film clips of rich senior executives doing the perp walk replayed endlessly. It was the Feds' favorite stunt and they indulged it every chance they got.

Bellweather in particular was a big hit,

especially on YouTube, where the stream of filthy curses pouring out his mouth weren't in any way censored.

Mitch Walters wasn't nearly as popular, logging a comparatively puny seven million hits. Mitch, the tough-guy wannabe, was shaking and blubbering as he tried to hide his face by draping a trench coat over his head.

Mia, on behalf of her client, did as few interviews as possible. She appeared thoroughly uninterested and came off dry and boring. The newspeople were attracted to her beauty, but it was obvious that TV time didn't float her boat, like so many in the legal profession. Her answers were brisk and not overly educational, and the news bureaus quickly lost interest.

Jack stayed in seclusion. Mia offered the thin excuse that her client needed to remain out of the limelight for legal reasons. There would be many trials, and Jack needed to avoid any risk of tainting the evidence, she insisted.

The defendants had already hired the most flamboyant legal guns in the country. The big D.C. law firms loved Jack, and adored Mia. Gift horses like them came along once a decade. Business promised to be great for the foreseeable future.

At the end of week three, a major city in California got torched by a raging wildfire. The damage and horrendous tales of suddenly homeless families displaced Capitolgate, as the scandal had inevitably been named by the imagination-deprived press.

Occasional stories continued to crop up — Martie O'Neal's attempted prison escape and subsequent recapture in a restroom in Richmond, for instance — but the public became bored and the press moved on.

After a three-week orgy, the press grew tired of Capitolgate, too.

They would rest for a while, until the slew of trials began with the promise of more sensationalism.

Mitch Walters was seated at a table at the Cosmos Club, across from Phil Jackson, now his lawyer.

Jackson was one of the lucky few to avoid an indictment, a strong tribute, he was sure, to his own legal ferocity. When the first arrests occurred, he held a rambunctious press conference where he snarled into the cameras and threatened a record-breaking lawsuit if any attempt was made to arrest or indict him. Yes, he was a director of the company, but he also served as legal counsel. Any involvement he had in the polymer fiasco was merely a by-product of that. All his conversations and associations occurred under that blanket, and were fully protected under the broad, immutable rubric of attorney-client privilege.

Two days later he was hired by Walters to be his legal counsel. He tried to refuse, but Walters offered him a magical incentive — get him off, or Walters would sing and offer enough damning material to ensnare Jackson and ensure him a rope on the gallows beside him. Throwing in some of his own money, Jackson posted bail to get Walters sprung.

They were discussing the case over a lunch of Peking duck, boiled asparagus, and fried wild rice when the couple appeared out of nowhere.

Jack was holding Mia's hand as they approached the table. "Hi, Mitch, Phil," Jack said, smiling broadly, as if they had just happened to bump into each other, and wasn't it a lovely coincidence.

Walters dropped his fork, took one look at them, and felt like throwing up. He thought about landing a punch in Jack's face, or maybe wrapping his hands around his neck. Knowing Jack, though, there was bound to be a hidden camera nearby. He would only end up with more charges.

"You're a lousy, lying bastard," Walters snarled. "You ruined my life."

"Get lost," Jack told him with a dismissive wave. "We're here to talk with Phil."

"Who the hell do you think you are?"

Jack looked at Jackson and hooked a finger at the exit. "Tell him to get lost. We need to talk."

Jackson considered the request for a moment, then said to Walters, "Do as he says."

Walters stood up, and for a moment he considered telling them all to screw off. Unfortunately, Jackson was his only hope for freedom. He bit down hard on his tongue and stomped off.

Jack and Mia fell into two chairs.

"Are you wired?" Jackson asked Jack in a taunting tone.

"Not today. Should I be?"

Jackson studied their faces and knew with a blinding flash something he should have recognized from the beginning. Jack and Mia were lovers.

"Isn't this sweet? How did you two meet?" he asked, dripping sarcasm.

"We met three years ago," Mia said, surprisingly open. "A company my law firm was representing was being bought by Jack's firm. After the deal closed, we began dating. We're in love, Jackson. Doesn't that melt your heart? For various reasons we decided to keep it quiet and low-key."

"Why?" Jackson asked.

"Why what? Why you? Why me? Why did we keep it quiet?"

"Start with why you?"

"I have a twin sister, Janet. Born a minute ahead of me, so we always call her my big sister. Like many twins, Janet and I were inseparable until it came time for college. I went to Dickinson, she went to Notre Dame."

"Nice story. Is there a point to this?"

"Listen and learn something for a change, Jackson. At Notre Dame, Janet fell in love. He was a football player, a big bear of a man who adored her back. He was wonderful, intelligent, incredibly talented, and had so much to live for. Anything he tried he was good at. Senior year, he and Janet couldn't wait, they were so much in love, and they married."

"Is there a point to this?" Jackson prodded, totally uninterested in this nice little love story.

"You asked why and I'm telling you. Come graduation, Bill turned down a wonderfully lucrative offer to go to Wall Street and instead chose an Army commission. He stayed in when the war started. He and Janet had two lovely little girls they both adored, big money on Wall Street still beckoned, but Bill didn't want to run out on his men when they deployed to Iraq. How do you think this story ends, Jackson?"

Jackson had no idea. "Go on."

"A little over two years ago, Bill was leading a convoy of his troops through an Iraqi village. This was less than two weeks before he was to return to Janet and his little girls. He was riding in a Humvee, a model that had yet to be uparmored with the latest protection. His battalion had been scheduled to get upgraded models eight months before, but the contractor kept falling behind. The soldiers riding in the death traps complained endlessly, but the contractor cared less. The upgrading program was understaffed, its employees notoriously lazy, the management dreadfully inept. The only thing the contractor accomplished on time were the billings to the Pentagon, after they were stuffed with nonexistent overtime, ghost employees, and as much double billing as it felt it could get away with. Would you care to guess the name of the company?"

"So this is a vendetta?" Jackson asked in a disappointed voice.

"Bill Forrest died horribly, Jackson. He

was blown out of his seat. He landed on a dusty street, his legs amputated by the blast, his stomach blown open, and he bled out within minutes. Only two weeks from home, he died in agony, staring at a picture of Janet and the girls."

"How sad," Jackson said, as if to say, Screw you.

"I spent the month of the funeral with Janet and the kids. They cried the whole month. Janet fainted at the funeral. Do you have any idea how horrible it is to lose a husband and a father who might so easily have been saved by a few extra pounds of armor?"

"Don't sound so noble, Jenson. You two make me sick. It was always about the money. Blood money. The one-billion-dollar prize, the biggest whistleblower jackpot ever."

"Well, here's the surprise, Jackson. Every dollar of that money is going into a fund Jack and I founded this week. The Bill Forrest Fund. You'll be happy to learn that it'll all be used to fund college scholarships for the wives and kids of servicepeople who died in this war."

"So that's why you chose us."

"You see, I went crazy for a while. I quit my law firm and joined DCIS, because I wanted to hurt you. I didn't care how, or how long it took. I would go after you, one by one. Anytime you made a mistake, I would be there. I would haunt the acquisition office, pore over their files, find every corner you cut. Every instance of overbilling, of cheating, of graft. I was confident you would give me plenty of opportunities and I intended to pounce on every one of them. The death of a thousand cuts, I called it."

"What changed your mind?"

"It was Jack's idea. Rather than waste my life chasing small cases, why not go for the big bang? So we decided to test your greed. You always had a choice. We'd offer you a deal only a scoundrel would take. Every step of the way, you people could always stop, always have second thoughts, always do the right thing. You never disappointed us, Jackson. You surpassed all our expectations."

"And Arvan Chemicals was the lure."

"Poor Perry. He was facing an almost certain bankruptcy, but he wasn't very comfortable with the arrangement. An honorable man. We dragged him into it kicking and screaming. He didn't fully change his mind until Walters paid him that nasty visit."

Jackson looked at her and said, "The correct legal terminology is conspiracy and graft. When this comes to court I'll prove it and shove it up your rear, Jenson."

"I don't think so. Any first-year law school student would look at the evidence and know how screwed you people are."

Jackson was too cold-blooded to get flustered, and too much the bully himself to be bullied. He turned his eyes to Jack. "This whole case rests on your shoulders. The tapes you provided, the testimony you've given. You're the only real prosecution witness."

"I do my best."

"Pretty soon you'll see my best, Wiley. I'll destroy you on the stand."

"Through Edith Warbinger?" Jack asked.

"Yes, because you're a murderer and a thief. I'll wait, Wiley. I'll bide my time till we're in a nice little federal court, with a judge and twelve impressionable jurors. I'll share my evidence and bring in your old friend Wallerman. Then I'll put you on the stand, pull out all my evidence, and drag you through the mud."

Jack said nothing for a moment. He seemed at a loss for words. He stared at a far wall long enough that Jackson thought he was in a coma.

"How did you find out about Edith?" Jack

finally asked, almost choking on his own words. He sounded sad and tired.

"A source," Jackson said with a tight, confident smile.

"Who? Who was your source?"

"You'll learn that in court, Wiley."

"Charles? Oh, please tell me it wasn't him."

Jackson chose not to answer. It was no surprise that Jack knew the name. He had the CG building so juiced he probably knew the names of the janitor's mistresses. But so what?

"Did you ever track him down?" Jack asked. "I know he was elusive. Ever learn his last name, his profession, how he learned about Edith and me?"

To answer those questions would reveal vulnerabilities that might come back to haunt him in court. Jackson was too smart a lawyer to fall for such an obvious taunt. He scraped back his chair and kept his mouth shut.

Jack leaned his elbows on the table and came forward. "Let me help you, Jackson. Charles Palmer. A Broadway actor, not overly successful, but I think you'll agree his talents are underrated."

"You're lying."

"Look him up. He's in the Manhattan

phone book. Since you're paying his rent this year, I'm sure he'll take your call. Fifty grand for a two-night performance, the best money he ever made."

"I don't believe you, Wiley."

"Or take Lew Wallerman. My old pal from Princeton. One of my best friends then, and now. Poor Lew has had a string of bad luck. His career on Wall Street was souring, a nasty divorce that cleaned him out. The past few years have been awful. So I offered Lew this one golden chance to make millions. He asked me to thank you. You boys came through like champs."

Jackson now was looking like the kid who just had his candy stolen. After all that happened with the polymer, he didn't doubt one word Jack was saying. It was going to be so beautiful, Jack on the stand, sweating and squirming, Jackson flashing his evidence that exposed the government's main witness as a cad and a murderer, the prosecutors wilting, the judge frowning with disgust, the jurors sneering and shaking their heads. Jack's credibility would be shredded. Jackson had plotted an epic mistrial and was sure he would get it.

Only a minute before, it had all been so clear in his mind, so within reach.

Jack crossed his legs and shook his head.

"After the break-in, the dope in my home, the bugging, your TFAC boys crawling through my past, it seemed like a good idea to create a diversion. You see, I needed to get your people off my tail. With enough people, time, and energy you might've discovered Mia. I couldn't afford that."

"Was there ever an Edith?"

"The best lies are always built on a grain of truth. Any decent lawyer knows that. Yes, there was an Edith and she did disappear from her cruise. She was missing for seven months."

Only out of idle curiosity at this stage, Jackson asked, "Where did she turn up?"

"Amsterdam. Met another old gent on the cruise, they snuck off, eloped, and were married in a small Greek chapel under the shadow of the Acropolis. A last fling for poor Edith. She was a mental wreck by then. I was worried about her so I hired a Dutch detective outfit after I left Primo. The CEO and CFO were crooks. They were after her money, and when I accused them, they gave me a million-dollar bonus to disappear. They didn't want Edith found, so I took it into my own hands."

"I see."

"She died five years ago, if you're interested."

"Uh-huh," was all he could manage to say.

"Complications from Parkinson's. She's buried in a well-tended grave out on Long Island, beside her first husband."

Jackson buried his face in his hands. He knew Jack was telling the truth and he knew his last hope for a brilliant defense — for any defense — was in shambles.

"But we didn't come here to gloat," Jack informed him.

"Yes you did, you bastard."

"Okay, maybe a little. You have one final thing to do for us. One last job."

Slowly the face came out of the hands. "I wouldn't piss in your mouth if you were dying of thirst. Not if my life depended on it."

"Oh, but it does," Mia told him. "It very much does."

"Are you wondering why you alone weren't arrested or indicted?" Jack asked him. "You don't really believe it was due to your brilliant legal skills, do you? That blustery press conference, those nasty threats you threw around? Please tell me you're not that naïve and stupid, Jackson."

It was a one-two punch. Mia barely allowed that thought to sink in before she lowered the hammer. "Of course we screened the tapes before we handed them over. If you're interested, we kept about thirty of them."

Jack's turn again. "Thirty tapes in which you are flagrantly breaking several serious laws, Jackson. Any one of them will get you disbarred and some prison time. Your career in Washington will be over. But the entire collected works . . . no, you really don't want them heard by a jury of twelve impressionable jurors."

Jackson was beyond arguing or resisting at this point. They had it all figured out. In a way he admired these two, their brilliance, their trickery, their persistence; in a much larger way he loathed and feared them. "Tell me what you want."

"What lawyers do best: settle," Jack told him very firmly. "When the Defense Department comes after the Capitol Group, you'll persuade the board to settle. It will cost you another five and a half billion. We want to be sure you pay back the taxpayers every penny you stole from them."

He tried to suppress it, tried his best to force it down, but a weak smile began to form on Jackson's face. The number didn't surprise him. Of course Jack knew exactly how much had been paid; CG's offices had been wired like a porn studio. But a friendly settlement was the best way out of this mess anyway. The board was already brought on.

Three billion had been placed in reserve. Jackson and the boys from legal counsel already had their defensive strategy laid out; they would fight every penny, itemize and inflate every expense, whittle it down until three billion felt like an incredible act of contrition and remorse on CG's part. With any luck, they'd get away with far less.

As if reading his mind, Mia added, "Don't even dream of counteroffers. You'll pay the full 5.5 billion, Jackson. We'll be listening closely. At the slightest hesitation, even a hint of resistance, Jack will suddenly remember the thirty tapes he sloppily misplaced."

Jackson locked eyes with her and had no doubt they meant it. His mind immediately turned to ways to reverse his earlier advice to the board. The Capitol Group's earnings this year were already an unsalvageable wreck. Now, after a month of wretched press coverage, the last thing CG wanted was a long, contentious brawl that only further dragged its name through the mud and antagonized an already furious Pentagon.

Jack added, "The Defense Department is also going to try to throw a one-billion-dollar penalty at you. Coincidentally, that equals my reward. You'll smile and pay every single dime of that, too."

Jackson grabbed his throat and looked like he was going to be sick. Six and a half billion dollars! That was the cost of keeping him out of prison. The board was going to howl, yet there was not the slightest doubt in his mind that he'd find a way to force them to pay it.

Mia said, "Somehow, we enjoy the thought of you paying our bill."

"Up yours."

"Don't be that way. Think of the good cause it's going to when you sign the check."

"Anything else?"

"Yes, one other thing," Jack told him as he got to his feet.

Mia stood also. She looked down at him and said, "Tell all your friends out there in the big defense companies that we're here. We're not going away, Jackson. Now we have a boatload of cash, and plenty of clever ideas. We'll be keeping a close eye on you and them."

ABOUT THE AUTHOR

Brian Haig is the *New York Times* bestselling author of six novels featuring JAG attorney Sean Drummond and his first standalone thriller *The Hunted.* A former special assistant to the chairman of the Joint Chiefs of Staff, he also has had articles published in journals ranging from the *New York Times* to *USA Today* to *Details.* Haig lives in New Jersey with his wife and four children. For more information you can visit his website at www.brianhaig.com.

The employees of Thorndike Press hope you have enjoyed this Large Print book. All our Thorndike, Wheeler, and Kennebec Large Print titles are designed for easy reading, and all our books are made to last. Other Thorndike Press Large Print books are available at your library, through selected bookstores, or directly from us.

For information about titles, please call:
(800) 223-1244

or visit our Web site at:
http://gale.cengage.com/thorndike

To share your comments, please write:
Publisher
Thorndike Press
295 Kennedy Memorial Drive
Waterville, ME 04901